Echoes
of the
Stones

Echoes
of the Stones

CHRISTINE KING

To Paddy
Hope you enjoy the book
Much love
Christine
x

Published in paperback in 2017 by Sixth Element Publishing
on behalf of Christine King

Sixth Element Publishing
Arthur Robinson House
13-14 The Green
Billingham TS23 1EU
Tel: 01642 360253
www.6epublishing.net

ISBN 978-1-912218-01-1

British Library Cataloguing in Publication Data. A catalogue record for this book is
available from the British Library.

This is a work of fiction. Names, characters, businesses, places, events and incidents
are either the products of the author's imagination or used in a fictitious manner.
Any resemblance to actual persons, living or dead, or actual events and places is
purely coincidental.

Printed in Great Britain.

*Dedicated to all my family, friends and the Horsemen
for all their love, encouragement and support.
Thank you all.*

Lihanna 1

She was running, her breath coming in short jagged gasps as she pushed her way through the undergrowth of the forest. She could hear her pursuers behind her, their shouts audible despite the distance between them.

Branches caught at her clothing, scratching her face, her bare arms and legs, but she ran on, oblivious to the pain, intent only on escaping her pursuers, intent on getting away to the safety of the dense heart of the forest.

Blood ran down her face, blurring her vision as it ran into her eyes, but she wiped it away with a hasty, impatient gesture. Her feet were bare, the rough shoes she had worn earlier being left far behind and she held up the thick woollen material of her smock, gathered in her arms to enable her to run all the faster, unhindered.

Finally, at last, she reached the comparative safety of the secluded cave she had been seeking. Praying that the men who sought her were unaware of its existence, with the remnants of her strength she pulled the boulder away from the entrance of the small cave, no bigger than a hole in the side of the great hill in the heart of the forest. She crawled behind the boulder and pulled at it with shaking arms to hide.

She pushed herself back against the curved wall of her small shelter and hugged her knees, burying her face in the material of her dress, breathing in the smell of sweat and blood and the faint aroma of ash from the campfire.

Gradually, her breathing eased, her shaking limbs became calmer and she brushed the mud from where it clung to the fine hairs of her bare legs.

Her thoughts strayed briefly to the events of the past few weeks.

The battle between her people and the Romans – they had been ruthless, her tribe had fought bravely, but the superior forces of the Roman army had decimated them.

The Romans. Invaders determined to conquer her land the way they had invaded and conquered the rest of the known world. They had fought their way across Britain, fighting, defeating and subduing the population, come at last to this part of her land, a stronghold of the Celtic warrior race she was a part of.

The noise of feet crashing through the undergrowth brought her mind back to the present. She held her breath, not daring to make a sound as the voices of her hunters echoed around the forest clearing.

The Romans had descended on her village weeks earlier, the men of her tribe defeated in a battle of epic proportions. Some stragglers of her defeated warrior army had returned to warn the women and children and village elders to pack up and run, hide from the murderous might of the invaders. She had hurried to pack her few belongings, helping her friends and neighbours, but too late.

"Too late..." she whispered into her knees, unwanted tears springing to her eyes, dashed away impatiently.

Her world had descended into chaos. The Romans had come and the Celts had fought them, the few remaining warriors, the old men, and women like herself. Young, proud and fierce she had fought them with the sword given to her by her father. Her people had been cut down before her eyes, roaring their defiance of these aggressors. She had screamed in her hatred and grief and had hacked at the soldiers, before being overcome and disarmed. She had struggled against them, biting, kicking, and screaming and, bemused at the furious hellcat they had captured, they had bound her and thrown her, protesting and fighting every inch of the way, into the compound hastily erected for the prisoners.

Lihanna shuddered as the cold of the cave permeated the damp material of her dress. She hugged her knees tighter and hardly dared to breathe as the voices outside her shelter paused and fell silent.

She strained her ears to listen to them but could hear nothing. She waited, listening for the sound of footsteps going away from the glade. She heard no movements and her head went up hardly daring to hope that her pursuers had given up their search and gone away.

She had run this day, into the forest. A place she knew well, she had grown up amongst the shelter of its trees; she had gathered herbs and flowers and plants from its glades; she had climbed the trees, swam in the small river which ran through it and hidden as she did now, crouching silently in the small cave which sheltered her.

Her hopes turned to horror as the stone she had struggled to pull in front of her small shelter was rolled away and she found herself facing the white robed Druids, the priests she and her people had put their hope and trust in.

Without taking his eyes from the girl crouching on the ground before him, the tall, dark haired young man barked out an order. His companions came forward and bending, dragged the protesting girl from her hiding place. They were all dressed alike, in flowing white robes, their hair long and uncovered, prepared for the ceremonies she had interrupted by escaping from them in a moment of inattention. She struggled against their hold but they held her firmly and stood before their leader, awaiting his orders.

"Is this any way for a Celtic Princess to behave?" he demanded, silencing her protests.

She ceased her struggling and looked up at him, dirty, bedraggled, covered in mud and blood, her tangled hair full of leaves and dirt and her wide green eyes snapping hatred into his face.

She drew herself up to her full height and stared at him with all the disdain her royal position could command.

"And is this how you treat your Princess?" she replied, glaring at her two captors.

He smiled at her, a cold humourless smile which did not quite reach his pale blue eyes.

"You will stop these senseless objections, Princess. You will return with me to the Stones and there we will complete the rituals which you have so unwisely disturbed."

She glared at him, hatred and despair in equal measures. "No ritual will bring back my father, or drive the invaders from our

3

lands," she retorted. "The Romans will kill you all unless you give up this madness and release me."

The young Druid looked down at her. He saw beyond the dirt and the blood, he saw only the untouched pure bred noble beauty of a Celtic Princess. He saw in her the salvation for their people.

"Release me," she continued, her voice clear and loud in the hushed silence of the great forest, "otherwise, if the Romans do not kill you then my mother surely will."

A slight frown marred the clear beauty of his face at the mention of her mother, the Queen.

"We will not continue with this discussion, Lihanna." His voice was harsh now. "It is pointless. Come, we still have time to complete our work before sundown."

He nodded to his men and they bound her hands behind her, tying them tightly. They walked with her between them, following their leader as he led the way out of the clearing and back towards the ring of stones she had escaped from earlier. The two who held her had once been good friends, their leader one of her best friends, but she walked silently between them now, her head held high. They did not look at her nor she them. She remained silent as she was taken out of this glade in the deepest heart of the dark forest and back to where the secret ceremonies of her Druid priests could continue unhindered and undisturbed.

Chapter One

The bright white light of the cold winter morning shone through the thin material of her curtains and awoke the girl sleeping in the narrow single bed.

A clatter heralded the arrival of the scullery maid whose job it was to light the fires in the family bedrooms prior to their awakening, dressing and descending to the heavily laden breakfast table.

Callista's fire was always the last to be lit. She was, after all, not "proper" family as the scullery maid had explained to her, much to her wry amusement. That she was allowed a fire at all was a consideration allowed by her Aunt, eager to prove that although Callista was only an extremely poor relation, reliant on her Aunt's family for their charity, she was, at least, afforded some measure of comfort, if not luxury.

Sighing, Callista rolled over onto her back and stared at the plain white ceiling. Her thoughts strayed briefly to memories of her bedroom at home in the rambling vicarage in which she had been born and brought up. It was cluttered and cosy, stuffed full of her belongings, her books, clothes, and much loved old toys she had never quite been able to part with. All were gone now, of course. Permitted to bring only the barest minimum of belongings, she had packed her clothes and a few beloved books and had arrived at Wetherby Court with only one trunk and a small bag of possessions to her name.

She sat up and, shivering slightly as she waited for the fire to catch and warm the small room, she wrapped her thick woollen shawl around her shoulders. Aggie, the maid, returned a short while later with a jug of clean water for Callista to wash herself in.

She smiled at Callista, her broad country face lighting up as she saw the young lady was awake.

"Good morning, Miss," she said as she deposited the jug in the bowl on the small chest of drawers in front of the window. She drew back the thin curtains and let the morning sun flood the narrow confines of the room.

Callista pushed back the covers and swung her legs over the side of the bed, shivering again as her bare feet touched the rough rug.

The dream had troubled her. Tonight it had been one of her running away from a terrible danger, running through forests, branches catching at her, her feet bleeding. Running for her life, knowing she was unable to escape the inevitable fate awaiting her. It was a dream she had had since childhood, but where in the past she had been able to go to her Papa and have him soothe away her fears and worries, these days she had no one. She smiled slightly as she considered what her Aunt would say if she tried to confide in her. She dismissed the thought immediately.

"Good morning, Aggie," she replied, standing and stretching.

"Would you like me to help you, Miss?" Aggie asked hopefully.

Smiling ruefully at the young scullery maid, Callista shook her head. "Thank you – much as I would love your assistance, Aggie, I'm afraid Cook would have something to say if I kept you from your duties." She moved swiftly over to the small fire now finally sending out some heat into the chilly morning air. "Go along, Aggie, I can manage very well thank you."

Callista watched her leave, a wry smile on her face. Aggie was nothing if not transparent in her sympathies for the Wetherbys' poor relation. Callista was aware of the feelings of Aggie and most of the other servants in the house. Callista's unfailingly pleasant nature, her calm politeness and gentle energy had made her friends amongst the staff. She knew they felt sorry for her but in no way did she ever acknowledge or manipulate their sympathies. She went about her daily life helping her Aunt and cousin where she could and reflected with a hint of humour that the staff considered her a grey dove compared to the dazzling peacock brilliance of her cousin, Georgiana.

As Aggie returned to her kitchen sinks, Callista washed and dressed in one of her usual day dresses, a plain dark blue gown with a white scarf that tucked around her neck and covered her bosom. Her clothes were good, well-made but plain, as befitted the daughter of a clergyman. With no mother to guide her in the ways of fashion, Callista had grown up totally oblivious to the latest styles in vogue in London and had relied entirely on the local dressmaker in the small village where she had lived most of her life to provide her wardrobe with the half dozen or so gowns in which she lived.

The dress was spotlessly clean, brushed nightly to ensure all marks and creases were obliterated before retiring to bed. She pulled on sturdy shoes over plain white stockings and completed her toilette by brushing out the thick tangled curls of her auburn hair. Her Aunt disapproved of her hair left loose so Callista struggled daily to keep her curls under control.

Staring at herself in the slightly dimpled mirror above the small dressing table, she recalled how the girl in her dream looked so like her. Wide green eyes, thick unruly auburn hair, a few freckles over the bridge of her nose, a full rosy lipped mouth. The dream came back to her mind in its clarity. Papa had always dismissed it and told her not to worry but it was so clear – so real.

She sighed and pulled the warm woollen shawl around her shoulders. Glancing at the smooth covers of her bed, noting that the room was as tidy as she could possibly leave it, she opened the door and stepped out into the hallway, preparing herself to descend the wide staircase to join the rest of her family in the breakfast room.

Her family. A brief smile touched her lips at the thought of her only relatives. By no stretch of the imagination could they be labelled "family". Family was a dear departed Mama, dying before Callista had reached her fifth birthday, giving birth to the baby sister who had outlived their mother by only a few hours.

Her family thereafter consisted of Papa, a loving gentle father, and Nanna, her nursemaid. Nanna had retired and gone to live with her sister in a little cottage by the sea three years ago, and Papa – pneumonia had carried him away some six months earlier. Her eyes clouded over briefly at the thought of losing her darling Papa. They had been the world to one another, and upon his death, she had thought herself quite alone in the world.

However, Samuel had made plans. A letter despatched a few days before his untimely death had brought her Aunt to the vicarage. Estranged from her only sister by Alicia's marriage to the wholly unsuitable Samuel, Aunt Amelia had arrived in time to attend the funeral and instruct Callista to pack up in preparation to return to Wetherby Court with her.

Remonstration and protests had counted for nothing. Callista was virtually penniless, the new Vicar and his family would require her home to live in and she had nowhere else to go. Poverty and penury were not attractive prospects and reluctantly Callista had packed her few possessions and returned with her Aunt to live with her only relatives.

Introduced a few days later to her Uncle Augustus and cousins Simon and Georgiana, Callista had found herself being coolly welcomed to Wetherby Court. Within days she had found herself in the unenviable position of the ubiquitous poor relation and the pattern of her life had changed irrevocably.

Entering the breakfast room, Callista found herself in the company of her Uncle Augustus. She curtsied politely to him and wished him a pleasant good morning.

Augustus barely looked up at her. "Morning," he replied, applying himself to a heaped plateful of sausage and eggs.

"Did you sleep well, Uncle?" she enquired.

"Tolerably," he replied between mouthfuls.

She seated herself along the table from her Uncle, leaving room for her Aunt and cousins. She began to eat her breakfast in silence, chewing thoughtfully on a piece of toast.

Her Aunt joined them a few minutes later, her face puckered in a deeper than normal frown. Callista had very rarely seen her Aunt smile, but this morning Amelia seemed particularly annoyed.

"Good morning, Aunt Amelia," Callista ventured, determined not to let her Aunt's bad temper spoil her own mood.

Amelia looked at her niece with ill-concealed impatience. "I am glad to see you are up at last, Callista," she said.

"Indeed, Aunt. May I get you some tea?"

"The servants can do that," Amelia replied shortly and a Footman hurried forward to serve his mistress with her morning cup of tea.

Amelia turned to her husband. "Augustus, have you sent orders to the Steward at Portland Square?" she demanded.

Her husband raised his eyes from his breakfast and took a draught of ale from the large tankard in front of him. Callista sipped her hot tea, listening with downcast eyes.

"Not yet, there is no rush, surely."

Amelia bristled, her indignation rising. "Augustus, it is less than a month until the Season. We must go to London as soon as possible. Georgiana and I both need new gowns if we are not to look like country bumpkins at Court."

No mention was made of Callista, for which she was truly grateful. Poor relations were not invited to Court and, thankfully, were not expected to appear any of the Balls or parties Georgiana could not wait to attend.

Georgiana intended, Callista had been informed, on making a brilliant match. She was determined to be a Duchess at least. Callista had remonstrated gently with her cousin, citing the possibility that Georgie might, actually, fall in love with someone far less grand than a Duke.

"Love?" Georgiana had been scornful. "Marriage has nothing to do with love, Callie. It is about position and power and I intend to make the most advantageous match I possibly can."

Callista hid a smile as she continued with her breakfast. At least in this ambition, Georgiana and her mother were in complete agreement.

She looked up to see her Aunt glaring at her, eyes narrowed

as she sipped her tea. Callista knew better than to provoke her Aunt, and merely smiled at her. "May I ask if there is anything in particular you wish me to do today, Aunt Amelia?" she asked innocently.

Amelia frowned slightly as she started to eat her breakfast. She was firmly of the opinion that poor relations should earn their keep and generally, she found plenty of tasks to keep Callista occupied.

"I believe Mrs Jarvis has recently been delivered of her latest child, Aunt," Callista continued. "Would you like me to visit with some provisions for her and the other children?"

As Amelia was only too aware of her position in the neighbourhood, it behove her to make sure the tenants on the Wetherby estate were seen to be well cared for by their landlords.

"Of course," she agreed, "please see Cook and take a basket over to the Jarvis farm. Pass on our best wishes to Mrs Jarvis and tell her I will visit as soon as I can."

"Certainly, Aunt." Callista hid her relief and kept the expression on her face strictly neutral. She could escape the house for a few hours; a brisk walk over to the Jarvis farm in the wintry sunshine would suit her mood.

"Will Callie be coming to London with us?" her Uncle startled her by asking, directing his enquiry to his wife.

Amelia swallowed her morsel of breakfast and sipped her tea before replying. "Of course Augustus, Georgiana will require a companion or chaperone on occasions when I cannot accompany her. Callista will certainly be coming with us."

Callista felt her heart sink. She had known this was coming but had hoped, forlornly, that she may be allowed to remain in the country for the Season. She had no desire for city life, especially in the company of her relatives.

She forced a smile to her lips. "I hope I may be useful, Aunt Amelia," she said. "But surely you would not need me to accompany Georgiana to Balls?"

Amelia's permanent scowl deepened. Her daughter was beautiful but Callista, drab and poor though she was, had a glowing spiritual beauty that no amount of dowdy, ill-fitting gowns could disguise.

"Only if I am indisposed," she conceded, "and of course, at Georgiana's Ball. It will be expected that you be there." She managed to force a smile onto her face. "I am sure we can find a suitable gown for the occasion."

"Thank you, Aunt," Callista murmured, good manners forcing the reply to her lips.

"Is Georgie up yet?" her Uncle demanded.

"I think so. Callista, if you have finished perhaps you would be good enough to inform Georgiana that her father wishes to speak to her."

Callista drank her tea and rose from the breakfast table. "Of course, Aunt Amelia," she replied, and left them to finish their breakfast alone.

She went back upstairs to her cousin's bedchamber. Georgiana was just finishing dressing as Callista entered, her maid completing the last minute touches to her hair, pinning long golden ringlets into place.

"Good morning, Georgie," Callista greeted her cousin.

Georgiana continued to survey herself in the mirror, turning her head and pouting into the glass. Huge blue eyes framed by a heart-shaped face returned her gaze. She nodded briefly, dismissing her maid. "Morning, Callie. What do you think of this dress?" she asked.

She stood up and turned to face her cousin, brushing the creases out of the new gown she was wearing. It was a beautiful blue muslin, embroidered with an intricate flower pattern across the bosom. Trimmed with white lace, it was a pretty dress and the blue enhanced the clear blue of her eyes.

"It's a lovely dress, Georgiana. It suits you very well," Callista complimented her sincerely.

"It will do, I suppose." Georgiana looked at herself in the long mirror again. "I just wish I was going somewhere to show it." She sighed. "Has my mother told you when we are to go to London?"

"No, but she has asked your Papa to prepare the house in

Portland Square. She wants to remove to London within the next few weeks."

"Good – I am tired of the country. All this winter weather and country living is so dull. I want some excitement in my life, Callie."

Callista smiled indulgently at her young cousin. Only two years separated them but sometimes she felt years older than the eighteen-year-old Georgiana. Georgiana could be selfish and capricious and she was certainly spoiled but she could also be kind to her frumpy old cousin.

"You will have excitement enough in a few weeks' time, Georgie," she replied. "King George himself will be dazzled by you, my dear."

"Lord, I do not want to attract that particular man's attention, thank you, Callie." Georgiana laughed as she finished admiring herself in front of the mirror. She picked up the shawl to cover her shoulders.

"Your Papa was asking for you, Georgie," Callista said as she helped to straighten the thick woollen shawl about Georgiana's slim shoulders.

"I will go down now. What are you doing today?"

Callista accompanied her to the door. "I am going down to the Jarvis farm and taking some gifts for Mrs Jarvis and the children."

"Are you taking the carriage?"

"No, indeed not." Callista laughed. "It is only a mile or so, I will walk. The fresh air will do me good. Would you like to accompany me?"

A petulant frown crossed Georgiana's beautiful countenance. "Heavens no," she cried. "Muddy fields and all those children at the end of it. I think not. Enjoy your walk, Callie."

She turned and ran lightly down the stairs to join her parents in the breakfast room. Callista returned to her room to exchange her shawl for her sensible winter coat. It was a heavy dark blue coat, thick and warm enough to protect her from the cold and frosty weather outside. Stout walking shoes and a dark velvet bonnet completed her outfit.

Picking up the velvet muff, she made her way down to the kitchen and after exchanging pleasantries with the Cook, she picked up a full basket of provisions for Mrs Jarvis – bread and cheese, cold meats and jars of preserves, sweets for the children and a small bottle of port for Mr Jarvis. It was heavy but the farm was not far and she set out from the Manor house with a light step.

She could see her breath as she walked. There was a light dusting of snow on the ground and all around her, ice and snow glistened on trees and hedges.

Crunching through the newly fallen snow, she made her way steadily down the country lane, pausing occasionally to rest her burden and take in the views of the countryside around Wetherby Court.

Brought up in the wilder mountainous regions of the Cumberland fells, she longed to explore further the flatter, more open countryside of her new home in this part of North Yorkshire. Not permitted to venture too far, she had nonetheless visited the coastal area and had delighted in the open aspect of the North Sea when her Aunt had visited an old friend in the harbour town of Whitby. She smiled as she recalled how Aunt Amelia's nose had wrinkled in disgust at the strong pervading fish smell from the quayside and how horrified she had been as Callista and Georgiana had gone further and walked along the beach at low tide.

Georgiana was full of stories of places she longed to visit once she had been presented at Court along with all the other debutantes. She would then host her very own party, a "Coming Out in Society Ball" as it was known followed by six months in London with its excitements. She would go to all the Ton parties and Balls and, of course, Almacks – the pinnacle of success for any society debutante. The summer was to be spent in Bath – far superior apparently to their more local (and humble) Harrogate. As Callista's only visit to Harrogate had aroused in her an interest to explore further and return as soon as possible, she could share Georgiana's longings for excitement and adventure. Dismissing

Whitby as being inferior to the exceptional charms of Brighton, Georgiana could only hope that she could prevail upon her Mama to take a house there for at least part of the summer.

Picking up her basket, Callista started back on the track towards the Jarvis farm. As she made her way along, she noticed that one of the fields on the outskirts of the farm looked occupied. She saw smoke curling into the air, the sure sign of a campfire and as she drew closer, she saw the unmistakeable signs of occupation by a band of Romany gypsies.

Callista's father had brought her up to be open minded and generous and she had no fear of the Romanies. Her relatives, however, were not fond of them and she wondered what her Uncle would do when he found out about them camping in one of his tenant farmer's fields.

A group of the travellers were sitting around the campfire, an old woman was stirring a large iron pot and the savoury smell of rabbit stew wafted through the air as Callista approached.

The old woman lifted her head and turned towards Callista. There were three caravans in total, and Callista found herself the scrutiny of a dozen pairs of eyes, suspicion and wariness in their expressions. Children were running around and two men were grooming the horses tied up near the caravans but all movement stopped and all eyes turned towards her.

She felt herself blushing slightly under their gaze but she kept her head up and smiled at the old woman.

"Good morning, Madam," she ventured.

The old woman nodded and, to the general surprise of the others, she held out her hand towards Callista.

"Would you come over here, my dear?" she asked.

Imagining the horror her Aunt Amelia would have felt had she been present, Callista paused in her journey to the farm. She had heard tales of robbery and violence surrounding gypsy families but it was not rumour that made her hesitate. Rather, the sudden intense expression in the old woman's face made her uncertain as to what to do.

The hand was still outstretched. "You will come to no harm,

my dear." She seemed to be seeking to offer her reassurance and Callista, wary but intrigued, put down her basket by the open gate and went into the field towards the old woman.

Silently, the group of women and seated men watched as their matriarch stood up and approached the stranger.

Callista met the old woman a few feet inside the field and wide green eyes stared into ancient brown ones. The old gypsy held out her hand once more and slowly Callista held out her own.

"I do not have funds or time for fortune telling," she smiled at the old woman.

Soundlessly the old one's hand closed around Callista's – a brown claw of a hand tightened its hold on Callista's small white one.

The world whirled around her – images spun in her mind and Callista felt sick and dizzy – it was as if her dream had come back to haunt her and she saw the old woman dressed in strange white garb, her grey hair long and straight, a flower garland around her head.

"Lihanna of the Stones…" The old woman's voice seemed to come from far away. "The wheel of fortune has turned, your time is at hand."

Callista found she could hardly breathe. She closed her eyes and saw a dozen more people – all in the long white robes, all surrounding her and behind them were tall, monolithic structures, stones taller than men, a ring of stones – she was in the middle of them and surrounded by the white robed people.

"Who are you?" she whispered to the old woman.

"I am the High Priestess," was the reply. "I tried to save you but it was too late – one betrayed you, and one who loved you lost you; but you will have your revenge. He is close; he loved you then and will love you now. Your time is near."

Callista opened her eyes and pulled her hand out of the firm grasp. Immediately the world stopped tipping, her head stopped spinning and she was back in the gypsy encampment in a snowy field in Yorkshire.

The long white robes were now dirty black skirts and

15

shawl, and the long grey hair tidily tucked beneath a black headscarf.

The old woman smiled at her. "I did not mean to frighten you, my dear," she said softly, "but I just wanted to speak to you. You have experienced a great loss and you have suffered grief, but that time is ending soon." She paused, taking a deep breath, her face, beneath the wrinkles and lines, suddenly pale. "There are two people in the shadows. They are close – one to fear, the other to trust. Beware my dear." She was trembling and Callista waited. The old woman seemed to want to say more but two of the women seated with her next to the fire were suddenly beside her, holding her arms as she swayed gently.

"Come, Mother," one said, staring hard at Callista. "Stop tiring yourself." She nodded to Callista. "I'm sorry she bothered you, Miss. Please do not let us stop you going on your way."

Callista stepped back and stared around at the silent campsite. She shivered and nodded in response. "Thank you, I must go now."

She turned and hurried, on legs suddenly trembling, back to the gate where she had abandoned her basket. Picking it up, she carried on with her walk and within a few minutes she was entering the farmyard.

Mr Jarvis was there to meet her, welcoming her into the warmth of the farmhouse kitchen. His three children greeted her with curious glances at the large basket that she put down upon the kitchen table, before removing her bonnet and coat and accepting a refreshing hot drink from Mr Jarvis' mother.

"Did the gypsies bother you, Miss?" Mrs Jarvis Senior enquired. "They only arrived last night and Tom here said they could stay for a day or two."

"No, not at all. There was an elderly woman who spoke to me but apart from her, they did not harm me in any way. Now, may I see the new arrival?"

Callista busied herself with distributing the gifts from her Aunt to the family. Mrs Jarvis presented her newborn son for inspection and Callista spent a pleasant morning with the family. She did not speak of her strange encounter with the old gypsy woman. It was disturbing and disquieting and it brought memories flooding back of the dream of last night, similar dreams that had haunted her all her life. She pushed the memory of that meeting to the back of her mind, forcing herself not to think of the words, or the strange landscape where she had found herself transported.

Lihanna of the Stones the old woman had called her and for an instant she had been taken to that alien place, surrounded by standing stones of ancient and mystical power.

Fresh snow was falling as Callista stood to leave and Mr Jarvis would not hear of her walking home alone in the cold winter weather.

He readied the pony and trap and despite her protests, Callista found herself grateful for his concern. She did not relish the thought of passing the gypsy encampment again. The old woman had unsettled her and she found herself not wishing to face her again.

The family waved as they set off and as they passed the field where the travellers were camped, Callista found her eyes drawn to the campfire. The old woman was standing and as Callista passed, their eyes locked in the briefest moment of recognition, leaving Callista uncharacteristically troubled for the remainder of the day.

Chapter Two

Georgiana's excitement grew beyond all reasoning as the time grew closer to the events that would officially introduce her to the cream of London society.

They had arrived in London two weeks earlier in the final week of January. The date for Georgiana's presentation at Court was not until early March and until then, due to the strict code of etiquette rigorously enforced by her mother, she was forced to attend only the quietest of parties, pay morning visits to friends of her parents and spend afternoons with dressmakers. This was, however, a most satisfactory occupation, surrounded by a rich tapestry of silks, satins and velvet, spending hours at a time choosing the latest fashionable gowns, matching accessories, and agonising over the choice of her coming out gown.

Even Callista's calm temper was stretched to breaking point after days on end of Georgiana's hysteria at her mother's refusal to allow her to attend any of the many Balls she was invited to.

Callista herself was duty bound to accompany Georgiana and her Aunt to many of their morning visits. She conducted herself in her usual manner, finding amusement in the excitement of Georgiana and her friends, talking endlessly about their presentation, followed by the start of rounds of Balls, fancy dress parties, and – of course – Almacks.

Her Aunt felt obliged to ensure that Callista was suitably attired for the upcoming Season. Callista, therefore, suddenly found herself the recipient of a bewildering amount of Georgiana's cast off clothing. She received a day dress of the deepest emerald green, suitable for paying morning visits, several muslins for receiving visitors, a travelling dress and coat and no fewer than four evening gowns. She even received, in an example of generosity that astounded her, a new gown for Georgiana's Ball.

She was aware that her Uncle Augustus had intervened in this respect. He was fond of her in his own quiet, gruff way and when he found his wife and daughter studying the latest fashion plates and discussing the merits of silk over satin, he asked Callista what she was wearing for Georgie's party. Learning she was contemplating wearing one of Georgiana's old outfits, worn once only it was true, he frowned at his wife and asked exactly how much it was costing for all this frippery. On being reassured it was only a trifling sum, he had smiled slightly, winked at his niece and had firmly stated that as it was so reasonable then of course Callie had to have one too.

Her Aunt knew better than to argue with Augustus. On the matter of her daughter making a brilliant match she was dogmatic; if it meant spending a small fortune to attract the right kind of husband then she needed Augustus to fund it – and if that meant dressing Callista appropriately then she could only acquiesce.

She had no intention, however, of allowing Callista to outshine her daughter in any way and whilst Georgiana was arrayed in the finest white silk, embroidered lavishly with seed pearls and French lace, Callista's gown was of a plain ivory silk, modestly embroidered and trimmed with matching ribbons.

Callista was bemused and bewildered by this sudden change in her life and could not help but find herself being swept along by Georgiana's irrepressible enthusiasm. She tried to keep her cousin's feet on the ground by suggesting they fill their days visiting many of London's attractions and even her Aunt, driven to distraction by Georgiana's endless demand for amusement, was grateful that Callista could intervene and take Georgie out for an hour. Georgiana, however, once the various tours of the capital city had been undertaken, soon became bored and it was with some relief all around when the day of her presentation at Court finally arrived.

Callista was not accompanying her relatives to this momentous event, for which she could only be grateful. She had already been informed by her Aunt that she must not expect to attend all the social events Georgiana was invited to, it did not do for someone in her position in life to push herself forward.

Callista was not offended. It was no more than she expected from her Aunt and she bade farewell to her vivacious cousin with no rancour or bitterness.

She kissed Georgiana's pale face as they waited for the carriage to arrive to take them to Court.

"You look beautiful, Georgie," she assured her cousin.

Georgiana, now that her moment had finally arrived, was inexplicably nervous and she clutched her cousin's hand. "I wish you were coming too, Callie," she whispered urgently.

Callista smilingly shook her head. "You will do very well dearest; all your friends will be there and you will have a wonderful time."

Uncle Augustus was not amused. Dressed in all his finery, he was attending Court very much against his will and had only agreed due to the incessant nagging from his wife. Although he bore the title of Sir Augustus Wetherby, they were only minor nobles and he was aware that they were likely to be overshadowed by those members of the Ton attending Court that evening.

"Wish I was staying home with you, Callie," he muttered to her. "Devilishly uncomfortable at Court, one does not sit in the presence of Royalty, there's no refreshment to speak of and the whole thing drags on for hours."

Callista's eyes sparkled at her Uncle's quiet aside. "I will make sure Cook leaves you some supper, Uncle Augustus," she replied.

Aunt Amelia, however, was in her element. Dressed in her finest mauve and lilac gown, matching feathers in her hair and wearing a glittering necklace of diamonds, she looked resplendent.

"Good night, Callista," she said to her niece as the carriage finally arrived for them. "Pray do not wait up for us."

Callista curtsied politely to her Aunt and smiled again at her cousin. "Enjoy yourself, Georgiana," she said and stood back as the Butler opened the front door, watching as the whole party swept out and into their carriage, conveying them to Court.

She watched them leave and was aware that she was the object of pitying glances from the staff of the London house.

She merely smiled at them, drew her shawl more tightly around her shoulders and went into the Drawing Room. There, she picked up the embroidery she had abandoned some hours earlier and sat quietly beside the fire, steadfastly sewing and keeping her thoughts to herself. She spoke to Cook and arranged for a light supper to be laid out in the dining room for the revellers upon their return and retired to bed as the night drew in, looking out of her bedroom window at the street below, the moonlight shining brightly on the square of fenced gardens outside the house. She undressed and sat herself on the wide window seat, not tired enough to sleep but curious as to how Georgiana's evening had gone, wondering if her cousin would come in that night to regale her with all her news.

Georgiana's Ball was due to take place in a few days' time. Invitations were issued and a gratifyingly high number of acceptances received. It was causing her Aunt as many headaches as this evening at Court and Callista had been called upon to help with the organisation of the event as Georgiana was totally incapable of putting her mind to such mundane matters. The problem of how many servants to hire, what livery the footmen should wear, what refreshments to offer, Callista had taken all in her stride. The arrangements of the party were in full swing, most of which being decided between Callista and the Housekeeper, with Aunt Amelia being consulted occasionally – often enough to believe she was organising the whole event but not enough to interfere with the smooth running of the upcoming party.

Callista consulted the lists on her small bureau as she sat up waiting for the return of her cousin and made notes in the margins to discuss with the Housekeeper and Cook the following day.

Looking up from her notes, she watched the occasional walker passing by. It was normally a quiet square but tonight the light, spring weather had attracted more pedestrians than normal.

She watched as a tall, dark haired man turned the corner into the Square. He was walking slowly, apparently deep in thought as he walked along. He was dressed in fine eveningwear, a dark cutaway coat, silk pantaloons, a fine silk shirt and carefully styled cravat above his waistcoat. He was carrying a cane and gloves and Callista found she was taking in all these details as she watched him strolling along the pavement outside the houses. She could not see his face, his head was down and he did not look up as two men turned the corner behind him. Callista watched in horror as the two men hurried after him, one of the men holding something that looked suspiciously like a small club. Without stopping to think, Callista swiftly turned. Kneeling up on her padded seat, she pulled at the window catch and pushed the window sash up. She leaned out of the window and screamed down into the Square below.

"Look out – behind you, sir!"

His head came up, taking in the sight of a girl in a nightdress leaning out of a window and as if roused from his reverie, he heard the running footsteps behind him. Whirling around, the cane became a sword and he found himself face to face with the two footpads. The man holding the club raised his hand and tried to bring it down on the head of their would-be victim. The gentleman sidestepped the blow and his sword came up to protect himself against a renewed onslaught.

Callista meanwhile had left the window and was running out of her bedroom, shouting for assistance. The Butler, hearing the commotion and roused from his seat in the hall where he awaited the return of his master, became instantly awake at the sight of Miss Callista flying down the stairs, her hair streaming behind her, clutching her shawl around herself.

"Quickly James, a gentleman is being attacked!" she called out, running towards the front door.

James caught her before she could pull the door open.

"Miss, please, wait here," he demanded and put her behind him as he pulled open the door.

The man had despatched one of the footpads, who lay groaning on the floor, injured by a wound to his arm.

The other assailant was lifting his club to bring it down on their victim once again as James and Callista hurtled out of the house. James threw himself at the attacker as Callista ran to assist the injured man.

The footpad, taken by surprise, had the club wrestled from his hand and as James struggled with him, other members of the Wetherby staff aroused by the commotion came out to assist and the attackers were quickly overpowered.

The gentleman meanwhile was kneeling down on the pavement, holding his shoulder. There was a trickle of blood on his forehead and Callista realised he had sustained a blow to the head. He was shaking it, as if to clear some dizziness.

Callista crouched beside him and gently touched him on the arm.

"Sir," she said quietly, "Sir, please let us help you into the house."

Without looking up, he touched his head, wincing slightly as he felt the cut. "I would be grateful if your men could assist me to my own home," he replied, his voice low. "I live nearby and have no wish to be a nuisance to your Master."

He thought she was a servant, Callista realised, but swallowing down her retort, she turned to James who instantly came to her assistance. He joined her next to the injured man. "Sir, we have apprehended the villains; how can we help you?"

The man took a deep breath and held out his hand to James to assist him to his feet.

"I wish to go home where my Valet can deal with my injuries," he said. "Can one of your men help me?"

"Of course, sir," James replied and at a signal, one of the footmen came over at once.

"Thank you for your help," the man said, and for the first time, he raised his head and looked directly at Callista.

She suddenly felt dizzy as if she too had suffered a blow to her head.

The dark hair, the deep blue eyes, and the tanned face – she knew his face as well as she knew her own she had dreamed of it so often.

He frowned as he looked at her – the wild haired servant girl in the cheap cotton nightdress and shabby shawl.

He stumbled slightly. James and the Footman held him, preventing him from falling again.

"Which way, sir?" James asked.

The man pointed a shaky finger to the far end of Portland Square and he managed a slight bow to the shocked girl. "Thank you," he said quietly. "I think you may have saved my life." He smiled slightly and moved away, James and the Footman helping him, leaving her standing silently watching him stumbling away from her.

"Miss…" The Footman brought her attention back to the present. "Please go back inside and let the Steward know that we are taking these men to the constable."

The two Footmen were tall, burly young men and they held firmly onto the would-be robbers.

Suddenly aware of her state of undress, Callista let them go and returned to the hallway of the house where more servants had gathered to see what was happening.

"Miss? Are you all right?" Mrs Bates the Housekeeper came bustling up to her.

Callista looked down and realised there was blood on her hands from where she had touched the man's head.

Pulling herself together, she took a deep breath. "I am quite well, Mrs Bates, thank you. I think the excitement is over for one night now." She smiled reassuringly at the Housekeeper. "Please send everyone back to bed, but in the meantime can someone wait for my Uncle's return until James gets back?"

Mrs Bates despatched the servants quickly and appointed one of the stable lads to wait in the hallway until the rest of the male servants returned. Order was restored and peace descended on the house once again.

"Do you need anything else, Miss Callista?" Mrs Bates enquired, concerned for the young lady who seemed unnaturally pale after the recent events.

Callista shook her head. "No," she replied, "Nothing, thank

you, Mrs Bates. If everything is in order now I'll go back to bed."

Mrs Bates left her and Callista took a candle from the sconce on the wall to light her way back to her bedroom.

She climbed slowly back up the stairs and returned to her room. She closed the open window and drew the heavy curtains before going over to her bed and climbing in, pulling the coverlet up as she sat with her arms around her knees.

She found she was shaking slightly as she remembered the events of earlier. The man – she did not know his name but his face – his face was so familiar to her. She had dreamed of him for years, in another time, another place but it was he.

Blowing out the candle, she lay back in the bed. Sleep was going to elude her for some time but she knew, before she finally closed her eyes and let sleep claim her, that she was going to dream of him again tonight.

Lihanna 2

The Romans were nothing if not efficient. Within hours of capturing the village, they had taken it over, and the large central dwelling was now where the prisoners were kept, closely guarded by their conquerors. Formerly Lihanna's family home, it was now stripped of its belongings and all that remained was bare earth around the central fire.

Taken from the guarded compound, she was pushed inside with the rest of the prisoners and as she stumbled to the floor, strong hands reached out to save her.

She looked up into the soft blue eyes of Daveth, one of the young men of her people, dressed in the white robes which proclaimed him to be one of the Druid priests to whom they looked for spiritual guidance. He was young and strong and he too, like her, was covered in mud and dishevelled. He had dried blood on the corner of his mouth, and his upper arm was bandaged in bloody white material where a sword had gouged him. He had fought them as hard as any other man in the village, overcome as they all had been, by superior numbers and the ruthless killing machine that was the Roman army.

He smiled down at her. "Princess, I thought you were dead," he murmured.

A spasm of grief gripped her, fighting to keep herself from crying aloud. She swallowed hard and clenched her trembling hands together. "My father…" she whispered, "I have heard that he has been killed. Have you seen or heard anything of my mother?"

He held her hands between his own and crouched beside her. "She would not listen to us," he said, his voice suddenly harsh, revealing the depth of his bitterness. "The priests warned this would happen –

26

we tried to persuade her – Lihanna, I am so sorry, your father was a good man." He squeezed her hands. "I have not seen your mother. I heard she had been captured but everything is so chaotic, so confused, I do not know who has survived – who has been killed."

Lihanna's head dropped, her shoulders sagged but immediately Daveth was beside her. He sat down and put his arm around her shoulders. She felt safer at once.

She and Daveth had known each other since childhood. Only a year separating them, he had been groomed to become one of the Druid priests from early childhood and she had been raised as the daughter of the King. Her brothers had followed their father into battles and her eldest brother Carmag was now King, if he, too, had survived the momentous battles. She had been the favoured daughter of her parents, their only girl and as such, she had been expected to marry the son of a neighbouring king. In her heart, however, she had hoped her parents would reconsider and allow her to make a choice closer to home. She looked up into his eyes and smiled, their futures now looked extremely bleak but at least tonight they were together.

"What did the Druids want my parents to do?" she asked him.

He did not answer at once. He stared into the flames of the fire in front of them and held her closer in the sheltering comfort of his arm. "There are... rituals we could have performed." He spoke softly so that no one could overhear them. "The priests have many sacred rites and ceremonies which could have saved our people. We begged your mother to permit us to carry them out – but she refused." He paused and turned his head to stare deeply into her eyes. "She preferred to lead our people into battle with these – marauders..." He almost spat out the word. "She said no ritual could help now, we had to face them on the battlefield. Leave our gods to watch over and protect us; and the priests to leave their ceremonies and join her in combat."

Lihanna could imagine her mother speaking those words. Her mother was both fierce and proud and as brave as any man. She and her father had been well suited. They had led their people well and had presided over many years of peaceful co-existence with the other kingdoms within their lands; the land the Romans called Britannia. The peace had been hard won, and Lihanna had loved to listen to her parents tell tales of how they had fought to keep their tribe safe, how they had won wars against would-be conquerors, to finally achieve the peace and harmony Lihanna had grown up to accept as normal. Nothing could have prepared her for the savagery of the war she now found herself caught up in.

She shivered and Daveth held her closer. She clung to him for warmth and for the briefest of times she felt safe, protected by his strength.

"Would the rituals have worked?" she asked him.

He sighed. "We still think they would work," he said firmly. "If we can get out of here, Lihanna, we can regroup with the other Druids. They are in hiding but I know where we can reach them."

His eyes shone, with a light she had never seen before. His beliefs were so strong she felt almost in awe of his conviction. "We can call on the power of the gods, Lihanna," he whispered fiercely. "They will help us to drive these invaders out of our country. We can defeat them!"

He raised his hand and gently touched her, brushing thick tangled curls away from her face. She held her breath as he traced his finger down her cheek, coming to rest against her lips. He bent forward and replaced his finger with his lips and kissed her.

It was brief, a mere whisper of a kiss, a feather touch against her mouth. She was trembling once more when he lifted his head.

"We must escape, Lihanna," he murmured. "You and I – we must get away."

They sat together for a while, gazing silently into the dancing flames. Each wrapped up in their own thoughts, Lihanna's mind crowded with swirling thoughts, of Daveth, of her father – of her missing mother and the silent brooding gaze of the Roman who had captured her village and ordered them to be imprisoned.

As if he had heard her thoughts, the Roman himself came into the dwelling. At his entrance, the guards suddenly straightened, standing to attention as he walked in, seeking out and finding the Celtic princess he had captured.

He walked over to where she was seated. Daveth bristled immediately as the Roman stood before them, staring down at the couple.

"Stand up, Princess," he ordered.

She glared up at him but not wanting the indignity of being dragged to her feet by his Centurions, she pushed Daveth's arm from her shoulder and rose to her feet. Daveth rose with her and stood beside her, not touching her but only inches separated them.

"Where is my mother?" she demanded.

She had to look up into his face, he was tall this Roman. He glanced at Daveth and that curious, cold smile touched his lips.

"Come with me, I have had more appropriate quarters prepared for you." He stepped back to allow her to pass him and as she hesitated, he put out his hand to take hold of her upper arm.

She pulled her arm out of his grasp and Daveth took a step forward. The look in the Roman's eyes was enough to make him pause.

The Roman smiled. "Sensible boy," he said, a note of genuine amusement in the dry tone of his voice.

Lihanna stepped forward, not wanting Daveth injured on her behalf.

She stopped in front of her captor and stared up at him, her gaze direct and unwavering.

"Will my people be safe if I leave them here?" she demanded, indicating the prisoners all around them.

He looked around at the crowd of vanquished Celts. They presented no immediate threat to his authority or his forces. They were dispirited and demoralised from their recent defeat. They were mainly women, children and the elderly; the men who were not wounded or dying were too few to cause him any concern. He nodded shortly.

"They will come to no harm; I give you my word," he promised her and with a few words to the guards, he despatched them to bring food and water for the prisoners.

Despite the fact he was her enemy, something about him reassured her that she could trust his promise. She followed him out of the improvised prison.

The camp was full of Roman soldiers, a few of her people were amongst them, but prisoners, some were wounded, their bodies and clothes blood-stained and the Romans were making them drag the dead bodies of her people out of the clearing.

Defeat briefly made her shoulders droop. The General waited and seeing the fleeting glimpse of pity in his eyes, she immediately straightened and followed him to a separate tent.

She felt the eyes of the Roman following her. She returned his gaze, glaring at him with all the imperious arrogance of a true princess. She marched in front of him, barefoot, dirty, her smock-like dress covered in blood and mud. She barely reached his shoulder yet to his evident amusement she managed to look down her small nose at him as she entered the large square tent.

"These are my quarters?" she demanded, looking around her at the cushioned bed, the table and chairs, the chests bearing strange carvings and a separate curtained off area.

"No," he replied, "these are my quarters. You will sleep over there." He indicated the curtained area. "You are too valuable a hostage, Princess, to leave unguarded."

"Who are you?" she asked, bristling immediately.

"I am Julius Maximus Aurelius, I am the General of the 10th Cohort of the Fourth Legion," he replied.

Two servants were standing inside the tent. They came forward and started to unbuckle their General's armour, lifting it from him to leave him standing in front of her in the short toga. He suddenly looked weary and older than his years.

He put on the robe they held out to him and speaking to them in his own language, he issued his orders. As they left to obey him, he turned back to Lihanna.

"I have sent for water for you to bathe, Princess," he said. "And food and drink for us both." He held up his hand as she started to protest. "It has been a long day – I am weary and there is still much to attend to. A messenger has been sent to your brother's camp – I hope to have your mother here before daybreak."

"She will never surrender." Lihanna almost snarled at him.

He was close to her; his deep blue eyes looked into hers, the cool indifference no longer there. She could almost feel his unspoken urge to reach out and touch the contours of her upturned face.

She caught her breath, knowing she was completely in his power; she was his prisoner, his hostage. He could refuse to hand her over in return for her mother's complete surrender. He could keep her as his prisoner, his slave, for as long as he wanted. He could do anything he wanted.

"She will surrender, you will be returned to her and you will be allowed to live in peace, under our rule." His voice was harsh, uncompromising and she flinched as if he had struck her.

She could not help but let the fear she felt flicker briefly in her eyes. She stepped away from him, not wanting to let him see her fear. He was a soldier, she was his prisoner and she prayed he had a duty to his men, to Rome, to his Roman code of honour to keep control of any situation; and himself.

His servants returned, carrying their General's bath and jugs of hot water.

"You can bathe now, Princess." He spoke softly, and watched as she followed his servants to the small curtained section, behind which lay a bed which had obviously been taken from one of the village thatches, somebody's bed — somebody who would probably never return to claim it again.

She was thoughtful as she walked away from him. She turned her head and gazed at him once more before following the servants into her bedchamber. There had been a moment when she had almost expected something to happen — she had expected much harsher treatment from her captors. This courtesy, this civility was most unexpected and she was unprepared for it, she did not know how to react. This man was her enemy, his armies had decimated hundreds of her people, including her own father and he was treating her as a truly royal princess, an honoured guest almost, rather than his prisoner.

He remained standing still where she had left him. Turning away, she closed the curtains and, waiting for the servants to leave her, she slipped off her smock and stepped into the bath, shocked by the warmth of the water but grateful nonetheless. It was with a growing sense of guilt that she allowed herself to relax and wash away the grime and blood of that horrendous day. Her feet were bloody and sore and she found countless bruises covering her body, but the warmth of the water performed its magic and she found herself almost slipping into unconsciousness.

Pulling herself out of the water, she emptied the final jug of water over her head to rinse out her hair, wrapping herself in the soft white linen his servants had left for her. She dried and sat down on the bed, intending to dress once more in her soiled dress. Instead, a great weariness overcame her and she closed her eyes. Within minutes, she was asleep.

Chapter Three

He slept badly. By the time his Valet had seen to his bruised shoulder and the cut on his head, it was almost two in the morning before he was able to fall into bed.

He groaned as he opened his eyes when the curtains shielding him from the clear March sunshine were drawn back. He rolled over onto his side, away from the brightness, burying his head in the downy comfort of his pillow and wincing when his injured forehead came into contact with his hand.

His head hurt, not only from the blow he had sustained but also from the amount of alcohol he had consumed the night before. He had drunk far more than normal. Leaving his club and deciding to walk home alone to clear his head of the smoky alcohol-fuelled fuzziness, he had not noticed the footpads following him. Normally his senses were alert and sharp but the circumstances of the previous evening had sent him out in a temper and he was too wrapped up in his own thoughts to realise he was about to be attacked. He had not enjoyed his evening. The argument with his mother before he left the house had left a sour taste in his mouth, and there were fewer of his friends than normal in the club, most of them gone to the opening of the Seasonal round of fashionable parties by attending Court. They had gone to Court to inspect the latest crop of debutantes about to be inflicted on the unsuspecting young men of the Ton.

It was a ritual he objected to. He had no wish to saddle himself with a wife and the increasingly urgent demands of his mother to do so had made him leave the house in a foul temper. His mood had not improved by his attendance at White's, culminating in the violent end to the evening when he had almost been murdered on his way home.

He vaguely remembered the call, the scream, which had saved his life and the half-dressed firebrand who had exploded out of the building, followed by a veritable army of footmen.

He had managed to account for one of the villains before he had fallen, the other one being overcome by the servants from the house and he had found himself on the ground, being helped to sit up by the girl with a mass of tumbling auburn curls and dressed in her nightclothes. It had been dark, the only light being from the huge white moon and the gentle candle glow from inside the house. He had not seen her face clearly, but she had been concerned for him, she had helped him and when the footmen had helped him to his feet he recalled the way she looked at him. She looked as if she had seen a ghost whilst he fought to remember where he had met her before. It was too much, he was in pain, his head hurt and together with the amount of alcohol he had consumed that evening he felt nauseous and was fighting to prevent himself from being violently sick in front of her.

He sat up in bed now and closed his eyes as the room swam dizzily around him.

His Valet was moving quietly around the room, preparing a washbowl and setting out his shaving brush and razors.

"Sir Maxim." The Valet came towards him and seeing how pale his master was looking, frowned down at him. "Perhaps you should remain in bed a little longer, sir."

Max sat on the edge of his bed and put his head in his hands.

Wincing slightly, he looked up into the concerned face of his manservant. He managed a crooked grin. "I would like nothing more than to remain in bed for a few more hours, Benson," he replied. "Unfortunately Lady Langley has demanded I attend her at 10am sharp."

He pulled himself to his feet, still a little unsteady. His Valet held a supporting hand on his young master's arm.

"Thank you, Benson." Max straightened and made his way over to the dressing table. Bending down, he stared at himself in the mirror for a moment, taking in the dark bruise on his forehead above black eyebrows and dark sapphire blue eyes. He frowned at the pallor of his cheeks, pale against the beginning of dark stubble. "I am not looking my best," he murmured to his Valet, "but I had better pull myself together fast before my mother comes looking for me."

His Valet suppressed a smile. He had served Max for several years, since the young Marquis had been eighteen years old and had watched the callow youth develop into a fine young man. Lady Langley was quite capable of bursting in on her son should he indeed be late for their scheduled appointment and he went to his master at once, holding up a towel and indicating the seat Max needed to take next to the shaving implements.

"Indeed, Sir Maxim," he replied, "perhaps we should attempt to make you look presentable?"

Max seated himself as directed and sat back, letting Benson wrap the towel around his neck. He was still frowning. "Benson, the young men who escorted me home last night, did anyone make a note of their address? I will have to pay a visit to thank the owners for their staff's prompt action in saving my life." He sighed and a rueful laugh escaped him. "You never know, they may actually have a daughter of the house of marriageable age – that would please my mother."

"Yes, sir. That would be most – fortuitous?" Benson agreed in a perfectly sober voice.

The frown cleared from between Max's eyes. "Yes, it would," he replied, his voice suddenly serious. "A nice milksop of a girl who will live quietly in the country and look after the children and leave me to pursue my interests in town with no fuss or interruption."

It was Benson's turn to frown, but carefully schooling his features, he began to lather the soap onto his young master's face. "I daresay there is a young lady out there somewhere who will not object to such an arrangement," he said carefully, hiding the genuine distaste he felt for his young master's sentiments.

Max was not fooled. Benson had been with him too long

35

for him not to understand the older man's opinion. He held his tongue however, and sat back whilst his Valet continued to shave him and help him to dress and turn him once again into the stylishly attired Marquis of Langley, fit to grace his mother's elegant Drawing Room.

He entered that Drawing Room, promptly at 10 o'clock, to find his mother waiting for him, seated on her sofa, drinking her morning tea whilst examining the pile of invitations and letters on the small table before her.

Taking a deep breath, he walked forward and bent down to kiss his mother's proffered cheek.

"Good morning, Mama," he said.

"Good morning, Max." She reached up and touched the bruise on his forehead. "My dear, I heard about your little fracas, I had no idea you had been hurt."

He straightened and moved away to sit on the sofa opposite her. "It was an unfortunate incident, Mama," he replied. "Luckily the servants of the house outside where the attack occurred came to my assistance."

She laid down her correspondence and poured a cup of tea for her son. He accepted it and sipped at it distractedly. His thoughts were miles away and it was with an effort that he brought his attention back to his mother.

"Will you return to thank the master of the house for his men's swift action?" she enquired. "I think a gift of some kind would be appropriate?"

He nodded his head. "Of course I will," he replied. "I will attend to it this morning."

His mother drank from her cup. Silently she observed her son, taking in the pale face, the shadows beneath his eyes, the bruised forehead. He looked troubled, but she knew his mood had nothing to do with the attack. Something else lay heavily upon her son and she knew very well what it was.

"Have you given our discussion any further thought, Max?" she asked him gently.

She was a formidable woman. Tall, grey haired and grey eyed, she had been a considerable beauty in her youth and even now, in her late fifties, she was still an extremely attractive woman. Widowed for some five years she had watched over her son and seen him inherit his father's title and estate with mixed feelings. She had thought him too young then to take on the duties of his estate but now the time had come for him to accept his responsibilities.

"I have thought of nothing else," he replied.

She sighed. "It was your father's dearest wish to see you happily married and settled at Langley," she said. "That is why he added that condition into his will."

Her son's face clouded with the suppressed anger he had been feeling ever since he had been informed of his father's wishes.

"I would have been delighted to accede to my father's wishes." He seemed to grind out the words. "Unfortunately as the only woman I wish to marry is – unacceptable – I find the whole subject extremely repugnant."

His mother's face darkened at his words. Her eyes were snapping with the fury she felt as her son dared to mention that woman in her presence.

"Your father's fortune was not entailed," she managed to speak at last. "He could leave it to anyone or anything he chose. Your title and the estate are yours to do with what you will but your fortune, Maxim, is only to be released to you on your thirtieth birthday, provided you are married." She took another deep, steadying breath. "And as you will be thirty before the end of the year, my dear, I suggest you find a suitable bride as soon as possible."

She indicated the pile of invitations on the table before her. "I am sure," she said, "that somewhere here we will find you such a young lady." Her voice held a note of steely purpose in her words.

He was frowning again as his mother continued. "I will make it quite clear, Max, that only a young lady from a respectable family with good connections will be acceptable to both your father's executors and myself."

He stood up and slammed the cup onto the table, the tea splashing out over the carefully scribed invitations.

Anger flashed into his eyes, reflected in the stiff posture of his body. "This is intolerable!" he exclaimed. "How could my father be so – so – controlling, so selfish as to expect me to marry someone just to inherit his money?"

His mother bit down her own temper, quite as volatile as her son's.

"He wanted to see you happy, Max. Happy, settled and living peacefully on your estates, not racketing around town like an overgrown schoolboy. I cannot bear to think of your inheritance being given away but if that means you must marry to achieve it then marry you must."

Max was by now pacing up and down the confined space of his mother's Drawing Room. The urge to leave, to find some action to satisfy his restlessness and calm himself down was almost overwhelming. He forced himself to pause, however. The situation was insufferable but he recognised the anguish in his mother's words and he knew it was not her fault.

He took a deep, steadying breath. "Very well, Mama," he agreed. "Accept the invitations, I will go to every party, every Ball, every damn Assembly in the Season's calendar." The words were forced out of him. "I will find a bride this Season and marry before Christmas or die trying."

His mother's body sagged in relief against the padded upholstery of her sofa.

"Thank you, my darling," she said softly.

He bowed to her and picked up her hand. "I will go to Portland Square now, Mama. When I return, you can inform me of where I will be going tonight."

He pressed a gentle kiss onto his mother's hand. "Farewell, Mama. I trust between us we will find someone suitable."

A slight smile touched the corners of his mouth and bowing once more, he left her.

In the Drawing Room of the Wetherby family home, an excited Georgiana was regaling her cousin with her adventures of the previous night, being presented to King George, the extravagance of Court, the elegant courtiers, the beautiful gowns of the young ladies being presented and, of course, the handsome young men.

Amelia was smiling indulgently at her daughter whilst perusing the gratifyingly large number of invitations that had arrived that morning, requesting the pleasure of the company of Miss Georgiana Wetherby to several of the most influential houses in London.

Callista was listening intently to her cousin, but her attention was not wholly upon the entertaining tales of the Palace. Dressed soberly in her dark green day dress, her hair tied severely back in green velvet ribbons, dark shadows under her eyes were testament to her sleepless night and she picked listlessly at the embroidery in her lap as Georgie described the grandeur of her presentation.

James the Butler entered the Salon bearing a visiting card upon a silver salver, interrupting Miss Georgiana's artless chatter. Amelia almost preened with delight as she read the card inscribed with the name of Sir Maxim Langley, Marquis of Moreland.

"Please show him in," she agreed, graciously.

A Marquis. She could not have wished for better. The young ladies rose as their visitor entered and curtsied formally as the young man bowed over his hostess' hand and bowed in turn to Augustus who rose to shake hands with his caller.

Callista looked up and was shocked once again to see the stranger from last night standing in their Drawing Room, introducing himself to her Uncle.

Georgiana's eyes were sparkling as she gazed upon the devastatingly handsome young man. Being careful not to stare, nevertheless her glance took in the height of the dark haired man, the width of his shoulders in the immaculately cut Weston riding jacket, the tightly honed stomach and muscular thighs in his riding breeches.

"I have come to thank your household for their prompt action in saving my life last night," he was explaining to Augustus.

"I heard all about it from my Butler, Sir Maxim," Augustus replied.

Georgiana had not heard about the dramatic events of the previous night. Wrapped up in her own excitements, she had retired straight to bed and had not stayed up to listen to her father's discussion with his manservants.

"Papa," she interjected. "Pray what happened?"

Augustus turned his attention away from Max and smiled at his daughter.

"Why your cousin here alerted the household to the villainous attack being perpetrated on Sir Maxim outside our home last night."

All eyes turned to Callista. She was blushing and she lowered her head.

Max stared at her; he had been convinced she was a servant. She looked up and for a moment their eyes locked and he felt a strange shiver of recognition go through him as her wide green eyes stared straight into his. Where did he know her from?

"Then I must thank you for your assistance, Miss Wetherby."

"Wingrove," she replied. "Callista Wingrove. I am happy to have been of service, sir. I trust you have no ill effects after the blows those villains inflicted upon you."

"No," he replied, "none whatsoever. I am a little bruised, but that will pass in due course."

She looked directly at him and she felt that strange, dizzying sensation she had experienced when the old gypsy woman had clutched her hand.

Georgiana, none too pleased at the attention taken from her, cast an impatient glance towards her mother.

Amelia intervened immediately.

"Sir Maxim," she diverted his attention away from her niece. "May I also introduce you to my daughter, The Honourable Georgiana Wetherby."

Georgie curtsied prettily to their guest and gazed up at him from limpid blue eyes. She held out her hand and he took it, bowing over it and kissing the pale slim hand.

Callista took a step back and returned to her seat on the sofa.

Augustus recognised the look from his wife and inviting his guest to sit, engaged him in conversation.

"We were away at Court last night, Sir Maxim," he said. "My daughter here was presented to King George."

Max forced a smile to his stiff features and turned to his host's attractive daughter. "I am sorry to have missed the occasion, Miss Wetherby," he smiled at her.

"It would have saved you a blow to the head," Callista said and blushed again at the angry glance her Aunt cast her way.

Max smiled again, this time genuinely amused. "You are quite right, Miss Wingrove. Pray, why were you not also at Court?"

An uncomfortable silence lasted for a moment until her Uncle intervened. "Callista has not lived with us for long," he explained. "The request for presentation at Court had already been sent before she joined us." He smiled and patted her hand. "She will, of course, be joining us for the rest of the entertainments the Season has to offer."

Callista returned his smile.

"In fact," her Aunt took up the theme, "we are holding a Ball this weekend, and we would be delighted if you could join us. It is Georgiana's Coming Out Ball, but of course Callista will be in attendance."

For all the world it sounded as though Amelia Wetherby was promoting both her daughter and niece equally. Max was quite well aware that in reality she was deciding that unless her daughter attracted the attention of a Duke perhaps this particular Marquis would do very well.

The Marquis had taken in the situation at a glance. He recognised all the signs of a wealthy family and their poor relation. Georgiana was stunningly beautiful, dressed in the latest fashion, her hair professionally styled. Everything about her screamed wealth, beauty and the pampered daughter of indulgent parents. Callista, with her pale face, eyes shadowed, her hair scraped back into a severe style she had obviously done herself, and her dress, smart but last year's style – everything about her told him she was not only poor but embarrassed to have to accept the charity of her wealthy relatives. There was some affection from her cousin and Uncle but the Aunt was ambitious and did not intend to let the dowdy niece outshine her beloved daughter.

Max's eyes narrowed slightly as he observed the family group. Chatting amiably to Sir Augustus, he was well aware of the predatory nature of the glances cast his way by both Lady Amelia and Georgiana. Only Callista, working diligently at her sewing, head down, eyes firmly avoiding looking at him, seemed aloof and unaffected by his presence.

After staying the requisite half an hour, he declined the offer of refreshment and stood to take his leave. Bowing solicitously over his hostess' extended hand, he promised to see them again at Georgiana's party and turned once more to Callista.

"Miss Wingrove," he murmured, holding her hand for far longer than necessary. "Once again, my sincere thanks. Your actions certainly saved my life. If there is ever anything I can do for you, please do not hesitate to ask."

She looked up at him, her clear green eyes looking directly into his. A jolt of recognition momentarily took him by surprise. "I am sorry, Miss Wingrove, but I must ask have we ever met?"

Acutely aware of the narrowed gaze of her Aunt looking her way, Callista smiled slightly and shook her head. "I think not, sir," she replied. "I am sure I would have remembered."

He bowed once more, punctiliously polite and left them. Two of the ladies agog with excitement, Sir Augustus pleased with the young man's manners and obvious good breeding, and Callista left with a frown between her eyes, trying desperately to remember those dreams which had haunted her all her life. They were vague, frightening nightmares – full of fighting and horror and death. Why was this man so important, his features so clear in her mind that even now as he left them, she could close her eyes and see him as clearly as if he stood in front of her.

"Callie." Georgiana's voice brought her back to earth. "What on earth happened? Why didn't you tell me you had met the Marquis?"

Aware that her relatives were staring at her, Callista fought to control the blush she could again feel spreading from her neck upwards. "Your news seemed much more interesting than mine, Georgie," she replied. "Besides, I had no idea who he was or whether we would see him again. I was just glad I could help prevent a murder on our doorstep." She smiled at them, the frown disappearing, the colour on her cheeks returning to normal.

Lady Amelia was still looking thoughtful but as she looked at her daughter and niece, seeing for herself the difference the young Marquis had noticed earlier, one so glowingly beautiful, the other no more than passably pretty, dowdy even, she relaxed slightly.

"A fine start to our Season, girls." She magnanimously included Callista in her statement. "If our first visitor is a Marquis, no less, imagine who else we can expect?" She preened herself, picking up the raft of invitations spread out before them. Her eyes shone briefly and she bestowed a glowing smile on her beloved daughter. "You will be a Duchess yet, my love," she exclaimed.

Augustus sighed, suddenly realising the extent of the social events his wife was determined to make him attend, and thought longingly of his estates where even now his son would be returning from school to take advantage of the hunting and shooting in Yorkshire.

"Hmph," he growled. "Let's try and get Callie married off as well Amelia." He picked up his newspaper and shook it out. "I don't think I could stand more than one London Season."

Callista and Georgiana laughed.

Amelia was outraged, as if she would ever go to the expense and trouble of a further Season for a mere niece.

"Pray, do not worry about me, Uncle Augustus," Callista replied. "I'm sure I can manage quite well without a husband and once Georgie here is married to her Duke it will suit me very well to return and live quietly in the country."

Georgiana smiled at her cousin's jesting. "Do you not wish to marry, Callie?" she asked, puzzled slightly. "Don't you want your own establishment, your own carriage, horses, and servants?"

Callista shook her head, her eyes sparkling with merriment. "I am sure I would attract no such rich young man, Georgie," she replied. "I may one day be worthy enough to attract the attention of a clergyman perhaps, or a schoolmaster and join them in their life's work – in the meantime I am quite content, I assure you."

Georgiana actually shuddered at the thought of such a lowly station in life, grateful that such a future was never to be hers. Her ambition was almost as great as her mother's and even though the young Marquis was by no means as great a catch as she was hoping for, there was something very attractive about the tall, handsome and extremely virile young man who had recently left her Drawing Room.

She wondered perhaps if she ought to lower her sights slightly.

Suddenly the importance of her Ball seemed to take on an even greater significance and looking at the calm face of her cousin, she wondered, not for the first time, what Callista was thinking. Perhaps Callista thought she might possibly win the interest of the young man herself, and Georgiana smiled to herself at the impossibility of such a thing happening. The ringing of the front door bell interrupted her thoughts and her eyes sparkled as the stream of visitors started to arrive. Sir Augustus groaned and her mother rose excitedly to greet their next guests. Georgiana's Season was about to become a great success.

Chapter Four

The Ballroom of the Wetherby mansion glittered with the lights of a thousand candles. The huge gold-framed mirrors sparkled, reflecting the gathered throng of dancers and the air was redolent with the smell of enormous bouquets of freshly cut flowers. The footmen in their green and gold livery circulated around the edge of the Ballroom, bearing silver salvers full of glasses of the best champagne. The orchestra played and the guests indulged in the latest dance craze, waltzing around the large, opulent room, the men elegantly attired, the women beautiful in gowns of silk, all the colours of the rainbow reflected in their finery.

Most of the unmarried young women present were wearing either stark virginal white or, like Callista, the softer muted ivory colour considered suitable for their age and status in life.

The Ton had turned out in force to welcome Lady Georgiana Wetherby into their ranks. She, in turn, outshone every other debutante. Her gown was the richest, her jewellery the finest, her hair dressed in the latest style, interwoven with diamond clips, a sparkling bejewelled pampered beauty whose eyes outshone even the diamond necklace around her throat.

Callista, in her turn had surprised everyone, including her Aunt, by appearing in her new ivory satin gown, wearing the silk gloves and the few diamond star hair pins bequeathed to her by her dear departed mother. Georgie's maid had styled her hair, so that it hung in smooth ringlets halfway down her back. Whilst a few untamed curls escaped the maid's ministrations and framed her face, she looked elegant and serene and although her own looks could never outshine those of her cousin's, she nevertheless attracted many admiring glances from the young men present.

Georgie had already gathered about her a crowd of potential suitors and Lady Amelia watched with undisguised pleasure as her daughter danced her way around the Ballroom with one after another of the young men, vying for her attention.

Even Callista, to her great amusement, found herself in demand and dancing almost every dance with a variety of the young men invited to Georgiana's spectacularly successful debut.

The arrival of some latecomers caused a stir amongst the assembled guests and Callista was quick to notice a frown creasing the smooth brow of her Aunt. Over the shoulder of her dance partner she followed her Aunt's gaze to the entrance.

A party of three stood there and she caught her breath as she realised one of the latecomers was none other than Sir Maxim Langley, the man she had saved from the villainous footpads four nights earlier.

He was standing with another couple and in the few moments her eyes lingered on them, she could not help but compare him with every other man in the room, finding them all wanting. He was tall, his dark hair glistening, his clothes showing the impeccable cut only Weston, the Ton's favourite tailor could achieve, his dark evening jacket stretched closely over broad shoulders, his linen white, his pantaloons tight against the muscular hardness of his abdomen. His eyes roamed the room, a kind of bored arrogance about his stance that made her instantly prickle, her back straightening, unconsciously disapproving of his perceived weariness.

Her partner, The Honourable Freddie Acheson followed the direction of her gaze and she found herself turning with the movement of the dance so her back was to the newcomers.

She smiled up at him. "I beg your pardon, Mr Acheson," she apologised. "I was distracted by the entrance of some new guests."

Freddie was an affable young man, slightly older than Callista, the veteran of several London Seasons and he frowned slightly, before his brow cleared and he returned her smile.

"Not at all, Miss Wingrove, perfectly understandable, Sir Maxim is very well known to me, it is his – companions I am surprised to see."

The movement of the dance afforded her a further view of Max's companions. They were a striking couple, they looked curiously alike and whilst the man was a tall, fair-haired good-looking man, it was the lady beside him who drew everyone's attention.

She was stunning. Dressed provocatively in a tight gown of midnight blue, her creamy breasts rose above the low neckline, trimmed with sparkling crystals that shimmered and glittered in the candlelight. She carried a huge fan of midnight blue ostrich feathers, perfectly matching the feathers adorning the white blonde sweep of hair above a heart-shaped face. Her eyes were as blue as the sapphires around her neck. She surveyed the scene before her with the same bored expression worn by Max, until she turned her head to him and her face lit up with a smile that transformed her features from mere beauty to an animation Callista had seldom seen before.

The newcomers were causing somewhat of a stir. She watched as her Aunt and Uncle went over to greet them.

"Who are they, Mr Acheson?" she enquired. "I have met Sir Maxim; it is the other couple I have never seen before."

As they waltzed around the room, Callista could see other people staring at the woman in blue. She was being introduced to her relatives seemingly unaware of the disturbance caused by her presence.

Freddie's boyish, good-looking face was marred momentarily by the slightest of frowns. He seemed to be struggling with the thoughts going through his mind, as if wondering how much he could actually tell the innocent young woman with whom he was currently dancing.

He was a forthright young man and if not blessed with a high degree of intelligence, he could not deny his innate honesty any longer.

"That, Miss Wingrove," he explained, raising his voice slightly above the music, "is Sir Damon Fortescue and his sister the Lady Davina Fitzpatrick. Max's estate borders the Fortescue's and the families are old friends."

"I thought they looked alike," Callista replied.

"Twins." Freddie whirled her to a sudden stop as the music ended. She smiled up at him once more and took his arm as he escorted her to the edge of the Ballroom where he enquired if he could interest her in some refreshment.

They seated themselves on one of the comfortable sofas that bordered the room and together sipped champagne as they surveyed the room.

Sir Maxim was currently bowing over Georgiana's hand and Callista watched as her cousin curtsied in response before bestowing a brilliant smile on him, and a much cooler greeting for the Fortescue twins. She was obviously privy to more information about the family than was Callista and as she drank her wine, Callista's curiosity prompted her to quiz Mr Acheson further.

"They seem to have caused quite a commotion by their presence," she said softly to him. "Is it remiss of me to enquire as to their history?"

Freddie sighed, but like her, he could not take his eyes off the trio. Lady Davina was as exotic as a bird of paradise; she was astoundingly attractive and there was about her a vibrancy, an air of suppressed excitement that she could barely contain.

"Old established family," Freddie explained. "Member of the Top 500 families – father was a rake and gambled away most of the family fortune. Damon inherited the estate a couple of years ago and he's now trying to repair years' worth of neglect – Davina was married off to an Irish Peer when she was barely seventeen – for a huge settlement apparently which saved the rest of the family from going bankrupt." He stopped abruptly and Callista followed his eyes to see Max leading Lady Davina out onto the dance floor.

The music started again and soon the dance floor filled with couples, her cousin amongst them.

"Is her husband not with her?" Callista enquired, watching the possessive way Max was holding Lady Davina, his eyes never leaving hers. She, in turn, was laughing up at something he had said.

They made a striking couple and danced as though they were the only people in the room. Callista envied them their composure, their total self-confidence if not the arrogant way they held themselves.

She watched as Georgiana started to dance with Sir Damon and Callista shivered as the strangest feeling engulfed her when she saw the way Georgie was looking at Damon.

"No, Callum Fitzpatrick rarely leaves Ireland these days – he was injured a few years ago and his health never really recovered."

"How tragic," she exclaimed, her sympathy aroused. "How was he injured?"

Her innocent question seemed to cause Freddie some consternation.

Eventually he coughed slightly and replied, "He was shot in a duel. His injuries were life threatening and he developed some kind of fever. He recovered but it left him maimed."

Appalled, Callista shook her head. "Oh I am so sorry – I should not have pressed you to tell me that. Was Callum a friend of yours?"

Freddie shook his head. "No, he is considerably older than me; he was not one of my circle. He is also a lot older than his wife and it was one of his wife's lovers he challenged to a duel."

"One of... oh!" Innocent of the world and society as she was, Callista suddenly became aware of the reason for Lady Davina's guarded welcome and the shocked expression on the faces of most of the other women in the Ballroom.

She was from one of the oldest, most respected families in London and therefore no doors would ever be closed to her, but the scandal which surrounded her was obviously well known and disapproval bristled from every respectable lady in the room.

"And Sir Maxim?" she asked, her voice sounding strained even to her own ears.

"Childhood sweethearts, apparently." Freddie shrugged and swallowed the rest of his wine. "He was sent abroad after the fall of the French at Waterloo. His father sent him to sort out their Italian estates over there, and when he got back Davina had been married and packed off to Dublin. She divides her time now between her husband's home in Ireland and her brother's English estates and London house."

He did not enlighten her as to the current rumours which surrounded Lady Davina – and Max. It was not his business and he did not want to be the one to sully the ears of such an innocent as Callista Wingrove with rumour and conjecture. Although he knew, as did most of Max's contemporaries that Max and Lady Davina were certainly embroiled in some kind of relationship.

Watching the dancers, Callista's attention returned to her cousin, dancing lightly and effortlessly with Sir Damon Fortescue.

"Are the fortunes of the Fortescue family improving now that Sir Damon is in charge?" she enquired.

Damon Fortescue was a good-looking man, although his own fair handsomeness was only a pale imitation of the vibrant beauty of his sister.

"I believe so," Freddie replied. "Although rumour has it that marriage to a suitable heiress might go a long way to getting the estate properly back on its feet." He stood up and offered her his hand to help her to stand. "Now, Miss Wingrove," he asserted suddenly, "as no one has claimed you for this dance, I think a further waltz is in order and you can tell me all about your own family."

Instantly aware that her interest in Max Langley and his companions had overshadowed her normal good manners, a faint rosy tinge touched her cheeks. "Of course, Mr Acheson. I should be delighted."

With her hand in his, they joined the other dancers circulating the floor, and anyone seeing Callista chatting naturally and smiling up at her companion would have mistaken the pink cheeks as nothing more than the exertions of the dance and the heat of the room.

The Ball was a success, the crush of people crowded into the Wetherby's mansion was a confirmation of the popularity of the latest debutante, and Georgiana's face blushed most becomingly from her triumphant acceptance into the world she had so longed for.

She had attracted a good deal of attention from many of the young men present. Several of the most influential and titled men in England had danced with her, paid her compliments and requested permission to call on her; her mother exulting in the knowledge that her daughter was undeniably the belle of the Ball.

With one notable exception, of course.

An invitation had most certainly not been sent to Lady Davina Fitzpatrick. However, her brother and Maxim Langley had been invited and where they went, Lady Davina accompanied them. No one, no hostess would ever refuse her entry; even the formidable Patronesses of Almacks, that bastion of respectability, did not turn her away and her requests for vouchers for admittance were always granted immediately.

They strolled together out onto the terrace of the Ballroom, the cool March evening a pleasant escape from the overheated room.

"You have another six months, Max," Davina said softly, not wanting to be overheard by the other guests who had also left the Ballroom seeking a breath of air. "There is still time."

His face was still and serious. "Time for what? Time for your husband to die? He would not be so obliging."

"Unfortunately not, my dear," she replied. "Besides, my reputation is bad enough already – if I were to remarry within a few days of his death, I would be ostracised for the rest of my life."

She smiled up at him, a dazzling, cold and calculated smile. "Callum has clung to life since his duel two years ago – he will live forever just to thwart me, I fear."

She pressed his arm through the superfine cloth of his

immaculately cut jacket. "No, I am afraid we must find you a wife, Max," she sighed. "I am sure there is someone…"

She stopped at one of the open French windows and looked in at the opulent and crowded Ballroom.

"Somewhere in there…" she nodded at the throng, "is the perfect girl."

He smiled back at her, suddenly amused. "Lady Georgiana?" he asked.

She laughed softly, a husky, throaty sound. "Oh dear me no – she will insist on staying in town and attending every Ball, every party – she will be far too demanding, Max – she will have you dancing a merry tune, I think."

Her eyes lifted to his and the message conveyed between them needed no explanation.

"Our pleasant – interludes – would have to be postponed – indefinitely… I could not possibly allow that. No, perhaps the companion, the poor relation would be a far more suitable choice."

Her lips pouted and he stared at them, mesmerised, seized with a desire to press a kiss against them.

"She would not dare to contradict or demand anything of you, my darling Max."

"What if my wife were to demand children?" he teased her. "I would be obliged to fulfil certain conjugal duties in order to satisfy her wishes."

Her eyes flashed sapphire fire.

"And what if I were to demand your presence to satisfy me – on your wedding night?"

She put a long finger up to his cheek and stroked it gently. He caught it and pressed a kiss against the palm of her hand.

"Your wish is my command," he whispered.

Her throaty laughter echoed along the deserted balcony and threading her arm through his, he escorted her back into the Ballroom.

After another dance with Lady Davina, Max excused himself and made his way over to Lady Amelia and Sir Augustus. He bowed to Callista who was standing with her Aunt, her face a little pink. Her eyes, however, were sparkling with enjoyment and a few more curls had escaped from her carefully styled hair to frame her face. She curtsied in response and when he requested the pleasure of the next dance, she nodded and placed her hand carefully on his arm to follow him onto the dance floor.

The orchestra started playing the strains of a waltz, a slow, melodic dance and despite the heat of the evening, Callista shivered slightly as his arm went around her waist, pulling her close to him. She looked up into his face and found his eyes looking down into her own. He was frowning slightly, and the expression on his face startled her.

"Why do I have this feeling we have met before?" he asked quietly.

She smiled, a little uncertainly. "I'm not sure, Sir Maxim," she replied. "I don't think we have ever moved in the same circles until now. I have lived all my life in the North and did not go out much in Society."

They moved together around the room, unconsciously graceful, their feet moving together in perfect harmony, and their bodies totally in tune with each other. They were attracting interest as they danced together, but they were unaware of the curious stares and Max certainly did not see the frown and glare of pure malice directed their way by Davina.

"Please, call me Max," he said. "Maxim is such a mouthful." He smiled and for a heart stopping moment, as she returned his smile, a faint memory, an echo of some long forgotten time touched the edge of his mind, gone in a moment, as faint, as ethereal as a morning mist burned away by the touch of the sun.

"Very well, Max, you must call me Callie in that case," she replied.

"Why did you not go out much in Society, Callie?" he asked.

"My father was the local Vicar and my mother died when I was a child. Until Aunt Amelia asked me to live with them my entertainments consisted of village fetes and organising Christmas parties for the local children."

He laughed, a genuine laugh of pure amusement, finding her self-deprecating humour highly diverting.

"Then no," he replied, "I do not think we will have met – my upbringing was sadly lacking in Church Christmas parties. My family hold a Christmas Ball every year for the local people – that is as close as I get to the village children."

"Where is it you live, when not in London?" she enquired.

In perfect time with the music, they danced on together. "In the South West of England," he replied. "On the borders of Somerset and Devon to be exact."

"I have heard it is a beautiful area," she said. "My cousin is determined to go to Bath at the end of the Season."

"Then you must call to see me," he continued. "There is much to visit and explore near where I live."

She smiled but at his words, she closed her eyes and a vision appeared. She saw an image of tall, silent, standing stones, rough-hewn columns of infinite history and power – and horror.

"Callie, are you all right?" His voice seemed to be coming from a long way off.

She rallied immediately, shaking her head slightly to dispel the vision, ignoring the feeling of foreboding that always accompanied her thoughts of the Stones. The gypsy woman's warnings were still vividly clear.

"Yes, thank you, I am perfectly well, Max," she said softly. "It is just the heat, I think."

The waltz continued. They danced together in perfect rhythm, their steps mirroring the others, perfectly synchronised. Callista did not see the narrow-eyed glances directed towards her by both her Aunt and Lady Davina. The music entranced her, as did the sheer pleasure of being in the arms of a man she had dreamed about so often for so many years. A pleasure tinged with a kind of darkness – a premonition that all was not as it should be. But, as she found herself caught up in his arms, looking into his eyes, conversing with him, laughing at something he said, she had the strangest feeling she was exactly where she belonged.

The dance was over far too quickly. He escorted her back to her Aunt and, with the slightest of bows, smiled down at her once more. He addressed his remarks to her Uncle, however.

"I hope I may have the pleasure of calling upon you once more, Sir Augustus," he said. "And, of course, seeing you at Almacks, Lady Wetherby."

Amelia smiled fondly at him. Even though he had not, so far, danced or paid any particular attention to Georgiana, she was not immune to his charm.

"We have, indeed, secured vouchers for Almacks," she replied. "We will be attending the next Assembly on Wednesday."

He smiled at Callista once more, his blue eyes crinkling slightly as if sharing a secret joke between them. "I look forward to seeing you again, Miss Wingrove." He took her hand and bowed over it once more.

"And I you, Sir Maxim," she replied, reverting to the more formal use of his name.

He left them then to return to his companions. Her Aunt rounded on Callista and Augustus immediately.

"I had no idea he was such an – intimate – friend of Lady Fitzpatrick." Amelia was smiling but the tone of her voice left no room for doubt. She was not amused.

Augustus sighed heavily and swallowed his now warm wine.

"Callista, in future please be sure to check a man's background before you are tempted to save them from being murdered," he scolded her.

Callista hid a smile at her Uncle's words but her eyes sparkled and she agreed in as sober a voice as she could summon that indeed she would be sure to rescue no further young men from being attacked on their doorstep.

Amelia was too busy observing Lady Davina to realise she was being mocked and drew her husband's attention to that lady once again.

"She is the talk of London," she whispered. "I have heard she has a different lover every week."

Augustus rolled his eyes heavenwards. "Amelia – do not be ridiculous. You know how the old pussies of this town love to gossip. She comes from one of the most respectable families in England, her brother is a fine upstanding gentleman – I am sure what you have heard is nothing but rumour and hearsay."

As the fine, upstanding man in question was currently escorting her daughter out onto the dance floor, Amelia kept her opinions to herself. She knew Augustus well enough not to carry on with this kind of discussion. His voice held a note of exasperation and annoyance and she did not want to provoke a show of bad manners and temper at this, their daughter's triumphant party.

Callista accepted an invitation for another waltz and as she danced close to her cousin, she could not help but observe the way Sir Damon was looking at Georgie and Georgie – for once Georgiana surprised her cousin. She was looking up at Damon with an expression on her face Callista had never seen before. Georgiana had never looked more radiant in her life.

Callista was smiling, but as she circled the floor in the arms of her latest partner, the smile left her face as she found herself being observed, with a kind of mocking, cool expression by Lady Davina Fitzpatrick and the thoughtful, serious eyes of Max Langley. She felt a cold finger of presentiment touch her spine and she shivered. There was something about Lady Davina that left her with that same strange sense of familiarity she felt when meeting Max, although in Davina's case, it was one of darkness and, somehow, fear.

She remembered the feeling she had experienced whilst dancing with Max earlier and despite the fact that he seemed to be more than a close friend of the most notorious woman in London, Callista felt a sense of ambivalence towards him.

Part of her was glad that this was just the beginning of the Season. Thanks to Georgiana, she was going to attend all the same Balls, routs, assemblies and parties where, if she was not much mistaken, she would be seeing a lot of Max over the coming months. On the other hand, she was seriously disturbed for exactly the same reasons.

Lihanna 3

Lihanna stretched and stirred several hours later. She was warm and cosy under heavy covers and as she put her hand out, she felt the unmistakable luxury of a fur weighting down the rough woollen blankets. She sleepily opened her eyes and as her vision grew accustomed to the dim morning light, she realised someone was observing her.

Julius was seated on a low stool beside the pulled back curtain. He was wearing a heavy fur robe, protection against the cold early morning. Drinking from a goblet, he was silently watching her sleep and as she opened her eyes and stared directly at him, she saw a slight smile lift the corners of his mouth.

"Good morning, Princess," he said quietly.

She found herself staring at him properly for the first time. He was not as old as she had first thought, perhaps only in his late twenties – his hair was cropped short, almost black, his skin was tanned and his eyes were the deepest blue she had ever seen in her life. Even sitting still he seemed to exude suppressed energy – he was staring at her with an intensity she found disturbing.

"Did you sleep well?" he asked, his voice low, speaking her language perfectly with no hint of an accent.

She felt curious about him for the first time.

"I did, I thank you. "

"My servants will bring you food and drink shortly, and they have procured some clothes for you. Your dress was stained and torn; they have taken it away to clean and repair it for you."

She sat up, keeping the covers wrapped around her, suddenly aware of her nakedness.

"You are well provided for, General," she said. "You travel with remarkable luxury for a man leading an invasion."

That slight sardonic smile played around his lips again. He leaned back against the pillar of the tent – the pillar was stout and solid and the tent was made of a leather material, stretched thinly over poles.

"I am not leading the invasion, Princess," he replied, "I merely follow the orders of my superiors and lead the men under my command. I do not wage war against civilians and my role now is to secure this area and await the arrival of my Generals – we will be here for some time until peace is restored."

She frowned, scowling at him. "What about my people? Are they being as well cared for as I?"

He stood up. "They have been provided with food, drink and shelter. Once your mother has surrendered, we can begin the process of rebuilding your homes and setting up a fort in this area." He paused, looking down into her upturned face.

"I am to remain here to oversee the settlement," he said. "I have no desire for more bloodshed, but I will stamp out any rebellion, have no fear of that."

He was close to her, beside her low bed and to her surprise, he crouched beside her, so his face was on a level with her own.

She did not flinch or move away but held her breath as he reached out long fingers and gently touched her hand that held the fur covering her breasts. A strange, shocking sensation went through her at his touch. He was clean-shaven and she stared at his lips, her own mouth suddenly very dry.

He took her hand in his and held it very gently. "Do not fear me, Lihanna," he murmured. "I will return you unharmed to your mother and I will negotiate a real peace with your people."

She was sitting facing him. He bowed his head and gently kissed her hand. Their heads were almost touching and an irrational desire to reach out and touch him filled her.

He looked up and the moment passed. She pulled her hand out of his and hugged the furs around her closely.

"You give me your word you will not harm my people, or my mother?" she demanded, imperious once again.

He smiled, genuine amusement lighting up his face. "I give you my word, Princess," he agreed and, standing, he left her in her small bedchamber and returned to the main room of his quarters.

Voices heralded the arrival of his servants and a few minutes later, clean clothes, shoes and combs were presented to tame the wildness of her hair. She rose and dressed and it was a true princess who joined her captor shortly afterwards.

The small table held food and water and as the rumbling in her stomach reminded her that it was almost twenty-four hours since she had eaten, she seated herself next to the General and picked up a slice of the meat laid on the platters. She had never thought she would actually eat with one of these invaders but the trauma and heartbreak of the previous day suddenly seemed a million miles away.

To all outward appearances, she seemed calm, composed and accepting of her fate. Her mind, however, was whirling with thoughts and ideas. She found herself scanning the tented quarters looking for a way out, wondering if she could manage to escape to try to find her brother.

Julius seemed amused by her subdued demeanour, and saw the imperceptible glances around the tent. He knew exactly what she was thinking.

"No, Princess," he said. "The camp is well guarded. Even if you were allowed out of these quarters, you would not get far. Accept you are my prisoner and await the arrival of your mother – or one of your brothers – they are said to be close by and I hope they will be here soon. They will want to negotiate for your freedom and I want their surrender. It is a simple business arrangement."

He sighed. "I grow weary of wars and battles," he said. "I have fought my way across this land of yours. The rest of this Island is now under Roman occupation and we seek nothing more than a lasting peace – accept it, Lihanna."

She glared defiantly at him but he returned her stare calmly. "Make yourself comfortable." His voice hardened. "Do not try to escape, do not cause any trouble and do not try my patience. I told you, I grow weary of constant fighting but I will brook no disobedience from you."

She lowered her eyes. "And what if they do not seek to release me?" she whispered.

"Then you will remain my prisoner until I decide what to do with you," he replied and the amusement was back in his voice. "I will bring peace to this country and if it means I must marry the local Princess to do it, then so be it."

She gasped in outrage at his words but he merely laughed, his eyes sparkling. He stood up to leave her and before she could move, protest, or turn away, he stooped down and captured her face in his hands. His smile disappeared as he lowered his head to hers and kissed her full on the mouth. A long, hard, scorching kiss that seared into her heart and soul.

She started to struggle and he released her immediately. He pulled away from her and left her, to stare after him in shocked disbelief. She raised a trembling hand to her mouth – the second time in two days that she had been kissed.

Once by Daveth – the softest, briefest of touches, reverential almost. Now this – this masterful, demanding assault on her senses which left her head reeling and caused strange feelings to stir within her.

More troubled than ever, she ate some more of the food laid before her, drank the water, and went over to the door of the tent. She was well guarded and had to content herself with sitting in the doorway watching as the camp and village came to life all around her.

She could not leave, she could not rejoin her friends, and she could only sit and impatiently wonder what further twist of fate awaited her.

Chapter Five

Davina Fitzpatrick lay back on the pillows of her huge bed as her lover dressed in the half light of the dawn streaming through the partially opened shutters.

She yawned and stretched luxuriously, a cat who had feasted on cream, and she watched through half opened eyes as Max carefully tied his cravat, a frown creasing the smoothness of his brow.

"I wish you did not have to rush away," she said softly, her voice low, husky.

Realising she was awake, he turned back to her and smiled, the frown easing immediately. He crossed back over to the bed and bending down, pressed the lightest of kisses on her pouting lips.

"Your reputation, my dear," he explained, "will not be helped if the servants gossip about me leaving your bedchamber at this hour. I should have left long ago."

She laughed, a throaty growl of laughter. "My reputation is already ruined," she replied. "Callum saw to that years ago with his meddling and interfering."

Interfering with her numerous affaires, she added to herself. As far as Max was concerned, it suited her to let him think Callum was the possessive jealous husband he thought him.

He touched her cheek gently, his eyes going lower to the partially exposed bosom, as pale as alabaster. His mouth felt dry with the desire she invoked in him.

"I must go," he murmured, "but I will see you later, I think?"

She rolled over onto her back, arching it just enough to let the long silver sheen of hair fall from her breasts, exposing more of her silken body to his view.

"Of course. Do you intend to go riding today? I believe Damon was speaking of it last night."

"Yes, he was wishing to ride on the Heath. Will you accompany us?"

Davina was an excellent rider however she had other plans. "No, I think not. I have an appointment with Madame Duvall and then I believe we go to Almacks."

Madame Duvall was the most exclusive, most expensive dressmaker in London. One did not miss an appointment with her. Her dresses were more than just clothing, they were art. Davina was the perfect canvas for Madam Duvall's creativity.

The stirrings of desire were making themselves felt as Max stared down at the pale, slim body of his lover. She was the most attractive, the most seductive of creatures and he knew he had to leave before his resolve totally crumbled. He kissed her again and she wrapped her arms around his neck.

"Come back to me, Max," she whispered, "tonight after Almacks, come back."

It was not a request, it was a fiercely whispered demand and he knew that despite the disapproval of his mother and the unspoken censure of his best friend, he was powerless to resist her demands.

He left a few minutes later, letting himself out of the elegant Fortescue mansion, in the attractive Mayfair area of London. His own home was only a few streets away and no one else stirred on the streets as he made his way homeward. He was deep in thought, the events of the previous night still uppermost in his mind.

He had attended the coming out Ball of Georgiana Wetherby. He had danced with every possible candidate for the position of his bride. The only woman to stir his interest had been Callista

Wingrove, the poor relation. She had been shy but not shrinking, witty and amusing and had captured his undivided attention whilst they danced.

She was extremely pretty; if not in the same league as her beautiful cousin or the dazzling Lady Davina, she had the kind of face he could not forget. He could recall in vivid detail her huge green eyes and the way her hair fell about her shoulders in a glorious tumble of dark auburn curls that night she had saved him from his attackers. He frowned, wondering why he could so easily summon her face and figure to his mind. He had met dozens of pretty girls in his life and apart from Davina, he could recall practically nothing about any of them, until now.

Last night, when he and Davina had discussed the various young women attending the Ball, Davina had actually originally suggested Callista as a likely bride but strangely, when he had returned from dancing with Callie, Davina had changed her mind. She had smiled but it was a cool, calculating smile, that had not quite reached her eyes. She had coldly dismissed Miss Wingrove as being just a little too poor and not quite well born enough to become the Marchioness of Moreland.

A slight smile lifted the corners of his mouth. He wondered what his mother would think if she met Callista – she may not be as well born as Davina but her relief at him finding someone would probably far outweigh any misgivings she may have about Callista's background.

His thoughts were in turmoil as he reached home and he went into his study to pour himself a small glass of brandy. He took it over to his favourite chair beside the fire. It was still smouldering, banked up as it had been the previous night. He threw another log onto it and sat back in his chair, watching as the log sparked and caught fire in the embers. He sipped the brandy, not really wanting it but it was too early to summon a servant to bring him anything else. He watched the flames come to life as he remembered the night he had spent with Davina. He knew of her reputation, the notorious Lady Fitzpatrick. He also remembered the girl he had grown up with, his childhood sweetheart, the girl he had wanted to marry when he was twenty and she was seventeen. His mother had disapproved of her even then. Davina had always been too wild, too impetuous, and too headstrong ever to win his mother's favour. She had always said Damon should have been the girl, he was quieter, more controlled, polite, a complete gentleman.

Max's father had sent him away to Italy on some family business – to check on their estate in Sorrento following the fall of Napoleon. By the time he returned, Davina had gone, married off to an Irish Peer old enough to be her father. He had been furious, inconsolable and not even his friend assuring him that Davina had gone into the marriage willingly could dissuade him that she had been forced into an arranged marriage against her will.

He had never met Callum Fitzpatrick. All he knew of the man was what Davina told him two years ago on her return to London. He was jealous, possessive and bitter; she had sought solace from his cruelty in the arms of a young lover. Callum had found out about his wife's indiscretion and had challenged the young man to a duel. Callum had killed the young man and he sustained a serious injury that should have killed him. Max had believed her implicitly. His friend Damon never corrected him, family loyalty and love for his twin sister would not allow him to betray her trust.

Max had heard rumours, he was no fool and he knew Davina well enough to know that she was a passionate, sensual woman and if she had had other lovers before him, he could not blame her. He had wanted her as soon as they met again and she – Max smiled at the memory – had made her interest in him very obvious.

He sighed; this damnable clause in his father's will had come as a total shock. He had resolved to wait until Davina was free of her disabled husband before making her his wife, but this timescale held over his head was intolerable. The thought that his inheritance, the bulk of his father's fortune would go to a distant cousin was insufferable. How could he improve his estates, put into place his plans for modernisation, without the money to pay for it all?

Frustrated, angry, he raked his hands through his hair and leaned his head back on the padded upholstery of the chair. He closed his eyes and sighed once more. Weariness was starting to creep over him but he could not bring himself to move. Warmth and tiredness seeped through his body and gradually he slipped into a restless sleep. Strangely, although his thoughts were full of Davina, it was a pair of flashing green eyes that were the last things on his mind before unconsciousness claimed him.

The cold late February wind blew across the Heath as the two gentlemen of the Ton braved the weather and blew off the cobwebs with a vigorous gallop across the open moorland. Few people were around, the Heath on a good day was a popular destination and one could very often bump into friends and acquaintances. Today the blustery weather and gathering clouds were keeping the crowds away.

They slowed to a gentle walk after the first few miles of thundering gallops and crested the rise of a hill together to behold the strangest of scenes below them.

They could see an open carriage, driven by a Coachman and escorted by a Footman, within which were two young women.

Or, rather, one young woman screaming hysterically as she pressed herself back into the upholstered cushions of the carriage. There was a Footman lying prone on the ground and the second young woman was standing up in the carriage, beating a would-be highwayman about his bare head with a rolled up parasol. She was loudly berating him (in no uncertain terms) as to his character, his manners, and his impertinence in attacking them in broad daylight. The Coachman, attending to his injured colleague was pleading with the young lady to desist and stop provoking the villain but Callista, for it was she, was so incensed at the effrontery of the attempted robbery that his words only served to increase the strength of the blows she was raining down on the head of the masked man.

His gun was lying on the ground near the Footman, whose shoulder was bleeding and who had obviously been hurt in the attack. The attack had simply infuriated the Vicar's daughter and despite Georgiana's fear and hysteria, temper had overcome her sensibilities and the ferocity of her attack on the highwayman had taken them all by surprise. His gun, once emptied into the shoulder of their unfortunate guard was on the floor, summarily knocked out of his hand with the parasol and Callista had launched a furious attack on the disarmed highwayman.

The villain had a mask over his mouth but his hat was on the ground and he was doing his best to wrest the offending weapon from the grasp of the virago wielding it as though it were indeed a stout club.

Max and Damon reined in their horses and took in the scene at a glance. Suppressing a sudden desire to laugh at the absurdity of the hapless highwayman's plight, Max spurred his horse and the two of them started down the hill at a gallop.

Startled by the thunderous sound of horses' hooves, the highwayman looked up and taking in the sight of two well-dressed and furious looking men bearing down on him, he pulled away from the carriage, turned on his heel and ran towards his waiting horse, without waiting to pick up either his pistol or his hat. He pulled himself up into his saddle and angrily wheeled his horse around, kicking it hard to ride away as quickly as he could, making his escape before the two men could reach him. Max saw him on his way, chasing after him for a few hundred yards before letting him go and returning to the carriage.

Damon rode straight to the ladies, throwing himself off his horse and going immediately to the injured man.

Callista, meanwhile, her breast heaving with emotion, her cheeks flushed with temper, turned to her cousin and taking her by the shoulders, shook her fiercely. "Be quiet, Georgie," she demanded. "He's gone. No one will harm us now."

Georgiana, however, had worked herself up into a state of

hysteria and without another word, Callista slapped her cousin's cheek.

"Oh!" Shocked into silence, Georgie put her hand to her stinging cheek and stared uncomprehendingly at Callista.

Max dismounted and opened the carriage door. He held out his hand and Callista placed her hand in his as he helped her out of the carriage. A sudden urge to sweep her into his arms and hug her assailed him, but, restraining himself, he merely held her hand and looked into her face, his eyes sparkling with suppressed humour.

"Miss Wingrove." His voice was shaking with the effort of keeping his laughter under control. "You were magnificent. You were very courageous – defending your cousin and yourself in such a – a vigorous manner."

She did not look amused and turned away from him instead to help her shaking cousin out of the carriage.

"Sir Maxim, Lord Fortescue – how can we ever thank you?" Georgiana, with a red mark on her cheek and tear-stained face still managed to look absurdly attractive.

"We merely frightened the ruffian away," Max replied, turning away from the ladies to join Damon in checking on the injured Footman.

The man was pale but conscious and between them the Coachman and Damon had stemmed the bleeding and were helping him to his feet.

"Miss Wingrove – I think you were getting the better of the encounter," Damon complimented her and he made a sketchy bow to the ladies. "Miss Wetherby, I trust you too are unharmed."

Georgiana was wiping her eyes in a most effective way. Damon wanted nothing more than to rush to her side, to comfort the obviously distressed young woman, but the Footman was injured and leaning heavily on him and the Coachman.

Together, they helped the Footman into the ladies' carriage and Max saw Callista looking down at the parasol that had fallen to the floor, its pink satin sadly stained and spokes sticking out at strange angles.

Bending down, he retrieved it from the dusty path and with a bow, presented it to her.

"I fear it is broken beyond repair, Miss Wingrove," he said, a note of regret in his voice.

She sighed, "It was my favourite parasol too."

Max could help it no longer. With shaking shoulders, he started to laugh. The sight of Callista and the helpless highwayman would stay with him forever. She scowled at him but when Damon joined in with the laughter, her face cleared and she smiled, albeit sheepishly at the assembled company. Even Georgiana, relieved at being spared the ordeal of robbery recovered her sense of humour and went over to her cousin to put her arms around her and hug her.

"Callie, you were so brave," she exclaimed and although puzzled by the gentlemen's obvious merriment, managed a shaky smile. "She would not let him rob us," she went on. "And when John was shot through the shoulder, Callie simply – exploded."

Gradually getting his merriment under control, Max recovered himself to enquire as to why they had chosen such a remote spot to take their afternoon drive.

Georgiana's cheeks coloured slightly. "Why, we merely understood it was a fashionable route for exercise, we had no idea it was so – wild – so desolate."

Damon suddenly was avoiding his friend's eyes; he went over to Georgiana and took her hand in his.

"I trust you have suffered no ill effects, Miss Wetherby," he said softly.

For a moment it was as though they were alone on the windswept heath. Her smile was glowing as she gazed up into his eyes. "I am perfectly well, I thank you. And it was so fortuitous of you to arrive when you did." She smiled across at Callista. "I don't know how much longer we could have held him at bay."

"I think he was just grateful we arrived when we did," Max said drily. "He could make his escape without too much loss of face." He had stopped laughing but his lips twitched.

"Come, let us escort you back home. Coachman – what is your name?"

"Hudson, sir," replied the Coachman, brushing grass from his coat and picking up the discarded pistol.

"Hudson, can you drive the ladies home without John to help you?"

Hudson picked up his whip and climbed back onto the box; he picked up the reins and soothed the restless horses with a few softly spoken words.

"Aye, sir, we can start back as soon as the ladies are settled."

Still pink, Georgiana allowed Damon to help her back into the carriage and arrange the travelling rug over her knees. Callista stepped inside and, seating herself next to the Footman, checked the wound in his shoulder.

Smiling reassuringly at him, she patted his hand. "Don't worry, it's not too serious. We will soon have you home, John," she said. "Hudson, please drive carefully, try not to jolt the carriage too much – we don't want John to lose any more blood."

She lifted her head to look across at Max who was closing the carriage door and fastening it carefully.

"Thank you," she said quietly.

Max bowed silently, still smiling. He knew that despite her bravery, the outcome if he and Damon had not arrived when they did could have been very different.

"We will escort you back to town," he reassured them and mounting their horses, the two gentlemen rode either side of the carriage, ensuring the two ladies were well protected.

Callista was concerned about the injured man, but he bravely held his shoulder and made no complaint.

Gradually Georgiana regained her composure and by the time they turned into Portland Square, she was quite recovered.

Ensuring that the Footman was handed over to the Housekeeper to attend to his injuries, their two rescuers declined her invitation to come in, it was getting late and past the hour for visiting.

"We will leave you now, Miss Wetherby," Damon reassured her, "but we will see you tonight at Almacks, will we not?"

Shaking hands with him, Georgiana assured him that indeed they would both be attending Almacks that evening and thanked him once more for his well-timed arrival earlier.

Disturbed by the commotion in the Hallway, Amelia arrived just in time to see her daughter and niece saying their farewells to the two men. Her sensibilities affronted at the lack of chaperonage, she rounded on Callista as soon as the door closed behind the departing escort.

"What on earth has happened, Callista? I cannot believe you would be so thoughtless to bring those gentlemen here – what if anyone had seen you? Your reputations could have been irreparably damaged."

"Mama, pray be quiet." Georgiana was exasperated at her mother's outburst. "If it had not been for Callie, we could both have been robbed or murdered and the gentlemen escorted us home to ensure our safety."

Silenced by her daughter's spirited words, Amelia stared from one to the other in wide-eyed surprise.

"And what on earth has happened to your best parasol?" she demanded, indicating the offending article with a pointed finger.

Callista and Georgiana exchanged a look and, like the gentlemen earlier, suddenly saw the absurdity of their situation and peals of laughter rang through the hallway, echoing all around the house for some time, before they retired upstairs to their bedrooms to bathe and ready themselves for the next important event in the social calendar. Their first visit to Almacks.

Several hours later, Georgiana appeared dressed in one of her dazzling new gowns of the palest pink satin. Pink ribbons were threaded through her hair which was hanging down in thick blonde ringlets, diamonds were in her ears and around her neck, and she was so stunningly beautiful she even took her father's breath away as she came down the sweeping staircase of the Portland Square mansion to join her family waiting for her in the hallway.

Sir Augustus came forward and kissed his daughter on her cheek. "You look lovely, my dear," he complimented her.

Amelia beamed with pride as her daughter twirled around to show them the back of her dress, the wide pink satin sash ending in a huge bow, the ribbons of which trailed to the hem.

"Where is Callie?" Augustus asked, looking around for his niece. "Is she not accompanying us?"

Amelia was careful not to scowl at the mention of her niece's name. She knew how fond Augustus was becoming of Callista and the events of earlier that afternoon when Callista had so courageously and single-handedly fought off a would-be highwayman – saving their daughter from robbery – or worse – had raised his estimation of the girl to new heights.

At his words, a movement from the door at the side of the staircase alerted them to the fact that Callista was approaching. She started as she realised they were waiting for her and smiled a little uncertainly at her Uncle.

"Uncle Augustus, I am sorry to have kept you waiting," she apologised. "I was just visiting John to make sure he was recovering."

"And how is he, my dear?"

She smiled again. "Very well, Uncle, the doctor has removed the bullet and he is sleeping now. The other members of staff are making sure he is well looked after – he is hoping to return to his duties in a day or so."

Augustus nodded, pleased with her concern. "I will visit him myself tomorrow," he promised. "There's no need for him to rush back too soon. He must rest until he is fully recovered."

Callista's smile broadened. "Thank you, Uncle," she beamed at him.

"Callista," Amelia's voice cut in. "Are you ready to leave?" she asked.

Callista was dressed in one of Georgiana's old dresses. Worn only a few times before and never in London, it was nevertheless a year old and although its pale blue colour complemented her colouring, the lace trim was slightly limp and the style was certainly not the latest.

"I just need to get my shawl, Aunt Amelia," she replied and made for the stairs.

Georgiana exchanged a frowning look with her father. "Callie, wait," she said. "I'll come with you." She accompanied her cousin upstairs and at her room, she took Callista's hand and pulled her inside.

"What is it, Georgie?" Callista was genuinely puzzled. "We must not keep your parents waiting any longer."

Georgiana meanwhile had crossed the room and was pulling open her wardrobe door, searching through the dozens of gowns that hung there. After a moment, she made her choice and drew out one of her new gowns, never before worn, in the prettiest of mint greens. The bodice, covered in crystals, shimmered and sparkled in the light. It fell to the floor in the softest shimmer of chiffon over silk and it was quite one of the loveliest dresses she owned.

With a sigh, she held it out to Callista. "Come along, Callie, get changed," she said firmly. "This is our first visit to Almacks – we are going to make an entrance."

Callista shook her head. "But Georgie – it is your new dress – I cannot take it – you have not worn it yet."

Georgiana smiled and shrugged her shoulders. "It is yours now, dearest – my thank you for saving us this afternoon. Now hurry, Callie, get changed, Mama was looking very impatient."

After a few moments of looking at her cousin and the beautiful creation that was the new gown, Callista gave in to her cousin's urging and reached behind her to unbutton the blue dress she was wearing.

The dress had been made to fit Georgiana but with a few simple adjustments, tightening of the ribbons beneath her breasts, and changing into a pair of Georgiana's low-heeled slippers she was soon ready. Her jewellery consisted of a simple gold locket that her father had given her years earlier, containing a picture of her mother and a lock of hair belonging to her baby sister.

Her hair was brushed out and the tumbling mass of curls were held back by the band of green silk which accompanied the dress, studded with the same crystals which embroidered the bodice.

In a matter of minutes, the transformation was complete and Callista shyly accompanied her cousin back downstairs to join her Aunt and Uncle waiting for them. Aunt Amelia's lips tightened as she saw the changes that had been made, but said nothing.

Augustus, however, complimented them both effusively and swept them out into the night into the waiting carriage. Amelia followed behind, adjusting her shawl and determined to speak to her husband at the first opportunity about encouraging poor relations into thinking they were rising above their situation in life.

Their entrance into Almacks was as sensational as Georgiana could have wished. Slightly late because of the unexpected delay while Callista had changed, they were the last to arrive.

All eyes were upon them as they entered and Amelia was gratified at the amount of attention her daughter received.

Georgiana was indeed attracting a lot of attention but so was Callista. Dressed as stylishly and as fashionably as anyone there, she was the recipient of as many compliments and bows from as many young men as Georgiana.

She felt, rather than saw, the glare of malice directed at her and she turned as they made their way through the crowds to find herself facing the tall, pale and cold beauty of Lady Davina Fitzpatrick. Callista bowed her head to Lady Davina and passed by, aware that Amelia would not approve of her speaking to that lady and glad that she did not need to acknowledge her.

That strange half remembered memory Max invoked in her was echoed when she saw Davina, but with an added malevolence she could not understand or explain.

They made their bows to the Patronesses and were gratified by Lady Jersey complimenting Georgiana on the success of her Coming Out Ball.

Refreshments at Almacks were strictly non-alcoholic and they had barely had chance to sip at the tepid punch before both young ladies were claimed for the first dance of the evening, a spirited country dance which left them breathless and laughing as they performed the figures of the dance.

The dance ended and they were returned to their relatives and as Callista's eyes swept around the room she saw, on the other side of the dance floor, the man she had unconsciously been seeking. Max was staring at her. His face was unreadable but the strange expression it bore made her stand up straighter and hold her head higher. He was making his way over to her and she waited standing perfectly still amongst the jostling crowds for him to reach her. Damon Fortescue was with him and together they bowed to her Uncle and Aunt.

Damon spoke first, and with a warm smile and a bow to her, he asked if she were quite recovered from her ordeal earlier that day.

Max stifled a laugh. "I think it is the highwayman you should be asking that question of, Damon."

Augustus was amused, Amelia's lips tightened to her customary thin line and Georgiana gazed at Damon adoringly.

"We are both quite recovered thank you, Sir Damon," Georgiana replied for them both.

"Then may I request the pleasure of this waltz?" Max bowed to Callista and held out his hand.

She curtsied in response and placed her hand in his in acceptance of the dance.

They made their way out to the Ballroom floor as the music began and they danced together, once again in perfect time with each other, albeit totally unknowingly.

"Tell me, Miss Wingrove…" Max looked directly into her eyes. "Have you always been so brave – or foolhardy, depending on which way you look at it?"

She stared back and a slight frown appeared between her eyes as she considered his question. "I have never thought of myself as brave," she replied, "but my father always brought me up to stand up for what I believed in and not allow injustice of any kind to prevail."

He swept her around the floor in his arms, the crystals on her bodice shimmering and sparkling in the brilliant candlelit room. "Did you not think of the consequences?" he asked her. "The night you saved me from the footpads and today fighting off that scoundrel?"

"I confess I did not think at all," she replied. "I just followed my instincts – I could no sooner allow us to be robbed as I could stand by and watch you being murdered."

Her forthright honesty made him smile once more. "For which I will always be supremely grateful," he said.

Her brow cleared, she saw the smile on his face and in his eyes and she laughed with him.

"May I also compliment you, Miss Wingrove?" he went on. "You look absolutely lovely tonight."

Incurably honest, Callista glanced down at her new gown. "That would be the dress," she answered. "It is very pretty, is it not?"

His laughter as he danced around the room with her elicited smiles from his acquaintances, an anxious frown from Lady Amelia, afraid that her niece had said something quite outrageous, and with a cold, furious expression from Lady Davina. Not only had the poor little relation been the subject of unwarranted praise from her brother since his return from the ride, she now had the effrontery to appear dressed in a gown which far surpassed her own and, moreover, was amusing Max with her nonsense. The sooner she found him a suitable mouse to marry the better. The more interested in Callista Wingrove he was becoming, the less she liked it.

The dance ended, Max escorted her back to her relatives and, with a bow and a smile, he kissed her hand. She looked down at her hand and then up into his eyes. That strange, now familiar, feeling of recognition passed between them again. She found her hand had curled around in his, holding on to it and for a moment they made no move to separate.

He found he could not tear his eyes from hers. He had observed her during the country dance, watching the way her hair

75

had bounced around her shoulders, thick curling ringlets falling down onto her breast, held back by the green silk band. He had been entranced by her, he had followed her with his eyes and despite the displeasure emanating from Davina, he had been powerless to prevent himself making his way across to speak to and dance with Callie.

It was all part of his plan, of course, he told himself as with another smile, he released her hand, bowed once again and moved away.

Augustus raised an arched eyebrow at his wife. "I think our niece has an admirer, Amelia."

Not pleased that her niece appeared to have attracted a Marquis whilst her own daughter was ignoring Dukes and Earls in favour of a mere Baron, Amelia could only fan herself furiously, cooling her burning cheeks as she watched Georgiana being led out again by that young upstart Damon Fortescue.

"And I think our daughter has attracted the attention of a fortune hunter, Augustus," she snapped in response.

Augustus followed his wife's eyes and saw for himself the way his normally animated daughter was shyly dancing with Damon. He considered the young couple thoughtfully. Damon Fortescue might not be quite what Amelia had in mind for their daughter and, it was true, her adoring parents had spoilt their daughter over the years. He knew, however, that she had a good heart and if she lost it to a lowly Lord rather than some exalted Duke, then he would not stand in the way of her happiness.

"Don't worry, Amelia," he reassured his wife. "It is early days yet, the girl's barely been out a week – give her credit for not throwing herself at the first handsome face that comes her way."

He patted Amelia's hand and managed to ease his wife's fears slightly. They watched in companionable silence as the dancers whirled past, Georgiana totally absorbed in Damon Fortescue, her eyes alight with happiness as she gazed up at him and her smile lighting up the room.

Callista, too, watched the dancers, but her eyes strayed, almost against her will, to the couple on the other side of the Ballroom floor; Max and Lady Davina were dancing, he was frowning and she did not look her normal serene, cool self.

They looked, in fact, as if they had just had a disagreement and despite chiding herself for her uncharitable thoughts, she could not help the swift rush of happiness at the thought of discord between the couple. Humming softly, she smiled as a handsome young man bowed and requested the pleasure of a dance. She accepted willingly and danced around the Ballroom floor, lightly and happily, chatting naturally to her partner, totally at ease.

She did not see the looks directed her way, a sharp look of something like envy from Max Langley and pure dislike from Davina Fitzpatrick.

Unconsciously, happily, Callista danced the night through with one partner after another. She did not see Max and his party leave, and when Georgiana declared she had a headache, they left; their first visit to Almacks a total success. Amelia was well pleased with the events of the evening and her daughter's triumphant acceptance into the cream of London Society.

Chapter Six

Amelia need not have worried. Over the course of the next few weeks, no less than two Dukes and the son and heir to an Earldom called at Portland Square to pay court to the lovely Georgiana Wetherby. Georgiana welcomed them all, prettily accepting their compliments and joining them on carefully arranged drives, or to picnics in the Park, accompanied by her cousin and occasionally her Mama on full chaperone duty. Georgiana was feted wherever she went, truly the belle of every Ball and debutante of the Season – it was enough to turn anyone's head. Strangely enough, Georgiana remained extremely down to earth and laughed with Callista at some of the more outrageous attempts to win her favour. Bouquets of hot house flowers were exclaimed over and turned aside for smaller posies of sweet smelling freesias, sent by one admirer she never tired of receiving. Extravagant gifts were returned with polite thank you notes, whilst a small, carved ivory fan was exclaimed over and carried everywhere.

Callista, too, had attracted admirers who called often to see her. Freddie Acheson was quite smitten with her and she looked forward to seeing his friendly face on his morning round of visits. He was attentive and polite and they danced at the various events where they would often meet but Callista never felt that same frisson of excitement she experienced whenever Max Langley was near. He only had to enter the room for her to know he was close; she only had to look around to see those piercing blue eyes resting thoughtfully on her to realise that he was thinking about her. He made every other man pale into insignificance. He was supremely attractive and as his arms went around her when they danced together, she could not help but wonder how it would feel to be held closely against that firm, muscular body. She banished such thoughts immediately, blushing at the very thought of the idea a man like Max would be interested in a girl like her with no money, no prospects and nothing much else to recommend her.

They attended the same Balls, the same routs and Assemblies. They met at house parties and afternoon Soirees. Max, accompanied by Damon Fortescue and Lady Davina Fitzpatrick, always arrived and left together. During the course of the evening, Max was careful to dance with practically every young girl being paraded in front of the Ton by proud Mamas anxious to attract the notice of such eligible bachelors as himself.

However, Callista knew that sooner or later, they would inexorably, inevitably, be drawn together to dance at least once, to converse, to laugh, to quiz each other and, more and more, for him to compliment her. Her wardrobe had certainly improved. Thanks to her bravery in foiling the highwayman and her growing closeness to Georgiana, her cousin had insisted on her being better dressed in order that Callista could accompany her to the dozens of social events they attended. Callista, therefore, found herself the recipient of several new and exceedingly attractive evening gowns. Amelia did not protest against this new extravagance; anything that kept Georgiana happy was sufficient to please her Mama.

Callista could argue against Georgiana's generosity as much as she liked, but she knew that when she danced with Max Langley she was secretly very relieved to be well dressed and elegant and, if not as startlingly beautiful as Lady Davina, she was quietly confident of her own attractiveness.

The weeks passed, each one crowded with more and more social engagements. The girls attended them all. Callista, knowing that this would probably be her one and only Season, relished the attention she received and whilst at times she longed for the peace and serenity of her life in the country, nevertheless she accompanied Georgiana and her Aunt and thoroughly enjoyed herself.

Even Aunt Amelia was thawing towards her niece. Grateful for the respite, occasionally she allowed the girls to go out alone, with only a servant to accompany them. She forbade them to ever go near the Heath again and so they contented themselves with drives in the Park, walks and afternoon visits to some of the other debutantes currently enjoying their first Season.

It was at one such innocent afternoon that the young lady they were visiting announced that it was her birthday and as a treat her mother was allowing her to take a party to Vauxhall Gardens.

"Oh, how exciting." Georgiana was envious. "Mama has never taken us there." She sighed and smiled at her new friend. "Perhaps your Mama could reassure mine that we would be perfectly safe and well chaperoned?" she enquired innocently.

Vauxhall Gardens was well known to the girls. They had heard tales of it being slightly risqué, which of course, only added to its allure. People from all walks of life and society mingled together in the gardens. The girls had heard many tales of the art exhibitions, the music, the lights, the suppers and as it could only be reached by taking a boat across the Thames to enter, its popularity as a destination was thought of as being one of the most exciting and romantic in London.

"Oh, do you think your Mama could be persuaded to allow you to come along?" Sophia Charles asked, her pale pretty face lighting up with pleasure. "It will be so exciting – it is a Masquerade, we will all wear Dominoes and there will be quite a party of us."

"How many will be coming, Sophia?" Callista interjected at this point. She knew Aunt Amelia would not approve of them going to Vauxhall, but as guests of the Charles family, part of a larger group, she might be persuaded.

"There will be ten of us, plus Mama and Papa to chaperone us. Papa has chartered the boats to take us up the river at 7 o'clock."

She clapped her hands with excitement; she was a pleasant and charming girl and Georgiana and Callista were often in her company. As they took their leave, armed with invitations and assurances from Sophia's mother, she hugged them both. "It will be such a thrilling evening – I have heard so much about Vauxhall, I cannot wait to see it."

Callista drew on her gloves and waited by the front door as Georgiana paused to speak softly to Sophia before taking her leave. Her eyes were sparkling with mischief and her mouth was set in a firm, stubborn line as they made their farewell and set off walking home.

"Do you think Aunt Amelia will allow us to go?" Callista asked her cousin as they walked together the few streets back to Portland Square.

Georgiana put her hand through the crook of Callista's arm, and hugged her cousin slightly. "I am sure she will," she replied confidently. "And if she objects then I will go without her permission."

"Georgie, you would not dare." Callista was shocked.

Georgiana was smiling, and Callista had never seen her so determined. "Oh yes, I would, Callie," she replied and exclaiming over the time, hurried her cousin homeward.

Amelia, however, presented with the invitation and letter from Mrs Charles, was quite amenable to the girls' evening out. In truth, she was tired and an evening at home appealed to her. She knew the Charles family, trusted them implicitly with the care of her precious daughter, and raised no objections as the girls went to bathe and change and pick out the heavy cloak Dominoes suitable for the masked event.

Georgiana's cloak was a heavy damask silk of deep rose, worn with a pale pink lace mask, tendrils of blonde hair escaping from under the hood as she waited in the hallway for their carriage to arrive to escort them to the Charles' home. Callista joined her cousin dressed in a burgundy red Domino, with a black lace eyemask, her gown beneath the cloak a matching dark red evening dress of silk, trimmed with black lace.

They left the house together and were taken to the Charles' home in Sir Augustus' carriage and there they joined eight other suitably nervous and excited girls to begin their journey to Vauxhall.

Mr Charles' carriages drove the whole party to Whitehall where the hired boat was waiting to ferry them up river to Vauxhall Stairs, on the Surrey Bank just south of Lambeth Palace. The river crossing was calm but the passengers were anything but as they approached Vauxhall Stairs. There was an indefinable atmosphere of adventure in the boat, the thrill of the unknown, that frisson of danger before reaching the delights of the gardens.

The visitors arrived and walked the last few yards to the entrance. Mr Charles paid the obligatory shilling per person and they entered the Grove, the central area of the gardens. They made their way to the supper boxes and took their seats in the box hired for them for the evening just as the orchestra struck up the first musical interlude of the night. The girls sat back, entranced by their surroundings. Georgiana seemed restless, however, and after a hasty, whispered conversation with Sophia, she settled back into her seat next to Callista and drank the cold lemonade provided for them, included of course in their entrance fee.

Callista gazed around her, her eyes wide with wonder at the sights and sounds of the famous gardens. The gardens were filling up rapidly and crowds of people were making their way up from the river to take their seats in the supper boxes. Men in black Dominoes and black masks, ladies in cloaks of different colours, all in disguise, all flocking in to enjoy the thrills of Vauxhall. From her seat, Callista could see the famous marble statue of the composer Handel and, like Georgiana, she felt restless, anxious to explore the rest of the gardens and take in their surroundings.

During the interval when the orchestra stopped playing, Mr Charles gave the young ladies permission to leave the box and explore, with strict instructions to return by 9pm in time for the famous Vauxhall Gardens supper, and as a special treat for Sophia's birthday, champagne.

Seizing Callista's hand, Georgiana pulled her cousin to her feet and within moments, they had left the box, going together in small groups of two to wander down the Grove, to gaze in wonder at the works of art on display. Georgiana, however, would not allow Callista to pause until they reached the end of the Grand Walk and there, waiting beside the golden statue of Aurora was a tall man wearing a tricorn hat, black cloak and mask. He saw them approaching and a huge smile lit up his face as he walked hurriedly towards them. He reached them, bowed and taking Georgiana's hand in his, raised it to his lips, pressing a light kiss onto the back of her hand.

"Georgie," Callista scolded, not pleased by this sudden turn of events. "You did not tell me Sir Damon would be here."

Georgiana turned to her cousin, her face alight and wreathed in smiles.

Sir Damon Fortescue bowed to Callista, his face serious, his demeanour immediately apologetic.

"Miss Wingrove, please accept my apologies, but we have so little opportunity to be together, I could not resist Miss Charles' advice that you would be here tonight."

Callista sighed but she was not impervious to the joy on her cousin's face. She realised now what the whispered conversation between Georgie and Sophia was about.

"Indeed I cannot censure you," she replied, "but what, pray, am I to do while you enjoy the gardens together?"

A movement behind her, a cough, and a voice, which sent her heart thudding in her breast.

"I think that is where I may prove useful," Max Langley said.

She whirled around and there behind her was Max, dressed as was Damon in a black evening cloak, but bareheaded, a black mask covering his eyes.

For a moment they stared at each other. He took in the pale beauty of her face, the wide green eyes beneath the black lace mask and the riot of tumbling curls falling over her shoulders onto the deep red of the cloak. She could see the strangest expression in his eyes and saw the way his fingers curled into a fist as if to stop himself from touching her.

He seemed to pull himself together, and, bowing, offered her his arm. "I believe we have until 9 o'clock before we must return you to your hosts?" he smiled at her.

She tentatively put her hand on his arm and looked around

at her cousin who, oblivious to everything and everyone around them, had already started down the overgrown and romantic Druids Walk; she was deep in conversation with Damon and was holding his arm, and he too, was completely engrossed in Georgiana.

Max and Callista looked from the other couple to each other and smiled. She shook her head, laughing softly.

"Aunt Amelia was sure her interest in him was waning," she sighed.

Max took her hand and drew it through the crook of his arm. "I fear it is the complete opposite," he replied seriously. "Damon has had eyes for no one else all Season." He paused and looked around him at the crowds of people walking around them. "He is a good man," he went on. "He is no fortune hunter and your cousin is completely safe with him."

Callista looked up at him, her eyes locked with his. She found it difficult to breathe suddenly. "I – I am sure she is…" she faltered.

A movement from the crowds jostled them and forced them to move, breaking the mood of the moment. Max smiled that dazzling smile of his and she relaxed as he led her down the same pathway as that taken by his friend and her cousin.

She found herself looking around her at the crowds promenading as they were doing and without thinking she asked innocently, "Where is Lady Davina tonight, Sir Maxim? Does she not normally accompany her brother and yourself to most social events?"

At the mention of Davina's name, Max's lips tightened. It was a momentary expression and his eyes hardened slightly, but Callista saw it nevertheless.

"Lady Davina had a previous engagement this evening," he replied smoothly, glossing over the angry exchange between brother and sister he had heard about from Damon.

His relationship with Davina was unchanged. Whilst they were together, she was the vivacious, sensual woman he had loved since childhood; he very rarely heard about the tempestuous rages that Damon experienced. Tonight was one such occasion. She had been furious that her brother and Max were going to Vauxhall without her and incensed to learn that Georgiana Wetherby was being chaperoned by her cousin.

Time was slipping by – it was May already and he had only six more months before his thirtieth birthday to find a bride. Davina had suggested more than one candidate for the role – including the young lady whose birthday it was – Sophia Charles, a gentle, easy going girl of good breeding and excellent manners. Davina recognised at once that Sophia could be manipulated and intimidated. She was perfect – even if Max did not yet think so.

Callista felt a huge relief that the exquisite Lady Davina was not around. She felt animosity coming from Davina every time she met her, despite the friendly smiles and elegant nods.

"You are a good friend to the Fortescues," she said as they started their own walk along the overgrown Walk.

"We have been neighbours all our lives, and friends from childhood," he replied. "Damon is one of the most honourable men I know; he has saved the family estate from ruin despite the efforts of his father to bankrupt them."

"He is fortunate to have such a good friend," she went on and they walked slowly down the path.

"I would like to help him more, but he is a proud man – he will not accept what he thinks is charity and he has turned down a surprising number of caps thrown at him from young ladies of considerable fortune."

"You assured me he was not a fortune hunter and I believe you. And what about you, Max, how many caps have been set at you?"

He laughed at her question. "More than I care to think about," he replied modestly, making her laugh with him.

In perfect accord they walked on together, Callista exclaiming over the exhibits and listening to his knowledgeable description of the gardens. They sat together on one of the garden benches as the orchestra started up again and listened in the growing twilight to the music, as the stars started to appear one by one in the deepening darkness of the skies. It was a lovely evening and the crowds were all good humoured and good-natured.

The different classes of people mixing freely and unselfconsciously fascinated Callista. Everyone from the nobility to the most ordinary of families were promenading along the Great Walk and the romantic Druids Walk. An occasional female would pass them and smile at Max with a roguish twinkle in their eyes, prompting Callista to innocently enquire if he knew the ladies in question. Max almost choked but laughed and denied immediately any acquaintance with the forward young women.

During an interval, as they were about to leave their bench and move on, they overheard a heated exchange coming from the overgrown wooded gardens behind them.

Max stood up and held out his hand to her. "Come, Miss Wingrove," he said firmly. "I think it is time we rejoined your hosts."

Callista meanwhile had heard the sound of a sharp slap, a cry and a rough looking man pushed his way out of the undergrowth and started quickly down the path.

"Come back, you thief!" The cry of a woman made her pause and she turned to see a woman following the man out of the overgrown wood, calling after him, her cheek red where she had been struck. She was dressed in ill-fitting clothes, they were dirty and unkempt and the girl was fastening the bodice of her dress, hastily covering partially revealed breasts.

Tears had sprung to her eyes and she looked angry and distraught.

Max took in the situation at a glance. The doxy's customer had obviously run off without paying, after their business had concluded.

"Come along, Callie," he said firmly and taking her hand tried to usher her away from the scene.

Callista, however, was not to be moved.

"Can I help you, Miss?" she asked the girl.

The girl glared at her, her eyes wary and when she saw Max, she cringed away from them.

"I've been robbed!" she exclaimed, "but I don't expect you or anyone else to care." Her voice broke on a sob and instinctively Callista stepped forward to take the girl's hand.

She snatched it away from her and pulled her faded shawl around her shoulders.

Her face and hair were not clean, and sores around her mouth alerted Max to the reality of her situation.

"Callista," he said again, "come along – let us leave this young lady in peace."

Callista's eyes snapped furious fire at him. "I will not leave until I have helped this unfortunate young woman," she exclaimed.

Firmly taking the girl's hand in hers, she led her to the bench and sat her down, and searching in her reticule, brought out a small square white handkerchief and handed it to the girl.

Within moments, the girl was talking to Callista, and Callista was wiping tears from the dirty cheeks and listening intently whilst Max looked on in silent exasperation.

Callista finally opened her reticule once more and drew out of it a small purse. She opened it and emptied the few coins within into the girl's hand.

She then took out a small white card and pressed that into the girl's hand also.

"When the time comes, Annie," she said quietly, "send Joe to this address. It is my Uncle's home, we will find a position for him, have no fear."

To Max's amazement, the doxy took Callista's hand in hers and kissed it fervently.

"Thank you, my Lady," the girl said and, standing, smiled gratefully at them and turning, walked quickly away into the crowd.

Max watched her go and shook his head at Callista.

"What on earth have you done now?" he asked her as she stood up and brushed the creases out of her Domino.

"The girl is a whore," Callista said coldly. "Her name is Annie and that – that – creature who ran away used her for his pleasure and did not pay her."

Max closed his eyes. He could not, in a million years, imagine any one of the other young women of his acquaintance even recognising a prostitute, let alone speaking with one.

"Callista, it is not our business to interfere," he said quietly.

Her eyes blazed. "Not our business?" She was incensed. "She has no husband and a child to feed. The least I could do was give her a few pennies to buy food for her child."

"The money will no doubt be spent in the first gin tavern she can get to," he replied grimly.

She shook her head, not sure with whom she was more angry; Annie's dishonest customer or Max's cynicism.

"Whatever you say, Max. I chose to believe her. She has a son, he is seven years old and she fears for his future." She paused and her eyes went to his. "I have told her to send him to my Uncle. We will find a position for him somewhere."

He felt something inside him give a lurch and melt. He looked up but Annie was gone, swallowed up by the crowds.

"And if your Uncle does not," he said softly, "send him to me. I can always use another stable lad."

Her anger faded, the sparks in her eyes turned into molten green fire.

"Oh Max, would you?" She clutched at his arm and suddenly in the overgrown Druids Walk, surrounded by people, they were looking into each other's eyes and could have been alone.

She amazed him. There was something so different about this girl. No other female he had ever known in his life would do what Callista had done. They would have ignored the prostitute and walked away in disgust at her plight. Callista had given her all the money she had in her purse.

"She has syphilis, you know, Callie," he said gently.

Callista nodded. "I know. She will not live long – that is why I wanted to help her son."

She realised that she was still clutching his arm and removed her hands. He stopped her. He held her hands and they faced each other, inches apart. She looked up at him wordlessly, watching the expression on his face change from one of admiration to one she had never seen before.

He stepped closer still and lowered his head to kiss her lips.

It was gentle at first but then something in her erupted; something exploded like a firework. His kiss hardened, and his arms went around her to pull her against his lean, muscular body. Her arms went around his neck and she responded to him with some previously unknown passion. As his lips moved against hers a vague ethereal memory surfaced and she suddenly felt an upsurge of feelings which threatened to overwhelm her.

She knew from the way his kiss deepened and became even more intimate that he felt it too – that something in him also felt this strange, hazy memory – this elusive mist hiding whatever it was that drew them together.

He kissed her with a kind of despairing need he had never felt before, she felt so good in his arms, so – right somehow. All thoughts of Davina and her plans and plots went out of his head, all he wanted right at this very moment was to hold Callista, kiss her, and make love to her.

The sound of the orchestra starting to play once again brought them back down to earth. He lifted his head and looked down at her with eyes glazed with desire. He groaned. "Callie, I'm – sorry – I should not have…" His voice was hoarse. He did not know what had come over him – all he knew was that he wanted to do it again – he wanted her with a hunger he could not explain.

Her arms withdrew from around his neck and she stepped away from him. She laughed a little shakily.

"No – I don't know what came over me either," she replied.

For a moment, they gazed silently at each other; the yearning to hold each other again was almost overpowering but with a great effort of will, Max took a deep shaky breath and offered her his arm.

"I think it is time to return you to your hosts, Callista," he said quietly. "It's almost time for supper."

She nodded, and was suddenly grateful to the deepening twilight that hid the rosy blush that was spreading across her cheeks. She took his arm and they turned as one to continue down the Walk to return to the supper boxes. Ahead of them on the walk, Georgiana and Damon were standing close together. They were talking earnestly to each other and Damon was bowing over Georgie's hand, raising it to his lips in a gesture of farewell.

Suddenly Max stopped her and turning to her, his eyes sought hers once more.

"Callista, may I ask where your next social engagement is?"

Frowning slightly, she tried to drag her brain back to the present, desperately trying to think.

"Why, I believe it is Sophia's Ball at the weekend. It is her birthday today but the official Ball is on Saturday."

He took her hand and pressed a kiss against her skin. "Look for me there," he whispered.

Damon was walking towards them and she nodded. "I will. Goodnight, Max."

"Goodnight, Callie," he replied and as his friend joined them, he bowed and waited, watching as she walked back to Georgiana.

The two girls turned to see Max and Damon deep in conversation and then, with a wave the two men bowed in their direction, turned and walked away.

Georgiana turned to her cousin and smiled, a little uncertainly. "Will you tell Mama?" she asked.

"Why did you not tell me, Georgie?" Callista asked.

"I was too afraid you would try and stop me," Georgiana replied.

"No, Georgia, I would not." Callista sighed. "But if your Mama asks me if Damon was here this evening, I cannot lie."

Georgiana smiled and seized her cousin's hand. "Why I would not expect you to lie to Mama," she said. "Of course you must say Damon was here if she asks, but then so are hundreds of other people here tonight."

Callista laughed softly. Her head and heart and mind were still coming down to earth after the kiss she had shared with Max. She could not find it in her to blame Georgiana for her subterfuge.

She suddenly realised she would have done the same if it had been Max she had wanted to meet. It was almost 9 o'clock and the famous Vauxhall suppers were about to be served. As the two girls made their way back to the Charles party, a signal was heard and the entire gardens were suddenly light up by thousands of lanterns being illuminated at the same time. The effect was stunning and Georgiana clapped her hands in delight at the spectacle.

"I wish Damon were with me now," she exclaimed. "It would have been wonderful to have shared this moment with him."

Callista found herself thinking exactly the same thing about Max.

"And you, Callie…" Georgiana smiled happily at her cousin. "What did you and Sir Maxim find to do?"

With a guilty start, Callista came back to earth. "Hmm, I will have to speak to your Papa when we return home," she started. "We may be receiving a new member of staff arriving soon."

Intrigued, Georgiana threaded her arm through Callista's and demanded to know exactly what her cousin had done now.

In complete harmony, the girls returned to their supper box, pausing only when Georgiana's shout of laughter rang out above the hubbub. Her amusement caused by the thought of her dear Mama's reaction at the entry into their service of the guttersnipe son of a Vauxhall prostitute.

Lihanna 4

Despite her misgivings and worries about what was happening to her people and the rest of her family, Lihanna spent the next few weeks a hostage in the unusual luxury of her tented prison.

She was reassured to see for herself that her friends had come to no further harm. Under the strict supervision of their General Aurelius, the Legion were turning her once peaceful village into a military stronghold.

There were hundreds of men in control of this part of her world and she watched, from the confines of the tent as they slowly rebuilt her village, transforming it into a Roman fort. Her tribespeople were amongst them, working alongside the Romans, forced into assisting them, but the General would allow no mistreatment of his captives and for that she was grateful. She was uneasy, however, awaiting news of her mother, and wondering what was going on in the outside world.

Julius spent his evenings with her and in a strange way, now that she had accepted the inevitability of the overwhelming defeat by the Romans, she did not rail against him, but spoke civilly to him. She grieved for the loss of her father and longed for the presence of her mother but she listened with growing interest to the stories of his life.

He had been born into a rich Roman family. The son of a Senator, he had wealth and fortune of his own, but had chosen to become a soldier. He had fought his way through Europe and half of the known world, to come finally to this last outpost of barbarity – this western point of Britannia. It was the last of the main kingdoms to be conquered before pressing on West to the Celtic strongholds in the wild Brecon Mountains.

He had been quickly promoted during his time in the ranks of the army, until now he commanded part of the most powerful army in the world, outranked only by those Generals even now making their way across to join him, to put their Legions together to crush the Celts once and for all.

He did not dwell on the subject of wars and conquest, however. When he was with Lihanna, he set out to charm her, to allay her fears and reassure her that no matter what happened, he would make sure no harm came to her.

He did not repeat his joking words about marriage. Sometimes though, she found his gaze lingering on her during the times they spent together. He spoke gently to her and treated her with kindness, and as the days passed with no sign of her family, he comforted her with the promise that no harm would befall her.

She began to feel ambivalent towards him. On the one hand he was her enemy, the invader, the conqueror of her land, destroyer of her birthright and she knew she should hate him for that; on the other hand he was cultured, educated and intelligent. He was kind to his servants, strict with the men under his command and compassionate to her people. He had none of the fanaticism she realised lurked under the surface of Daveth's personality, and she could argue reasonably with him long into the night on many varied topics. In fact, as the days passed, she felt her feelings changing toward him and she began to look forward to his presence, anticipating his return with something like impatience, until he was once again with her.

She began to wonder if her mother or brothers had indeed survived the battle against the Romans as she received no word from them, heard nothing from them and Julius told her that his envoys had not yet returned from their forays to parley with them.

He would not allow her to leave the safety of his quarters but left alone for most of the day, she would sit at the entrance, watching the world from the limits of her captivity. Some of the older women would approach her and sit with her, speaking to her, asking if she was being well cared for and asking after her welfare.

She would blush as she realised what they asked but she would reassure them that she was unharmed and untouched. Her captor *had not repeated his behaviour of that first morning. He had not so much as touched her hand since then and, as the nights followed days, sitting on the low stool at the doorway of the tent, she would watch the sun go down behind the trees of the great forest to the West and wonder how long his patience would last.*

Chapter Seven

Whilst the Ball celebrating the eighteenth birthday of Miss Sophia Charles was not quite as grand or as well attended as Georgiana's, it did, nevertheless, attract enough of the Ton's cream of society for it to be declared a resounding success.

The Charles family, moreover, received the Honourable Lady Joanna Langley with some surprise. The mother of the present Marquis of Moreland, Maxim Langley, arrived escorted by her son, and swept into the Charles' mansion as regal as a queen and twice as haughty. Neither Sir Damon Fortescue nor his sister accompanied them. It was well known that Lady Langley did not approve of Lady Davina and it was with some relief on behalf of Mrs Charles that the brother and sister had not yet put in an appearance.

Max had endured almost a week of constant harassment. From being unremittingly bombarded with questions from his mother asking if he had found anyone suitable to become her daughter in law, and from Davina urging him with almost desperate insistence that he make an offer for Miss Sophia Charles.

She assured him that Sophia was by far the best choice of bride. She was a gentle, well brought up young woman, heiress to a fortune in her own right and of such limited intelligence that she would never suspect her husband of carrying on a liaison with another woman. Davina had spelt out his future – marry the milksop, get her pregnant and install her at Moreland, miles away from London, thus enabling him to carry on his life with Davina uninterrupted by the inconvenience of a wife and with his father's funds firmly in his hands.

With all the feeling of a condemned man approaching the gallows, Max attended the Ball in the foulest of moods, carefully schooling his features to disguise his feelings and introduced his mother to the Charles family, and to Sophia, whom he immediately asked to dance and whisked around the Ballroom floor.

Within five minutes of her stilted conversation, her chronic shyness and stumbling steps, Max had decided he would rather end up penniless than marry the girl.

The sound of laughter assaulted his ears as he concentrated on some inane remark Sophia was making about the weather. He looked up to see Callista and her cousin Georgiana at the centre of a group of admirers. Callie was laughing at something Freddie Acheson had said and he almost stumbled over Sophia's feet as Freddie led Callista out onto the dance floor. He watched as the couple took their places in the figures of the dance and smiled grimly to himself as Callie and Freddie joined hands to dance down the centre of the lines. Freddie was holding her hands rather possessively and she was smiling up at him rather too intimately, he thought.

The dance dragged on for what seemed like hours but was, in fact, only another few minutes. He escorted Sophia back to her mother, bowed politely and thanked her and moved away to join his mother where she stood talking to some of her friends, sipping iced champagne. She smiled at the furious expression on her son's face.

"Ahh," she sighed, "I take it you will not be offering for Miss Charles tonight then, my dear?"

"Miss Charles would, no doubt, be a perfectly amiable daughter in law, Mother," he replied waspishly, "however, I would die of boredom in a week."

Lady Joanna smiled indulgently at her son. She followed his eyes to where he was looking over at a lively party of young people. They consisted of a stunning blonde young lady, a vivacious girl with dark auburn curls and several young men vying for their attention.

She sipped thoughtfully at her champagne. "I think it is time we circulated, Max," she said holding her hand out for her son to take. "Pray introduce me to some more of your friends and their parents."

Sir Augustus and Lady Amelia Wetherby were suitably impressed with Max's aristocratic mother. She, in turn, found Amelia to be a total snob but quite liked the bluff, no nonsense Augustus and within a few minutes she discovered they shared a similar sense of humour.

Georgiana and Callista were, in turn, presented to Lady Joanna and when she met the young ladies she was quietly surprised that Max's interest was not in the beautiful blonde Georgiana. She, it seemed to Lady Joanna, was more his type. He, however, was quizzing the other young lady in Freddie Acheson's interest in her.

"Congratulations, Miss Wingrove," he said drily. "I declare I have never seen Freddie so smitten with anyone before."

Callista's eyes were sparkling as she smiled up at him. "Freddie is truly a charming gentleman," was her rejoinder, "and such an accomplished dancer."

Before he could reply, the music started and the son of the Earl who had been paying particular interest in Georgiana came to claim her for the dance.

Max could see Freddie was making his way over, with a determined expression on his face. Exasperated, he took Callista's hand. "My dance, I think, Miss Wingrove," he snapped and virtually pulled her to the dance floor, leaving Freddie to stare after them with such a look of disappointment on his face that it left Max feeling triumphant and Callista sorry for him.

Lady Joanna watched her son with a strange smile on her face. Max was acting most oddly. He was behaving in the manner of a man who was almost jealous of the attention being received by the girl he was currently dancing with.

She smiled as the young lady appeared to be scolding him for his bad manners, but as she watched, her son actually seemed to pull the young lady a little closer and bend his head to whisper something in her ear. She drew back her head and the two of them shared a moment of amusement; she was smiling at him and he too seemed to relax and start to enjoy the dance.

Lady Joanna smiled and nodded with satisfaction.

"May I congratulate you, Sir Augustus, Lady Amelia," she said to them. "Your daughter and niece both seem very accomplished young ladies. I wonder if I may prevail upon you to bring them to my next Soiree?" She smiled at the dumbstruck Amelia. "I will send the invitation tomorrow."

Her eyes went once more to her son on the dance floor and smiled again. "I understand your niece is the young lady who saved Max from serious injury some time ago?"

"Indeed, Lady Langley," Amelia replied. "My niece was quite the heroine." She beamed with pride, causing Augustus to look at his wife in some astonishment.

Whilst the son of an Earl was so interested in their daughter, Amelia was quite prepared to promote her niece's interest in a mere Marquis. Even one who seemed to have an equal and disturbing interest in the most notorious woman in London. No one would ever accuse her of failing to look after the interests of her family, poor relation or not.

Max and Callista, meanwhile, were dancing together to the strains of a waltz. He was enquiring as to whether she had jumped to the assistance of any other good causes since they had last met, had she rescued a colony of cats or come to the aid of a downtrodden flower seller?

"Although," he added thoughtfully, "judging from the flowers in your hair, Miss Wingrove, they were not supplied by any ordinary flower seller, downtrodden or not."

She found herself laughing at his nonsense. The tiny cream rosebuds had been expertly woven into her hair, caught up with matching cream silk ribbons which perfectly complemented the demure cream silk gown she was wearing. Her whole outfit was pretty, understated elegance and, as usual, she felt unaccountably pleased that she had not had to wear Georgiana's cast off clothes, perfectly respectable though they were.

"No sir, indeed I have been most circumspect. I have respected my poor Aunt's shattered nerves by doing nothing to upset her this week. Although," a slight frown appeared on her brow, "I have not yet told her about upsetting Madame Duvall the dressmaker."

As Max knew very well who Madame Duvall was, and had indeed purchased a gown from that lady not too long ago, as a present to Lady Fitzpatrick, he raised a quizzical eyebrow.

"That sounds ominous, Miss Wingrove," he remarked.

"Well, the woman is quite frightful, you know." She spoke quietly, her tone one of confiding in a friend. "She is a total bully and she was shouting at one of her young seamstresses because the poor girl was hemming a seam crookedly."

Max whirled her around the dance floor, intrigued despite himself. "What happened?" he asked.

"We were in her shop and the room was very badly lit. The poor girl could hardly see straight and from the look of her, she had not slept – Madame Duvall's girls live on the premises, you know, and apparently the girl had been up until the early hours finishing off a most beautiful gown. Georgiana was being fitted for another evening dress and the hem was uneven and Madam Duvall was so cross with the seamstress that she raised her hand to slap her."

Max listened with growing horror. "Then what?"

"Why, I simply stopped her, that is all," she replied. "I caught hold of her hand and pulled her away and told her that if she ever struck the poor child again, I would make it my personal business to make sure every society hostess of my acquaintance boycotted her shop."

She spoke so calmly, so matter of factly that for a moment Max could only stare in silent astonishment at her.

"And how, pray," he asked faintly, "would you know if she kept her word?"

"I made sure every girl in the room knew who I was and where I could be found and they were to come to me if anything like it happened again. I also told that dreadful woman to dismiss them all at once and let them get to their rooms for some sleep. The girls were all totally exhausted."

"And did she?" He was by now fascinated.

"Why of course." She smiled at him, her brow clearing. "Although I fully expected her to make them get up again later so Georgiana and I stayed in the shop for much longer than necessary just to make sure."

"A – protest, in fact?" Max felt his lips start to twitch.

"Absolutely. By the time we left, Madame Duvall had gone from looking fit to murder me to complete resignation. I do not think she will be mistreating her girls again in the future. Also when we returned the following day to collect Georgiana's gown, the girls seemed much happier."

"I thought Madame Duvall delivered," he managed to say.

"Normally she does but we wanted to be sure she was keeping her word. That poor girl had been up for nights on end working on a very expensive dress. Madame Duvall does nothing herself, you know. I do not believe she is a true Frenchwoman either."

She sounded so shocked, so outraged, that Max could help it no longer. His eyes were sparkling with merriment and he threw back his head in the middle of the Charles' Ballroom and laughed out loud.

Puzzled by his amusement, Callista smiled but the smiled disappeared abruptly.

He looked down at her and restrained his laughter. "What is it, Callie?" he asked.

"That dress. The one which nearly blinded the poor seamstress – someone has just walked in wearing it." She sounded almost incensed and, curious, Max spun her round to see indeed, the most exquisite of gowns – a brilliant peacock blue studded with pearls and heavily embroidered with beaded work around the hem and bodice; being worn by Lady Davina Fitzpatrick.

His amusement disappeared immediately. Davina was with her brother, making a graceful bow to their hosts. Mrs Charles did not look pleased at receiving the newcomers.

"Oh." Callista was suddenly subdued. "It is your friend," she said, her voice totally devoid of emotion.

The dance ended and Max escorted her back over to her Aunt.

His mother was still standing with the Wetherbys. She, too, had seen the new arrivals.

"Maxim," her voice was cold. Her haughtiness had returned with a vengeance. "I fear I do not feel well enough to remain." She glanced fleetingly over at Davina Fitzpatrick. "I wish to leave and you must escort me."

"Of course, Mother," he replied, just as formally.

They made their bows and farewells to the Wetherby party and Max accompanied his mother over to their hosts. He nodded to Damon and Davina but his mother merely acknowledged Sir Damon with a stiff, formal bow of the head. She held her skirts and swept past Davina without so much as a glance in her direction.

Max waited until they were seated together in their carriage before speaking to his mother.

"That was rude," he admonished her coolly.

Lady Joanna merely sniffed. "I will not remain in the same room as that woman. How dare she turn up at a Ball to which I am invited?"

"As you decline more invitations than you accept, how could she possibly have known you would be there tonight?" he replied, his voice still cold, annoyed with his mother.

Lady Joanna turned her head to stare, just as coldly, at her son. "As you seem to prefer the company of that family to your own, I presumed you would have told them."

"That is totally ridiculous, Mother." His irritation with his mother was threatening to become real anger.

"Is it?" she asked, arching her eyebrow at him.

Furious, he did not answer. Lady Joanna observed her son silently for a moment.

"I have invited the Wetherbys to my Soiree tomorrow evening," she informed him. "I expect you to be present – I am quite happy for you to bring along Damon Fortescue, he is your friend and our neighbour and I have no argument with him. However, Lady Fitzpatrick will not be welcome, pray have no misunderstanding about this. I will not have that woman in my home. Either here or at Moreland – she is not welcome."

Lady Joanna's mouth closed on a firm line. Her face was set and resolute, she would brook no argument and Max realised that it would be pointless to argue. He sat back in the corner of the carriage, temporarily defeated.

Davina had looked stunning this evening. Her delicate heart-shaped face had seemed even more entrancing; her huge blue eyes had turned to him as he was leaving and the expression he saw there made him feel as though he had wounded her deeply. Large sapphires had glittered at her throat and the dress of peacock blue had been the same exquisite colour of her eyes. How could his mother, or anyone else, think her cold and hard – she was neither of those things – but apart from Damon, he seemed to be the only person in the world who did not think ill of her. However, even momentarily thinking of the beautiful beaded dress made him smile as he recalled Callista's description of her dealings with Madame Duvall. Despite himself, despite the animosity he currently felt towards his mother, he could not help but smile in the darkness of the carriage as he thought of Callista's spirited defence of the seamstresses.

"Is something amusing you, Max?" his mother asked him, curiosity overcoming her coldness.

"Callista Wingrove – she does not think Madam Duvall is a true Frenchwoman," he told her, his mouth beginning to twitch once more.

Lady Joanna smiled in agreement with her son. "I believe Miss Wingrove may be correct in her assumptions. I think Madame Duvall is in fact more Pimlico than Paris."

She chuckled to herself softly. Max laughed too, the tension between mother and son evaporating in their shared humour.

"Is Miss Wingrove included in the Wetherby party tomorrow evening?" he enquired.

"Of course," his mother replied and determined that she would personally ensure Callista Wingrove's name be added to the invitation.

–❦–

"That evil, scheming bitch – she hates me." Davina's voice rose with fury and picking up the nearest object to her, threw it with all her strength at the unfortunate maid currently hanging the beautiful blue dress into the already full wardrobe.

The silver backed hairbrush bounced harmlessly off the wardrobe door but with a scared look at her mistress, the maid backed away and looked at Damon imploringly.

With a wave of his hand, he dismissed the maid and tried to placate his furious sister.

"Davina, calm down my dear," he urged gently.

"Calm down?" She was almost screeching. "How can you ask me to calm down when everything I have ever dreamed of is being denied me?"

She turned away from her brother and started to pace the floor of her bedroom.

"She humiliated me in front of the whole Ton," Davina went on. "She swept past me like the Queen herself, refusing to even acknowledge me – it was a total insult and her snub meant that half the people in there tonight turned their back on me."

It was useless to remonstrate with her when she had worked herself up into this kind of temper. Useless to remind her that half the people in every Ballroom would not receive her or acknowledge her but due to her position and title no doors were ever closed to her. Except one.

Lady Joanna had disliked Davina for years, since childhood in fact. She had watched Davina grow up and had disapproved of Max's attachment to her even then. Damon knew, and recognised the reason behind Lady Joanna's disapproval, but brotherly love and loyalty refused to let him admit what both he and Her Ladyship knew to be the truth.

Davina had inherited their father's temper, his waywardness, his unpredictability. Damon preferred to call his sister headstrong and wilful; Lady Joanna called it madness.

Davina, however, had never let Max see that side of her. Damon had long suspected her of playing a waiting game. She had a chronically sick husband she had left behind in Ireland

and whom she never visited, preferring to live with her brother and spend her husband's money in London. She had a close relationship with Max and he knew that she was just waiting for the death of her estranged husband before announcing to the Ton her engagement and subsequent marriage to Max.

Something had happened though, to change all that. Max had not confided in him but Damon knew something was amiss – and whatever it was had served only to make Davina angrier and more erratic than ever.

Damon stopped her furious pacing and held her shoulders, forcing her to stand still.

"Davina, you must calm down." He spoke slowly, looking into her eyes, forcing her to look at him. "You cannot let Lady Joanna affect you in this way. You will always be received everywhere – people will always talk and you must always act as though you have not a care in the world."

She took a deep, shuddering breath. She closed her eyes and forced herself to relax.

"Yes, I know you are right. It is just so – unfair," she cried, real tears springing to her eyes.

Damon hugged her, his love for his sister overcoming the unease he always felt when he witnessed her ferocious temper tantrums.

"And I miss Max," she went on. "We have not seen him for days."

What she meant was that it was over a week since he had spent the night with her. He visited, he went riding with Damon, he had gone with them to the theatre a few nights earlier, but since Damon had returned alone from Vauxhall, Max had not come to her room at night when the house had been silent and asleep. He had spent every night in his own home and something had unsettled her. She had thought she had him exactly where she wanted, but this business about him finding a wife had disturbed the equanimity of their relationship.

Damon laughed softly. "Don't worry, Davina." He kissed her forehead. "I am sure whatever it is that is bothering him will soon be resolved. He will be back to normal and we will be seeing as much of him as we ever did."

She smiled up at her brother, her face calm once more. "Of course we will," she exclaimed and moving away from him, seated herself at her dressing table in a flurry of her white lace dressing gown. "Now send that silly girl back in to help me get ready for bed."

Her good humour restored, Damon sighed with relief and left his sister's room, summoning the maid back to attend her.

Waiting until she settled, Damon retired to his own room; he was restless and could not sleep. His own thoughts were also of the Ball from where they had just returned.

He had danced only once with Georgiana before the Wetherbys had left, but that one dance was enough to make him happy. He held her in his arms for the few minutes of the dance. They had spoken in urgent whispers; she had carried the fan he had given her and wore the corsage of pink rosebuds he had sent earlier. He had kissed her hand and for one heart-stopping, trembling moment he had almost swept her out onto the terrace of that house and kissed her with all the urgency he was feeling. It was only when they realised her Mama was watching them with ill-disguised displeasure that prevented him from acting so rashly.

He had made up his mind to speak to his men of business to see exactly what kind of condition he and his estate were currently in. He had worked hard over the past few years to repair the damage caused by his father; he was not penniless but, he had to admit, he was not the best catch for a beautiful young woman and her ambitious mother.

Sighing, he sent for his Valet and got ready for bed; he had not told his sister he was going to Lady Langley's Soiree the following evening, not wanting to provoke another scene.

At least, he told himself, he would not be tortured by the presence of the one girl in London who he longed to see with all his heart. She, no doubt, would be attending one of the numerous other social engagements going on in London that Season. Gloomily he stared into his bedroom fire and wondered how long it would be before he heard about the engagement of Miss Georgiana Wetherby to some elderly Duke or heir apparent to an Earl.

In another part of London, Max Langley sat alone in his bedroom, staring out of his window onto the moonlight garden below. He was deep in thought, and he did not see the way the shadows played across the beauty of the silent stone statues, or how the moonlight turned the water in the fountain to silver, shimmering seductively in the cool night air. For once, Davina was not the sole occupier of his thoughts. She had been his childhood sweetheart and for years he had felt cheated and angry at the way she had been spirited away and married off the moment his back was turned. She had returned to London eventually and within weeks of their meeting they had become lovers. He had worshipped her, adored her and had been more than happy with their arrangement until this unexpected turn of events.

Then, a green-eyed auburn haired girl had literally exploded into his life and his world had turned upside down yet again. Callista was the most unusual girl he had ever met and he found himself comparing her to Davina more and more. Where Davina would sneer, Callie would help.

Where Davina would ignore, Callie would intervene; where Davina would mock, Callie would turn on those who mocked and give them a thorough dressing down.

He knew Davina disliked Callista Wingrove and despite the urgency of his need to find a wife, she had dismissed Callista out of hand because she was too poor, too lacking in social graces, someone who would never be accepted by his Trustees. She wanted him to marry Sophia Charles or someone of that ilk. Well brought up young women, heiresses, of good family background and totally without the backbone to make a fuss when they found themselves left alone in the country for most of the year.

Unfortunately, with the best of intentions, he had spent

months trying to find the kind of young woman Davina would approve of. He had failed miserably; the Sophia Charles types of this world irked him and bored him to tears. The Season had only a few more weeks to run until the heat of the summer sent all the members of the Ton to disappear to their country estates, or the cool sea air of Brighton; he was running out of time.

He sighed, recalling the expression in the clear blue eyes of Davina. She had been so disappointed when he had left the Ball earlier, without even speaking to her. He loved her – he had always loved her. Why then could he not do as she bade him, why was he so obsessed with Callista Wingrove? He could not forget the moment he had kissed her in the gardens at Vauxhall. The memory of that kiss lingered in his mind long after any of the encounters he had experienced with Davina.

Sighing, he realised that since the moment he had kissed Callista, he had not spent another night with Davina.

Sitting on the window seat, one leg propped up, he leaned back against the glass and turned his head away from the unseen gardens below him. He had been perfectly happy with his life until that moment six months earlier when his mother had explained to him the clause in his father's will.

He had enjoyed his life, his friendships, and his love affair with Davina. He had managed to forget about Davina's past, her husband had been a vague inconvenience he never thought about. He considered her former lover no more than an unhappy wife's comforter, and in her arms, in her bed, he gave no more than a passing thought to their future, except to reassure himself and her that eventually their futures lay together.

On the other hand, he felt consumed with a feeling he had never experienced before when he thought of Callista – what if she were to accept someone like Freddie Acheson, or one of her other admirers? He did not want her, he told himself, but neither did he want anyone else to have her.

Common sense told him he was talking nonsense. Instinct told him otherwise.

Chapter Eight

Davina was a superb rider. Fearless, skilful, she rode her spirited horse as gracefully as the Goddess Diana as she galloped along beside Max over the Heath. It was early morning and no other riders were around to spoil their enjoyment. Damon had declined their invitation and they had set out alone, eager for the moment they could give their horses their heads and let them gallop unrestrained over the deserted parkland.

Her face was alive with excitement, her eyes sparkled and her rose pink lips were smiling as they finally brought their horses to a stop.

She was laughing and he thought she had never seemed so beautiful.

"Is this not the perfect morning?" he asked her, stopping to admire the view and the sun coming up over the distant trees.

"I only wish we were hunting," she replied. "There is nothing more exciting than the thrill of the chase, the dogs and the hunt."

"You truly are Diana reborn," he responded.

"Ah – the eternal Huntress, "she smiled at him. "What a perfect life that would be. Hunting all day, feasting and dancing all evening…" She lowered her voice and leant forward in her saddle to reach out her hand to take his. "And making love all night."

He returned her smile and leaning forward, kissed her fully on the lips, feeling her instant response.

"Will you return to Moreland at the end of the Season?" she asked him as they walked their horses along together.

"I have to," he replied, "there are several estate matters I need to attend to and my Steward is pressing for my return. Will you be accompanying Damon to your estate?"

She smiled at him. "Of course, my love," she purred to him, her voice throaty with desire. "We will be able to see much more of each other in the quiet of the country."

He bent across and kissed her once more, feeling the desire for her rising in him.

"And if I am accompanied by my wife?" he teased her and watched the shadow of anger cross her face.

She lifted her eyes to his; the shadow passed and a calculated expression marred the beauty of her features.

"Do you intend to be faithful to the little milksop, my darling?"

"Not if I marry a milksop," he replied.

She laughed again, a throaty sound, full of confidence that came with knowing he was hers, completely.

"Sophia?" she asked, smiling.

"Perhaps," he replied. "She certainly meets all the requirements."

Davina was delighted. "Don't forget," she murmured, "your wedding night – is mine."

He laughed along with her, wondering how he could ever bear to marry another woman while she was in his life.

They finished their ride in harmony and returned to the Fortescue town house together. Max left her at her door and rode home alone, smiling and content that Davina was happy. If Davina was happy, that was all he cared about.

Lady Joanna Langley, Dowager Marchioness of Moreland, graciously welcomed her guests that evening to her intimate Soiree. She seldom entertained and her Soirees were filled with carefully invited guests, where they could expect music, good food, conversation and fine wines.

Her rooms were full and the atmosphere was one of genteel enjoyment. There was no dancing, but her guests had the opportunity to mingle and talk and, at one point in the evening, they were invited to sit in the Salon and listen to a piano recital by an eminent musician. The whole evening was sociable and congenial and Lady Joanna's guests were all very affable well-mannered members of society. Lady Amelia Wetherby, accompanied by her family, felt transported to the highest echelons of the Ton by virtue of the invitation they had received that morning, scribed by hand from no less than Lady Joanna herself.

Augustus went along with his wife with good grace, relieved that the Soiree was not going to be yet another Ball, or noisy party, where he would do his best to be sociable for the girls' sake, but secretly long for the comfort of his own home and bed. This time he was relieved to find that he was expected to do no more than converse politely with other men of his own age, comparing notes on the vagaries of the Season and talk longingly of the anticipated end of the festivities and a return to the relative calm of their country estates. Lady Amelia meanwhile could gossip unreservedly with other women of her acquaintance, safe in the knowledge that there was no need to keep such a strict eye on her daughter in the home of the Langley family.

Her daughter, meanwhile, accompanied by Callista, mingled with the other guests, doing her best not to start or look up every time the door opened, managing to look up naturally as new people arrived and not downcast or unhappy when each newcomer was announced and it was not the one person she most wanted to see.

Callista, greeted by Max with a bow and a kiss of her hand, was perfectly satisfied. Curious as to where he lived, she was pleasantly surprised by the interior of his home and had wandered the rooms with Georgie, admiring the understated elegance of the décor and the spacious refinement evident in every room.

Max seemed a little cool when he received them, and she was slightly disconcerted when he did not meet her eyes or welcome them with more enthusiasm. Callista watched him and wondered what had occurred to cause the sudden reserve in his manner.

She shook her head at such nonsensical ideas; why should he single her out and treat her differently from any other guest present that evening. She was nothing to him, a mere poor relation of the Wetherby family he had been kind to occasionally. She firmly put out of her mind the night he had kissed her. That was a one-off, an aberration on his part that he had obviously regretted as there had been no repeat of his behaviour and she certainly could not encourage him.

Determinedly she accepted a glass of champagne and joined Georgiana in their tour of the Drawing Room and Salons of the Moreland family mansion. With her head held high, she turned away from Max and left him at the door, her thoughts and feelings in turmoil.

Damon arrived accompanied by other young men deliberately invited by his mother. Max was surprised to find Freddie Acheson amongst the group, together with other of his friends. All young, single eligible bachelors and he frowned wondering what on earth his mother thought she was doing, asking them to her Soiree.

He welcomed them, summoned footmen bearing trays of champagne and furnished his guests with glasses of the finest wines his cellar could offer. Damon remained by his side as the others went into the Salon, making their bows to their hostess and joining the small group of young ladies on the balcony outside the Salon.

"I did not know your mother had invited the Duke of Rutland tonight?" Damon questioned him as together they watched the Duke and Freddie singling out Georgiana and Callista.

"Neither did I," Max replied, watching with slightly narrowed eyes the proprietary way in which Freddie was taking Callista's hand and leading her to the bench overlooking the garden.

"Her mother will be overjoyed," Damon remarked coldly as he watched the young Duke flirting shamelessly with Georgiana. "She has ambitions to see her daughter a Duchess," he went on, unable to take his eyes off the scene unfolding before him.

Max tipped his glass and swallowed its contents in one. He was riveted by the sight of Callista and Freddie sitting close together, their heads almost touching, whispering together; Callista had a serious, thoughtful expression on her face. Max felt as if a cold hand had suddenly squeezed his heart. It could not be. Was Freddie proposing to her?

She suddenly looked up and a peal of laughter escaped her. Freddie too was smiling and they seemed to be greatly enjoying a joke together. Relief flooded his body and it was with an extraordinary effort of will that he stopped himself from marching out onto the balcony and removing her from Freddie's side, forcibly if need be.

The announcement was made that the musical interlude was about to start and the four young people on the balcony came back inside and made their way into the Salon where chairs had been set out in rows behind the grand piano, where a young man was seated, ready to start his recitation.

Max groaned inwardly. He loved music but right now he could not think of anything worse than sitting for half an hour, enduring the sound of his mother's latest protégé entertaining her guests.

Georgiana walked back into the Salon and started in surprise as the first person she saw, positively glowering at her from his place beside the pillar, next to Max, was Damon Fortescue. A smile lit up her face as she saw him, and she had the satisfaction of seeing the darkness lift from his brow as he returned her smile and bowed slightly in her direction.

Freddie, as usual, proved an informative and pleasant companion, and he kept Callista amused by a commentary on the various people who were in attendance that evening. She was rather distracted, however, by the feeling of being watched and when she turned her head quickly, she saw it was Max who was observing her tete-a-tete with Freddie.

Silence reigned as the pianist started playing and for half an hour, the company were entertained and entranced by the melodies emanating from the talented young man. Callista closed her eyes and swayed in time with the music, listening to the haunting melody, which for some reason reminded her of the wild expanse and changing moods of the sea, then it changed and she was transported to the wide open countryside, the cry of the birds circling overhead, and the wailing of the winds across desolate plains. It was evocative and poignant and she felt incredibly moved by the music. Memories of her parents came to mind and the tiny baby who she had held in her arms, as a child, who had died within hours of birth. Other, deeper held memories stirred and the old gypsy woman came back to her mind, as did the thoughts of those tall, forbidding standing stones, awesome and powerful. The music swelled, came to a crescendo and finally, ended.

Silence followed the performance for a few moments whilst the audience came back down to earth and thunderous applause filled the room. Lady Joanna approached her protégé and joined him as he stood up next to the grand piano and took a bow.

Callista realised her cheeks felt damp and she put her hand to her face and was startled to find that tears had started to roll down her cheeks. She wiped her eyes surreptitiously; the shy young musician bowed again to his audience and allowed Lady Joanna to introduce him to her friends as she circulated the room with him. Callista stood up and searching in her reticule for her handkerchief, she laughed softly.

"Oh excuse me, Mr Acheson," she apologised, "I don't know what has come over me."

Freddie stood also and offered her his arm. "May I escort you to the balcony to cool down, Miss Wingrove?"

Callista suddenly felt a tug at her elbow, and without missing a beat she shook her head. "Thank you, Freddie, but I think Georgiana and I must find my Aunt," she replied.

Georgiana, too, was excusing herself from the Duke and together the two young women left their erstwhile admirers. "Callie, whatever is the matter?" Georgie exclaimed as she saw the red eyes and damp cheeks Callista was hastily wiping.

"I – I don't know," Callista replied, "I think I must find a withdrawing room to tidy myself." Together they moved towards the door which led out into the hallway. Finding a maid, Callista left Georgiana seeking her mother and followed the maid to the room set aside for the women of the party to freshen themselves up.

She splashed water over her face, and wiped her eyes, dried her face and made herself presentable once again. Shaking her head at her emotional reaction to the music, she stood up, brushed the creases out of her gown and left.

Max was waiting for her. He was alone on the landing outside the room and he stepped forward as she walked out.

His face was stern, the look one of deep concern. "Callie…?" He stopped her from descending the stairs. "What has upset you? Has Freddie said something?"

"I – no – thank you for your concern, Sir Maxim, but I am quite well." She managed a shaky smile. "It was so silly really."

He indicated a small sofa and leading her to it, they sat together. "What was it? You were weeping – I saw you." He sounded anxious.

She looked up into his face, so clear, so handsome, his blue eyes dark with concern, his dark hair brushed back from his clear brow, marred now by a frown.

"It was silly, really," she repeated. "It was the music, I found it very emotional." She sighed.

He took her hand in his. "As did I," he agreed. "I was transported to another time, another place – does that sound odd?"

She shook her head, "No – I thought of a great plain with standing stones – I dream of them sometimes."

His cheeks paled and his hand tightened in hers. "Stones?" he whispered. "Tall standing stones?"

She nodded. "I have dreamed of them all my life," she said quietly.

"There are tall standing stones on a plain near where I live," he told her. "I have always been fascinated by them. When I was a boy I used to go there – it was strange; I felt I needed to find something there."

She gazed up at him. "I always feel afraid when I dream of them," she admitted slowly, "but just then, listening to the music, it was not fear I felt, just overwhelming sadness."

The words came out slowly, falteringly, but her eyes never left his and his hand held hers firmly. He looked down into her wide

114

green eyes and for a long moment he was lost in their emerald pools.

"I will show them to you, Callie," he said softly. "I will take you to the Stones and you will see there is nothing to be afraid of and nothing to feel sad about."

He lifted her hand to his mouth and kissed it gently.

Silently her eyes never left his and when he bent his head to kiss her, she lifted her face up to meet his lips. The kiss was brief, but he reluctantly lifted his lips from hers, wanting to linger but knowing they would not remain alone for long. "I will look after you, Callie," he whispered, "I will protect you from the ghosts of the Stones…"

She did not smile; his words resonated with something deep within her. "Don't make promises you may not be able to keep, Max."

Their eyes met, that strange silent recognition passed between them again, something faint, nebulous, something just out of sight, just out of reach.

Loath though he was to move, he stood up and pulled her to her feet.

"I would never break a promise to you, Callista," he said and meant it.

Drawing her arm through his, he held her hand as they walked down the curved staircase to the hall below. They made a striking couple. Tall and handsome, his athletic body clothed in immaculate evening clothes, Callista in her ivory silk evening gown, the colour of her dress almost exactly matching his waistcoat, smiling up at him as they rejoined the party. Lady Joanne was speaking to Sir Augustus as the couple came downstairs. Sir Augustus raised his eyebrows at them both; Callista blushed rosily but turned laughing eyes to her Uncle. Lady Joanna's smile was more circumspect, but she was, nevertheless, most pleased with developments.

"I am escorting Callista into the Salon," Max said to the other couple. "She has not yet eaten," he explained.

"Indeed, Uncle, will you join us?" Callista asked politely.

A stern look from the formidable Lady Joanna stopped

Augustus in his tracks. "No, thank you, my dear, you go along and get something to eat, I will join you later."

Many eyes turned to look at the couple as Max and Callista entered the Salon. They moved together to the dining table where a light supper was set out for the guests. Georgiana was there already, with her mother beside her. Georgiana looked annoyed and Lady Amelia was frowning. They moved away as Max and Callista approached. The look Amelia sent in her niece's direction was sufficient to make Callista's spirits dip.

"Would you like something to eat, Callie?" Max asked, noticing her change of expression.

She sighed. "No, I have lost my appetite," she said quietly.

He appropriated two glasses of champagne from the nearby Butler and handed one to her. He took her free hand in his and led her out of the open French doors onto the balcony. It was a quiet, still summer night, the warmth of the evening redolent with the scents from the garden, night scented stock and honeysuckle mingled with roses.

"Has your Aunt upset you, Callie?" he asked.

"Not exactly." She paused and sipped her drink before putting the glass down on the stone balustrade of the balcony. Turning back to him, she sat down on the balustrade and looked up at him, her face resolute.

"I must be frank with you, Max," she said, her tone matter of fact. "You must be aware that I am wholly reliant on the charity of my Aunt for my life here."

He nodded, not interrupting her.

"She rescued me from poverty when my father died; I had no future except as perhaps a governess or a companion. My father was a Vicar, he was a good man but he was not rich and he left nothing to support me after his death." She took a deep breath. "I did not want to accept my Aunt's charity but she left me little choice and for a while I resented her. Sir Augustus has been very kind to me and I love Georgie dearly – but," she paused and frowned again. "We fully expect Georgiana to make a good match by the end of this Season and afterwards, I shall be her unpaid child minder when Georgie brings her children to stay."

A shaky laugh escaped her, but it was without humour. "I am a poor relation and I have been so lucky to have had the opportunity to come to London and enjoy this Season – and meet you. That look Amelia just gave me was a reminder that I must remember who and what I am and not monopolise the son of the house any further."

She stood up. "Thank you, Max, for your attention and your company but I must leave you now and return to my Aunt. I must remember my place in society and unfortunately it is not out here with you."

She smiled at him, and made to walk past him but he put out his hand and stopped her. Side by side, she facing the Ballroom, he facing the garden, he turned his head and looked down at her.

"I know exactly who and what you are, Callista Wingrove," he said quietly. "You are the daughter of a man who taught you how to be brave in the face of adversity and he would be proud of you. I have seen you fight off footpads and highwaymen, stand up for people others would have ignored and you deal with your relatives with charm and discretion and love." He paused and turned to her; putting his hand on her shoulders, he turned her to face him.

She looked up at him, his face clear and resolute in the shining moonlight.

"You have no need to be embarrassed or ashamed of who you are and what you are, despite your Aunt Amelia."

He dropped his hand from her shoulders and took her hand in his. Taking a deep breath, his eyes sought hers again. "Callista Wingrove, will you do me the honour of becoming my wife?"

She pulled her hand out of his. "Pray do not jest with me, Max," she said sharply.

"I am not joking with you, Callie," he replied. "I want you to be my wife."

She stood, irresolute – not knowing what to do or say.

His mouth set in a straight, firm line. "I will call upon your

Uncle in the morning, Callista." He bowed. "I am sure between us we can come to some suitable arrangement."

"But – I am penniless – I will bring no dowry or land… Your mother will not approve of me – she will want a young lady of better connections than me to be your wife."

He put a gentle finger against her lips. "She likes you already," he assured her. "And no other young lady of my acquaintance would suit me as well as you…"

For a moment they gazed at each other and with a sound almost like a groan he pulled her into his arms and kissed her once again. His mouth moved against hers, her lips parted under the pressure and she felt the same heat explode within her as she had felt that night in Vauxhall Gardens. His hands pulled her closer and she felt the warmth of his hands through the thin material of her dress. She pressed herself against him and her arms went around him holding him as tightly as he held her, clinging to him, returning his kiss with an ardour she did not think herself capable of feeling. He was kissing her with a deepening passion and intimacy and he did not know where it was coming from. He only knew that, like the night at Vauxhall, he did not want to stop, but wanted to keep on kissing her, holding her in his arms and make love to her. Callie, despite her initial shyness, was responding to him with a passion and a hunger that matched his own.

"Callista!" The shocked tones of Aunt Amelia made her jump out of his arms.

They turned to see Lady Wetherby standing in the doorway, and Max, shivering suddenly, managed to pull himself together, to face her. He kept hold of Callista's hand and bowed to her Aunt.

"Aunt Amelia, I – I'm sorry to have kept you waiting…"

Max squeezed her hand. "Lady Wetherby, please inform Sir Augustus that I will give myself the pleasure of calling on him tomorrow morning." He bowed to both women, raised Callista's hand to his lips and kissed it once more before walking back into the Salon, leaving them both alone on the balcony.

Almost speechless with fury, Amelia turned on her niece. "Am I to understand Sir Maxim has offered for you?"

"I – I believe he has," Callista replied, totally bewildered by this sudden change in her circumstances.

Lady Amelia took a deep breath, shaking with the effort of suppressing her temper.

"We are leaving, Callista – come along at once."

She turned on her heels and walked back into the Salon, followed by Callista. Max was speaking to Damon and there was no sign of either Augustus or Georgiana. They said their farewells to Lady Joanna and joined a stern-looking Augustus and a red-eyed Georgiana in the hallway. It was a silent, chastened party who left the Moreland mansion and returned home and Callista, not sure if the preceding hour had been a dream, and longing to talk to Georgie alone, hugged the knowledge of her proposal to herself all the way home.

The anger emanating from her Aunt was unlike any other mood Callista had ever experienced. Her tight-lipped silence fairly seethed with annoyance and it was with relief that they finally entered the hallway of the Wetherbys home.

Georgiana turned on her heels and headed towards the stairs, but before she had gone two steps, Amelia finally erupted.

"Georgiana Wetherby come into the Drawing Room at once," she demanded. "And you, Callista – I want to speak to you most urgently."

Augustus exchanged a puzzled glance with his daughter but they all went into the Drawing Room and closed the door against the ears and eyes of the servants.

"Did Georgie tell you what happened at Lady Joanna's this evening?" She turned to her husband, her voice cold.

"No, my dear, she did not." Augustus sighed, and sat down heavily in his armchair.

"I heard our daughter planning to go riding with Damon Fortescue." Her voice was hard, accusing. "Which," she silenced her husband with a cold glance, "which in itself is not unacceptable, however, I also heard her refuse a marriage proposal from the

Duke of Rutland. And Callista – why I found her acting like a common strumpet and kissing Maxim Langley."

The two accused young women stared at each other. "But, Aunt Amelia – he had just proposed to me," Callista protested.

Augustus held up his hand to silence them as Georgiana and Amelia started to argue once again.

"Am I to understand Amelia that you are angry because both our daughter and niece have been proposed to this evening? That is most improper." He shook his head sombrely, his eyes downcast.

Amelia smiled grimly at her husband. "Most improper," Augustus continued. "It is I they should have approached first."

Callista hid a smile. "Sir Maxim will be calling upon you in the morning, sir," she said quietly.

"I look forward to speaking to him, Callista," her Uncle replied. "Am I to understand we are to wish you happy, my dear?"

"I – er – I did not actually respond to his proposal," she admitted.

Georgiana caught her hand, her eyes shining, her own troubles forgotten.

"And what is your answer, Callie?" Georgie asked.

Callista had thought of nothing else all the way home. She was confused – she thought of no one else but Max when they were apart, and was overwhelmingly happy when she was in his company. She did not think he was in love with her, but her feelings for him had done nothing but grow steadily since the first time they had met. She wondered if she could possibly make him happy – she was not sophisticated or worldly wise, just a poor parson's daughter from a quiet country parish. He was a Marquis, a member of one of the noblest families of Society, why he should single her out and propose to her she had no idea, but the thought of spending the rest of her life with him was so seductive, it felt right somehow, something about it made perfect sense.

"I think I would be honoured to become his wife," she replied quietly.

"Callie!" Georgia exclaimed and hugged her cousin with genuine love and happiness for her.

Amelia, however, was not happy. She turned to Augustus. "Say something," she demanded. "Your niece will be married before your daughter and your daughter has just turned down the opportunity of becoming a Duchess." She was incensed.

"Am I to understand you want me to send young Langley away?" Augustus demanded of his wife.

Amelia looked from her niece's suddenly anxious face to her husband's expressionless one.

"Yes, I do," she exclaimed. "I will not have Callista married before Georgiana."

Georgiana however, rounded on her mother. "You cannot ask Papa to do that," she said vehemently. "I will not marry anyone except Damon Fortescue and if he never proposes to me then it is grossly unfair to expect Callie to remain unmarried."

Amelia almost screamed in anger and sat down in a nearby armchair, fanning herself furiously and exclaiming over the misery of having such an ungrateful family, tears of self-pity and anger springing to her eyes.

Alarmed by his wife's sudden collapse, Augustus finally roused himself. Standing, he went to his wife's side and took her hand.

"Calm yourself, my dear," he urged her.

He patted her shoulder and gave her the large white handkerchief that he produced from his waistcoat pocket as Callista and Georgiana held hands and stared anxiously down at Lady Amelia.

"I will not have you make yourself ill, my dear," he said kindly. "You have worked tirelessly to make sure Georgiana and Callista have had a wonderful Season."

Amelia sniffed, smiling appreciatively up at him. "I have tried," she agreed, wiping her eyes.

"You should be proud of yourself, my love," he said. "Look what you have achieved. Callista has the opportunity to become a Marchioness and Georgiana – well, she could be a Duchess."

Amelia looked up, tears sparkling on her wet eyelashes, nodding furiously in agreement with her husband.

"Our girls have been a success; they are welcomed everywhere, why our daughter is the Debutante of the year. And it is all down to your efforts. Amelia."

She nodded. "It is, Augustus," she agreed.

"Well then," he continued reasonably, "you will now have the pleasure of organising the wedding of the Season when Callista marries her Max."

Georgiana's hand tightened and squeezed Callista's suddenly.

"And it may well be before Georgiana marries," he went on, "because I tell you, my love, I will be the happiest father in Christendom the day I walk my daughter down the aisle to marry Damon Fortescue. However, I give you fair warning, if that snivelling little snob Rutland dares to repeat his proposal to me, I will eject him out of this house without a second thought."

"Augustus," Amelia wailed anew, but Augustus turned to receive his daughter as she threw herself into his arms and covered his bluff, kind face with kisses.

Augustus put his daughter aside and held out his hand to Callista. Without a word, she went to him and he enfolded the second girl into his embrace.

Tears of happiness shone in both girls' eyes.

"Send word to Damon that you will go riding with him," he told his daughter. "And when Maxim arrives tomorrow, I will be happy to receive him, my dear."

Amelia blew her nose, defeated. She knew when not to argue with Augustus any further.

"And you, Madam," he said to his wife, "I expect my niece to be provided with a complete trousseau for her wedding. Will you arrange it?"

She sniffed. "Of course I will," she replied snappishly. "Now go to bed, girls, it is getting late."

Dutifully they curtsied goodnight and kissing Augustus once more, Georgiana and Callista left the Drawing Room.

The last thing Callista saw as she closed the door behind her was her Uncle draw Amelia to her feet and put his arms around her, kissing her gently on her damp cheeks and holding her close. She smiled at this unexpected show of affection and gently closed the door with a quiet snap.

Lihanna 5

Held in the confines of her prison, the restriction began to irk her. Used to the freedom allowed by her Royal position, being unable to leave and visit the forest or see for herself how her people were surviving was a constant source of unhappiness to her. Finally, her daily request that she be allowed to exercise was unexpectedly granted.

Eating their evening meal together, she once again made her request and watched as the usual frown appeared between his eyes. This time however, he seemed to be considering her request.

"I expected that we would have heard from your mother by now, Princess," he said slowly. "But our envoys have been unable to locate the rest of your tribe. I thought to travel around the edge of the great forest tomorrow, to investigate for myself what lies beyond. Perhaps you can be my guide?"

A light sprang into her eyes at the thought of leaving the camp and possibly finding her family. The area he spoke about was well known to her. It led to a place of great power and beauty, held in reverential esteem by her people.

"I can be your guide if you wish, General," she replied. "I will be happy to leave the confines of this camp for a little while."

Julius smiled, relaxing back on his cushioned seat. He was eating one of the apples that grew so prolifically in this area. "We will be escorted by a guard of some of my most trusted men," he continued. "So please have no thoughts of running away from us."

She bridled as she considered his words. "You have my word, General," she said stiffly, bowing her head briefly.

"Ah, my prickly Princess is offended by my words." He teased her,

still smiling at her demeanour. "Can you ride? It will be faster than a wagon."

She nodded. "Yes, I can," she replied. "My father treated me as equal to my brothers in all things. He taught me to ride." For a moment her brow furrowed at the memory of her father, remembering his tall, broad frame, his energy, his laughter. Unexpected, unwanted tears sprang to her eyes and Julius leaned forward, covering her hands with his own.

"I'm sorry, Lihanna," he whispered. "Your father was a brave man, a fierce warrior. He died fighting for what he believed in."

She pulled her hands away and dashed the traitorous tears from her eyes. Her eyes flashed green fury as she glared up at him. "He believed in freedom," she replied.

She stood up, all thoughts of food and drink deserting her. "I give you my word I will not try and escape," she said quietly. "But I do not feel easy about breaking bread with my father's killers."

She turned away from him and went towards her small quarters. Pulling the curtain to one side, she bent her head to enter when she heard a movement and felt his hands grasp her shoulders, pulling her back against the taut coiled muscles of his body. "I was not his murderer." His whisper was low, controlled, fierce. "I am a soldier of the Roman Empire. I fight because my country demands it of me and I am loyal to my Emperor."

She could feel the heat of his breath against the nape of her neck. His hands held her firmly and she trembled as he held her close. "I do not kill unarmed men nor do I ravish unprotected women." His lips were close to her, she could feel them brush against her skin as he spoke. She felt a heat rise in her that had nothing to do with the anger of a few moments earlier. "But believe me, Lihanna, neither will I be insulted."

She twisted slightly in his grasp and turned her head to look into his midnight dark eyes. She could not bring herself to apologise but she could see the anger and frustration in his face and for the first time since her capture she felt a frisson of fear go through her.

"I will not insult you further, General," she whispered. "I will guide you tomorrow as you have requested but I would like to rest now if you please."

He held her unmoving for another moment before releasing her and allowing her to enter her quarters. "We leave at dawn, Princess," he said and walked away from her, leaving her to drop the curtain and sit, shaking on the small bed.

He had not attempted to join her since her capture but for the first time she wondered if she had pushed him too far and she would feel the consequences of his anger this night. She pulled the fur cover from the bed and, wrapping it around herself, remained upright, forcing herself to stop trembling and reminding herself that she was not just a common prisoner, she was a princess and he had given his word he would hand her unharmed back to her mother. For all his anger, she did not think he would ever easily break his word and it was with this scant comfort that she finally relaxed enough to fall into a fitful sleep.

Chapter Nine

Max had concluded his business with Sir Augustus the following morning and been allowed to speak to Callista for a few moments, under the strict chaperonage of her Aunt, when he had invited the Wetherby family to dinner with himself, his mother and a few close friends to celebrate their engagement. He had left without being allowed to see Callista alone, but as he bent over her hand and kissed it farewell, she had squeezed his hand and looked anxiously up into his eyes. He had smiled reassuringly at her and had the satisfaction of seeing her relax and return his smile.

"I will see you tonight, Callie," he had murmured to her and for a moment, they had exchanged a look that had sent a shiver of anticipation down her spine. Her stomach tightened at the thought of seeing him again and her hand trembled slightly. Her mouth was dry and she licked her lips, an action which caused him to gaze silently down at those lips and wish for privacy so he could press a kiss against them.

Even though he was under no obligation to do so, Augustus settled a generous dowry on Callista, together with a sum of five hundred pounds a year. Max had demurred, assuring Augustus he had no need of any monetary settlement on his future wife but Augustus had been adamant and the matter was concluded with instructions being sent to his lawyers to draw up the agreements and a separate formal announcement sent to The Times.

Reading the announcement in The Times of the engagement of Sir Maxim Langley and Miss Callista Wingrove was met with the worst explosion of temper Damon had ever witnessed from his sister. Davina was beside herself with fury. Max had allied himself with the one girl in London that Davina hated with a passion. She had recognised Max's interest in the girl and had done her best to dissuade him from offering for Callista. All to no avail it seemed.

Davina was pacing the Drawing Room of her brother's home; she could not rest, she saw her carefully planned life with Max falling apart before her eyes. She had been determined no one else would have him and if she had to share him with anyone, it was not supposed to be that wretched girl from that appalling family, the crass snob who was Lady Amelia and the country bumpkin husband of hers. As for Georgiana, she was an empty-headed nincompoop who if Max had to marry anybody, would have suited him far better than the poor relation.

Why had that damnable husband of hers not died like he was supposed to? When the duel had not killed him, she had hoped the fever that followed would have succeeded. Unfortunately, the determined ministrations of his doctor and sisters had made sure that he had survived and as she was not allowed anywhere near his sickbed, she could only look on in frustration as he slowly recovered.

Damon had returned from a most enjoyable hour of riding with Georgiana, her groom acting as unofficial chaperone, when he had listened with growing delight as she had relayed to him the fact that her father approved of him and he had permission to call on them at any time he wished.

He had been extremely happy on his return. His meeting with his lawyers a few days earlier had given him cause to view the future with cautious optimism, Georgiana had turned down the offer of marriage to a Duke and her father supported the courtship of his daughter. His cheerfulness evaporated however on hearing, as he entered the hallway, the sound of breaking china coming from the Drawing Room. He had heard his sister's angry screech at some hapless Footman, and had entered to find Davina wild eyed and red with temper.

Seriously alarmed by Davina's show of anger, he went quickly over to her – seeing for himself the discarded newspaper. He had heard Callista's news from Georgiana not half an hour earlier; he knew Davina would be upset but he had not expected this. It was as if she had taken total leave of her senses. Her tantrums were legendary, but this was beyond anything he had ever witnessed before.

Vases were smashed against the walls, flowers and water in puddles all around the room, tables were overturned, chairs kicked out of place, she had scratch marks on her arms where she had clawed at herself in frustration.

He caught her arms and shook her fiercely. She struggled against him but he was firm. He held her and shook her and shouted at her until she stopped the high, keening wailing noise that was coming from her.

He was appalled and alarmed, worried that this latest news had finally tipped his beautiful, highly-strung sister totally over the edge of reason.

Finally, she was silent, recognition crept back into the frightening emptiness of her eyes and she slumped against him. Her descent into unhinged madness had drained the energy out of her and totally spent, she let him hold her and guide her to a seat.

The Footman who had been cowering in the corner trying to get away from his mistress came hesitantly forward and with a nod from Damon, started putting the room to rights, picking up the tables and broken pieces of pottery that had once been beautiful, valuable vases.

Damon left her briefly to pour her a small glass of brandy that he forced her to drink.

"You have had a shock, my dear," he said soothingly. "Drink this, you will feel better."

She shuddered but obediently swallowed the fiery liquid. She lay back on the sofa, her eyes closed, until some colour finally returned to her cheeks.

"We cannot prevent Max from marrying," he said gently. "You are married already, Davina – I know he cares for you but he cannot go on forever waiting for you to be free."

"His mother is forcing him to get married," she retorted, her voice shaking but calmer now.

Damon looked down at her quizzically. "Nonsense! Max is nearly thirty years old, how can his mother force him to do anything?"

She looked almost pityingly at her brother.

"The terms of his father's Will says that he cannot inherit the bulk of his fortune until Max is married, provided he is wed before his thirtieth birthday."

Damon was frowning now. "Do you mean Max is only marrying Callista to inherit his father's money?"

"Of course – you do not think Max would marry anyone but me unless he was being forced into it, do you?"

Damon seemed to be struggling to accept this latest bit of information.

"He seems genuinely fond of Callista," he argued.

"Callista Wingrove is a poor relation, and a poor substitute for me, I can assure you of that, Damon." She sat up again, her colour quite restored, and gave a shaky, humourless laugh. "He will not be happy with her and she will wish she had never laid eyes on him."

She stood up and brushed down her dress, pulling her sleeves down to cover the marks on her arms and smoothing her immaculate hair back into place.

"Nevertheless, it is remiss of him to let me find out about his engagement in this way. I deserve a personal visit at least, do I not?"

Damon was still contemplating the fact that his best friend was about to marry for money. He could hardly believe it, yet somehow, it made sense. It explained Max's odd behaviour at the various social events they had attended, his insistence of speaking to and dancing with the various debutantes, his whispered, urgent conversations with Davina; and finally his engagement to Callista. He was puzzled though, Max had seemed, to him, to be genuinely attracted to Callista and he had observed the way Max behaved with her, the way they laughed together, their unusual closeness. Surely Max was not cold-blooded enough to enter into marriage with an innocent girl purely for money, and with the intention of carrying on his relationship with Davina.

Watching his sister now, preening in front of the mirror, totally devoid of emotion following the turmoil of a few minutes earlier, Damon had the strangest feeling of foreboding creeping over him. He loved Davina but he had no illusions about her and he hoped, for her sake, that Callista Wingrove was strong enough to be able to hold her husband by her side and away from his childhood sweetheart.

The knock on the front door heralded the arrival of their friend and Max entered the Drawing Room to find calm restored, debris removed and brother and sister sitting in frosty harmony.

Max saw the newspaper, folded up on the side table next to Damon.

Damon stood up and held out his hand to his friend. "I believe congratulations are in order," he said drily.

Max seemed to flush slightly. "Thank you."

"Callista is a delightful girl," Damon went on, his voice steady, his eyes level with Max. "I hope you will both be very happy."

Davina had said nothing but she stood up and turned to her brother. "Damon, would you be so kind as to leave us? I wish to speak to Max alone."

She was perfectly calm, serene almost. The violence of earlier completely gone, to be replaced by the tranquil, unflustered exterior of the beautiful Lady Davina.

Damon looked from his friend to his sister and felt the urgency between them; they obviously had things to say to each other. Davina was completely calm now; he had no need to worry that her mood might change. Mercurial she might be, but she had never completely lost control when Max was with her.

He nodded. "I will be in the library," he said and left them, his disapproval evident in the stiffness of his gait as he walked out of the room, closing the door behind him.

For a moment silence hung in the air between them. "Davina," Max said softly, "I am sorry – I tried to find someone else but really – she was the only one suitable."

She smiled, a gentle wistful tremulous smile of unspoken bravery and sacrifice. She stepped closer to him and raised her hand to press a finger against his lips.

"Hush, my love," she whispered. "I understand – you had no choice, I know."

She put her arms around his neck, pressed herself against him and kissed him.

He hesitated, then pulled her hard into his arms and kissed her back, feeling the pliant sensuous body mould itself against his. Her fingers entwined in his hair and she pulled his head closer, putting every ounce of passion she felt for him into that kiss.

Reluctantly she pulled away and out of his arms. "I have missed you, Max," she said softly. "I have not seen you for some days – and nights – my heart and bed are cold without you."

Her voice was low, that throaty, husky quality which in the past had never failed to arouse him.

"I know." He ran his fingers through his hair. "I haven't been able to come to you," he said ruefully. "My mother insisted on my attendance at various events and it has been impossible to get away."

"No matter – you know I am here when you need me, my darling."

He sighed and watched her move gracefully away to pick up the newspaper and read again the notice of his engagement.

"I fear I will not see much of you over the next few weeks," he admitted.

"When is the wedding to take place?" she asked him

"We are to be married at the end of July, and honeymoon in Cornwall at my cousin Hugo's residence; then return to Moreland in September."

"Six weeks?" She was surprised. "That is not long to arrange a wedding."

"Long enough," he said shortly.

"Will you visit me before your marriage?" she asked, moving closer to him again.

The exotic scent she wore suddenly assailed his senses. He

felt torn between desire for her and the love he had always felt, and guilt that he was to marry another woman. She was being so courageous, so accepting of their fate that he could not help himself. He reached out for her and drew her to him, kissing her deeply once again.

"Before, during and after," he promised in a whisper.

Delighted, sure of her eventual victory over him and the minor setback of his marriage, she wound her arms around his neck and pressed herself against him once more.

It was some time later before he left and despite himself, as he hurried home to change in time for dinner with his fiancée and her family, he felt a curious ambivalence towards Davina. Her body was smooth as silk, enticing, inviting, everything about her screamed temptation, from the heavy curtain of silken hair to the tips of her perfectly manicured toes and yet he found himself wondering for perhaps the thousandth time, what Callista would feel like in his arms, in his bed.

He belonged with Davina, he told himself firmly as he made his way homeward. This was going to be a marriage of convenience only – but for all her experience and sensuality, the memory of her kiss did not linger with him in the way that Callista's had.

Lady Joanna Langley was seated in her Drawing Room awaiting the arrival of her guests when Max entered. He greeted her with a nod and went to stand at the window, to look out over the garden, silently contemplating the beauty of the summer scene.

He looked unusually stern, immaculately dressed in his evening clothes; his hands were behind his back, clenched tightly together, the only outward sign of his inner turmoil.

His mother smiled to herself. She recognised the symptoms of his unease; she knew where he had been that afternoon and had hoped his visit was to inform Lady Davina Fitzpatrick of his forthcoming marriage and break off all contact with that woman. Her relief at the news of his engagement was immense, she actually liked Callista, and there was something fresh, original and unusual about the young woman. She felt a connection to her she had not felt with any of the other girls to whom she had been introduced. She had met dozens of prospective brides, all of whom were perfectly pleasant and polite; Callista had been different and she was unaccountably happy with Max's choice.

"My dear, will you come over here please?"

He spun on his heel and for a moment, whatever dark thoughts were pressing in on him were obvious in his face and in the solemn expression in his eyes. With a deep breath, however, he seemed to pull himself together and forced a smile onto his face.

He walked over to where his mother was seated and looked down at the small box she was holding out to him.

"What is it, Mama?" he enquired, curiously picking the box up.

"It is the Langley engagement ring," she replied. "I had it cleaned and prepared for such an occasion."

He opened the box to find a small circle of gold, intricately woven in an open Celtic design with three diamonds in a triangular shape sparkling up at him.

"Your ring, Mother?" He looked up quickly at her face; it held a hint of sadness as she observed it.

"It belongs to your fiancée now, Max. It was given to me by your father and his mother had passed it on to him – it goes back generations and now it is Callista's."

He picked the ring up out of the box. He recognised it at once; he had seen it upon his mother's finger all his life. She had loved the ring almost as much as she had loved his father.

He was moved by her gesture. He had thought to buy Callista a new ring as a token of their betrothment but looking down at the intricate open gold work, he felt an overwhelming feeling of love for his mother at her unselfish giving up of her favourite ring.

"It is perfect," he said quietly. "I think Callista will love it."

He bent and kissed his mother's cheek. She caught hold of his hand and indicated he should sit down beside her.

"She is the right girl for you, Max," his mother said sincerely. "She will be the making of you, you know."

He laughed softly at her words.

"Max, I know how difficult this is for you – I know you have felt torn between your feelings for Davina and your duty to Moreland. But the fact is, even if I could approve of you marrying Lady Fitzpatrick, she remains a married woman and as such is out of your reach."

He looked down again at the ring, wondering if Davina would ever have worn it. He had bought her sapphires the colour of her eyes and she had exclaimed over them in delight. However, she wore them only occasionally, treating them with a casual indifference that would have been insulting in any other woman.

"Thank you again for the ring, Mama," he said, standing up again, as if the thought of Davina was truly painful for him. "I think our guests have just arrived."

Callista, when presented with the ring later that evening, when he finally had chance to speak to her alone, on the same balcony outside the Salon where he had proposed to her, had gasped with delight at it. She had trembled when he placed it on her finger and tears had sprung into her eyes as she held her hand up to the moonlight to see the diamonds sparkling in the silver light.

Her whole face was suffused with pleasure and she had unselfconsciously thrown her arms around him and hugged him tightly, speechless with happiness.

He had laughed softly at her reaction. "It is very old," he explained. "I had thought of buying you something more modern, something bigger perhaps."

She stood in the circle of his arms and stayed still as he wiped the tears from her eyes.

"I love it and will wear it always," she said simply. "It is perfect. Thank you."

He followed her gaze to the ring on her finger and indeed, it did look perfect on her slim hand. It even fitted perfectly.

"It is almost as if it were made for me," she said musingly. "How old is it?"

He was loath to remove his arms from around her, but after drying her eyes he could do no more than thread her hand through his arm and begin to escort her back into the Salon where her family and the rest of the guests were drinking their champagne.

"Rumour has it that the first owner of Moreland had it made for his bride, back in the Dark Ages. It is certainly very old but I do not think it goes back that far."

She looked at the ring and felt generations of emotion and love emanating from its band of gold and simple diamonds. "It is older than that, I think," she said.

He looked at her curiously but the moment passed and she smiled back up at him, returning with him back into the room where she left him to go to Georgiana and show her the small diamond ring.

He watched her as he sipped a fresh glass of champagne. She looked beautiful in a dark rose gown, with sparkling diamond stars threaded through her hair. She had been introduced to his uncles and aunts and the various other members of his family his mother had summoned to the house this evening. Her family had been slightly overwhelmed by the gathered Langley clan, but Amelia had soon found an ally in his Great Aunt Emily. His mother and Augustus were talking like long lost old friends, Georgiana and Damon had been quietly flirting all evening despite the disapproving glances from her mother and, as Callista showed them her new ring, he felt an odd surge of protectiveness towards her. Despite the incongruity of his situation, he felt strangely happy that evening. Callista would occasionally catch his eye, they would smile at each other and he wished everyone would leave them so he could finally be alone with her.

As the evening drew to a close, he bade farewell to the members of his family he would not see again until his wedding day. He caught Damon frowning thoughtfully at him from time to time but as they had no chance to converse in private, he had no idea what was wrong with his oldest friend.

"I take it you will not be joining me tonight at the Club?" Damon asked as he was taking his leave.

As their visits to the club invariably led Max home with Damon, and of course Davina, Max shook his head.

"Unfortunately, I cannot. We have guests staying the night and my mother has insisted I remain to entertain them." He nodded over in the direction of his Great Aunt and Uncle, currently still in conversation with Lady Amelia.

Damon smiled, genuinely pleased at his friend's decision.

Strangely, Max felt almost relieved at his decision not to go with Damon or see Davina once more that evening. He knew Davina would not make a scene – she was far too dignified to remonstrate with him regarding his marriage. She loved him and only wanted what was best for him; he was convinced of her devotion to him. However, he knew she was hurt by his choice of bride – she had not openly condemned his decision but he had seen the looks of dislike Davina had given Callista. She had brushed off his concerns, laughed at his disquiet – assured her lover that it was a slight feeling of pique only that she felt – annoyed that she could not take her rightful place at his side as his true bride of Moreland.

Finally all the guests were gone and he was able to say goodnight to his betrothed. She had been delightful this evening, modest but friendly with his family, well-mannered and polite to his elderly and starchy relatives, she had been respectful towards his mother and seemed genuinely pleased to have been with him.

As they stood alone for a few moments saying their farewells, he was struck by a new and disturbing thought. What, if anything, did Callista feel for him?

Etiquette forbade him to do any more than squeeze her hand, bow over it and kiss it but he found himself requesting permission from her Uncle to take Callista for a drive on the following day.

"Why of course, Max," Sir Augustus agreed. "I am sure that would be quite in order now you two are actually engaged."

Callista felt a familiar rosy blush stain her cheeks but she turned laughing eyes to her betrothed and smiled with pleasure.

"Augustus!" Amelia scolded. "Callista cannot go unchaperoned."

Augustus frowned at this but his brow cleared as he came up with the perfect solution. "Nonsense, my dear, she will have a

Coachman and Footman to ensure they are not left alone. Why, what possible harm can come to her going for a respectable drive in Hyde Park?" He seemed pleased with his decision, grinning broadly at the remaining company. "You forget we allowed Georgiana to go for drives with that repellent little Duke you liked so much."

Amelia scowled but seeing the eyes of the remaining Langley family on her, she quickly turned it into a smile. "Of course Callista may accompany you, Sir Maxim," she replied. "What time may we expect you?"

Georgiana smiled at the way her father had outmanoeuvred Lady Amelia. Thanks to him, she had been allowed to go riding with Damon, albeit accompanied by a groom, but these last few days had been the happiest of her life.

Max found himself urgently wanting to talk to Callista; he longed to whisk her back into the study, or the Salon for five minutes of private talk. However, etiquette and good manners forbade such intimacy and he was forced to content himself with escorting her to the Wetherby carriage and handing her in, with a promise to see her the following morning.

Callista knocked quietly on her cousin's door an hour later.

"Georgie, are you awake?" she asked softly.

Georgiana was at her writing desk, the room lit by a single candle as she finished her letter and sealed it as Callista entered.

"Come in, Callie," she replied, yawning and stretching.

Callista came in and followed Georgie over to the bed as Georgie climbed underneath her covers, patting the space beside her for Callista to join her.

"Is that another letter to Damon?" Callista teased her.

"Of course, just a little note saying how much I enjoyed your betrothal party."

Callista laughed softly, but her eyes were shadowed and she felt troubled somehow.

"What is it, Callie?" Georgiana asked her, noticing the signs of strain on her cousin's face.

"It – it's probably nothing but…" She hesitated wondering how to go on.

"But?" Georgie took her cousin's hand and squeezed it.

"But why would Max offer to marry me? He has never given me any expression of love or any other reason to offer for me?" She paused again, her brows knitted together in genuine bewilderment.

Georgiana sighed. "Why should he not offer for you? He has shown nothing but pleasure in your company since you first met and you have captured his interest far more than any other young lady ever has, according to Damon that is."

Callista hesitated once more. "That is just it, I thought he had a particular interest in Damon's sister. In fact, I heard a rumour that he and Lady Davina were more than good friends."

"Callie." Georgiana was shocked. "Where on earth did you hear that?"

Callista sighed. "Freddie told me the first time I saw Davina. She was with Max and Damon and Freddie said they went everywhere together."

Georgiana turned to face her cousin and took both her hands.

"Davina is a married woman," she said gently. "Her husband was cruel to her so she came back to live in London with her brother. She and Max are nothing but old friends; that is all. They were childhood sweethearts but that all ended when she married Lord Fitzpatrick."

She reached up and touched Callista's hair in a gesture of affection. "He would not have offered for you if he did not care about you, Callie. Lady Davina has a bit of a reputation but Damon loves her dearly and he says it is wholly unjustified."

Her eyes shone with happiness at the thought of Damon Fortescue, and if he asserted his sister's notoriety was without foundation, she, of course, believed him.

Callista smiled. She still felt uneasy at the thought of Max and

Davina being more than close friends but if Davina's brother had refuted that particular rumour, it would have to reassure her.

"Thank you, Georgie," she said. "I feel better now." She reached forward, kissed her cousin goodnight, and left the room to return to her own bed.

She still wore the engagement ring Max had placed on her finger earlier that evening and she held her hand up to the candlelight to admire the way the diamonds sparkled in the shimmering light.

It was beautiful and she felt comforted as she looked at it – the feeling of generations of love suffused her as she finally drifted off to a deep, dreamless sleep.

Chapter Ten

The scene that met Max's eyes the following morning, as he drew his carriage up outside the Wetherby residence on Portland Square, was nothing short of comical.

The Wetherby Butler was an extremely affable man but faced as he was on this occasion, with an urchin, dressed in rags and clutching a bundle of – presumably – more rags, he had drawn himself up to his full height and was looking down on the child with a mixture of disbelief and utter horror. Apparently, not only had the urchin the temerity to call at the front door but also to stand there and demand entrance.

Passers-by were looking on in amusement at the sight of the tall man and the small boy staring at each other, neither one giving way and the child demanding in a high pitched voice to see "'Er Ladyship Callista." Because "me ma sent me."

James was doing his best to shoo the child from the front step, telling him in no uncertain terms to go round to the back of the house immediately and the child refusing to budge until he had seen 'Er Ladyship.

The altercation would probably have gone on indefinitely had intervention not occurred in the arrival of Callista who had heard the commotion and had come out from the Drawing Room to see what was happening.

"What is it, James?" she asked, seeing the small, ragged and decidedly dirty child on the doorstep.

Relieved to be able to hand over responsibility for the disturbance, James turned to her.

"This – guttersnipe is demanding to see you, Miss Wingrove," he said, handing over a small card that had once been white but which was now hardly distinguishable, folded and held tightly in a grubby fist as it had been until reluctantly handed over by the child.

Callista raised her eyebrows at the card and looked down at the boy. Her eyes were kind but sad as she smiled down at him.

"Your mother is Annie, I presume? How is she – Joe – is it?"

"Are you 'Er Ladyship?" he demanded.

"I am Callista Wingrove, yes," she replied

"Me ma said I had to come to you, Miss."

Callista was suddenly aware of another presence as Max alighted from his open Phaeton and came up the stairs to stand with them.

"Joe," she continued gently. "Is your mother still alive?"

Joe was scowling, his face screwed up in a desperate attempt not to cry.

"Yes, Miss," he said, "but she sent me away last night so Ole Man Grady wouldn't get me."

Callista and Max exchanged looks of alarm and amusement.

"Old man Grady?" Max enquired.

"E's a chimbley sweep," Joe answered. "Look – can I come in or not?"

Startled, Callista turned to James. "I think we need to get this young man inside – we are causing something of a spectacle for our neighbours."

James' scowl was as pronounced as Joe's but he stepped aside and permitted entrance to the house of the child, bowing to Max and apologising for keeping him waiting.

"Not at all," Max was highly diverted, "I am all agog to hear about this Old Man Grady character."

"Shall we go into the library?" Callista was faintly aware that her Aunt would be distraught at the thought of the dirtiest child she had ever seen in her life having access to the fine upholstery and pale carpet in the Drawing Room.

"Miss," James coughed politely, "may I suggest my pantry? It is less likely to become – contaminated by anything this young man may have brought in with him."

Callista had to lower her eyes, and bite her lip to prevent a laugh escaping her. Joe was extremely serious, but as he scratched an unknown itch, she realised the sense in James' suggestion.

"Of – of course." Her voice was shaky. "Please come this way, Joe."

Joe followed her across the hall, staring around at the luxury of his surroundings with wide eyes and open mouth.

James stared down fiercely at the child. "Keep your eyes off and hands to yourself, young man," he admonished, receiving a look of pained effrontery at the insult.

"I ain't no fief," he retorted.

They went through the side door down into the servant's quarters where they passed the amused and horrified gaze of several below stairs staff.

They went into the Butler's Pantry, a small private sitting room containing a desk, a chair and a cabinet.

James pulled the chair out for Callista to sit down and, face to face with Joe, she gently urged him to tell his story.

Joe looked around at his new surroundings and, deciding he could trust the lady he had been sent to meet, he dumped his bundle on the floor.

"Me ma said yer tole 'er to send me to yer when it was 'er time, like," he explained. "She's got worse these last coupla weeks and was coughing fit to bust yesterday."

He glared up at her, a fierce expression on his face. "I tole 'er I wasn't leavin' 'er – not while she was still alive – I wanted to look after 'er see?"

Callista nodded, "Yes, I see. Quite right too." She smiled again, encouraging him to continue.

"What happened then?"

"Ole man Grady was sniffin' about, sayin' he would take me wiv 'im and look after me – he's lost his last lad and needed a new one."

"Lost?" she enquired raising an eyebrow and looking up at Max. Max and James, however, both suddenly looked extremely grim-faced.

"Up a chimbley," Joe went on, "'e got stuck, I fink."

Horrified, Callista tried not to let her emotions show on her face, "Oh, I see. And he wanted you to replace him. Your mother did not want you sweeping chimneys though?"

Joe shook his head. "Said she would die first…" He stopped and looked around at them. "Then she gave me your card and tole me where to come and – 'ere I am."

"How long did it take you to find me?" she asked.

"I walked all night – kept 'aving to stop and ask directions – but I found yer. And yer just like she said."

Faintly bemused by this exchange, Callista asked what his mother had said she was like.

"A toff," was the reply, "but yer looked like an angel."

Callista shook her head, amused at the compliment but her attention was taken by Max who, after glancing from the child to Callista, decided to interject.

"Joe," he began. "How old are you?"

Joe looked across from Callista up to where Max was standing beside her chair.

"Go on, Joe," she urged gently, "answer Sir Maxim."

"Seven," he replied. "Why?" His suspicions were aroused.

Max tried not to smile at the child. "Do you like horses, Joe?" he asked.

Joe was still frowning, his thin face serious and drawn. He certainly seemed older than his years.

"Yeah – I do – I ain't afraid of 'em at any rate."

"Good. Do you think you could help me out then, at my stables? I need a new stable lad."

Joe was silent, his eyes going from the lady opposite him to the tall man standing at her side.

"Me ma said I was to come to 'Er Ladyship," he repeated.

Callista ignored the horrified glance from James and leaning forward took hold of Joe's thin shoulders. "You will be with me, Joe." She smiled at him, encouragingly. "Sir Max and I are to be married." She looked up briefly at her betrothed before turning her attention back to the child. "You can work for me at Sir Max's

Estate and we can train you to be my groom. How does that sound – do you think your Mama would approve of that?"

Joe was still frowning, appearing to be deep in thought but before he could reply a disturbance in the corridor outside James' pantry announced the arrival of Lady Amelia, accompanied by her Housekeeper. The parlour maid had informed Her Ladyship of the altercation that had taken place on her doorstep and Amelia had left the Morning Room immediately, leaving Cook with only half the instructions for meals for the household and gone to seek out the Housekeeper to escort her to the Servants' Quarters and catch the miscreant red-handed.

The door opened abruptly and Lady Amelia stood there, bristling with indignation at the sight of the grubby child.

Her cold, affronted glare took in Callista, the child and finally, Max. She was taken aback at the sight of her niece's betrothed and found herself being forced to temper her annoyance.

"Callista," she began. "I cannot believe you have allowed this – this child to come into my house in this fashion."

Before Callista could respond, Max interjected smoothly.

"Please accept my apologies, Lady Amelia," he replied. "Young Joe here has just agreed to become a trainee groom in my stables. If I could beg your indulgence and request that your servants attend to him whilst Callista and myself continue with our drive, I will collect him on our return."

"Attend… to him?" she asked faintly, holding a handkerchief to her nose as she became used to the pungent smell of the boy.

Max wrinkled his nose slightly in agreement with Her Ladyship. "Yes, a bath, I think, for you, young man."

Joe looked immediately horrified but Mrs Smith the Housekeeper, mother of several sons and in charge of a houseful of servants, took in the situation immediately.

Exchanging a glance with the Butler, Mrs Smith folded her arms. "You can leave the young man in my care, Miss Wingrove, Sir Maxim," she said firmly. "We'll get him bathed, dressed and fed ready for your return."

"I 'ad a bath at Christmas!" Joe protested loudly.

Callista turned him to face her once again. "Joe, listen to me. I very much want you to work for me and train to be my groom. However," she took a deep breath, "you need a bath and some clean clothes and some food. I will only be gone for an hour or so and when I get back, I will come for you."

Joe sniffed, suspiciously close to tears but instinct told him to trust her. His ma had said she was all right – and if his ma said so, then he believed her.

He nodded, and turned to Mrs Smith.

"Are you hungry, young man?" she enquired looking down at him, taking in his ragged, unkempt appearance, his bony body and thin face. This child had obviously not eaten well for some time.

"I could eat an 'orse," he replied.

"Come along then and try not to touch anything," Mrs Smith scolded, but not unkindly.

"I ain't no fief!" Joe retorted.

"I did not suggest you were, young man. I merely do not want to have to clean anything you might touch."

Mrs Smith held out her hand to Joe and he bent, picked up his bundle and walked slowly to the door. He turned his head and looked again at Callista, who smiled and nodded encouragingly at him.

"Go along, Joe," she urged him. "I will come back for you shortly. Go and have a good breakfast, young man."

The assembled group watched as the ragged child followed Mrs Smith out of the Butler's pantry. Lady Amelia was clearly still annoyed. However, as Sir Maxim was smiling urbanely at her, his dark eyes twinkling with what she thought was suspiciously like some kind of amusement, she very wisely did not rise to the bait.

Max turned to James. "Thank you for allowing us the privacy of your Pantry, James," he said. "I will be back shortly to collect the young scamp."

James nodded his head. "Very good, Sir Maxim," he replied. "I will ensure he is ready for collection."

Max hid a wry smile and turned to Lady Amelia. "I am sorry

to have inconvenienced you, Lady Amelia. Have no fear, I will remove the child as soon as we return."

Amelia was not immune to his considerable charm. She visibly thawed as he smiled winningly at her, his dark eyes twinkling.

"Thank you, Sir Maxim," she said. "But please, will you accompany me back to the Morning Room for tea, whilst Callista readies herself?"

Max held out his hand to Callista who promptly rose from her seat and took it. "Thank you, Max," she said quietly.

"I should be delighted to wait for Callista with you, Your Ladyship," he replied to Amelia.

"I will not keep you long," Callista promised as they made their way back up to the hallway.

She left them to go up to her room to put on a driving coat of the deepest sapphire blue and a most becoming matching bonnet. It had once belonged to Georgiana but had suited Callista so well she wore it as often as she could.

Returning to the morning room, she found Max refusing Amelia's offer of refreshment and he looked up with some relief as Callista rejoined them.

Bowing to Lady Amelia, they bade farewell to her. Max offered his arm to his betrothed and escorted her to the awaiting open carriage.

As he helped her into the Phaeton, he looked down at her face, becomingly framed by the dark blue bonnet. For a moment he was struck anew at the understated beauty of her face.

However, he did not miss the glint in her eye. "No Callista," he said, very seriously.

"No? Whatever do you mean, Max?" she asked, all innocence.

"No, we are not driving to Whitechapel to seek out and arrest Old Man Grady, nor are we going to rescue all the chimney sweeps in London – I only have so many horses to take care of you know."

A rueful smile answered his remarks and as she settled herself into the carriage, refusing the offer of a rug from the attentive groom, she turned to him in all seriousness.

"And Annie?" she asked him.

He seated himself beside her and the carriage finally departed from Portland Square. "I think Joe's mother is probably beyond our help by now, Callie," he replied quietly. "We have no idea how to find her and I would not ask Joe to escort us." He paused, taking her hand in his own. "I think it would upset him too much – better to take the child and do what his mother wished for him."

"And what is that?" she asked him, her fingers curling around his in a gesture he found oddly trusting.

"She wanted a better life for her child. We can give him that, Callista – we can make sure he grows up healthy and hopefully happily in the country."

She sighed, recognising the truth in his words. "I know you are right, Max," she said, settling back onto the upholstered seat. "I just wish we could see her to reassure her."

They drove along in silence for a few moments before Callista turned back to him and he saw a sadness in her eyes but she squeezed his hand. "I think she already knows he is safe, Max," she said softly.

He nodded, touched by her simple words but he found himself hoping the same thing himself.

The driver touched the whip to the flanks of his perfectly matched pair of bay horses and they set off at a trot out of the Square and towards the Park, to enjoy the morning sun in the wide open spaces, and the fresh air out of the crowded environs of the city.

The day was warm, the drive pleasant and as they drove into the open aspect of the Park, with Max pointing out the landmarks, Callista found herself relaxing in his company more and more.

"Am I to expect this a lot, Callista?" Max teased her.

"Whatever do you mean, Max?" She turned her innocent gaze onto him.

"You have a certain quality about you which I have never encountered in any other young lady," he continued. "I am just wondering what I might come home to once we are married?

A house full of reformed criminals, a home for Waifs and Strays or the Top Paddock turned over to a permanent gypsy encampment?"

She laughed softly and found she could not take her eyes away from his. "I hope that once we are married I may make a good impression on the people of your estates." She frowned thoughtfully. "I certainly hope that they will not dislike me at any rate and if I happen to find something which I think needs improving or if I feel it unjust or unfair – then I will certainly bring it to your notice."

He found himself extremely diverted by her reply. "I am sure my tenants will adore you, Callista. And I am even more certain that whatever faces us over the years, our life together will never be boring."

He stopped suddenly. It was the first time he had actually thought about a future with Callista. In all his torment over marrying someone other than Davina, he had never before wondered what his day to day married life would be like. He had imagined marrying and, once the honeymoon was over, leaving his bride at his estates in the country and returning to take up his former life in town, with Davina by his side. Sitting beside Callista now, laughing with her, talking about a future with her, he wondered what was happening to him.

"Callie…" The laughter stopped and he found he was still holding her hand. "I have never asked you – is this what you want?"

Her open, honest eyes gazed into his. Her smile faltered slightly but the frown disappeared.

"I did wonder…" she began, then, taking a steadying breath, "I thought your – interests lay in a different direction. I was surprised when you proposed, but I could not imagine that a man of your morality would offer for another woman if your affections were already engaged. You are a man of honour, Max, and I am honoured to be your betrothed."

Her words only served to increase the self-reproach he had been feeling.

"Callista," he said softly. "Do you care for me at all?"

A rosy blush suffused her cheeks, but she did not falter as she gazed directly into his eyes.

"From the moment we met, I felt a connection to you, something so powerful I have been unable to resist it – or you."

He was taken off guard by her words. They were spoken with such simple conviction and so honestly that he could not doubt her sincerity.

"Callie," he murmured and in broad daylight, in front of the amused glances from the occupants of passing carriages, he pulled her into his arms and kissed her.

He raised his head, wanting nothing more than to carry on kissing her but aware that he was in grave danger of ruining both their reputations if he did so.

"Callie – I promise I will do my best to make you happy," he said softly.

She did not smile; she was serious as she was held in the safety of his encircling arms.

"I am sure you will, Max. But please, I have said it before and I mean it. Do not make promises you cannot keep."

He smiled and kissed her cheek. "I will never break a promise to you," he said softly.

Her words had resonated with him; he, too had felt that connection between them. He did not know where it came from but as Callista had said, it was very powerful.

With an effort, he withdrew his arms from around her and settled back again into the comfortable seats of the carriage. He kept hold of her hand and raised it to his lips. He gave a low, shaky murmur of a laugh.

"I tell you what I am looking forward to coming home to," he said softly. "If you have no objections, of course."

"What is that?" she asked.

"A houseful of children would be most agreeable."

He spoke in a low, husky whisper that had the oddest effect on her. Heat was spreading through her body, starting low down in her belly and rising up to her breasts. It was a kind of ache and as his eyes bored into hers, she knew he was feeling the same kind of heat, that if they were not out in public, he would be assuaging the hunger which was gripping both of them at that moment.

His face was flushed, his eyes were dark with desire, he wanted her at that moment with a passion he could not ever remember feeling before. All thoughts of Davina were wiped from his mind. All he wanted was to pull the bonnet from her head and run his hands through the luxurious curls of her hair. He wanted to bury his face in her neck, kiss her breasts, make love to her with an abandonment she had aroused in him. Where it had come from he had no idea, all he knew was that this woman – this girl he was marrying as a matter of convenience – was very inconveniently getting under his skin. She was winding emotional tendrils around his heart and he was being drawn in – reluctantly at first but now – now he found such pleasure in her company, such enjoyment in their time together that he wondered how much of a marriage of convenience this was going to be. He had talked of wanting children with her and, God help him, he meant every word. More than just a son and heir, more than just someone to carry on the family name, he wanted children with her – he wanted a family.

He was trembling slightly as he squeezed her hand again. She was still staring at him. Her eyes were so honest, so direct, he felt as though she could see into his heart, into his very soul.

"A house full of children would be my idea of heaven," she replied to his last remark. "I grew up an only child and I did not expect the pleasure I have experienced these last few months with Georgie. She is the sister I should have had."

They were sitting so still, so wrapped up in each other that they did not see the riders coming closer, did not hear the beat of horse's hooves and were unaware that riders had stopped beside their Phaeton until a voice penetrated through their reverie – a voice sharp with barely disguised annoyance.

"Max, why we have been calling you this age." Davina's voice shocked Max and he turned to see Davina and Damon beside his carriage, riding their matching horses. She looked magnificent, her blue eyes flashing, her slim figure upright and elegant in her black riding habit, contrasting vividly with the white blonde of her hair.

She nodded to Callista with a graceful bow of her head. "Miss Wingrove, I understand congratulations are in order."

Callista smiled at her. "Yes indeed, thank you, Lady Fitzpatrick."

Damon was his usual composed urbane self. He, too, bowed to Callista and raised his hat in greeting. "Good day, Max, Miss Wingrove. It is a pleasure to run into you like this."

Max forced a stiff smile to his face. "It is certainly a surprise. How are you, Lady Fitzpatrick?"

Davina's horse was restless, despite the urgent gallop she had put it through to catch up to the Phaeton. "I am very well, thank you. Are you to attend Lady Markham's Ball this evening?"

Her tone was casual, almost indifferent but Callista was aware that constant feeling of unease in Lady Davina's presence.

"We have been invited, I believe. Is that not so, Callista?"

Callista took a steadying breath. The intimacy of the few moments before had gone, they were no longer alone and she found herself straightening imperceptibly as she faced the other couple.

"I believe that is correct," she replied. "Lady Markham has been extremely kind, she has invited my Aunt and Uncle and, of course, Georgiana, will also be attending. May we expect to see you there this evening, Lady Fitzpatrick?"

"Of course." Davina was barely polite, almost dismissive, but at receiving a warning glance from her brother, tempered her reply and a smile suffused her features. "Do you ride, Miss Wingrove?"

Startled by this change of subject, Callista looked from Max to Davina in surprise.

"No – not at all, I am afraid," she replied. "I never learned as a child and I have not had the opportunity to learn since coming to live with my Aunt."

"We must do something to correct that." Davina was almost laughing. "We will be neighbours soon and once you are back from your honeymoon, Max must arrange riding lessons for you." She paused. "There is some wonderful countryside to explore – sometimes it is best done on horseback. Is that not correct, Max?"

Max's face was a mask of bland indifference. "We certainly have some beautiful countryside. I hope to show you, Callista," he replied. "If you would like to learn to ride, I am sure I can arrange it."

"You will be able to come hunting with us, Miss Wingrove – you will surely enjoy that."

At this, however, Callista shook her head firmly. "Whilst I would not dream of interfering with my husband's pleasure if he desires to go hunting, I am afraid this is one activity you must all excuse me from."

Davina's smile was almost a sneer. "Do you not approve of hunting, Miss Wingrove?"

"I am sure there is a need to keep vermin down on every country estate, and I have no problem with gamekeepers keeping them under control. I just dislike the thought of fox or stag hunting, that is all. I certainly would not enjoy myself riding to hounds."

To Davina, a born huntress, this was almost sacrilegious. Her eyes snapped fiercely at Callista's words but she kept her temper under control, careful not to antagonise either Max or her brother. Instead, she threw back her head and laughed. "Why, Max, I declare you are marrying a blue-stocking."

Max smiled and Callista, too, did not take offence at Davina's words. She merely smiled in response and shook her head. "No indeed, Lady Fitzpatrick. I am no intellectual, I just have no taste for blood sports." She turned to Max. "As for learning to ride, if you have the time and patience to teach me, I am sure I will be happy to learn."

He returned her smile with genuine warmth, a brief exchange not lost on Davina. Wheeling her horse around, she brought their attention back to herself. "Come Damon, I will race you to the Lake. Max, Miss Wingrove, we will see you this evening."

Damon bowed his head again, and touching his riding whip to his hat in farewell, kicked his horse and followed his sister.

Within seconds, they were galloping away, towards the lake in the distance.

Max followed them with his eyes, narrowed against the bright glare of the sun, and a feeling of guilt and confusion almost overwhelmed him. He closed his eyes briefly, opening them to find Callista watching him with a strange expression on her face.

He forced himself to relax, and ignoring the look on Callista's face, he spoke to the Coachman, ordering him to return to Portland Square.

"Time to go home," he smiled ruefully at his betrothed. "And I must collect my very first waif."

She nodded, returning his smile. "And I must reassure my dear Aunt that I will bring no more uninvited guests into her home. One of the nice things about marrying you, my dear Max, is that finally I will have my own home and I will be able to invite who I like into it."

A sudden vision of half the chimney sweeps in London taking up residence in his spare rooms assailed Max and he could not resist a throaty chuckle. He possessed himself of her hand once again and lifting it to his lips kissed it, as the sun shone brightly down, sparkling on the three small diamonds in her ring. In harmony once again, they drove back together to Portland Square.

Their waif, however, was not awaiting them in the hallway. On enquiring as to his whereabouts, a very disapproving Butler indicated the Library.

Walking into her Uncle's room, they were greeted by the sight of her Uncle Augustus having a very animated conversation with young Joe. Joe, by this time washed to within an inch of his life, his hair cut, his teeth cleaned and his nails scrubbed, was dressed in the cast off clothing of Mrs Smith's youngest son. He was entertaining Sir Augustus with a highly colourful description of some of the shady characters he had been brought up amongst all his life.

On their entrance, Joe immediately broke off from his discussion and ran over to Callista.

"Miss!" he exclaimed. "I fort you wasn't comin' back."

"I said I would Joe," she replied gently. "And I always keep my promises."

Joe's face was beaming with happiness at the sight of her.

"Make your bow, Joe, to Sir Maxim," she reminded him, touching him on his shoulder.

Obediently Joe turned to his future employer and bowed.

Joe screwed up his face and looked up at Callista. "Do I 'ave to go today?" he asked. "Can't I stay wiv you for a bit longer?"

Callista sighed. "I would love to keep you here, Joe, but it is not my house. I need my Aunt's permission to let you stay – and – besides, Sir Maxim has very kindly offered to train you to be my groom."

She did not see the look exchanged between her Uncle and her betrothed. Augustus coughed and she looked up at him enquiringly.

"Callie," Augustus said, "as you are to be married in only a few weeks, perhaps we could keep Joe here until then – he can run errands for you and help around the house before you move to Moreland. Plenty of time for Joe to learn how to be a groom then." He winked at Joe and looked up at Max. "I hope I can persuade Sir Maxim here to let you remain with us for a few weeks longer."

Max may have been immune to the hopeful looks on the faces of Sir Augustus and Joe, but it was the sparkle of amusement in his betrothed's eyes that swayed his decision.

"Of course," he bowed gracefully. "I am sure we may survive for a few more weeks without the addition of a new stable lad. However," he added, "I must insist that Joe spends a couple of hours every day in your stables, Sir Augustus. He can begin his training here in readiness for our move to Moreland."

"Of course, a capital idea. Callie, ring the bell for James – we must find a bed for this young man and then he can come with me to the stables."

With Joe safely returned to the reluctant care of the Butler, Augustus bade goodbye to Max and Callista escorted her betrothed to the door.

"I will see you this evening, Callie," he bowed over her hand.

"I am looking forward to it already," she replied. "Thank you for a lovely day, Max."

"It has certainly been – interesting." He nodded in the direction of the Servants' quarters where James was escorting young Joe by the ear to find him accommodation below stairs.

The howls of protest rang out through the hall and despite herself, Callie could not help but laugh. Max, too, was laughing as the door closed behind him.

It had been a very enjoyable day and as Callista made her way to the Drawing Room to find her cousin and Aunt, she found herself hoping that every day spent with Max would be as happy. She could only hope the evening that lay ahead of her, at Lady Markham's Ball, would prove to be as enjoyable, even with the promise of Lady Davina Fitzpatrick being present.

Her amusement suddenly left her at the thought of Davina. There was something about Davina – Callista instinctively knew that Davina disliked her – but then she reasoned, Davina would dislike anyone who was marrying Max. He had been her childhood sweetheart after all, and there was something possessive in the way she looked at Max which boded ill for anyone not strong enough to withstand her. She resolved for Max's sake that she would try her best to get along with his friends. If one of them was a beautiful, predatory, possessive creature such as Lady Fitzpatrick then so be it – she would have to accept her and do her best not to alienate her husband because of her.

Lihanna 6

Dawn arrived and Lihanna arose, determined to be ready when the Roman came for her to leave on their journey. She pulled her curtain aside to see Julius, already up, his back to her as his manservants helped him to dress in his armour.

Her slight movement alerted him to her presence and he turned, his face composed and stern.

"We leave in fifteen minutes, Princess," he said. "Will you be ready in time?"

She faced him, straight, proud. "Of course," she replied. "We can leave now if you wish."

A slight smile lifted his firm mouth. "We have time for you to dress and prepare yourself."

He indicated a platter of bread and meat that had been provided for their breakfast and a low growl in her stomach reminded her of the meal she had walked away from the previous night.

"I will return to collect you as soon as the horses are ready."

He picked up the gleaming helmet and, bowing his head in farewell, he left the tent. She had been prepared for his anger, for his displeasure, but this cold civility was something she had not expected. She felt almost deflated following his departure but the manservant interrupted her thoughts.

"I will bring you warm water to wash, my lady," he said quietly. "Please eat something before you leave."

She smiled, thanking him and moving towards the small table where the repast awaited her. She ate a little and washed herself in the warm water he brought her, before dressing in a warm woollen smock dress, tying a thin corded belt around her waist before pulling on a *heavy woollen cloak and moving to the entrance of the tent to await her captor's return.*

She did not wait long. She saw the small contingent of horses approaching her, watched with curious eyes by the members of her people who had not seen their Princess outside the tent for some time.

She felt an uprushing of emotion as she approached the riderless horse being led towards her. It had been many weeks since she had ridden; she had gone with her parents to meet with neighbours – to warn and plan for the threatened attack by the advancing Roman armies. It had been a serious matter and it had been a sombre meeting but she and her brother Carmag had raced their horses home, allowed them to have their heads and galloped away from the rest of the group and laughed as they felt the summer wind blow through their hair, relieving the tension of the previous few hours. Carmag, her amber eyed, golden haired brother whom she had loved above all her other brothers. He was the eldest child, she was the youngest and they shared a bond that overcame the difference in their ages and station in life. He would be the next King, she would be married to a neighbouring King and strengthen the ties between the two peoples.

All plans, of course, which would come to nothing now. Her father was dead, her mother and brothers in hiding somewhere with the rest of the armies of the Celts; and she held prisoner by their most deadly of enemies.

The leader of her enemies drew his horse up next to her and his eyes crinkled into smiles as she was helped into the soft Roman saddle of the horse. She sat astride as she had always done, grasping the reins and settling the horse, stroking the head and mane, leaning forward to whisper reassuring words into the horse's ears.

Her long tangled hair fell across the horse's mane and she brushed it to one side, looking up to find the Roman's eyes upon her, softened with an expression she had never seen before. She straightened and turned her head to face him.

"I am ready, General," she said clearly.

He bowed his head briefly in her direction and, taking up position next to her at the head of a column of his men, he raised his arm. At his signal, the party moved off, leaving the compound and allowing

Lihanna to see for herself the changes wrought in the countryside surrounding her home.

She could hardly contain her rising excitement as she felt the unaccustomed freedom of that first ride out of the encampment for many long weeks. The weather was changing, the leaves on the trees of the forest turning from verdant green to rich ruby reds and dark browns. Autumn was upon them, the seasons were changing and she realised that the festival of Lammas had passed. The Autumnal Equinox, long celebrated and revered amongst her people, was almost upon them and then it would be Samhain. Samhain was the great event celebrated before Yule. A time when the Druids led the people in a ceremony honouring their ancestors, the great festival of Darkness. Lihanna loved all the rites and ceremonies; she was old enough to take part in the celebrations and she remembered how proud her father had been as he had watched her leading all the other young women of their tribe into the centre of the great Standing Stones to take part in the rituals of worship.

She rode along next to Julius and for half an hour neither of them spoke. He, however, noticed the sparkle in her eyes and the rosy flush in her cheeks. He smiled, unable to resist speaking.

"You look well, Princess," he said, smiling at her.

Her ambivalence towards him had melted with the early morning frosts and she returned his smile. "I had forgotten how glorious the forest could look," she admitted.

"It is certainly impressive," he agreed. He pulled his cloak around his shoulders a little tighter. "Are you warm enough? There is a chill to the air today."

She breathed in and smiled once more at him. "Autumn, General," she said. "Soon, in a few more weeks, you will be riding through snow."

Relieved that their disagreement of the previous evening seemed to have been forgotten, Julius relaxed slightly.

"Where is it you are taking us this morning, Princess?" he asked, indicating the route they were now following, a long winding rutted track edging the forest.

"How far have you explored this area?" she countered.

"We have not yet gone to the other side of the forest," he admitted. "We have had skirmishes with various tribes of your Celtic people and it is only now that we feel we can go further. We have heard rumours of a huge flat plain that I would like to find."

She nodded slowly, wondering if she was in danger of betraying her family and friends by leading him to the Stones.

Lihanna comforted herself with the knowledge that a small force of Roman Centurions would be spotted well before they reached the Stones. She knew none of her Celtic people would actually live there, it was far too sacred a place to use as an encampment. They were far more likely to be hidden within the safety of the forest itself and would watch the Romans from afar rather than risk an encounter with them.

"I am taking you beyond the forest, General — to a site which is sacred to our priests and the people of our tribes. It lies on a great plain some miles from here — beyond it lies more forest and beyond the forest, the sea. We will need to ride for several hours to reach it." She leaned forward to stroke the horse's mane as it skittered slightly. "I imagine you will have provisions to last us the full day?"

He smiled at the question in her voice. "Of course, Princess, sufficient to last us two days at least."

She pressed her heels into the horse's side. It started to canter and a wider smile covered her face. "If we hurry, we will be there and back in a day," she told him.

Together they rode in harmony, she pointing out the various places along the way that until recently had been part of her father's lands. She showed him the lake she and her brothers had swam in as children, the burial mound of her ancestors, a holy place greatly revered. She spoke so solemnly that he found himself promising that he and the men under his command would respect the countryside surrounding their new encampment.

He asked her about her childhood and she told him of the restrictions placed upon her by her parents and how she and her brothers had rebelled against them, risking punishment by leaving the safety of their village to explore the great forests and the lush countryside around their home.

She laughed and her eyes sparkled and Julius found himself

enchanted by her animated face as she regaled him with tales of growing up in this wild and untamed kingdom. Her joy at the unrestricted and unexpected day of freedom was infectious and he laughed along with her, drawing amused glances from his men at arms who followed at a respectful distance.

Finally, after a brief rest period and a further two hours of riding, she led them through a part of the forest they had never visited and out onto a wide, flat plain. In front of them, some half a mile away, were the Standing Stones she had been leading them to. Great grey slabs of granite rising twenty feet into the air, twenty of them in a great circle, with a large flat altar-like stone at the furthest point from them, in line with the entrance made obvious by the wider gap between two of the largest monolithic structures.

The riders stopped their horses as they observed the scene before them. Grey scudding clouds added to the atmosphere of power and mystery that emanated from the great circle. Julius had seen similar structures in other countries the Romans had conquered as they passed through the lands of Europe but none as huge and as awe-inspiring as these.

Lihanna's enthusiasm dimmed a little as she gazed down at the sacred stones. For a moment she wondered if she had made a mistake in leading Julius to this place but there was no sign of any activity, the landscape before them was wild, uninhabited, untouched by any human occupation. It was bleak, terrible and beautiful and, as she always did, Lihanna caught her breath at the majesty of the panorama before her.

Julius raised his arm in a gesture to re-start the ride down to the Stones when Lihanna held her hand out to him.

"General, may I dismount please?" she asked.

He nodded, watching with undisguised curiosity as she slipped easily from the saddle and went to the trees. From around the base of the oak trees, she picked the wildflowers that had not yet fallen prey to the autumn frosts, before reaching up and trying to pull the mistletoe from where it grew twisting around branches. She could not quite reach until Julius dismounted and pulled down the branch, snapping off a huge bunch of mistletoe for her.

They were inches apart and he breathed in the scent of her, the faint perfume of apples and herbs that emanated from the lustrous curls of her hair. Her lips were inches from his and it took all his innate discipline to prevent himself from capturing them with his own.

"Thank you, General," she said softly and moved away, as if sensing his growing desire. Before the faintest of blushes on her cheeks gave away her own matching feelings.

He followed her to the horse and lifted her back onto it, waiting until she was settled before leading the way down the slope to the Stones, Lihanna's arms full of the wild flowers and mistletoe.

They reached the site and as Julius and his men circumnavigated the circle, she rode into the centre and dismounted once more, going to the altar stone and laying the flowers and mistletoe as an offering.

He watched as she knelt and raised her arms and face to the heavens. He saw her lips move in a prayer to the gods of her people. He did not know it but she was whispering a prayer of supplication, asking the gods to protect her family and friends. She paused, raising her eyes to his and adding an extra person to her prayer of protection. Her head fell back, the glorious weight of thick auburn curls falling to her waist as she looked upwards to the sky and begged her gods to spare the life of her Roman captor, Julius Maximus Aurelius.

Chapter Eleven

The warmth of the summer sun was fading as they arrived that evening at the Markham mansion in the fashionable and extremely genteel Grosvenor Square. They were meeting Lady Joanna Langley and her son at the Ball, and it was with pleasurable anticipation that Callista and her cousin prepared themselves for the evening ahead.

Wearing their newest gowns, for Sir Augustus, despite her protests at the extravagance, had been extremely generous in his instructions to provide Callista with a trousseau and wardrobe suitable for the wife of a Marquis, they had prepared themselves for the evening with a great deal of laughter and eagerness as they looked forward to meeting again Max, and, as promised, his dearest friend Damon Fortescue. Georgiana was looking particularly lovely that evening in a dress of palest pink, heavily beaded with pearls, wearing a choker of matchless pearls, with a pearl tiara to complete her outfit, thick blonde hair hanging in carefully arranged ringlets over one shoulder. Callista was wearing a dress of silver, with aqua coloured ribbons shimmering under her breasts, tying in a huge bow which cascaded down her back. It was simple but stunning and it was a very proud Sir Augustus who led his family into the Grosvenor Square home of Lady Sophia Markham that evening. The evening was still warm, the crush of people adding to the heat of the Ballroom and as they entered, Sir Augustus and his wife were greeted by old friends as they made their way over to join the small party around Max's mother.

Lady Joanna met them graciously and held her hand out to Callista as she curtsied to her future mother in law. Callista looked around for Max but could not see him in the crowd of people, but she realised that Lady Joanna was looking particularly displeased at this lapse of manners in her son.

"I apologise for the absence of your betrothed, my dear," she said to Callista. "I am sure he will be returning to us shortly. In the meantime, Sir Augustus, may I ask you to procure some champagne if you please? The warmth of this room makes one quite dry – I am parched."

Sir Augustus bowed to Her Ladyship and agreed that it was, indeed, extremely warm. His wife was fanning her face, pink already from the heat of the room, and the blaze of light from the huge chandelier and despite the open French windows, no cool breeze circulated around the Ballroom.

A Footman arrived carrying a silver tray of sparkling champagne and the party helped themselves to a glass each. Callista sipped hers and her eyes scanned the room for a sight of Sir Maxim, wondering where he was.

A dozen couples were circling the dance floor to the strains of the latest Viennese waltz and she found the smile on her face fading as she recognised her betrothed dancing with Lady Davina and they were looking at each other with such an intense expression on their faces that despite the heat of the room, she felt as though a finger of ice had touched her spine. Davina seemed to be clinging to him, her beautiful face uplifted, gazing into Max's eyes with such a look of fierce passion that Callista found herself wondering anew how Max could possibly have offered for any other woman. She looked away, and found Lady Joanna was watching her, a thoughtful expression in her eyes.

"Callista," she said, and Callista moved to stand next to her.

"Yes, Your Ladyship?" she enquired.

Joanna nodded in the direction of her son, her eyes serious, her mouth set in a straight grim line.

"She is a married woman, Callista," she said quietly, so Callista had to bend her head to hear her. "She is married and I thank God for it."

Callista was surprised by the vehemence behind Lady Joanna's words. "Indeed, Your Ladyship? I have never met her husband, I understand he is ill and has to remain in Ireland."

Lady Joanna's eyes never left the dancing couple. "She is deranged, Callista," she said quietly. "The girl is unbalanced and disturbed. She was a wild and unhappy child and has grown up to be a dangerous woman." She forced herself to relax suddenly and smiled at her future daughter in law. "But he is marrying you, my dear, and I think you will make him very happy." She squeezed Callista's hand and nodded at Georgiana who was engaged in a lively conversation with her mother.

"Tell your cousin to be careful," Lady Joanna went on, her voice still quiet. "Damon is the best of a bad bunch but there is a streak of wildness in the family – their father was as bad as Davina – let us hope it won't be passed on to his children."

Alarmed, Callista looked up as the subject of their conversation himself arrived, bowing to Lady Amelia and Georgiana.

Callista looked at the tall man, his face quietly handsome, his figure that of well dressed, understated elegance. He was calm and controlled, his blue eyes crinkling at the corners as he smiled down at Georgiana. He was attentive and polite and as Georgiana looked up at him, Callista saw the adoration shining out of her cousin's eyes. "I think it might already be too late, Your Ladyship," she said dryly.

Lady Joanna's smile was perfunctory and did not quite reach her eyes. She drew her breath in with a hiss as the music ended and they watched as Max bowed to Davina and offered her his arm to lead her from the dance floor. "He would not dare," she whispered loudly as they watched Max make his way over to rejoin his party.

Davina accompanied him to the group and Lady Joanna turned away, her icy glance towards her son saying more than any words her disapproval of the woman by his side. Davina, however, seemed unaffected by Lady Joanna's aloof snub. She smiled charmingly as she stood beside her brother and Damon introduced her to Georgiana. Lady Amelia acknowledged her with a barely perceptible nod, Sir Augustus shook hands with her and bowed politely and Georgiana curtsied to her.

"I am very pleased to meet you at last, Miss Wetherby." Davina was at her entrancing best, dressed beautifully in a gown of deepest red, which made her skin seem luminous in the glow of the bright candle lights. "My brother can hardly speak of anyone else, you have quite captivated him, my dear."

Georgiana blushed becomingly, a rose hue tinting her cheeks. "You are most kind, Lady Fitzpatrick, thank you."

Max bowed to Callista and captured her hand, raising it to his lips, raising his eyebrow at her cool gaze. "I was beginning to think you were not coming," he murmured. "You look lovely, Callie." He smiled. "You look like a mermaid. Come, dance with me."

She put down her glass of champagne and allowed him to lead her out onto the dance floor, where the silver and aqua coloured dress shimmered under the lights. Her hair, refusing as usual to stay in any tight formal arrangement, hung in riotous curls down over her shoulders, held back off her face by silver and crystal clips.

"How are you this evening?" he asked, his dark blue eyes seeking hers.

She gazed back up at him, her green eyes cool and composed.

"I am well, I thank you," she replied quietly.

He realised at once that something disturbed her. "What is it? Has something happened, Callie? You do not seem yourself tonight."

He swung her around in his arms, pulling her closer, his arm warm against her back.

"I am perfectly well, Max. I was – just…" she took a deep breath. "I confess I was – surprised – when I saw you dancing with Davina."

She turned her head away, and her eyes found the lady in question, still speaking with her cousin. Davina's eyes were sparkling with good humour, she was laughing and quite ignoring Lady Joanna who had stood up and moved away towards the wide staircase.

Callista looked back up to Max. "I think she is still in love with you, Max," she said speaking directly to him.

He had the grace to look discomfited. "Callie, she is not – she is married."

"I know, otherwise I think you would not be marrying me."

He spun her around and she saw the tightening of his mouth, the darkening of his eyes, the sudden flash of anger. "No!" he said vehemently, "I am extremely happy you have accepted my offer of marriage."

His hand caressed her back, he was holding her close and she became aware of that heat, that strange surge which was building up inside her and she caught her breath, her eyes darkening with desire. She found that she wanted to reach up and touch his face, she wanted him to kiss her – she wanted to be alone with him and give in to these feeling which threatened to suffuse her. She could see in his eyes that he was thinking the same and all thoughts of Davina Fitzpatrick vanished as he waltzed her out of the Ballroom onto the quiet balcony outside. He pulled her out of sight of the people within, and with the wall of the house against her back, she found herself being kissed with a ruthless disregard for the niceties of polite society. Without the bounds of chaperones or the watchful eyes of concerned relatives, she felt for the first time the strength of the passion he felt for her. His arms were bands of steel holding her, his mouth devoured hers, drawing from her the response he sought. She gave it willingly, her passion soaring to meet his, the urgency of his kiss greedily drinking from her lips, his body taut against hers, her breasts crushed against him. She could feel the hardness of him, the evidence of his arousal tight against her belly, she could feel it through the thin material of her gown. He had kissed her before, breaking every rule of courtship in doing so, but never before had she felt this urgency, this unrestrained, untamed wild passion from him. She gloried in it, revelled in the intensity of his feeling for her at that moment. She returned his embrace, gasping for breath when he finally raised his head, not to stop caressing her, he merely moved his mouth against the wildly beating pulse in her neck.

Her hands went up around his neck, her fingers entwining themselves in his hair, holding him as tightly as he held her. She was shaking with the intensity of her feelings, wanting this man, loving this man with all her heart and soul and from somewhere deep within her she knew this was meant to be, that they belonged together and she knew from his touch, from his eyes, from his kiss, that he felt the same way about her.

With a deep, shuddering breath, he finally drew away from her. His face was flushed, his eyes dark, his body was trembling and his hands were shaking as he put his hands on her shoulders and pushed himself away from her.

"God help me," his voice was hoarse. "You have bewitched me, Mermaid." He stepped away from her and ran unsteady hands through his hair, bringing some order back. He turned his back on her and walked over to the edge of the balcony, seeking to get himself under control once more.

She pressed her hands against her burning cheeks. Taking a deep breath, she too steadied herself.

"I think we had better return to the Ballroom," she said quietly. "My Aunt will be wondering where I am."

The music had finished, the hum of conversation came through the open French doors and finally the sounds of the outside world permeated their consciousness once more. They became aware of movement and realised other people were making their way onto the balcony. Straightening her gown, smoothing her hair, Callista moved away from the wall and waited until Max returned to her. His eyes still glittered with a strange light, but his face was less flushed, he was again in full control of himself and he offered her his arm to lead her back into the room.

"How many more of these damned events do we have to suffer before we can finally get married?" he whispered to her as they stood on the threshold of the balcony.

He looked up suddenly aware of being watched and he saw Davina a few feet away, her smile frozen on her face, her huge blue eyes staring into his with something like – reproach – accusation?

It was bad enough that Max seemed to be developing a

tenderness towards his fiancée, but to actually seek her out, dance with her and then – embrace her? Davina was furious, but the telltale signs were all there – the heightened colour, the ruffled clothes, the tousled hair. Rage was welling up inside her but she knew that in this place, in front of all these people, she could not vent her feelings. She forced a smile onto her face and gracefully bowed her head towards them before turning and walking quickly away.

Callista watched her go with something like foreboding. Davina had not looked pleased and Max – he was watching her walk away with a very troubled look on his face. Common courtesy towards his fiancée would not let him abandon her but Callista withdrew her arm.

"If you will excuse me, Max," she said carefully, "I must find my Aunt." She looked in the direction of where Lady Fitzpatrick had walked away, glanced up into his eyes once more and walked away from him.

She saw Georgiana standing at the edge of the Ballroom floor talking to her mother and Lady Markham. She made her way over to them and Georgiana saw at once that something was troubling her cousin. Taking her hand, the two young ladies excused themselves and went out into the cooler wide open hallway where they were able to speak quietly together without being overhead.

"What is wrong, Callie?" Georgiana asked her gently. "Is it Max – have you argued?"

Callista shook her head. "No, Georgie," she sighed. "We have not quarrelled."

"What is it then? He does not want to end your engagement surely?" Such a horrific idea struck Georgie so forcibly she was visibly paled at the thought of the scandal.

Callista almost laughed at her, but shook her head once more. "Indeed no, Georgie, he has – demons of his own to exorcise I fear, before we can be truly happy together."

Georgiana nodded. "You mean Damon's sister," she said. "I confess I do not find myself warming to Lady Fitzpatrick." She glanced around her, to ensure no one was eavesdropping before continuing. "She does not seem to like women very much. She has a bad reputation, I am sure most of it is unfounded and Damon of course, is totally loyal to her but – she has this way of – looking at one as if she is far superior to every other member of her sex."

Callista sighed. "Lady Joanna makes no secret of her dislike. Max, however, is clearly still very fond of her and I – well, I just wish she would return to her husband. I feel uneasy whilst she is so close."

Her head drooped and Georgiana was alarmed at this lowering of spirits. She had been delighted that her lovely, feisty, fearless cousin had won the heart of one of the Ton's most eligible bachelors and could not wait for the impending nuptials, but this sadness overpowering her was so unlike Callie that it worried her.

The sudden sharp scream which echoed all around the empty hallway shocked them into looking up the wide steep staircase. A lady was falling and without stopping to think, Callie lifted her skirts and ran to the stairs, running up them two at a time to try and prevent the lady from tumbling, over and over, all the way down to the bottom. She was closely followed by several of Lady Markham's servants and as she caught the falling woman, strong arms reached out to help her and stopped the force of the fall from taking her and the woman to the bottom of the stairs.

It was Lady Joanna Langley and Callista held her in her arms, alarmed at the sickly grey colour of her skin, her face drawn, etched with pain as she struggled to right herself and sit up.

"Stay still, Your Ladyship." Callista's voice was urgent. "You may have broken a bone. We should not move you yet."

Georgiana ran to help them, assisting Callista to help Lady Joanna to sit up. The Footman was despatched to find Lady Markham and summon a doctor.

Callista ran her hands over Lady Joanna's arms and shoulders. There did not seem to be any sign of a break, but as they attempted to lift her, she gave a cry and collapsed again.

"My hip." She bit her lip, to stop herself from crying out loud again.

Callista held onto her, supported her back and shoulders and glanced briefly upstairs from where Lady Joanna had fallen. A flash of red disappeared around the banisters and Callista frowned, surely she was mistaken. She dismissed the suspicions from her mind and turned her attention back to the injured woman.

A crowd had gathered, murmurs of concern spreading through the building and finally, Max arrived, shouldering people out of the way to reach the crowd gathered around his mother.

"What happened?" he demanded tersely

"Callie stopped me from breaking my neck," his mother returned, her voice weak, but she held Callista's hand and squeezed it gently. "I think I have injured my hip – but she stopped me halfway down the stairs so at least I was not killed."

"How did it happen? Did you slip?" Callista asked her, but she knew the answer before she heard it.

"I was pushed," Lady Joanna said weakly. "I did not see who did it. Max – can you please get me off these stairs?"

"Careful, Max," Callista said. "We must get a doctor to examine your mother at once – move her very slowly – she may have broken more than a hip. "

Lady Markham appeared at this juncture, summoned by the Footman, alarmed at the injury to her guest.

"Oh my dear Lady Joanna!" she exclaimed. "Please Max, can you carry her into the small Salon? I have sent my man to fetch a doctor – he will be here directly."

Between them, slowly and very carefully, Max, aided by Damon who had pushed his way through the crowds to assist them, lifted the injured woman and carried her, painfully slowly, down the rest of the stairs and into the small Salon, accompanied by Lady Markham.

Georgiana sought to reassure their hostess. "Please, Your Ladyship – return to your guests. We must not let this incident spoil your lovely party. We will inform you when the doctor arrives."

Lady Markham left, promising to return immediately and went out to the gathered crowd, alarmed at the news of the accident.

She soothed everyone's fears, assuring them all that Lady Joanna was indeed injured but thankfully had not been killed and was awaiting the services of a doctor. She calmed them, reassured them and ushered them all back into the Ballroom where, at a signal, the orchestra recommenced the music. Within a few minutes, the guests were once again dancing and enjoying their hostess' hospitality – whilst only a concerned few remained in the Salon, waiting for the doctor.

Max was almost as white as his mother. She, in turn, laid down on the large, luxuriously upholstered sofa, clung onto Callista's hands and tried bravely not to groan as the pain in her hip became excruciating.

"Max, Damon – would you leave the room please? Come back when the doctor arrives." Callista voice was firm and serious as she watched the pain spasming across Lady Joanna's face. She had some experience with nursing and knew from the signs that Her Ladyship was in a great deal more distress than she was saying.

Max and Damon exchanged worried glances but seeing his mother's white face and Callista's calm, determined one, Max nodded and the two men left.

Callista turned back to the injured woman and sat on the small stool beside the sofa.

"Lady Joanna," she said gently. "Will you let me examine your legs if you please?" Glancing up at Georgiana for support, she smiled again at Joanna. "I was used to nursing my father and various others when I lived in the North."

She did not go into details, even her cousin did not know of the reputation she had acquired in her home village. She had been looked on as something of a healer – her father had often joked that had she not been the Vicar's daughter she would have been thought of as a witch.

"It's true, Lady Joanna," Georgiana added, kneeling beside the stricken woman. "Our Footman was shot and he says Callie helped him enormously. Please let her look at you."

Lady Joanna's eyes were closed but she opened them to look

from one young lady to the other. She nodded slightly, grimacing as if the slightest movement caused her pain.

Gently, Callista helped Joanna to lay down flat and Georgiana moved to sit beside her, to hold her hand and smooth her forehead. Her cool hands soothed Lady Joanna's head and she watched silently as Callista moved to kneel beside the sofa and, bending over the prone woman, ran her hands gently up each leg, feeling through the delicate silken material of the dove grey gown. She could feel no break, no dislocations but as she felt the side of Lady Joanna's hip, she pressed softly and heard the quick intake of breath. The older lady's brows were knitted together in a state of extreme concentration and as Callista gently probed the site of the injury, her eyes were almost closed.

"I cannot feel a break, Your Ladyship," she said quietly, "but it is swollen and I fear you will be badly bruised. "

Lady Joanna opened her eyes and looked up at Georgiana. "Your hands feel so hot, Callie," she murmured. "I can feel such heat coming from them – my hip feels less painful already."

Georgiana's sigh of relief was audible. "Thank the Lord it is not broken," she exclaimed. "Such a bad fall too."

Lady Joanna's mouth was set in a tight line of displeasure. "I did not fall," she reiterated firmly. "I felt hands on my back and I was pushed."

Georgiana and Callista exchanged a look of discomfiture. "But, Your Ladyship." Callista said quietly. "You could have been killed – surely no one would deliberately do such a thing."

"You would think not, I obviously beg to differ." She sighed and looked directly at Callista. "You saved my life, my dear," she said softly, "And now you appear to be healing me – you are truly an amazing young woman, Callista Wingrove."

A knock on the door heralded the return of Lady Markham, accompanied by a well-dressed gentleman in black. He was of a serious disposition, his sober appearance declared him to be one of the medical profession and Callista was relieved that he was a fairly young man – he would be well versed and well trained in modern medical procedures.

He came over at once to the lady reclining on the sofa and bowed to the assembled ladies.

"Lady Joanna Langley," Lady Markham introduced him to his patient, "this is Doctor William Harvey."

Doctor Harvey waited until Callista and Georgiana stood up.

Callista smiled up at him. "I do not think Lady Joanna has broken any bones," she said, "but I felt swelling around her hip and she will be badly bruised."

Doctor Harvey raised his eyebrow at Callista's summation and she felt her cheeks redden slightly.

"Of course, you must ascertain for yourself, Doctor."

"Thank you. Now if I may examine my patient?"

The ladies moved out of his way and he smiled down at Lady Joanna. "Good evening, Lady Joanna," he began. "I believe you have experienced quite a nasty fall…"

"Somebody pushed me," she snapped back.

Dr Harvey did not seem perturbed by her words. He merely seated himself on the small seat recently vacated by Georgiana and turned to the other ladies.

"If one of you could remain, I would be grateful if the others left so I can examine my patient in private?"

"I will stay," Lady Markham offered at once. "Girls, please let Maxim know his mother is in good hands now."

Lady Joanna glared at her friend and the doctor. "I was in good hands already thank you," she retorted, but allowed herself to submit to the thorough examination by the doctor.

Callista and Georgiana withdrew from the room and found a reception party awaiting them. Max and Damon had been joined by Georgiana's parents and Lady Davina. Davina was clearly displeased that she had been forced to leave the Ballroom by her brother and Lady Amelia was not pleased to be in the company of Lady Davina.

Max turned anxiously to Callista as she came out of the room. "How is she?" he asked.

Callista took his hand and squeezed it, smiling reassuringly. "She is shaken and in pain, but I don't believe anything is broken."

He sighed with heartfelt relief. Maddening and autocratic she might be, but he loved his mother and wanted no harm to befall her.

They waited only a few minutes before the door opened and the doctor emerged.

He looked around and when Max stepped forward, the doctor directed his remarks to him.

"Your mother, sir?" he enquired.

"Yes, Doctor – Harvey, is it not?"

"It is, sir. Your mother has injured her hip in the fall. It is not broken but she will require complete rest for at least four weeks and ice packs on the injury every day to aid the healing process. Gentle exercise only, no dancing, no excitement. I would recommend removing her to somewhere in the country to recuperate if possible."

The doctor smiled grimly and turned to Callista. "My compliments, Miss Wingrove." He bowed in her direction. "Your diagnosis was entirely correct."

Callista's cheeks burned once again at his cool but sincerely meant compliment, causing Max to regard his betrothed with a thoughtful expression on his face.

Georgiana smiled up at Damon. "You should have seen her, Damon, she was wonderful."

Davina stared coldly at her brother and Georgiana. "Indeed, how so, Miss Wetherby?" she enquired.

"Why, of course, you did not see her, Lady Fitzpatrick," Georgiana explained. "She stopped Lady Joanna from falling more than half way down the stairs, then she found what was wrong before the doctor had even arrived." She laughed, her eyes sparkling with a mixture of merriment and relief after what could have been a tragic outcome. "Callie could feel the injury on your Mama's hip, Max, and Lady Joanna said she could feel the heat from Callie's hands – she was most annoyed when the Doctor arrived."

Doctor Harvey's smile was a little warmer. "I have heard of people with such healing abilities. Congratulations,

Miss Wingrove, you were certainly in the right place at the right time."

All this praise on the poor relation was more than Davina could stand. "Why Miss Wingrove," she snapped, "in another age you would have been called a witch."

To her astonishment, Callista actually laughed at this description; far from being offended, she was actually amused. "My father used to say the same, Lady Fitzpatrick, but when he had the headache or felt weary from his day's labours, he used to have me massage his shoulders and he was pleased with my abilities then, I assure you."

Whatever Davina's response to this would have been was never uttered as Damon, recognising the signs of her rapidly diminishing good humour, stepped forward. "Well you have certainly bewitched Max, Miss Wingrove. It was creditable indeed the way you prevented Lady Langley from falling further than she did, was it not, Max?"

Max had been gazing at his betrothed with a bemused expression on his face, mixed with relief that his mother had not been injured further. He stepped towards her and took her hands, the look in his eyes telling her that if they had been alone she would have been hugged closely to him. As it was, he could only raise both her hands and kiss them both.

"You are a remarkable woman, Callista," he murmured. "Words cannot express my feelings at this moment. My thanks for your quick thinking and your actions – I will be forever in your debt."

For a long, silent, heartfelt moment, he gazed into her eyes, oblivious to everyone around them. She returned his gaze steadily, unblinking, wide green eyes looking into his and it came again, that shiver of recognition, that faint, nebulous memory of something ancient, something overwhelming and powerful which drew them together and weaved around them as insubstantial as mist but real nonetheless.

A gasp from Davina brought them back down to earth. Her fury was being held in check but her eyes told another story. Damon gripped her elbow and sent a warning glance her way.

Before anyone else could speak, however, the door opened and Lady Markham stepped outside.

She smiled at the small gathering. "Doctor Harvey, thank you for coming so promptly. My Coachman is waiting to take you home whenever you are ready and Lady Joanna is anxious to go home too, Max."

He turned in her direction and held out his hand to the doctor, standing beside Lady Markham. "Doctor, my thanks – will you attend my mother tomorrow if you please? I will arrange to transport her to our country estate as soon as possible but until we can move her, I would appreciate your visits."

Doctor Harvey shook his hand in farewell. "Of course, Sir Maxim. I will call tomorrow morning. Please be careful when you move her, however, she is in a great deal of pain still."

He bowed to the assembled company and made his farewells, leaving to return home.

"Damon, would you be so kind as to order my carriage? I must get my mother home at once and get her settled."

Before anyone else could speak, Callista stepped forward. "Would you like me to accompany you, Max?" she asked quietly.

He was sorely tempted but propriety and good manners would not allow him to accept her offer.

"Thank you, Callie," he replied, conscious of the eyes and ears upon him. "I will not trespass on your good nature any further – please come and visit Mother tomorrow. We would be delighted to see you but you have done more than enough for one evening and I fear my mother would not be good company tonight."

Damon went to order the carriage, still keeping hold of his sister's arm so she was forced to accompany him. Lady Markham and Lady Amelia went in to assist Max's mother to make her comfortable for the journey home, Lady Markham sending harassed maids running for pillows and rugs and everything possible to cushion the carriage and prevent Lady Joanna from injuring herself further.

Upon Damon's return, he was alone, Davina having returned to the Ballroom. Max raised a silent eyebrow at his friend but

Damon merely shook his head. Sir Augustus, ready to leave insisted that they, too, would also go and as Max and Damon were leaving, neither Georgiana nor Callista felt any great desire to remain.

Damon bowed over Georgiana's hand. He seemed perturbed but he forced a smile to his lips and he drew her away from the rest of the party to exchange a few words in private with her.

"Georgiana," he said softly. "I had so hoped to speak with you this evening." He squeezed her hand and stared intently into her wide blue eyes. "Circumstances have conspired against us – but," he sighed and managed a soft laugh at the same time, "we will meet again soon, I promise."

"Perhaps we could go riding again?" Georgiana suggested hopefully.

His face was a closed book, his eyes guarded and his smile was wintry. "Yes, of course," he said softly, and raised her hands to press a gentle kiss upon it.

Max had gone into the Salon and upon being reassured his mother was ready to return home, he called Damon and together, they gently lifted her and carried her out of the Salon, out of the house and settled her onto the padded, cushioned and pillowed carriage.

Callista and her Aunt collected their cloaks from Lady Markham's servants and went out to say goodbye to Lady Joanna.

They watched as Max settled his mother, seating her carefully and wrapping her evening cloak around her shoulders. Her face was pale and drawn with pain, but she was composed and thanked him as he put a fur rug across her lap.

She held out her hand to Callista, who leaned into the carriage and took it. "Thank you once again, my dear," she said. "You saved my life – come see me tomorrow before Max whisks me off back to Moreland."

Callista glanced over to Max. "Will you accompany your mother?" she asked.

He stood beside the carriage and nodded, his face sombre. "I will take her in a day or so," he agreed, but he smiled again. "I will be back in time for our wedding," he said. He bowed to Amelia. "I am sorry this has curtailed your enjoyment of this evening, Lady Wetherby."

"Nonsense." Amelia was brisk and no-nonsense and Callista was grateful to her Aunt for her stoic understanding on this occasion. "I am only thankful this evening did not end in tragedy, Sir Maxim. I am sorry you were injured, Lady Joanna – we will call tomorrow if we may. Come along, Callista, let Sir Maxim get his Mama home."

She stepped away from the carriage and Callista stepped back with her. Max smiled at Callista and bowed to both ladies. He sprung up inside the carriage and seated himself opposite his mother. The waiting Footman slammed the door shut and the ladies watched as the carriage moved smoothly away from the Markham mansion.

They waited a few minutes and were joined shortly by Sir Augustus and Georgiana.

"What a strange day!" Augustus exclaimed. "Lady Markham has just told me that Lady Joanna has insisted she was pushed." He shook his head in disbelief. "Poor lady, the fall must have confused her."

Callista was watching the carriage driving away down the drive and briefly closed her eyes. She recalled the flash of red she had seen on the landing above the stairs and slowly turned her head to the front door of the house where Damon Fortescue and his sister were standing, also waiting for their carriage and ready to leave. Damon was clearly troubled, his brow furrowed, his mouth set in a straight, grim line. Lady Davina, however, was smiling, a strange light in her eyes. She held her brother's arm and was speaking softly to him.

She waved to them as the Wetherby party climbed into their carriage and drove away, but Callista did not return the wave. However, she could not take her eyes off Davina, watching her laughing up at Damon and pulling her shawl around her shoulders. The shawl was a dark red, perfectly matching the material of her dark red dress.

Callista felt cold. She recalled Lady Joanna's words and wondered exactly how deranged Lady Davina could be to try and kill someone for nothing more than refusing to acknowledge them.

She shivered slightly. She was not afraid of Davina but she realised that Davina would make an implacable enemy and she also realised that by marrying Max, she had just placed herself in the unenviable position of Davina's rival. She pressed her lips together firmly. She was no coward nor was she helpless. If Davina intended to try and intimidate her, then she would find that poor little relation Callista was more than ready for her.

Chapter Twelve

Georgiana gazed disconsolately out of the Drawing Room window at the rain-soaked garden of the Portland Square house.

She sighed and moved away, back to her recently vacated seat on the sofa where lay her discarded embroidery. Hers was not a particularly patient nature and the various occupations she had sought to distract herself with were wearing extremely thin.

She heard the unmistakeable sound of the front door knocker and brightened immediately. Surely this time it would be Damon. But no footsteps heralded the arrival of a visitor, no door opened announcing a guest and she sank down again, to pick up the discarded needlework and pick at it distractedly.

Her mother and Callista were visiting the Langley household, saying goodbye to Lady Joanna as Max prepared to escort his mother to their estates in Wiltshire.

Wedding preparations were in full swing, but owing to his mother's unexpected accident, the lavish event which both Lady Joanna and Lady Amelia were hoping for had been scaled down to a more private and, much to Callista's relief, more intimate affair. They were to be married in the chapel on the Moreland estate at the end of August and they were to honeymoon as planned for a month in Cornwall. Lady Joanna had invited a friend to come and live with her and keep her company whilst the newlyweds were on honeymoon and, upon their return, she planned to move into the Dower House at Moreland. She was handing over the reins of the household to Callista and going into semi-retirement, planning on inviting the friend to remain with her and act as companion from then on.

All was arranged, all was going ahead as planned, all was progressing smoothly. Callista was extremely happy. Even though Lady Joanna's accident prevented Max from attending any of the social events still taking place in London, she saw him every day, albeit briefly. She confided in Georgiana that she was content to wait until her wedding day to see him again. He had pressing estate matters to attend to, and the logistics involved in moving his partially disabled mother across the country to Moreland were proving to be more complex than he had at first imagined.

Georgiana and Callista found the final few weeks of the Season to be a gradual winding down of the social whirl. Callista was as relieved as her Uncle that they no longer attended every Ball, every Soiree, every party being held. She was busy with the wedding arrangements, although Lady Amelia, thwarted in her plans to make Georgiana the bride of the Season, was making the most of Callista's forthcoming nuptials. Despite her niece's alarmed protests at the amount of wedding clothes she was being provided with, Amelia had decided Callista was not going to embarrass the family by appearing in anything less than the best Madame Duvall could provide.

As Georgiana's first month in London had involved more time spent in the dressmakers than at home, so it was that Callista's final month was proving to be the same.

Georgiana felt no animosity towards her cousin. On the contrary, she was happy that Callista was to be married. She had felt sorry for Callie when the dowdy parson's daughter had been brought by Mama from the small country parish in Cumberland to their home all those months ago – now she could not imagine life without her and it was with a sharp pang of dismay that she realised that Callie's wedding was a matter of only a few weeks away and the cousins would be parted once again.

She had hoped – oh how she had hoped – that they would be neighbours as well as cousins. But Damon had been behaving most strangely over the last week. Up until the night of Lady Joanna's accident, he had been a most satisfactorily ardent suitor. They had gone riding together, driven in the park in his sporting curricle, danced together at every social event; he had sought her out and despite his initial reluctance to become involved with anyone, he had been so captivated by her that he had courted her and she had reciprocated with all her heart. All dreams and ambitions she had nurtured to become a Duchess had flown away and had been dismissed without a backward glance.

Ambition had been replaced by that most inconvenient and purest of emotions, she had fallen in love. He was no spoiled and arrogant Duke; he was quite simply an honourable man. He was an upright, respectable and decent man. He had rescued his family estate from the brink of bankruptcy; he had worked hard to restore his family's name and fortune and had turned the tide against penury by the force of his quiet, determined personality.

Added to that, he was a tall and devastatingly handsome man, with the brightest blue eyes, the broadest shoulders, the sort of physique which made Georgiana quite blush with her own boldness in even thinking about it – and on the one occasion where he had thrown caution to the winds and had swept her into his arms, pressing a passionate kiss upon her rosebud lips, she had experienced the strangest feeling and had been quite bereft when an approaching footstep had ended the embrace.

Since that night, however, she had not seen him. There had been no visits, no cards, no flowers, no gifts, no notes requesting the pleasure of her company on a curricle drive, or a ride in the park or a picnic.

She could not imagine what was wrong – she had gone over the events of that night, and up until Lady Joanna's accident, she and Damon had been dancing together, laughing over some amusing anecdote. They had been happy. He had pressed a kiss against her hand and escorted her back to her Mama, then excused himself to go in search of his sister. He had been worried about Davina – he knew how unpopular his notorious sister was and felt it his duty to ensure she was not abandoned, alone and unprotected in the Markham household.

As they took their leave later that evening, Georgiana recalled how strangely Damon had acted. He had been almost withdrawn.

He had promised to see her soon but since that night she had not seen nor heard from him.

The Drawing Room door opened and her head went up sharply, only to droop once more as her father entered.

"Good morning, Georgie," Sir Augustus beamed at his daughter. "Are you all alone, my dear?"

"Yes, Mama and Callie have gone to say farewell to Max and Lady Joanna. I thought I would remain here in case we received any visitors."

The tone of her voice left her doting Papa in no doubt which particular visitor Georgiana was referring to.

He came over to her and, bending, kissed her upturned cheek.

"No word from Damon, then?" he asked gently.

"No, Papa," she replied quietly.

Augustus frowned slightly at the lifeless tone apparent in his daughter's voice.

"Have you written to him, my dear?" he asked seating himself in the armchair opposite Georgiana.

She shook her head, lowering her eyes to her embroidery as a suspicious sparkle blurred her vision. "I wrote to him two days ago and have received no reply," she admitted. "I did not think it becoming of me to write again."

Augustus regarded his daughter's downcast eyes. He felt a stirring of emotion suspiciously like anger toward the absent Sir Damon. His daughter had turned down a perfectly respectable marriage proposal (conveniently forgetting he had detested the young man in question) to throw her cap at that young man from a decidedly questionable family – even he had to admit that the rumours surrounding Lady Davina had more than a hint of truth in them – and that Sir Damon had the effrontery to treat his daughter in this decidedly cavalier fashion was insupportable.

Standing up again, he walked over to the bell pull on the wall. Silently he waited, observing the studious application of attention Georgiana was giving the previously discarded embroidery.

James, the Butler, entered within moments. Augustus beamed at his manservant.

"Ah, James, is young Joe around at the moment?"

It was as much as James could do to prevent his lip from curling at the mention of the child's name but he managed to school his features.

"He is in the stables, My Lord," he replied, "in keeping with Sir Maxim's instructions."

"Excellent." August smiled. "Advise the stables that I wish to go out, I will need my horse and Joe can accompany me – if he is to be a groom, he may as well practise with me."

"Of course, my lord." James bowed and left the room, making his way to the stables to advise the head groomsman that his young protégé was to prepare himself and saddle up two of the horses at once.

In the meantime, Georgiana looked up in surprise at her father. "Where are you going, Papa?" she asked.

"I am going to pay a couple of overdue morning visits, my dear," he replied.

Georgiana stared at her father in astonishment. He hated the whole ritual of morning visits and avoided them like the plague.

"Do you wish me to accompany you, Papa?" she asked.

He shook his head and started walking towards the door. "No, my dear, I have a few errands to run, you will be extremely bored and I will not be long. If your Mama returns, tell her I will be back soon."

Georgiana sighed, she was bored already. However, the thought of visiting some of her father's cronies did not exactly fill her with enthusiasm either so she settled herself down again to await the return of her mother and cousin and listen hopefully for the announcement of a longed-for visitor.

Augustus returned to his room to change into suitable riding clothes and emerged twenty minutes later to find young Joe waiting for him in the hall.

Several weeks of good food, Mrs Smith's determined mothering and enforced bathing had transformed the young urchin who had first appeared on their doorstep.

He seemed to have grown a few inches, his unruly mop of

hair had been washed and cut and was now an almost respectable head of blond curls, contrasting with wide amber eyes. A stunning combination which, added to the angelic features, had changed the boy into an attractive child who showed promise to be an extremely handsome young man.

He was totally devoted to Callista and had formed an unlikely friendship with Sir Augustus who was amused by his chatter and description of his former life in the dark, seedy underbelly of London. A part of the world none of his new employers would ever see or could imagine.

Aware of the eagle eyes of his arch nemesis James the Butler upon him, Joe made his bow to Sir Augustus and wished him a good morning.

"Good morning, Joe," Augustus replied, his eyes twinkling as he took in the studied politeness of his young protégé. "How are my horses this morning?"

Joe beamed, his smile lighting up his whole countenance. "Very well, my lord," he replied. "Charlie's leg is almost healed and Misty's colic is nearly cured."

Augustus nodded, picking up his riding whip and gloves from the outstretched hands of his Butler.

"Good, very good. Which horses have you picked for us this morning, young man?"

Joe moved forward to open the front door for Sir Augustus. "Mr 'udson says I can't ride well enuff to have a decent 'orse, so's I 'ave to ride old Bishop and your 'orse is Milly as usual."

James raised his eyes to the ceiling as he bowed his master out of the house and Augustus emerged to find his gentle Bay Milly awaiting him, accompanied by the much older, more sedate and smaller Bishop, Joe's mount for the short ride.

In his few weeks in His Lordship's stables, Joe had learnt quickly, the head stable lad was quite pleased with his young assistant and lost no time in teaching Joe the basics of horse husbandry, and more importantly, had taught him to ride. Joe was a fast learner, he worked hard and as a reward for his days of toil in mucking out stables, polishing brasses, grooming the horses and cleaning the tack, he was allowed to ride the gentle Bishop around the courtyard and, occasionally, he would accompany the head lad on errands, riding the horse in a studious, careful manner until he gradually became used to the horse and started riding with more confidence until he was now quite proficient. The highlight of his day was when Callista came to visit him. Every evening without fail she would venture down into the kitchens and spend half an hour with him, talking to him and asking about his day. The other servants were scandalised at his free and easy way with Miss Wingrove, but she seemed happy to listen to his artless chat, laughing at his description of life as a stable lad, and commiserating with him over the various bruises and scrapes he would proudly show off to her, explaining how he acquired them with total honesty and using such language that Mrs Smith was forced to reprimand him so often that gradually he learned to moderate his language in front of the family of the house.

He took the reins of his horse from the other stable lad and climbed inelegantly onto his horse as the lad helped Sir Augustus to mount the Bay.

The street was busy but Augustus led the way and Joe followed at a respectful distance, concentrating hard on controlling his horse and doing his best to appear as experienced a rider as his master.

Joe trotted a respectful distance behind Sir Augustus but suddenly found himself side by side with his employer.

He drew his horse to a stop and looked up expectantly at Sir Augustus who was observing the house in front of them with a thoughtful expression on his face.

"Joe," he began, "Joe, this is the house we are visiting and I have a little – favour – to ask of you."

Joe straightened in his saddle, suddenly aware of the importance of the mission about to be requested of him.

"Yes, guv'nor?" he asked, his eyes brightening.

Augustus still looked thoughtful but he smiled at the child at his side. "It is nothing too difficult Joe, I just want you to – listen."

"Who to?" Joe asked, frowning slightly.

"Just the servants, my boy, that's all. Whilst I am visiting the master of the house, you will go to the kitchens and just – listen."

Sir Augustus dismounted and Joe followed suit. Joe took the reins of both horses and as his master was admitted through the front door, he was directed by the Butler around to the rear of the building where he tethered the horses outside the stables and after knocking politely on the kitchen door was let in by a harassed-looking scullery maid.

The kitchen was busy, a hive of activity as the Cook and the maids prepared the midday meal for their masters and for the houseful of servants. The Cook acknowledged his presence with a nod in his direction and a mug of milk, before ignoring him and continuing with her work. Unnoticed, unobserved and ignored, Joe settled himself down with his milk and awaited the summons to let him know his master was about to leave.

Sir Augustus had told him to listen, so he did. Being careful not to appear to be eavesdropping, Joe merely sat quietly and let the ebb and flow of the kitchen surround him and he very quickly learned more in half an hour from the servant's gossip than his master could have found out in a month.

Sir Augustus in the meantime was presently seating himself in the sun-filled morning room of the Fortescue mansion. He looked around in an appreciative silence at the understated elegance of the room. It looked to him as though the room had been recently decorated, the furnishings fairly new and the carpets and curtains certainly of a more modern design than that currently gracing his own home. He had heard that the Fortescues had been brought back from the brink of ruin by the current Baronet and from the look of the house, Damon had done a good job of it, replacing works of art sold off by his rakish father and refurbishing the house to a standard expected of such an old family name.

Damon himself came into the morning room a few minutes after Augustus' arrival. He looked slightly flustered, his face was pale and his eyes were glittering a bright pale blue.

"Sir Augustus..." He came forward with his hand outstretched.

"Please forgive me for not being here to greet you. I am afraid you find me somewhat distracted at the moment."

Augustus shook the outstretched hand. "I am sorry if I have intruded, Sir Damon – is this a difficult time?"

Damon seemed to gather himself together and walked to a small side table that held a decanter of sherry and crystal glasses.

"Please Augustus, be seated. May I offer you some refreshment?"

Augustus accepted the glass of sherry and sipped it thoughtfully. "A delightful beverage, Damon, thank you."

He silently watched his host pour himself a glass and noticed that Damon's hand shook slightly. He certainly did not seem himself.

"We were worried about you, Damon," he said quietly, watching as his host moved restlessly over to the large fireplace. He stood with his back to the fireplace whilst Augustus observed him and glanced at the large painting above the fireplace. It was a charming study of a woman and two small children. His mother, Augustus hazarded a guess, and the two children, the angelic fair-haired blue-eyed boy and girl were obviously Damon and his sister.

"Worried?" Damon asked and Augustus sensed rather than saw the effort with which he held himself.

"Why yes, Damon. Since the night of Lady Markham's Ball we have not seen you and we have wondered if you were quite well?"

Damon swallowed his sherry and gave a short laugh. It was a sound devoid of humour but he moved away from the fireplace and seated himself opposite Augustus. He leaned back in his armchair and crossed one elegantly shod leg over the other.

"I am quite well, thank you, Augustus," he answered and paused before going on. "My sister, however, has been ill and I have been forced to remain at home to ensure her wellbeing."

"Ah." Augustus watched Damon and tried to see beneath the pale, urbane exterior.

A muscle twitched in Damon's cheek and he appeared to be struggling to remain still.

"I am sorry to hear of it. How is Lady Davina at present, may I ask?"

A pause, Damon forced a smile to his lips. "She is still unable to receive visitors, I am afraid. She has an indisposition of her nerves and is confined to her room – I am hopeful that she is on the mend now though."

Augustus smiled at the younger man, an understanding paternalistic smile. "Oh these ladies and their nerves – how we suffer from them." He chuckled slightly. "I normally find a visit to the jewellers settles Lady Amelia's nervous indispositions."

Damon forced himself to join in with the joke. "Alas, my sister is impervious to the blandishments of a new item of jewellery."

He paused, as if wondering whether to explain further. Augustus smiled at him once again and with a sigh, Damon closed his eyes. He could not bring himself to unburden himself completely, but the strain of dealing with Davina's behaviour of the last week was beginning to tell.

"My sister has received a letter from her estranged husband demanding her return to Ireland and she is, not unnaturally, loathe to comply with his wishes."

Augustus sipped his sherry once again. "He cannot force her to return to him, surely," he said reasonably.

Damon opened his eyes again and looked over to his guest, his face pale but stern. "He can withdraw his financial support and instruct his lawyers here in London to refuse to pay her bills. It has taken me years to get this family's fortune back under control without the need to sell off vast tracts of my estates. I love my sister dearly but I simply cannot afford to support her extravagant lifestyle." He paused, but looked Augustus in the eyes. "I cannot pursue my own interests or fulfil my own desires until I have settled Davina's problems."

Augustus drained his glass. His voice was firm, his meaning unmistakeable. "I am sorry to hear that," he sighed. "You are a gentleman, Sir Damon." He went on quietly, "You have paid a considerable amount of attention to my daughter, you have given every indication of offering for her, so much so that she has refused an offer of marriage which was very much against her mother's wishes. Please excuse me for my plain speaking, but it seems to me that your sister and her marital problems are for her and her husband to sort out. If she is not to return to him, you need to get your lawyers involved and work out some form of separation agreement which will be mutually acceptable. In the meantime, if you are not going to continue your relationship with my daughter you will do her, and me, the courtesy of paying us a visit to break off the connection." He paused for breath. "Georgiana is extremely upset that you have not visited, or written to her in over a week. It distresses me to see my daughter in this state and whilst I would not normally dream of interfering in my children's affairs, I cannot stand by and watch her decline in this manner."

At the mention of Georgiana, Damon uncrossed his legs and leaned forward. "She is upset? I – I am sorry – I would not offend nor upset Georgiana for the world." His pale cheeks regained some colour. "I had every intention of calling on you, sir. I had been to see my lawyers, my affairs were all in order, my life was settled, and my estates were slowly recovering after the years of neglect inflicted upon them by my wastrel of a father."

He stood up again, pacing to and from the fireplace, his agitation obvious, his distress tangible.

"I love your daughter, Sir Augustus – but until this problem with my sister is settled, I am in no position to make an offer of marriage for her."

He stopped and faced Augustus again. "I beg you to accept my apologies, Sir Augustus. I had no intention of ever causing Georgiana any hurt or distress."

He seemed to struggle with his emotions for a few moments. "I will call tomorrow and speak to Georgiana if I may, sir?"

"And say what young man?"

They faced each other, the tall, strikingly handsome young man and the older, grey haired bluff Yorkshireman.

"I will tell Georgiana that I must take my sister to Ireland – I will be gone for some time and she must not feel that she has any obligation to me. If she should meet someone else then I have no right to expect her to wait for me or turn down any offers of marriage from another."

The words seemed to be wrung out of him, but his voice was steady, his demeanour quietly determined.

"You will not return for the wedding of your best friend and my niece?"

Damon shook his head. "I don't know," he admitted. "I have no idea how long we are likely to remain in Dublin."

Silence followed his words, but a sudden crash from above their heads made them both jump.

Damon closed his eyes briefly then looked up at the ceiling, forcing a smile to his lips. "My apologies again, Sir Augustus – my servants are getting careless."

Augustus smiled back at him. "I only hope it was nothing very valuable."

He reached down for his gloves and riding whip. "Thank you for being so frank, Sir Damon," he said, holding his hand out once more to his host. "I look forward to receiving you tomorrow," he continued, shaking hands with Damon before pulling his gloves on. "Would you mind sending your Butler to inform my young groom that I am ready to leave?"

"Of course." Damon moved to the bell pull and within a few moments the Butler arrived to receive his orders.

Damon accompanied Augustus to the front door and waited until Joe appeared around the corner of the building, trotting confidently on Bishop, leading Sir Augustus' horse to the mounting block.

"Until tomorrow, Sir Augustus," Damon said and watched as Augustus took his leave. Augustus mounted his horse and together, he and the youngest groom Damon had ever seen rode away.

Another crash sounded from upstairs and, muttering a curse, Damon closed the front door and started up the stairs back to Davina to calm her down once again before she completely destroyed every movable object in her bedroom.

Augustus and Joe rode in companionable silence for a few minutes until they turned the street out onto the thoroughfare leading back to Portland Square. Augustus waited for Joe to catch him up and observed with some concern the solemn expression on the boy's face.

"Well, Joe?" he asked quietly. "Did you hear anything of interest in the kitchens?"

Joe seemed troubled but he looked up at Sir Augustus and his young face seemed to take on an almost adult appearance. "Yes, guv'nor," he sighed, and Augustus saw him struggling to put into words what he had heard.

"Take your time, Joe," Augustus said as they walked the two horses slowly homeward. "Were they saying anything about Lady Davina? Her brother told me she was unwell."

"Unwell? I heard 'em talkin' about her orl right – sayin' as 'ow he should 'ave 'er locked up in Bedlam. That she was as mad as an 'atter and 'e was being run ragged tryin' to keep her under control."

Augustus was shocked by Joe's outburst, but there was more to come. As if a dam had burst, Joe continued, the words spilling out of him in a rush.

"They were sayin' how she was fumin' that Sir Max had stopped visitin' 'er cos of him getting' married to Miss Callie – and – and that…" Joe stopped, his emotions almost getting the better of him. His amber eyes had darkened, he was upset and angry and, child though he was, he knew the malicious gossip had an element of truth in it.

"Sir Augustus – they was sayin' as 'ow Lady Davina was goin' to do summat to 'urt our Miss Callie."

Augustus was alarmed at how upset Joe was getting and he reached out his hand to stop the boy's horse. He put his hand on the child's shoulder and pressed it reassuringly.

"Joe," he said firmly, "Lady Davina is unwell – she is ill and she will have no intention of harming our Callista. Besides, Callie has us to protect her and in a few weeks, she will be married to Max and he will keep her safe from any harm."

Joe did not look convinced. "What if Sir Max starts visitin' 'er again? Who's goin' to look after Miss Callie then?"

Augustus' mouth thinned to a straight line. "Sir Maxim is marrying Callista," he said firmly. "He will not be continuing his – er – visits to Lady Davina then." He paused. "And, of course, you will be there to look after Callista then, will you not?"

"Me?"

"Yes Joe – I do not think there is anyone more devoted to my niece than you, Joe. I am sure you will do your best to always protect and care for her."

Joe's expression lifted for the first time since leaving the Fortescue mansion. His brow cleared and the frown on his young face disappeared.

"Course I will," he exclaimed and he smiled. "I'll not let 'er down," he said and despite his youth and tender years, the determination in his voice and expression boded ill for anyone daring to try and harm his beloved mistress.

Augustus meanwhile was pondering what Joe had informed him about Davina. Most of it could be dismissed as idle servant's gossip. That Davina was ill there was no doubt, Damon had admitted as much. However, there was always some element of truth in the most salacious of gossip. Davina's reputation had been considered unsavoury for years. Rumours of her behaviour had reached even his ears; stories of her wildness, her recklessness had abounded. If the gossip was to be believed then Davina was indeed teetering on the edge of true madness and that could explain Damon's sudden reluctance to involve himself further with Georgiana.

Perhaps he was worried that the waywardness exhibited by both his father and sister could, actually, be hereditary. In which case he no doubt was worried of the possibility of passing on the instability to his own children.

Augustus sighed. Damon was doing his utmost to ensure Georgiana was never going to be hurt by something which might never happen – he was being brave and noble in giving up the woman he loved and Georgiana would probably never know the true reason behind his sacrifice.

Shaking his head, he gently urged his horse onward and side by side the two returned to Portland Square. They arrived at the same time as Lady Amelia and Callista, returning home after bidding farewell to Max and Lady Joanna. It had been, as far as Callie was concerned, a most unsatisfactory parting. She had not been able to speak privately to Max all morning. They had been forced to remain circumspect and formal for the entire, heavily chaperoned visit. There had been no stolen embraces, no whispered intimacies, no more than a gentle squeeze of the hand as he had raised it to his lips to formally kiss her farewell.

The two ladies were standing on the pavement as Augustus and Joe turned the corner and almost without thinking, Joe kicked his horse into a trot and upon reaching Callista, he jumped from the horse and it was a veritable volcano who threw himself into her arms, squeezing her tightly and letting the pent up emotions of the day release themselves in a short torrent of tears.

"Joe," Callista exclaimed, hugging the child to her. "Whatever is wrong?"

He struggled to pull himself together but with a determined sniff he released his somewhat bemused mistress.

"Sorry, Miss," he whispered fiercely. "I was just so 'appy to see ya."

She smiled down at him and producing a handkerchief from her reticule, she wiped his eyes and gently pushed the fair curls away from his face. "And I am happy to see you too, Joe," she replied. "Are you all right now?"

He sniffed and pulled away from the comforting circle of her arms. "Yes, Miss," he said. "I'm orl right now."

"Good boy – now take the horses to the stables and I will come and see you later, is that agreeable?"

He nodded, the sparkle of unshed tears glistening in the sunshine, turning his eyes into pools of clearest amber. "Yes Miss, fank you."

He turned away from her and took up the reins of Bishop and Milly, held out to him by Sir Augustus.

Sir Augustus smiled kindly down on him and with a slight imperceptible shake of his head, his message was conveyed to the boy. Joe recognised the meaning immediately and nodded in return. He would say nothing of the gossip he had overheard. It was a secret between himself and Augustus and not for the world would he give Miss Callista a moment of unease regarding her future or her safety.

He was going to protect her and he promised himself that no harm would ever become her for as long as he was around to prevent it.

Augustus watched the boy leading the horses away and smiled to himself – Callista had found herself a true little champion in the child. He followed the ladies into the house, Amelia scolding her niece for allowing the child to throw himself at her in such a forward manner. Callista was murmuring something in reply and Georgiana came out of the morning room to greet her family, her face lighting up and becoming wreathed in smiles as her mother and cousin greeted her.

Heavy hearted, Augustus watched his daughter as she smiled and laughed with her cousin. Her happiness was about to be shattered and he knew that there was nothing he could do to ease the pain of her broken heart. Forcing a smile to his lips, he joined his family as they made their way into the Dining Room for luncheon and he reached his daughter as she waited for him by the open door.

Silently he took her hand in his and patted it affectionately. Laughing, she leaned forward and kissed his cheek before turning to join her mother and cousin at the table.

He paused, taking in the scene before him, drinking in the joy and happiness in the room at that moment, capturing forever in his mind the scene before him and wishing with all his heart that he was not privy to the knowledge that in twenty four hours his daughter's laughter would soon be nothing more than a distant, fading memory.

Lihanna 7

Time passed and with it Lihanna's impatience at being held in captivity. The relationship between the Roman General and his captive thawed and he allowed her to leave the prison of his tent. She was able to see for herself that her people were not ill-treated and although they were as much prisoners as she was herself, they were free to move around and carry out their normal day to day tasks. The Romans allowed them to leave the compound to tend to their crops and gather in the harvest, she was able to visit and converse with the villagers and whilst the young men, Daveth included, had been put to work to help the Romans' building projects, she saw no evidence of brutality or violence against them.

She was well-guarded however and given no opportunity to speak to Daveth or the other young men. They could see her though. They watched as she moved around the fortress and returned each evening to the confines of her quarters.

Each evening Julius would return and, torn by a desire to keep her at a safe distance and a longing to have her accompany him, his resolve weakened when she did not abuse the trust he placed in her.

He returned from his day out of the fortress with his men, some two weeks following their visit to the Sacred Stones. He had continued his reconnoitre of the country he had helped to conquer and with his men they drew maps and routed out small bands of rebellious Celts.

He found her standing at the entrance of their quarters; she was wrapped in her heavy cloak and staring into the distance as he approached.

"Is something troubling you, Princess?" he enquired.

She turned her head towards him. "Samhain is almost here, General," she replied. "It is a time when we used to honour our ancestors with great celebrations at the Stones." She paused. "My mother and I used to visit the burial sites and take offerings to our ancestors."

She sighed and a tremulous smile lifted her lips. "It is many weeks since I have seen my mother," she said softly. "I do not know if she still survives. If she still lived, surely she would have come forward by now to parley for my release?"

As the same thought had been uppermost in the General's mind, he nodded.

"We have received no word from anyone. The only Celts we encounter are small bands, separate from any large forces. They pose no problem and they are unable to give us any information regarding your family."

He hesitated, not wanting to speak the thoughts which had assailed him, but she gazed at him with her direct clear eyes and spoke aloud his own fears.

"Do you think she is dead, General?" she asked.

His eyes did not waver from hers. "I do not know, Princess," he replied. "Until we receive confirmation then I will not make any guesses."

Her face turned away again to look out over the top of the high walls of the fortress.

"May I ask a favour, General?"

"If it is within my power to grant it, Princess," he replied.

"Take me out again," she said. "Take me to the burial mound so I may make an offering and grant peace to my ancestors."

He followed her gaze to the far horizon where the sun was now setting behind the trees beyond the safety of their fortress.

"Very well," he agreed. "We will go tomorrow."

She turned to him then, smiling at last. "Thank you, General."

"And Lihanna..." he continued.

"Yes, General?"

"Whether your family live or – or not... I promise you will always be safe and protected with me."

She put out her hand and he took it in his own.

"Thank you, Julius," she whispered.

He would have lingered there, her hand in his and his eyes fixed on hers when a movement disturbed them.

His manservants appeared and she returned to the confines of her small room as Julius changed from his armour. She knelt on the fur rug beside her narrow cot and prayed once more for the safety of her family and tried to forget the expression in his eyes as he had held her hand in his.

The following morning, true to his word, he had her horse prepared and they set off together on another clear, crisp autumn day to ride to the burial mounds of her ancestors. She found herself wishing it was just the two of them, alone together, but these were dangerous times and danger could be waiting for them at every twist in the road so they were accompanied by six of his men, riding behind them as she led the way towards their destination.

The ancient burial barrows had long been replaced by the burial mound which now held the bones of her ancestors. There was an entrance, guarded either side by a pile of stones, blessed by the Druids, granting safe passage to those who came in peace and meaning no harm.

As on their previous journey, Lihanna gathered the remaining wild flowers which were hardy enough to still grow amongst the shelter of the trees, though this time she asked Julius to cut some holly from the large bushes which grew in such proliferation throughout the forest. With holly, ivy and flowers, she entered the tomb and placed her offerings on a small altar holding crystals and the remains of former offerings which she removed and threw outside, to be caught up and carried away by the winds.

Julius and his men watched as she scattered herbs in the entrance and once again held her arms up to the sky, her head back, her eyes closed and murmured an incantation to bless the souls of her ancestors.

Ordering his men to dismount and rest, Julius waited while they built a small fire to ward off the chill wind that blew over the open countryside. There was little shelter and the small group gathered around the fire, producing flasks of water to drink and a small amount of food that they shared.

Lihanna and Julius sat a little distance away from the men, eating bread and drinking the water.

"How do you feel now, Princess?" he asked her as she huddled on the floor, her thick woollen cloak tight around her for warmth.

She smiled at him, brushing hair from her face as the wind caught at it and blew it across her eyes.

"Thank you for bringing me here, General," she replied. "I know our customs and rites must be strange to you but it has meant a great deal to me to come here today."

"Every country I visit I encounter different customs, yours are no more strange than those of my own lands."

"Do you worship any deity, General?" she asked him thoughtfully.

He was frowning slightly. "My men pray to Mars the God of War for victory when they go into battle. My mother worships the Goddess Vesta to ask for protection for her home and family. I however prefer not to place my faith or my trust in something I can neither see nor understand." His smile lifted the stern lines of his face, making him look ten years younger. "Does that make me a blasphemer?"

"It makes you a heathen," she replied, smiling in return.

Time stood still as deep blue eyes gazed into green. The clouds scudded across the heavens and the winds howled around them but neither noticed. All she knew was his face was close to hers, he was close enough to touch, close enough to go into the shelter of his strong arms and bury her head in his chest, knowing that he would protect her from the weather, from the world. He in turn trembled with the urge to touch her face, trace his fingers down the contours of her cheeks, her chin, her full rosebud lips.

"General." The voice of his Tribune interrupted them.

Julius stood up at once to face his second in command.

"What is it?" he demanded.

The Tribune saluted his commander. "The weather, sir. I suggest we return to camp if our business here is concluded."

He pointed towards the black clouds gathering above them.

"Are we finished, Lihanna?" he asked her.

She nodded and accepted his hand to help her to stand.

The first large heavy drops of rain started as she remounted her horse. She pulled the hood of her cloak over her head and at a signal from their General, the whole party started back to camp at a fast trot.

The storm broke in earnest about a mile from the fortress and it took little urging for the horses to speed up until they were almost at a full gallop as they entered the heavily guarded gate.

The General and Lihanna rode straight over to their quarters. He leapt from the back of his horse, handing it straight to his servants waiting in readiness for them. He turned to Lihanna and lifted her easily down to the ground but the rain had soaked them both and it was two very drenched riders who entered the tent.

Julius dismissed his manservant, sending him to bring warm food and drink for them both before turning back at the sound of laughter coming from Lihanna.

She was laughing at the sight of the great Roman General as he removed his helmet and brushed back the black hair from his face. He caught his breath as she removed her cloak to reveal the sodden dress beneath it, clinging to her form, almost transparent under his burning gaze.

They were alone and for once he did not consider his iron will, nor his self-imposed discipline. He took one step towards her and in another moment his arms were around her and his lips were claiming hers in a kiss of such passion and power that it took her breath away. She knew she should object; she knew she should push him away and scream for help. Instead, her arms snaked around his neck and she drew him closer to her, revelling in his touch, groaning as she felt the iron hard muscles of his body press against hers. He kissed her mouth, her face, his lips sought the pulse beating wildly in her neck and his hands caressed her with an urgency that excited her as much as it frightened her. She kissed him and felt her heart soar with pleasure as she heard him groan her name.

A flash of lightning lit up the darkened interior of the tent and she felt a shudder go through his body as he lifted his lips from hers and took a deep, steadying breath.

Still within the circle of his arms, she opened her eyes to look into his face.

"Julius…" she whispered. "What is it, what is wrong?"

He stepped away from her, holding her shoulders at arms length.

"Lihanna, I promised you I would look after you and protect you. I did not think you would be in any danger from me."

"Danger? Julius, I feel no enmity nor danger from you."

He smiled but shook his head. "Princess, you are a valuable hostage. I am ordered to guard you, not to take you as I would a common slave."

Her head swam at his words, she felt cold again and shivered.

"Is that all I am to you, General, nothing but a hostage to be bartered over?" she asked, bewildered by his sudden change of mind.

He hung his head, still holding her shoulders. When he looked up again, his eyes burned into hers.

"Lihanna – my heart is yours. I would give my life for you." His voice was an urgent low whisper. "I would kill anyone who threatened to harm you, I never want to be apart from you but I must obey my orders."

Her heart melted at his words and pushing his hands from her shoulders, she moved in to be close to him allowing him to cradle her in his arms.

"My heart and yours, Julius," she whispered. "They are one."

He trembled again at her embrace but he smiled against her hair.

"I want you as my wife, Lihanna," he said softly. "I once said that if it took marriage between us to bring peace to this land then I would do it. I was only half joking. Now I am entirely serious."

"Will we be allowed to marry?" she asked.

"I am a General in the Roman Army. The son of a Senator of Rome. My family are rich and powerful and my father has the ear of the Emperor. It would be a very brave man to refuse my request."

She smiled up at him. "There is my brother, the King, of course," she teased him.

"I will ask his permission, Lihanna. It will broker a peace between our people and he would be extremely foolish to refuse."

"My brother is not a fool," she replied.

"And in the meantime..." He moved away from her, kissing her briefly. *"I promised to protect you. That means from me as well."*

She walked away from him towards her curtained off quarters, squeezing the rainwater from her hair and looking over her shoulder at him. "Hurry and find my family, Julius," she said and, blowing him a kiss, went into her room to remove the soaking wet smock and wrap the warm fur robes around her body.

Chapter Thirteen

The morning of the last day of July dawned a bright, sun-filled summer's day. A low ground mist swirled around the grounds of the Moreland Estate and started to lift on a scene of hectic activity as the servants and tenants of the Langley family prepared the Hall and the local Church for the wedding of their Lord, Sir Maxim Langley to the unknown young lady he had met in London. Huge bunches of flowers were being carried into the Church, yards of white satin ribbons were being used to decorate the pews and in the Hall, the Dining Room and Ballroom were being similarly decorated in preparation for the ceremony due to take place later that morning.

As the sun burned away the lingering remnants of mist, the activity went on unceasingly. The open carriage was being polished to shining perfection, a fitting vehicle for the bride of Sir Maxim. The horses were being groomed, the grooms – including the smallest, newest addition to the stables – were all preparing themselves in readiness to escort the bride to the Church and the bride and groom back to the Hall for their wedding breakfast. His Lordship's travelling carriage was also being made ready for a journey, planned for the following day, to the country estate of his cousin, Sir Hugo Trevellyan, who was even now a guest at Moreland with his wife and their two children. Sir Hugo and his family were travelling north to spend the rest of the summer months with their friends in the North East of England, leaving the newlyweds the run of their Cornish estates for the next four weeks.

Lady Joanna Langley was supervising the preparations taking

place in the Hall itself, inspecting the Dining Room as the Butler organised the setting up of the dining table for the fifty guests, and checking on the Housekeeper as she harried the housemaids who were cleaning and polishing the Ballroom until every inch of the room sparkled with light and the scent of freshly cut roses filled the air. The house was filled to bursting with the gathered relatives of both families, although as Callista had no other relatives than her Aunt and Uncle, her side of the Church threatened to be a little on the sparse side, until Uncle Augustus had invited several of their London friends to the festivities to fill the pews.

Lady Joanna was in her element. This was her last chance to be a hostess in her own home, before retiring gracefully to the Dower House which had been redecorated and renovated by her son for her impending occupation. She had welcomed the wedding guests with undisguised happiness, introducing her daughter in law to be to the extended Langley clan with only a hint of pride in her son's choice. Callista, meanwhile, overwhelmed by the sudden realisation that her wedding day was upon her, greeted her new relatives with grace and dignity and not a few nerves.

Speculation about Miss Wingrove was rife. She had arrived with her family two days previously and had been introduced to the servants of the house. She had then been taken on a brief, somewhat limited tour of the estate, accompanied by her groom to be, and duly chaperoned by her Aunt and the pale-faced beauty who was her cousin. She had been charming and pleasant to the servants and tenants of the Moreland estates and they in turn had cautiously welcomed her to their community.

The subject of their intense curiosity was, as the morning progressed, being prepared for her forthcoming wedding by her increasingly manic Aunt and her distracted cousin.

Bathed and dressed in her underwear, a maid was tackling the mane of curling hair under the critical eye of Aunt Amelia, who was dividing her time between harassing the maid and scolding Georgiana.

"Really, Georgie, pull yourself together, girl." Amelia was

growing increasingly annoyed with her daughter. "Finish getting yourself dressed and come back here to help your cousin."

"Yes, Mama," Georgiana replied and left her post beside the window of Callista's room to come back over to the dressing table where she watched Callie's maid and her own devoted Milly trying to pin Callie's thick hair into some semblance of style. A faint smile lifted her lips at Callista's expression of resigned annoyance. They all knew that as soon as the wedding ceremony was over and the veil was removed, her hair would be once again bouncing untidily down over her shoulders. In vain had Callista demanded that her hair be simply pinned back with the diamond stars she loved so much. She had been overruled by Amelia's desire to see her fashionably and expensively attired and, with a sigh, Callista had accepted that after today Amelia would have no further influence over her and had acquiesced to her Aunt's wishes.

Callista looked up at her cousin. All the sparkle had left Georgiana's fine blue eyes. She seemed tired and Callista knew it was because night after night she had lain awake or had stayed up talking to her cousin late into the night. Georgiana was broken hearted. The man she loved had gone away. He had called to see her and, instead of the expected proposal, had quietly explained to her that he must leave the country for some time, in the service of his sister, and he did not know how long he would be absent.

Despite her objections, he had informed her that he could not, in all conscience, ask her to wait for him. He had left her with no further explanation and she had been left totally bewildered and in despair thinking she was never going to see Damon ever again.

Amelia was simply furious that her daughter had wasted the entire Season throwing her cap at a man who could so cruelly let her down and it was left to Augustus to smooth things over and try and ease his daughter's sorrow.

Callista held out her hand to Georgiana and squeezed it gently as Georgie held it briefly.

"I will go and dress and come back to help you get ready," Georgiana said quietly. "I will not be long."

She moved towards the door and on hearing a knock, she opened it to find Lady Elinor Trevellyan standing outside, accompanied by her small daughter, Caroline.

"May we come in for a moment?" Elinor smiled. She was a slim blonde haired woman with large, gentle grey eyes. She was holding Caroline's hand and the child was shyly peeping out from behind her mother's skirts of deep rose pink satin. The child was startlingly beautiful, as dark as her mother was fair, with green tinged hazel eyes. The two of them made an attractive tableau as they stood together framed in the doorway and as Georgiana held the door open wide for them, they stepped into the room together.

"Lady Elinor," Callista spoke from her dressing stool, "please forgive me for not getting up."

Elinor chuckled at the sight of the bride to be. "My dear Callista, pray do not even try. We must not undo all the hard work your maid is putting into your coiffure."

Callista grimaced but submitted to the ministrations of her maid as, finally, the last curl was pinned into place, the small tiara was set onto her head and the long veil was attached to the diamond headdress.

"You look like a Princess," Caroline Trevellyan lisped as curiosity overcame shyness and she let go of her mother's hand and came to stand in front of Callista.

Callista laughed. Sitting in her petticoat and shift with a diamond tiara on her head and yards of the finest lace cascading onto the floor, she certainly did not feel like a Princess.

"Why thank you, Lady Caroline," she replied and bending forward, took the child's hand.

"You look very pretty today, does she not, Georgiana?"

Georgiana agreed from her place by the door, and with a murmured farewell, she left the room.

"That girl." Amelia tutted. "Please excuse me, Lady Elinor, I must go and try to cheer her up before she disgraces us all at this wedding. She is going to be a bridesmaid – not attending a funeral."

She ran a critical eye over her niece. "I will return to help you into your dress, Callie. Please do not put it on yet, there is an hour to go and you will only crease it."

"Yes, Aunt Amelia," Callista agreed meekly and remained seated on her stool, as Amelia bustled out of the room, taking Milly with her and leaving Callista with her maid and her two visitors.

The maid pulled a chair up for Lady Elinor, before leaving them to attend to the rest of her duties and finishing her mistress' toilette.

Elinor seated herself opposite the bride to be and her fond Mama's eyes crinkled at the corners as she smiled at the way Caroline was staring fascinated at Callista's tiara.

"I can see I will have to find Caroline a replica," she said. "Although knowing Hugo, he is likely to want to give her the real thing."

"He must be a devoted father." Callista was amused by the way the child was gazing up at her. "I cannot remove it, Caroline, I'm afraid. Otherwise I would be happy to let you wear it."

"I have come to ask a favour, Miss Wingrove," Elinor continued.

Callista looked up at her guest, wondering what she could possibly do for such a lovely, refined woman as Elinor Trevellyan.

"Of course, anything I can do – I should be happy to oblige."

Elinor indicated her small daughter. "Would you allow Caroline to be your flower girl? One of her cousins was a flower girl at a wedding last year and Caroline has been talking about it ever since."

Callista and the small girl looked at each other. "Would you like that, Caroline?" Callista asked. "Will you walk down the aisle with me and scatter rose petals?"

Caroline nodded. "Yes please," she replied, her smile lighting up her whole face.

"Thank you, Miss Wingrove. I will get her dressed – I have a pale pink dress which I think will do very well."

"Excellent, Georgiana is wearing pink – they will match."

Elinor's brow creased suddenly in a slight frown. "Is Georgiana quite well? Her mother seems very concerned about her."

Callista paused but Lady Elinor's frank concerned gaze was sincere.

"Georgiana is not unwell, " she sighed. "She is a little – unhappy unfortunately."

Lady Elinor shook her head slightly, and glanced down at her daughter, still holding Callista's hands. "An affair of the heart, I suppose? It is a shame, she is such a beautiful young girl – she should have her pick of young men."

"She did," Callista replied. "She told me a year ago she was going to marry a Duke – but when one asked her she turned him down flat. Her heart had already been given to one who, I fear, has not deserved it."

Elinor gazed down at her daughter and for a moment seemed lost in her own thoughts. "I was married when I was scarcely Georgiana's age," she said quietly. "He never had my heart and all the riches and titles in the world mean nothing when one is unhappy."

Callista was startled. "Sir Hugo?" she asked and was relieved when the frown on Elinor's face lifted and a smile of pure happiness lit up her lovely features.

"No – I adore my darling Hugo," Elinor replied. "But he is my second husband. The Marquis died some years ago now."

Callista instinctively knew better than to offer condolences. Elinor was patently an extremely happy woman and the memories of her old life were obviously not pleasant ones.

A strange feeling suddenly came over Callista. She had experienced this swaying, light-headed sensation a few times in her life before. She had felt it that day the old gypsy woman had stopped her in the snowy field and talked to her about the standing stones; she had felt it the minute she had first laid eyes on Max and over the years she had been able to sense things that she could not have possibly known. That same, shivering sensation overcame her now.

She stood up, releasing Caroline's hand from hers and stepped towards Elinor. Her face was pale as she reached out to touch Elinor. She lifted Elinor's hands into her own and it was as if Elinor's life flashed into her mind in seconds. She saw the cruelty of a sadistic man, the love and gentleness and heroism of her husband and the joy that surrounded her now.

"You haven't told Hugo yet, have you?" she whispered.

Elinor was puzzled but not alarmed at Callista's words and actions.

"Told him what?" she asked.

Callista smiled, the colour returned to her face and she reached out her fingers to touch Elinor's cheek very gently.

"The baby," she said softly. "You are expecting another baby."

Elinor gazed in amazement at Callista. "How could you possibly know that?" she whispered. "I have only just realised it myself."

Callista shook her head. She shrugged slightly, clearing her mind and her thoughts.

"I don't know – I just get feelings sometimes."

Elinor's mouth twitched and she smiled. "I don't suppose you know the sex by any chance?" she asked.

"Oh – a boy of course," she replied without hesitation and watched as Elinor's pink cheeks grew pale.

Elinor's grey eyes suddenly filled with tears and she blinked quickly, turning her head away so her daughter could not see.

"We have two beautiful daughters," she managed to say eventually, "Caroline and Louisa – we absolutely love them both – Hugo dotes on them – he adores his girls. But – he would never say so but he has always longed for a son."

She stood up and for a long silent moment the two women stared at each other.

Callista gave a shaky laugh. "I have been called a witch many times," she said. "This is one time I hope my prediction is entirely correct."

Elinor reached for her and hugged Callista to her in a brief, hard embrace.

"Thank you, Callie," she said softly and released her.

She took Caroline's hand in her own and led her daughter towards the door.

"By the way, in case we do not get chance to speak in private later, I hope you and Max enjoy your honeymoon in Penhallow. It is a magical place – you and Max will be very happy there – you certainly deserve all the happiness in the world, my dear."

Elinor's voice was intense and Callista could feel the sincerity in every word.

She nodded her head. "Thank you," she replied and the light from the sunny window reflected on her diamond tiara, sending prisms of rainbow colours flashing around the room.

Elinor left her and for a moment, alone in her room in the house which was shortly to be hers, Callista closed her eyes and thought about Max and wished he were with her then. She wanted to feel his arms around her, wanted to feel his kiss, his breath on her face, wanted to hear him say how much he loved her. She sighed. Those were words he had never uttered and she wondered as she looked at the closed door Elinor had just gone through whether she would ever feel that same joy in her marriage as Elinor obviously felt in hers.

Closing her eyes, she put her hands together and for a brief moment she thought of her father, and offered up a prayer wishing he could be with her today. Her thoughts, however, flew once more to Max and she prayed again, more fervently than ever, that they would be happy together and that this wedding today would lead them to greater happiness in the future. She opened her eyes as the door opened and with another sigh, she forced a smile on her face and stood up as her Aunt returned, accompanied by the maid. Time to get dressed; time to ready herself, for what, according to her Aunt, was going to be the happiest day of her life.

In another part of the house, Max too was looking out of his bedroom window. He was watching the arrival of a swift moving horse and his eyes narrowed wondering who it could be. He leaned against the wall next to the window, his head resting against his arm as he watched the rider grow closer. The rider was covered in dust but as he dismounted from the large black stallion, he looked up at the windows of the house, as if suddenly aware he was being watched.

He swept off his hat and raised his hand to wave at Max and Max's brow cleared in an instant, a wide grin lighting up his frowning features. Damon Fortescue had returned, in the nick of time, to attend his best friend's wedding and Max was delighted to see him. He wondered briefly how Damon had managed to get here in time, as the last he heard, Damon was with his sister in Dublin. Obviously his friendship with Max and, perhaps, his feelings towards one of the other wedding guests, had finally been strong enough to overcome his reservations and here he was, and from the state of his dust covered clothes and tired horse, they had ridden all night to get here.

Max turned to his Valet who was, even then, arranging Max's wedding clothes ready for his master to step into.

"Benson, can you go down and make sure Damon is taken care of?" he asked

His Valet bowed and left the room to do as his master bade him and Max watched as Damon spoke to one of the footmen who had hurried forward to take his horse. Damon's estate bordered his own and his house was only a matter of a short twenty minute ride away. Benson went out to speak to his master's friend and after a brief exchange, Damon remounted his horse, waved once more to Max and galloped away turning at the end of the long drive in the direction of his own estates. The Valet was back in Max's bedroom a few minutes later and Max turned to greet him.

"What is it, Benson? What is he doing?" he demanded.

"Sir Damon wished you to know he was returning home to change and will meet you at the Church in time for your wedding. He trusts you have not appointed a replacement best man in his stead as he wishes very much to stand at your side as you wed Miss Wingrove."

Max laughed at his friend's message and his former sombre mood evaporated. He was smiling as he sat down for his Valet to shave him and all the doubts that had assailed him earlier that morning seemed to vanish. He was marrying a beautiful, spirited and unusual young woman, one that not only his mother whole-heartedly approved of, but one who had charmed his friends and family. She intrigued him, she baffled him, she made him laugh and she made him question things he had taken for granted all his life. Plus there was that strange sensation he had whenever he was with her. He had no idea where it had come from, but that vague, nebulous recognition tormented him, teased him, so that he was constantly wondering where and when they had met before; she haunted him and he found himself constantly wanting to look after her, protect her from – who knew what? She had demonstrated quite clearly that she needed no champion to rush to her defence but there was still that sense that she was not quite as independent as she appeared.

"I must pay a visit to my cousin Hugo," Max said to his Valet, "and advise him that his best man services are no longer required."

"I trust his lordship will not be too crushed by the news," his Valet murmured in response.

Bearing in mind Hugo's groaning acceptance of the honour of being his young cousin's best man, Max had no worries about hurting his feelings.

"Pray be careful, my lord," Benson continued, "I am sure Miss Wingrove is being kept safely out of sight by her Aunt, but it is considered bad luck to see the bride before the wedding – perhaps we should ask Sir Hugo to come here instead?"

Max closed his eyes and settled back in his chair, smiling to himself. "Excellent idea, Benson," he concurred, picturing his cousin's reaction to being summoned to the groom's bedchamber a few hours before the actual event. His cousin was the best of men, the best of cousins and Max knew that the news of his sudden demotion to a mere wedding guest was not going to offend him too gravely, being dragged away in the middle of his toilette might, however, just do it.

The morning sped by and in due course the wedding party, led by the groom and his mother left Moreland Hall and made their way to the small Church in the nearby village. Villagers and well-wishers lined the streets of the village waving to the procession of landau's and open carriages carrying the wedding guests. The sun was shining, the day was fair and sunny and the air was filled with the cheers of the gathered people as their young master drove past on his way to his wedding.

The final carriage carried Lady Amelia and her son Simon, home from school and genuinely astonished that it was his cousin's wedding he was attending and not, as everyone had so confidently predicted, his sister Georgiana.

Georgiana herself had remained behind with Callista and Sir Augustus. They were accompanied by Miss Caroline Trevellyan, both bridesmaids becomingly dressed in gowns of the palest shell pink. Caroline wore a dark rose coloured sash and matching ribbons which had been threaded through her ringlets by her adoring Mama and held a basket of rose petals, hastily picked by the Langley gardeners which she had shyly practised scattering, much to the amusement of the grown-ups. Caroline had even made Georgiana smile and Callista was relieved that her cousin seemed to have regained a little colour in her pale cheeks. She looked beautiful, her favourite pink silk suiting her blonde colouring, but she had lost weight in the last few weeks and no amount of jewellery or lovely clothes could make up for the shadows under her eyes and the sadness which had dimmed her natural vivaciousness. For perhaps the first time in their lives, Callista actually eclipsed her beautiful cousin.

Her gown of ivory silk was simple but beautiful, heavily beaded with sparkling crystals around the neckline and hem of the gown, lace sleeves covered her arms and she carried a bunch of cream and pink roses. Her eyes sparkled with happiness and outshone even the glittering diamond necklace around her throat, a wedding gift from her husband to be.

Sir Augustus stepped back to look at the three young ladies before him. He felt overcome with emotion suddenly and he was forced to wipe a single tear from his eye as he embraced his niece. Georgiana pulled the heavy lace veil down over Callista's face and she and Caroline led the way to the stairs, ready to descend to the hall where the servants of the house had gathered to see them off. Included in the gathering was a certain small boy, dressed in his smart new clothes. He was to ride on the bride's carriage on the way to Church, up beside the driver and in his uniform, smart new shoes and hat, he was resplendent.

He gazed in awe as the wedding party made their way downstairs and he caught the eye of six year old Caroline Trevellyan, sighing as the little girl smiled shyly at him, revealing pretty little dimples in her rosy cheeks. Joe fell in love there and then. Caroline had, unknowingly, made her very first conquest.

Callista was trembling slightly as she held her Uncle's arm as she walked downstairs. A sudden breeze lifted her veil slightly and something, some instinct made her pause and look behind her at the landing they had just left. She caught her breath as for an instant, for one moment out of time she saw a girl standing there. A girl with long tumbling auburn hair and wide green eyes, dressed in a strange long white robe. The girl was looking directly at Callista and as their eyes met, she smiled. Then she disappeared. Callie caught her breath and almost stumbled but her Uncle held her firm and together they continued their journey down to where the servants waited to see the bride, and to wish her happy as she made her way to the Church. In vain did Callista strain her head to try and see the girl again – the phantom was gone and she wondered if she had seen a reflection of herself, or if she had imagined the whole thing. A remark from Georgiana made her look outside where she saw the open carriage awaiting her, covered in flowers and garlands of ribbons and she smiled across to Joe to thank him for the effort he had put into the arrangements. Joe, meanwhile was not looking at her and Callie laughed to herself as the two children stared mesmerised at each other.

The day held fair and the sun blazed down on them as the carriage came to a stop outside the little Church. Joe jumped down from his seat beside the driver and he ran to open the carriage door, pulling out the small step for the passengers to climb down onto. He held out his hand and Georgiana descended first, smiling at last as the boy made a fuss of holding Caroline's hand as she stepped out of the carriage. Joe, holding the hand of his first love, was loath to release it but at a small cough from Sir Augustus, he stepped back and bowed to her instead. Augustus helped Callista out of the carriage and as her feet touched the path outside the Church she longed, not for the first time, for the comfort of her father's arm to lead her up the aisle to her husband.

Augustus sighed, looked across to Georgiana and wondered how she would feel if he were not the person to escort her down the aisle at her own wedding. He squeezed Callista's hand reassuringly and smiled down at her. "Your Papa would have been a very proud man today, Callie," he said softly and she smiled gratefully up at him.

"Thank you, Uncle," she replied and together, side by side they entered the small Church, packed to overflowing with friends and family and villagers.

Caroline walked in front of them, scattering rose petals and beaming at her delighted parents who were watching her every move with undisguised love and pride. At the sight of Caroline, Hugo Trevellyan turned to his wife with the biggest smile on his face she had ever seen. Elinor wiped away a tear and returned his smile, full of the love and happiness she felt for her husband and children.

Callista's head was down but as she walked towards Max, her head went up and she looked him in the eyes as she approached. He was dressed formally, his black coat stretched tight across his broad shoulders, his black hair brushed back and his eyes startlingly blue in his tanned face. He smiled as she walked towards him and she heard a slight gasp from Georgiana as Max's best man turned around to welcome the bride and bridesmaids.

Damon Fortescue was not smiling, but his eyes seemed to burn with molten fire as he stared at Georgiana, taking in her thin pale face, her sudden trembling hands and her hesitation before carrying on walking behind Callista and her father. She tore her gaze away from his. This was Callie's day, she reminded herself fiercely, and she would not, in any way, spoil it for her although her emotions were equally torn between turning and running out of the Church and throwing herself into his arms and kissing him as if her life depended on it.

Callista looked around at the guests and found Lady Joanna smiling fondly at her. She was standing and leaning heavily on a stick but Callista thought she had never seen Max's mother look so radiant. Even Aunt Amelia was preening herself on the success of her niece, although as she glared at Damon Fortescue, Callista could imagine the scolding Amelia would like to address to him.

Max stepped forward, Augustus bowed and stepped aside. Callista turned to hand her bouquet to Georgiana and paused to lift her veil off her face so she could look at Max unimpeded. Max took her hand in his and together they faced the priest.

The ceremony began and half an hour later, in a simple but beautiful service, they were husband and wife.

Chapter Fourteen

The music swelled and the orchestra played the opening strains of the waltz as the new Lady Langley was led out onto the Ballroom floor by her groom. He smiled down at her as she moved gracefully and easily into his arms and together, in perfect harmony, they started their first dance together.

It was evening, the crystal chandelier sparkled with the lights of a hundred candles, the wedding breakfast had been eaten and the guests had been wined and dined and now the finishing touch to their wedding day saw Max and Callista begin the Ball being held in their honour.

Their steps mirrored the other and for the first time since she had known him, she found herself feeling shy in his company.

"Have you enjoyed today, Callie?" he suddenly asked her, bending his head to speak softly in her ear.

"Every minute," she replied. "Thank you Max – it has been perfect."

His mouth twitched, a sudden smile lighting up his features. "It is not over yet," he murmured and was amused as a faint blush stole over her cheeks. "We can finally be alone together – it has been a very long six weeks, Callie."

She found herself laughing at his words. "It has indeed been a long time since we have been able to spend any time together. I only hope the month we will spend alone together will not totally bore you, my lord."

"I think we will find ways to amuse ourselves," he replied, drily and laughed with her as another blush stole over her cheeks.

"Lady Elinor told me Penhallow is a magical place for a honeymoon. Have you been there before?" she asked him.

"Not Penhallow, no. I stayed at my cousin James' estate when I was a child. Penhallow was left to Hugo when his mother died but was neglected for years while he was away in the army. The area is beautiful though – I hope you will like it as much as I do. You will get to meet more of my cousins when we get down there so we will not be too lonely."

She wanted to tell him that she could never be lonely while he was with her, but a shyness she had never before experienced with him left her suddenly tongue tied. She found herself looking up into his eyes, moving in time with him as they followed the steps of the dance, perfectly in time, perfect synchronicity in their movements as his arm tightened around her and he pulled her closer to his taut body. Her lips parted as she looked up at him, his eyes gazing down into hers and she felt again that heat between them. She found herself wishing the evening was over and that they could escape everyone and everything and finally be alone together.

They danced on together, totally oblivious to everyone else in that room, circling the Ballroom floor, the tall, well-built devastatingly handsome young man and his beautiful green-eyed bride.

In another part of the room, Damon Fortescue swallowed the glass of champagne with one gulp. He had had enough. He had kept his distance out of respect for Sir Augustus and his own strong sense of duty but he could stand it no longer. Georgiana was smiling up at a tall good-looking young man, dressed in the dashing uniform of an Officer in His Majesty's Hussars. He was paying her a great deal of attention, flattering her and amusing her with his light-hearted conversation.

Damon was aware that Georgiana was purposely ignoring him. He had broken her heart and she was repaying him by her show of interest in the officer. Even though he knew he had no right to be jealous, the sight of her flirting with another man was driving him to recklessness.

He edged his way around the crowded Ballroom, watching with half an eye at the way his friend was holding his new bride so possessively. He was relieved – Max had obviously got over his youthful infatuation with Davina and he was about to settle down with Callista to happy married life. He could only hope his sister had finally decided to leave well alone and let the newlyweds enjoy their lives together without any interference.

Georgiana was fluttering her fan in front of her face as she laughed up at something the officer was saying. She lowered her lashes and looked up again to see over the young man's shoulder the sight of Damon Fortescue glaring at her. His eyes burned into hers and she felt heightened colour stain her pale cheeks, the laughter dying on her lips.

The officer followed the direction of her gaze and turned to face him as Damon approached.

"Miss Wetherby, may I speak with you please?" Damon's voice was silky smooth but with an underlying steel which sent a frisson of anticipation down Georgiana's spine.

The officer drew himself up, tall and suddenly on guard as he felt the tension between the two. "Miss Wetherby, if I can be of any assistance?" he asked, his voice quiet but concerned.

Torn by indecision, Georgiana knew she should ignore Damon and walk away but she could not move. She smiled uncertainly up at the young man by her side.

"Thank you, Major Darwen, that is very kind of you – but Sir Damon and I have some – unfinished business?" She arched an eyebrow at Damon seeing the pulse beating in his cheek as he struggled to keep his emotions in check.

Coolly, she bowed her head to the Major and walked away from him, towards the edge of the room. Damon followed her and before she could protest, his hand closed around her arm and he propelled her out of the Ballroom onto the empty terrace outside.

He could not help himself. With a groan he turned her to face him and pulled her into his arms, his mouth pressing down onto hers in a searching searing kiss which sent her senses reeling and all arguments and protests flying out of her head as he took her breath away.

Pulling himself together, with a shuddering breath he lifted his head. His eyes were tormented. "I – I'm sorry Georgie…" he whispered. "I should not have – I have no right…"

Georgiana almost stamped her foot with frustration. "Damon Fortescue, how dare you," she snapped and before he could move and to his utter astonishment, she put her arms around his neck and pulled his head back down to hers, her lips finding his and kissing him back with a passion which equalled his own.

After a long, long moment, Georgie drew away to take a deep breath. Her eyes were shining with unshed tears as she glared up at him. "I love you, Damon," she said. "How could you be so cruel as to leave me?"

Damon touched her face with trembling hands. "I love you too, Georgie. I could not stand to be away from you another moment – but…"

"No, Damon – no buts. Whatever it is that is preventing us being together, you must tell me."

He had never seen Georgiana so animated, so determined. "I will explain everything, my dearest girl," he said softly. "But first…" Again his arms tightened around her and the pent up frustration of the weeks they had spent apart was relieved at last as his mouth found hers once more in a kiss of infinite tenderness and growing passion.

The newlyweds were separated often that evening, circulating the room, chatting to family and friends, and Callista found herself the object of more attention than she had ever received in her life. She danced a slow, sedate waltz with her Uncle, then found herself being whisked around the Ballroom by Sir Hugo, followed by several of Max's friends, each one more dashing than the next, each one flirting outrageously with her and she responding with a laugh and a twinkle in her eye her family had never before seen.

She saw Georgiana and Damon dancing, her Aunt scowling over in their direction and her Uncle looking thoughtful. She, however, only saw how radiant Georgiana was looking, how ardently Damon held her in his arms, how determined and resolute was his face as he danced with her all evening. Callista smiled as she observed her cousin. Georgiana was happy at last and from the expression on their faces, both she and Damon had resolved their problems. She had a good feeling about their reunion, and she had learned to trust her feelings over the years.

She danced happily with a very attractive young man and he made her laugh with his disclosure about Max's childhood indiscretions. She found herself being observed by a silently watching Max. He was looking at her from the edge of the Ballroom floor, sipping a glass of champagne and with a slight frown between his eyes. What he was thinking she could not imagine but for one moment she wondered if he was actually jealous. His smile was certainly forced when he was greeted by his friend who handed over the bride with the utmost reluctance, kissing her hand before she laughingly turned to her husband.

He took her hand and pulled her close to stand by his side, his arm resting possessively around her waist.

"I think I am tired of sharing you, Callie," he said softly. His voice was a low, husky growl which sent shivers of anticipation down her spine.

"What do you suggest?" she asked, her voice as low, velvet soft against his ear.

"This party is going to continue for several hours, I don't think anyone will actually notice if we slip away now."

The frown had disappeared, he was smiling again, his eyes alight with laughter.

"But it's only 10 o'clock," she whispered back.

"Late enough," he replied and taking her hand in his, he placed his champagne glass down and led her once again onto the dance floor.

The music was another waltz, the lively cotillions and country dances of earlier giving way to the slower, more sedate and intimate dance, and Callista found herself being steered slowly but surely around the room and towards the open doorway leading to the reception hall.

Max was smiling and she was laughing up at her groom as they circled the hallway in time to the music, watched by no one but a few curious footmen and a couple of maidservants watching the dance from behind the open doors. They all smiled indulgently at the newlyweds and the girls giggled as Max stopped dancing and drew Callista towards him to cup her face between his hands and place a gentle, velvet soft kiss against her lips. It was the briefest of caresses, but it seemed to seal forever the promises they had made to each other earlier that day in that small Church.

Hand in hand they left the Ballroom behind them and walked up the stairs together. Callista's eyes sought the point on the half landing where she had seen the girl – wishing that she could see her again. But no phantoms disturbed their gaze as they went softly together up to the master suite where Callista's maid awaited them, laying out her mistress' nightgown and arranging a beautiful bouquet of roses next to where an ice bucket stood on the dresser, containing an unopened bottle of champagne.

Max raised her hand to his lips, kissing it briefly. "Shall I leave you alone for a few minutes?" he asked, indicating her maid.

Callista shook her head. "No, I think tonight my husband should assist me," she whispered back.

Max's eyes sparkled and he dismissed her maid as he went across to open the bottle of champagne, a gift, he saw, from Sir Augustus.

The maid left and Callista went over to the French doors that led out onto a small balcony overlooking the front of the house. She opened them and stepped out to breathe in the cooling night air, listening to the sounds of the music coming faintly now from the ground floor – soft and melodic, the sound seemed to reach out and embrace her as she leaned against the balustrade, looking up at the silver moon just rising above the late summer stars. Other sounds reached her ears, the soft rustling of animals moving through the grass and shrubbery around the house, the neighing of horses as they awaited the return of their masters, the low murmurings of conversation between the drivers and grooms, the call of an owl as it swooped down onto an unsuspecting field mouse. The night was still warm, the last day of July about to give way to the lazy summer days of August, but the scents of the garden and the fields beyond drifted over to her full of the aromas of roses and freshly cut grass and hay. She breathed it all in deeply, trying, and failing, to recall ever feeling this happy before in her life.

Max paused in the doorway of the balcony as he watched her raising her face to the moon. He stood stock still for a moment as she closed her eyes and he saw, quite clearly, moonbeams light up her face, a strange beacon of light illuminating the pale, still beauty of her countenance – she glowed silver in the night and he hardly dared take a breath fearing to disturb the vision before him.

It lasted for only a moment and then she opened her eyes and turned her head to smile at him.

The silver light evaporated and he walked forward, holding out the tall champagne glass, filled with the sparkling wine; she took it and took a small sip of the champagne.

"Happy?" he asked her.

She was so close to him they were almost touching and she looked for a long, long moment into the depths of his deep blue eyes. She saw something there she had never seen before – something which touched a chord in her memories and she breathed his name. "Maxim…"

He dropped his glass of champagne and somewhere in the back of his mind he heard the explosion as the glass hit the stone floor of the balcony. His arms were around her and he pulled her close, his mouth seeking and finding hers, finally able to kiss her free of the restraints which had held them back over the last few weeks. He tried to rein in the sudden surge of passion which engulfed him, a rising tide of feelings which he found he had no control over, trying not to frighten her; trying not to alarm her with the strength of his emotions as he devoured her mouth with the hunger of a starving man.

She clung to him, dizzy from the unexpected urgency of the kiss, something inside her exploded into a million pieces as her arms went around his neck and she responded to his embrace with a passion which rose up to match his own.

This time there was no restraint, no relatives or jealous lovers to interrupt them. He released her just long enough to pull her back into the bedroom with him. He pulled off his tight fitting jacket and immaculate waistcoat, throwing them aside with little regard to neatness or propriety, before turning his attention to his bride. She carefully lifted the tiara from her head and turned her back to him, brushing her hair over one shoulder to present him with the buttons of her heavy silken wedding gown. With fingers that suddenly trembled, he slowly undid each button in turn, pausing to kiss her neck between each action. Finally undone, he pushed the bodice of the gown down and his mouth followed his fingers, kissing her shoulders as the dress fell from her body. She stepped out of it and picked it up – placing it over the nearest chair, with the diamond tiara on top of it.

Standing before him in her thin chemise, she watched as he pulled his shirt off. He saw her pupils dilate as he stood before her, his broad chest bare, the taut muscles of his stomach rising above the tight cream breeches, but she looked up, meeting his eyes, as, with shaking fingers, she undid the straps of her chemise, letting it fall to the ground revealing her naked except for the ivory coloured stockings kept in place with silken garters.

His mouth felt suddenly dry as his eyes took in the beauty of her nakedness. Her full breasts rose above a slim waist and neatly flaring hips, long slim legs, and her hair – those gloriously thick auburn curls hung in wild disarray down her back and over her shoulders, only partially covering her breasts. With a groan he reached for her again and lifting her into his arms, he walked the last few yards to the four poster bed and laid her down on the covers, tenderly pulling the pillows towards her to cushion her head.

He kneeled above her and forcing himself to slow down, he stroked his hands up her leg and rolled the silken stocking down, one at a time, sending shivers of pleasure through her. Lying down next to her, his hands gently caressed her breasts, his mouth finding hers. She raised her hands and touched his chest, all shyness gone in the heat of the passion which was building up again within her. Their kisses deepened. She felt his tongue in her mouth, probing, teasing, seeking and finding an answering response and as her hands roamed the bare expanse of his chest, she heard him groan as her hands slid up his body and around his neck, pressing herself closer. That strange heat – the aching she had experienced before when his kisses had aroused her – it came again, hotter, more urgent than ever and even in her innocence, she knew he was the only one who could assuage this burning throbbing desire.

He raised himself away from her and immediately she protested, bereft as he smiled and made her wait as he stripped off his final garments, releasing himself from the tightening restrictions of close fitting breeches. He was trembling slightly, forcing himself again to wait, slow down, not frighten her, his hands caressing her breasts, going lower, shocking her and making her stiffen as his fingers gently found and probed her silken opening.

He kissed her again and as his fingers gently stroked that deepest most intimate part of her, she felt the waves of pleasure starting to build up. She was moaning now, his expert hands and lips and tongue driving her over that edge where all reason fled, until all there was left was this writhing ecstatic sensual being who knew she wanted more but could not imagine what more there could be to equal or surpass what he was doing to her.

Then he showed her and she clung to him, feeling a sharp brief pain as he entered her and then that was gone in the rhythm and movement of their bodies moving together in perfect harmony, as synchronised and as perfect as their dancing. Even as she revelled in the passion and tenderness of their lovemaking, that deep seated feeling surfaced once more and she knew, without any doubt whatsoever in her mind or heart, that this was where she belonged, they were meant to be together, they had been drawn together by some fate, some destiny far beyond her understanding and as the passion rose and the tempo of their movements increased to a final, shattering conclusion she knew he felt it too.

Max did not understand the powerful surge of emotion he was experiencing – this all-encompassing feeling of togetherness was just so perfect, so right – Callista was responding to him with such a fierce passion which surprised and delighted him. She was all instinct and innocence and finally, when he could hold back no longer and brought them both to that explosive climax, he was shaking with the strength of the sensations which flooded through him. Somewhere, briefly, like a faint bitter taste in his mouth, the memory of Davina's lovemaking surfaced and disappeared – their lustful coupling was nothing like the intensity of this first wondrous night with Callie.

They clung together, spent and satiated, and he pulled the sheets over them, covering their nakedness, arms and legs entwined, her head cradled in his arms, his mouth pressed against her hair.

She raised her eyes to his, wide green and wondering. "Is it always like that?" she whispered.

He felt the grin spreading across his face, lighting up his eyes and they were twinkling with genuine amusement as he kissed her damp forehead. "I hope so," he murmured and captured her lips with his own once more. She laughed with him and returned his kiss with gentle pressure.

"How do you feel?" he asked her, suddenly anxious.

"Wonderful…" she sighed and snuggled down further into the bed and his arms.

Within minutes, they were asleep.

The dream came almost at once. He was fighting; he was dressed in a strange short robe, armour over his chest, leather sandals on his feet, with thongs that curled around his bare calves up to his knees. He was wearing a helmet, adorned with a scarlet plume and in his hand he carried a short, broadsword.

He was hacking his way through crowds of heavily armed men. Men wearing long white robes, men who were trying to stop him from getting through their ranks. Fear and fury had him in their grip, but the fear was not for himself, he had no fear of these men, they were just impeding him, stopping him from going forward, blocking his passage through to a huge slab of stone. The slab was an altar and on it – on it was Callista, bound and imprisoned – her limbs tied to the corners of the stone. Through the noise of the battle he could hear a voice, a loud chant, a ritual, a prayer of power that resonated across the field of conflict. His fury was directed at the owner of that voice. As long as the chant continued, he knew Callista was safe and as he fought his way towards her he was screaming above the noise telling her he was on his way, to hold on, he was coming for her.

Then the thunder started, the field was lit up by forked lightning and he was weeping, tears coursing down his cheeks, and Callista – his Callie – his bride, his sweet innocent love – she was lying in his arms and she was so still, she was lifeless. She was wearing her wedding gown, and blood was seeping out over her dress, running down his arms as he held her close against his chest.

He opened his eyes and sat up with a sudden jerky movement. There was thunder and lightning outside, rain was falling heavily and his bed was empty.

Panic tore at him, his heart pounded and his eyes darted around the room, searching for her. She was gone – Callie was gone.

Then a movement brought him back to reality. He saw a white figure pulling the French doors leading onto the balcony closed and pull heavy curtains across, shutting out the lightning bright night sky.

"Callie?" he called out softly.

She turned her head and smiled at him before walking back over to the bed. She had pulled her fine lawn nightdress on over her naked body and he could see the outline of her curves through the material.

"The thunder woke me," she whispered, climbing back into

the bed with him. "I saw the rain coming into the room so I thought I'd better close the window."

He took a deep shuddering breath and realised he had broken out into a sweat, induced by the nightmare. He lay down again and pulled her into his arms.

"I thought I had lost you," he murmured against her hair. "I woke up and you were gone…"

He smoothed down her hair as she rested her head on his chest. "You were dreaming," she whispered again. "You were so restless. Was it a bad dream?"

He shuddered and held her closer. "It was a nightmare – but it's over now. I'm sorry, I didn't mean to disturb you."

She reached up her hand and touched his cheek. "I wasn't disturbed; I have never felt so comfortable in my life."

He felt her smile against his chest. He hugged her and lowered his head to seek her lips once more. "You disturb me though," he whispered.

He felt her hands roam down from his face to his neck to his chest. Her touch was light but sure, she raised herself on her elbow and he opened his eyes to see her gazing down at him. He smiled at the expression on her face and he put his hand up to push the curls from her cheeks, pushing them behind her ear.

"What is it, Callie?" he asked.

"I have never been so happy in my life," she said, slowly. "I just wanted you to know it. From the moment I met you I felt as though we had known each other for ever and now, tonight, married to you, I – I can't explain it exactly but it's as though we were meant to be together." She paused, aware that the words were tumbling out. "This time last year, I was an orphan, a poor relation living on the charity of relatives. Tonight I am your wife – I don't know how it has happened, I am only so grateful that it has."

He put his finger against her lips. "No, Callie, don't say that. I don't want you to ever think you need be grateful to me."

In the darkness of the bedroom, lit up only by the occasional flash of lightning, she saw the serious expression on his face, intense and frowning.

She smiled again. "Very well then. Not gratitude – something else, something far deeper than that."

He remembered in vivid detail the picture in his mind of her lying in his arms, her blood staining her wedding dress as her life drained away. His mouth felt dry with the thought of it, a desperate foreboding overwhelming him.

"Something far deeper," he agreed and as her eyes widened in wonder, he pulled her head down, seeking and finding her lips, gentleness hardening into desire as the passion between them flared once again, brighter and stronger than before.

The storm outside rolled on but no noise, no flashing lights or pounding rain had the power to interrupt them again that night as Max made love to his beautiful, innocent, wondrous wife and Callista responded with every ounce of love and passion in her being.

Lihanna 8

Lihanna watched from her seat at the entrance to her quarters. Julius and his men were engaging in battle practice and she watched with interest as they fought with wooden broadswords in a well-planned and organised routine which had proved so successful in their unstoppable march across the continent.

She watched with interest and was surprised at both the efficiency and violence of the practice. Julius was as involved as any of his men and she stood up in alarm as a well-aimed blow sent him to his knees. With a roar between anger and laughter, the General sprang to his feet and dealt his attacker a responding blow with his fist that sent his Centurion onto his back in the sand. Roars of laughter accompanied this exchange and Lihanna found herself shaking slightly, unaware that she had stopped breathing in a mixture of fear and dismay as Julius had fallen.

It was almost dusk and as the sun began to set, she returned to the shelter of the tent. Winter was almost on them and she was grateful for the warmth of the brazier in the centre of their quarters.

Julius followed her and as she warmed herself, she watched as he stripped off his armour. He was slick with the sweat of his exertions and as he turned to face her, wearing nothing but the short toga which covered him from the waist downward, she saw the wetness which beaded his chest and stomach. Lihanna felt a lurch in her stomach, her pupils dilated as his eyes caught hers, he was smiling as he watched the effect his half naked torso was having on her. He came towards her, stopping an arm's length from her. Silently, he reached for her hand and brought it up to his damp chest where a smattering of dark hairs glistened in the twilight of the flickering brazier.

Her breasts rose and fell in swift succession, as a heat spread from her loins through her stomach and up to her face, becoming flushed with the strange feelings that burned through her.

Torn between the desires palpable between them and his promise to wait until she was officially betrothed to him, it was becoming increasingly difficult to restrain from giving in to their feelings.

"Julius..." she whispered and was powerless to resist as his hand cradled her face and he moved close enough to kiss her.

His lips moved gently against hers, a teasing promise at first which deepened and hardened into the ardour which she aroused in him. He pulled her against him and they gave in briefly to the moment, unable to prevent the rush of passion burning between them.

His lips moved to her cheeks, her throat, lingering over the pulse beating wildly against his mouth. She groaned softly as his hands caressed the smooth skin of her shoulders, her back, holding her against him, letting her feel the hardness of his body, revelling in the yielding softness of hers, aroused by her breasts pressing against his naked skin, excited by the feel of her lips against his. She was innocent and pure but her desire for him was as tangible and as real as his for her.

He shuddered as sense returned. He had made her a promise and despite their mutual desire he could not, would not, break that promise. She would be his as soon as their marriage was arranged and not before.

He lifted his head, his eyes dark with passion and smiled again.

"My heart and yours, Lihanna," he whispered.

"In this life and the next," she replied, her voice a murmur against his skin.

Her words troubled him but he dismissed them as no more than a lover's promise. He stepped away from her, kissing her hands and grinning, looking years younger.

"I must bathe and dress, my love," he said softly. "Then we will eat and you can entertain me with more tales of your childhood in this wild and wonderful land of yours."

She laughed gently. "And you can describe your life in Imperial Rome, my heart."

He moved away from her, leaving to join his men in the bathhouse, to bathe and wash away the sweat of their mock battle; she remained beside the brazier, watching him leave and despite the warmth of the room, a shiver went through her body.

Chapter Fifteen

Max could not remember a journey he had enjoyed more. The four days it took to travel from Moreland to Penhallow passed in a blur of happiness. They travelled through some of the most beautiful countryside in England, stopping at well-appointed Coaching Inns along the way where Callista was wined and dined and shown by an attentive groom how appreciative he was.

Callista had bid farewell with mixed feelings to her family on the morning of their departure. Her Aunt and Uncle had embraced her and kissed her most fondly as she was leaving; even her Aunt's normally frosty exterior became almost effusive in front of the gathered Langley clan. Her cousin Simon, a young man she had only met occasionally, was reserved but friendly and wished her very happy in her new life with Max. As for Georgiana – Callista could only smile as she recalled her cousin's farewell. She had been glowing with happiness, almost incandescent with the joy of her reconciliation with Damon. He had proposed to her and had promised to seek Augustus' approval before announcing their engagement to the world. Georgiana and Callista had managed only a few minutes alone together before they parted but Georgie promised to write to tell her everything that had occurred. Including, with a hushed voice and a frown, Damon's concern about passing on to his children any hint of instability that had so blighted his past when recalling his life with his father and, now, his sister. Georgiana confided to Callie that Damon had always been grateful that his sister and his best friend had never married. "She would never have suited him half as well as you, dearest Callie."

Whilst Callista whole-heartedly agreed with this sentiment, she nevertheless felt some apprehension at the thought of Max and Davina meeting once again. There was something so predatory, so possessive about the way Davina looked at Max that she could only hope that Davina's husband in Ireland had finally managed to keep his notorious wife by his side and safely out of England.

The newlyweds duly arrived in Penhallow. Travelling through the rugged Cornish countryside, Callista was delighted when the bleak moorland softened imperceptibly at first, becoming gradually greener, and then she caught sight of the coast and gazed with wonder at the sparkling expanse of the Atlantic Ocean. They passed through a picturesque fishing village, a prosperous, comfortable place well populated and well looked after by the Trevellyan families in whose land the village lay. St Milo's Bay lay half way between the town of Newquay and the smaller fishing village of St Ives and Callista loved it on sight. Driving on another five miles or so, they came at last to Penhallow, the country home of Sir Hugo and Lady Elinor Trevellyan and their two children. It was near to Max's other cousins, Sir James Trevellyan, the head of the Trevellyan clan and his family, and also James and Hugo's sister Sarah, a vivacious girl, happily married to her Henry and the proud mother of two lively sons. All was peaceful and calm and as they drove up to the Elizabethan Manor House, Callista caught hold of Max's hand and squeezed it gently. She gazed at it with eyes wide with pleasure.

"It is a beautiful house, Max," she said as their carriage came to a halt outside the wide front doors.

"It is indeed. I have never spent any time here, though," he replied. "All my visits were to my cousin James' house. We will be exploring this house and lands together, Callie; it will be a first for both of us."

For a moment, they stared into each other's eyes. Such moments of total unspoken communication were becoming almost natural. He found himself mesmerised by her sparkling green eyes, gazing so lovingly and confidently into his own. He returned the squeeze of her hand and raised it briefly to his lips. His eyes never left hers and, as his gaze dropped to her mouth, her lips suddenly parted with the same rush of desire that filled him as he kissed her hand.

He did not understand this feeling. He had deliberately set out to enter into a marriage of convenience and yet every passing day took him further away from that heartless cold-blooded decision. He found himself actually looking forward to spending his days with the unusual, loving, sensuous woman he had married and his nights with the passionate, almost wanton creature she became in his arms. Callista was correct, he reflected, it was as though destiny had conspired to bring them together. Being together just felt so right, so perfect somehow.

A cry of welcome diverted their attention and as the carriage door opened, they saw a tall vivacious dark-haired woman coming towards them. She was smiling broadly and, as Max jumped down from the carriage, he held out his arms and embraced his cousin Sarah before turning his attention back to helping Callista alight.

She held out her hand to Max's cousin but Sarah swept her into her arms and hugged her ruthlessly.

"Welcome to Penhallow, my dear," she exclaimed, kissing her on both cheeks. "Max, I am so sorry to have missed your wedding but Henry has been ill and I couldn't leave the children – but come in, come in, the house is all prepared for you and the servants are waiting to meet you."

Happily chattering away, Sarah kept her arm around Callista's waist and, bemused but delighted by her welcome, Callie allowed herself to be swept along into the wide hallway of the old house.

The hallway was welcoming, the scent of fresh flowers filled the air, mullioned windows sparkled with light and Callista looked up at the Elizabethan-style stairs and around at the panelled walls, and found herself feeling warm and welcomed even more. The Butler was directing a veritable army of footmen carrying in their luggage, and Max's Valet Benson and Callista's maid Alice hurried after the trunks to supervise the unpacking.

Max and Callista were introduced to the Butler and the Housekeeper and then the irrepressible Sarah led them through into the Drawing Room.

"How was your journey, Lady Langley?" she asked. "I have ordered tea for your arrival and once you have had some refreshments, I will leave you in peace and you can explore to your heart's content."

"Please, Lady Sarah," Callista replied. "Please call me Callista, or Callie – Lady Langley sounds so formal."

"And in that case, I am just Sarah." She smiled at her new cousin and waved a hand at the comfortable furnishings of Lady Elinor's Drawing Room.

"I have strict instructions from my brother to welcome you to Penhallow, make sure you are comfortable and then I must leave you in peace."

Callista laughed at the self-deprecating tone of her voice. Max's eyes were alight with laughter at her words and the mischievous twinkle in her eyes.

"That sounds like Hugo," he remarked, seating himself beside Callie on the well-padded seat of the Trevellyan's sofa.

Sarah sighed and seated herself opposite the couple. "It is his years of military life, I'm afraid. He likes to order us all around and feel as if he is in charge." She smiled at Callista and attractive dimples appeared in her cheeks. "The truth is, he is an absolute darling and Elinor can wrap him around her little finger. Discreetly of course – she adores him, you know."

Callista smiled at Sarah's artless chatter. "I know and it is so generous of them to lend us their house for a month."

They were interrupted by the arrival of the Butler and two housemaids carrying a tray bearing their afternoon tea. One tray held the silver teapot, milk, sugar and cups whilst the other positively groaned with the weight of sandwiches, scones, strawberry jam and fresh clotted cream.

"I see there is no fear of me fading away," Callista remarked as the Butler set the tea trays down in front of the bemused young couple.

"Indeed no, my dear," Sarah rejoined, picking up the teapot and pouring the tea. She looked at them from beneath lowered eyelids. "If there is one thing I can promise you, between Mrs

Sinclair's cooking and dinners with both Henry and I and your other cousins, you will never go hungry in Cornwall."

"And how is Henry now?" Max enquired, sipping the hot tea his cousin handed to him.

"Much better thank you – the foolish man managed to break his arm just before we were due to travel to your wedding. He was in a lot of pain but the local doctor has set it and it is just a matter of letting it heal now."

"You must let Callie look at it, Sarah," Max said. "My mother has nothing but praise for her healing abilities. Callie diagnosed her injury following a fall and said the only time she was free from pain was when Callie was with her."

"Really?" Sarah was interested and paused in her demolition of a particularly delicious scone to raise an eyebrow at Callista.

Callie felt herself blush slightly under their combined scrutiny but she smiled at them both and sipped her tea appreciatively. "I will certainly assist Sir Henry in any way I can," she agreed. "I think Max said we would be visiting his cousins over the next few days so I will look forward to meeting him."

"We will look forward to your visit – anything that will alleviate poor Henry's suffering would be greatly appreciated, by his wife if not by him."

She chuckled slightly, finished eating her scone and drank her tea. "I will leave you both to settle down now." She dabbed her mouth with her napkin and rose gracefully to her feet. "You are allowed a day or two to find your way around the estate, and then you must come to dinner with us on Saturday night. James and his wife will be there and they will be looking forward to meeting you, my dear."

She moved to the bell pull and rang it. "I must return to my family, Max, but it is wonderful to see you again. It has been too long."

The Butler entered the room barely before she finished speaking. Ordering her carriage to be brought round and sending for her bonnet and coat, she held out her hand to Max once again and he moved to stand beside her and took her hand in his.

"Thank you for your kind welcome, Sarah," he said bowing over her hand. "We are both very grateful."

"Nonsense," she responded. "Just enjoy your honeymoon and come to see us often and I will be happy. We love to entertain and love to see new people occasionally."

She took her cousin's arm and allowed him to escort her to the door of the Drawing Room. Looking around at where Callista sat, staring around the room and drinking her tea, she lowered her voice and whispered into his ears. "Rumours of your indiscretions had reached Cornwall, my dear," she said softly. "Let us hope no one sees fit to let your wife know."

He stared at her, all laughter gone from his eyes, suddenly serious. "That is all behind me now, Sarah," he said quite coolly. "I would not have Callista hurt for the world so please keep your rumours to yourself."

She smiled up at him, not a bit abashed. "Splendid. That is just what I wanted to hear. Come along, Max, take that look off your face, I was only testing you."

Curious as to the whispers, Callista stood up and moved over to her husband. Standing next to him, he sought and found her hand.

"Are you planning something, you two?" she asked, only half joking.

Sarah leaned forward and kissed Callista's soft cheek. "Not at all – I am just reminding Max to bring you over to visit – Saturday night dinner and after that come when you please, you must meet my sons and we are all invited to the Truro Assemblies next week so I hope you will join us for that?"

"Of course, I am sure we would be delighted to accept." She stole a glance at her new husband, the sudden scowl had gone, replaced by a relaxed smile once more.

The carriage arrived, Lady Sarah's coat and bonnet were brought in to her by her maid and she took her leave, accompanying her maid to the carriage, waving a fond farewell to the couple who stood together on the steps of the lovely old Elizabethan Manor house.

As her carriage left the drive, Max placed a protective arm around Callista's shoulders.

"Shall we start our exploration?" he asked her.

"I'd like to see the gardens – I understand they overlook the sea," she replied.

"Hmm, I had a different destination in mind," he growled softly in her ear, "but we must not shock the servants just yet."

She laughed up at him and he pressed a swift, gentle kiss on her upturned face before they went back inside to find their new Butler awaiting them.

"Ah, Peters, is it not?" Max enquired. "Lady Langley and I would be grateful if we could have an escort to show us around the house and garden – may we call upon your expert services?"

Callista smiled to herself, Max could be so charming when he wanted to be and she could see the Trevellyan's Butler almost melt with the flattery.

"Of course, My Lord." The Butler bowed and with a serious expression on his stern face, he led the way on a guided tour of the ground floor of the house.

He showed them the attractive morning room, as elegantly furnished as the Drawing Room, the Dining Room, the Library, the small study which Hugo had made his own, dominated by a large oak desk, with militaria adorning the walls, a portrait of the Duke of Wellington, and a painting of Hugo himself, astride a magnificent black stallion. The room was masculine and comfortable but odd little touches disturbed and lightened the atmosphere – a discarded doll on the leather chair, a child's toy on the window seat, and the painting above the fireplace where Hugo could see it whenever he sat at his desk, of Elinor and his daughters.

It was the room of a contented, happy man and as Max gazed round, he felt a sharp pang wondering if he would ever feel so comfortable and satisfied with his life. He put his hand on Callie's shoulder as he stood beside her and immediately that contact between them caused her to look around, smiling quizzically up at him. He returned the smile and knew, with a deep and sure certainty that whilst he could eventually achieve the same level of contentment as Hugo enjoyed, it was going to be with Callista and not, as he had long ago hoped and dreamed, the beautiful Davina Fitzpatrick.

The tour continued and the Butler led them into a large formal room that he explained was used as a Ballroom and where they held Christmas and birthday parties. The Ballroom had a wall made up of French windows, some of which were open, leading out onto a wide flat terrace overlooking the garden. Callista was entranced and walked over to the doors to gaze out at the stunning scenery outside the house.

The large garden was enclosed by a wall in front of which grew an abundance of colourful flowers, being tended as she watched by two gardeners, intent on weeding out any and all intruders within their carefully nurtured blooms. A summer house lay at the bottom of the garden and beyond the far wall, Callista could see the sea, a wide horizon of sparkling blue which beckoned and fascinated her.

Peters the Butler followed her across the Ballroom floor and a fond smile lifted the serious expression on his face.

"Sir Hugo had the summer house built as a gift for Lady Elinor after their wedding," he explained, a touch of pride in his voice. "It used to have an uninterrupted view of the bay," he went on, "but after the children were born, Her Ladyship insisted on a wall being built all around the garden so the view has been disrupted somewhat, but it is still a fine vantage point if you would care to visit it."

Callista smiled at the Butler. "Thank you, Peters. I think Sir Maxim and I will explore on our own now. Thank you for showing us around so far, but I feel like stretching my legs and going for a walk in the garden."

She stepped out onto the terrace and turned to Max, her hand outstretched.

He took it and joined her, stepping out onto the sun-warmed stones leaving the Butler to smile indulgently at the newlyweds as they walked hand in hand down the winding path to their romantic destination.

Max nodded his thanks to the Butler and wondered anew as he accompanied his bride towards the summer house what on earth had come over him. Six months ago he had been a confirmed bachelor, enjoying the delights of a liaison with the only woman he thought he could ever love. Now, here he was, strolling in the sunlight of a late summer day, holding the hand of a woman he had never, in his wildest dreams, ever imagined he would marry, and not only that, but he was actually feeling that strangest of all emotions, happiness at being in her company. A wave of guilt engulfed him, a vision of a cool, blue-eyed beauty suddenly swam into his vision and he realised with a start that Callista was speaking to him.

"I'm sorry, Callie," he apologised, having the grace to be embarrassed.

She was smiling at him though. Nothing, it seemed, could overshadow her happiness.

"You were lost in wonder at this magnificent view, no doubt," she teased him.

They had reached the steps leading up to the summer house. It was open to the elements, with a roof and side panels, a padded bench seat ran around the interior, and a small enclosed bookcase took up space against one of the panels. Freshly cut flowers adorned a small side table, filling the fresh sea-tanged air with the scent of roses. It was, like the rest of the house, attractive and charming, and Callista loved it.

She left his side and went over to the open side. Facing the sea, she leaned against one of the carved upright supports and lost herself for the moment in the view of the sea, of a ship in full sail about to disappear over the horizon. She watched, mesmerised as the gull circled overhead and listened to its cry, tipping her head back to follow its flight through the clear blue skies.

Max stood still and watched her – his eyes drank in the wild tumble of curls as her hair blew back in the gentle sea breeze, the curve of her breast, the upturned face, smiling softly at the bird, the way her hand rested against the pillar, the sparkle of the ring on her finger.

Suddenly aware of his scrutiny, she turned her head and for another of those moments they gazed at each other. He realised in that moment that what he felt for Davina paled in comparison to the sudden wave of emotion overwhelming him. Callista smiled, a little hesitantly, Max looked so serious, he was almost frowning.

He crossed the summer house in three strides, taking her breath away as he reached out and roughly pulled her towards him. His kiss, when it came, was a searing blaze of pure passion and when he finally raised his head she was almost shaken with the intensity of his embrace.

"Max?" she whispered, her eyes wide with surprise. She had experienced the passionate nature of his feelings over the past few days but this kiss was a revelation. It was almost a seal of possession, of ownership and it left her slightly shaken.

He placed his hands either side of her face and drew in a deep shuddering breath. He had shocked her and he forced himself to hold back the feelings, to reassure, to ease and he followed that wild kiss of possession with another, gentle kiss.

"It is a magnificent view," he whispered. "And tomorrow we will go to the beach and bathe and I will teach you to swim… oh Callie…" He could not continue. His feelings were threatening to overwhelm him once more and afraid of frightening her again, he bowed his head and pressed his forehead against hers.

He did not deserve her. He pulled her into his embrace and kissed the top of her head. How could he tell her how he felt when he could not explain to himself this overpowering wave of pure emotion that rocked him, knocked him completely off balance. He wanted her with a fierceness he had never felt before. Not even the early intensity of his relationship with Davina could match this yearning, this need he felt for Callista. He did not understand it and he had given up trying, he was just going to accept it.

She wriggled out of his embrace and stepped away from him, her eyes alight and her face alive with happiness and mischief.

"Come on then, show me now," she whispered and danced away from him, running down the steps of the summer house, her pale muslin dress streaming out behind her as she ran towards the door in the wall leading to the cliffs. He found himself laughing as he chased her and caught her just as she opened the heavy wooden door.

"Tomorrow," he said firmly. "It is too late and the tide is in – look." He pointed down over the cliff, holding her close, afraid of letting her go too near the edge.

She followed his pointing finger and looked over the edge to see the waves crashing against the foot of the cliffs, no sand visible, only the white topped foaming ocean.

She sighed. "I suppose one more day will not matter."

They stood for a moment on the cliff top path, staring out together at the perfect view. He held out his hand and folded her small white hand protectively in his own.

"We've been travelling for hours," he reminded her. "I think tonight we finish looking around the house, change, eat dinner, and relax. Despite what Sarah said about my family leaving us in peace, I don't think we are going to have many days alone." He smiled at her, his teeth showing white against the tanned skin, his blue eyes crinkling at the corners.

"But tomorrow," he promised, "tomorrow the beach."

He pushed a stray curl of her hair away from her face and still holding her hand, he led her back into the walled garden, closing the door in the wall behind them. They walked sedately back to the house and anyone watching them would have seen only the way the tall, handsome young man held the hand of his wife in a propriety, protective manner and how she smiled up at him, contented and glowing with happiness.

No one would ever have guessed at the emotions churning around the heart of the young man as he held on to her as though his very life depended on it.

Chapter Sixteen

True to his word, Max escorted his bride to the beach the following day. Following a comfortable night in Penhallow's best guest room, they spent a leisurely morning exploring the rest of the house. The Housekeeper was Mrs Peters and she, like her husband the previous afternoon, proudly showed them the bedrooms and nursery and took them up onto the roof where they could see the surrounding countryside for miles around. Callista was entranced by the house. It held an atmosphere of calm and mellow happiness. The rooms were spacious, elegantly furnished and comfortable and she listened fascinated as Mrs Peters told the story of how the house and land had been given to Sir Hugo's mother's ancestor by a grateful Queen Elizabeth. Exactly what service the first Penhallow had performed for the Queen had never been recorded, but suffice to say he had emerged from the encounter with several hundred acres of prime Cornish land.

They had lunch together in a small dining room that the family used when not entertaining and over the meal, Callista quizzed Max about his own estates.

"Do you have such a romantic tale as to how your ancestors acquired Moreland?" she enquired.

Max paused in his enjoyment of the fine Cornish cider he was drinking and wrinkled his brow as he recalled the history of his own inheritance.

"No, I think Moreland was in our family from before the Norman invasion," he said. "Apparently I had a very astute ancestor who knew where his best interest lay and he managed to keep both his head and his lands."

He laughed a light of pure amusement in his eyes. "I believe the house was built on the ruins of an old Roman fort once the Romans left Britain to defend their empire."

For an instant, the memory of a nightmare disturbed him. He had been dressed as a Roman in that dream and he recalled in vivid detail the blood staining his hands as he held a dying Callista in his arms.

"Do you think your family held Moreland even then?" Callista asked, fascinated.

He shrugged, suddenly not wanting to dwell on the history of his home. "I don't know," he admitted. "But over the years, various archaeologists have been very excited by finding remains of Roman pottery in our grounds."

He smiled again, not wishing to spoil her enjoyment of their discussions. "And when I was a child, my father allowed a dig to take place where they discovered a fine Roman helmet – they believed it had belonged to a high ranking officer and the archaeologist presented it to my father."

"Really?" Callista was wide eyed. "Do you still have it? May I see it when we return home?"

He smiled anew at her natural usage of the word home. "I have it in my study," he told her. "It was formerly my father's study and I found myself using it more and more since I returned to the estate with my mother so it is now officially mine. As is the helmet. Do you know, I tried it on once – when I was about eighteen – and it was a perfect fit." He shook his head with the reminiscences. "My father was annoyed with me for disturbing it - but even he had to admit it looked as if it had been made for me."

"I am sure you look very noble in it, my love," she laughed. "We must have a masquerade party for your birthday and we will have the rest of the Roman uniform made for you to match."

He smiled along with her, feeling a tinge of uneasiness at the thought of actually wearing the uniform he had so recently dreamed of. It was almost a shade too prophetic for his liking. Shrugging off his disquiet however, he went along with her joking mood.

"I don't know about that, Callie," he protested. "I have a winter birthday and I think the weather may be a little chilly to be wearing short togas."

"Nonsense, we will just make sure all the fires are lit and the house is thoroughly heated before we expose your legs to the world."

He stood up and walked around the table. Standing behind her, he put his hands on her shoulders and dropped a kiss on the top of her upturned head as she laughed up at him.

"My legs, dearest Callie," he said drily, "are going to be exposed to no one except my tailor, my doctor and, of course, my loving spouse."

"Very well, Sir Maxim, if you dislike the idea so much I will not insist on a masquerade. I would still like us to have a party though – it is your thirtieth birthday after all."

He grimaced. "I feel so old," he sighed, only half joking. "But if you would like to throw a party for our friends and family, I will not object. I'm sure my mother will be delighted to provide you with a guest list."

She wiped her mouth on the fine linen napkin and stood up to move away from the table. "I am sure she will," she agreed. "I will be happy to take her advice, however, this is going to be my first party at Moreland and I want to do it myself. Do you think she will be offended?" Suddenly anxious not to upset Lady Joanna, Callista turned worried eyes to him.

He held out his hand to her, to escort her from the small Salon, leaving the maidservant to clear the remains of their delicious lunch.

"My mother will do whatever you want her to do," Max said firmly. "She loves you, Callie, and she will help you in whatever you wish."

Extremely gratified by his words, Callista accompanied him as they strolled back through to the hallway.

"Now, Callie," he said, "I am going to ask Mrs Peters to provide us with a blanket and towels and something to drink and we are going to have a walk down to the beach. You will need a sun hat, my dear, and perhaps a parasol – the sun is extremely hot this afternoon."

Delighted, Callie clutched his arm and stood on tiptoes to kiss his cheek before turning to run lightly up the stairs to their room to search through her belongings for the required items.

She returned a few minutes later to find Max waiting for her. He was accompanied by a young Footman who was carrying a large wicker basket in which Mrs Peters had thoughtfully packed two large bottles of homemade lemonade, some fruit and a large cake.

Callie shook her head. "Mrs Peters is determined to fatten us up, Max," she sighed.

Max was carrying a blanket and towels and she smiled at the sight of him in his finest tailored clothing, his immaculate cream breeches and spotless white shirt and cravat. He was wearing a jacket which, whilst being the height of fashion and which moulded itself to his body like a second skin, was nevertheless wholly inappropriate for an afternoon on the beach. She hid her amusement however and together, accompanied by the attentive Footman, they walked through the grounds to the door leading to the cliff top path and very shortly afterwards found the steps leading down to the cove.

It was a small private beach belonging to the house, inaccessible from anywhere except the path they followed. The young Footman, albeit a little reserved in the presence of his employer's relatives, found himself answering Her Ladyship's questions about the area and what he knew about it. She learned more about St Milo's Bay in one short half hour walk than Max had ever known and he found himself greatly diverted by the way in which the Footman could not do enough for Callista as they finally reached the wide sandy expanse of the beach. The young man directed them to the most sheltered spot, spread the blanket out for them, advised them to watch out for the tide and gave them the tide times for the day. He laid the picnic basket down for them and unpacked a bottle of lemonade and two glasses before bowing and leaving them, promising to return to collect them and their basket in good time for dinner that evening.

The sun was extremely hot and Callista was relieved that she had chosen to wear one of her fine muslin sprigged dresses. It was light and comfortable and the pale blue of the dress highlighted the creaminess of her skin, already starting to acquire a faint golden tan. Max, however, looked more than a little uncomfortable and with a muttered curse, he peeled off the jacket and pulled the cravat from around his neck, casting it down on the sand without the slightest concern of what Benson was going to say to him. In his Valet's opinion, a gentleman was correctly dressed at all times of the day and night and the sight of his young employer discarding his clothing in such a cavalier manner would have distressed him beyond measure.

He sat on the blanket next to Callista and divested himself of his boots next. Finally, with his shirt undone and barefoot, he lay back on the blanket with his hands behind his head and sighed with utter contentment, causing his wife to explode in a peal of laughter.

He opened one eye and squinted up at her. "And what, exactly, Madam, is so amusing you?" he enquired, coolly.

"You look like a schoolboy, Max," she replied and reaching out she ruffled his hair, completing the total destruction of Benson's best efforts of several hours earlier.

He rolled over onto his stomach and she found herself looking down into eyes that were alight with mischief. Before she could stop him, he reached out his hands and caught one of her feet in his hand and with a few deft movements, he removed her thin shoe before turning his attention to her other foot, unbuckling the shoe and divesting her of that one also.

He stood up in one swift movement and grasping her hand, pulled her to her feet and before she could make a sound or protest, she found herself pulled along, running, and breathless down to where the surf and the waves pounded against the beach.

The air was filled with the tang of salt and the breeze blew the sea spray of the incoming tide onto them, cooling them as they ran together into the shallow waters. Despite the heat of the day, Callista was shocked at the coldness of the water but she lifted her skirts and followed Max into the sea. The water came up to her knees and she watched as he pulled his shirt off, tossing that onto the dry sand before turning away from her and diving, headlong into the oncoming waves.

He disappeared and she watched without breathing for a moment until his dark head, wet and as slick as a seal appeared again several yards out to sea. He floated on his back and she watched in envy as he swam back towards her with easy fluid strokes.

He reached her and stood up, shaking the water out of his hair, his face and body wet with rivulets of water running down. He was grinning at her and he looked so happy and carefree that her heart lurched with love for him. She had never felt so close to him as she did at that moment when he took her face between his hands and kissed her upturned face.

Her laughter turned to screams as he grinned suddenly and swept her into his arms and picked her up. She clung to his neck as he spun her round until she was dizzy and she gasped for air as a wave caught them and the force of the tide knocked him off his feet plunging them both beneath the water.

He hauled her to her feet, and they stood facing each other, soaked through to the skin, Callista spluttering and brushing her hair out of her face as the water had loosened it from its carefully arranged style.

He pulled her towards the shore, and she held on to his hand, stumbling over her skirts as they emerged from the water.

She fell onto the sand as he threw himself down beside her and she turned her head to look into his deep blue eyes, suddenly finding him inches away from her. They moved together as one and the kiss tasted of the sea as his lips devoured hers.

He lifted his head and gazed down at her lying beside him on the beach, her hair spread out on the sand, her dress clinging to her, the buttons undone, the bodice awry revealing damp breasts, her nipples showing clearly through the wet material.

She looked wild and wanton and his mouth was suddenly dry as he touched her breast, his eyes never leaving hers as his fingers traced the outline of her nipple. She caught her breath, her pupils dilating with desire as his fingers gently played over her skin, teasing a groan out of her as he slowly aroused her, his tongue following his fingers to tantalise and excite, undoing the remaining buttons, peeling damp clothes from her helpless, clinging body. She lay still, defenceless against the relentlessly sensual assault. He held her still, not allowing her to move or touch him. His lips and tongue followed his fingers, licking her breasts and rolling his tongue around her nipples, sucking them softly as she moaned in pleasure at his ruthless dominance of her body.

His hands reached down and pulled her skirts up and she reeled with shock as she felt his hands pulling at her underclothes, pulling the ribbons undone and pulling the silken material down over her buttocks and down until they were discarded next to his sand covered shirt.

His fingers caressed her legs, her thighs, parting them to slide his hand up over her stomach and then down, through the crisp damp hair and into her, rubbing slowly, oh so slowly, as slowly and as sensually as he had caressed her breasts. His eyes stared into hers, watching her reaction as she gave herself up to the waves of pleasure his hands induced in her. She pressed the back of her hand against her mouth to stop a scream escaping her as his fingers continued their relentless onslaught bringing her to the peak of ecstasy once more.

She was shaking with the intensity of his attentions and she took a deep shuddering breath as he removed his hands to lie back in the sand and pull her with him. Confused at first but as he pulled her across him so that she straddled his body, her hands caressed his tightly muscled body and she realised what he wanted. She lowered herself onto him as a shiver of anticipation and excitement coursed through her body and he waited as she started to move against him, lying still, allowing her to set the pace of their lovemaking. She sat astride him, her eyes never leaving his, silently communicating her love for him as his hands played with her naked breasts.

They moved in harmony, and building up to that wonderful release, she cried out in ecstasy as he held on to her hips to still her when he gasped, shuddered and she felt the rush of heat as his seed spilled into her.

He sat up carefully and pulled her head down to seek and find her lips, kissing her once more and pulling her down onto the sand beside him. She lay next to him, held tightly in his arms, her head swimming, her body aching with pleasure, her breathing shallow.

Through a haze, she vaguely heard the waves lapping against the shoreline. She closed her eyes, listening to the gentle sounds, to the cries of the seagulls circling overhead, to Max's deep breathing as he held her close. Contented, at peace with the world, Callista slipped into sleep.

Max awoke her as he stirred, awakened by the water coming in and covering his feet. He sat up and looked around, suddenly aware of their state of undress. He knew the cove was private and not overlooked but as he gazed down on her half naked form, he wondered how she would feel at the thought of being spied on. Davina would have revelled in it, he realised, proud of her form and totally uninhibited. Callista was not shy, nor was she a shrinking Miss, but she would be mortified at the thought of such behaviour being observed.

She sat up and, like him, realised the state of her clothing and blushed rosily as she pulled her bodice up to cover her naked breasts, buttoning it with suddenly shaking fingers.

"Don't worry, Callie," he said softly, pulling on his breeches as he spoke, "No one can see us."

"I should hope not," she replied. "My Aunt would be horrified by my behaviour." She paused in straightening her clothing and stood up, assisted to her feet by her husband. "It is not the way a lady should conduct herself, you know."

Max grinned at her, boyish and relaxed once more. "She will not hear of your disgraceful exhibition from me," he promised.

In response to his outrageous statement, she pushed him away from her and had the satisfaction of seeing him fall back into the sea. She ran out of the way of retaliation and returned to the smooth blanket lying undisturbed in the shade of some large rocks. The bottles of lemonade remained cool inside the basket and she uncorked one of them, pouring its contents into a tall tankard provided by their Cook. She drank greedily, the salty sea air and the heat of the sun combining to make her thirsty. Almost three hours had passed since they had eaten and whilst not hungry, she found herself drinking the sharp cold drink with relish. Max joined her and she passed a tankard of the drink to him. He threw himself down onto the rug and stretched out beside her, totally relaxed, totally at ease.

They sat in companionable silence, enjoying the day, enjoying the view, enjoying just being together.

She sighed. "This is just perfect. Every day I feel as though I could not be happier – and then I am."

He laughed at her statement and leaning back on the rug, propped up on one elbow he looked at her face. She was perfectly serious.

He had to admit to himself, he did not know how it had happened, but he, too, felt absurdly, incredibly happy.

"I hope you will be just as happy once we are home, settling into our normal day to day living," he replied.

"I am looking forward to it," she said. "I know there is a lot involved in running an estate as large as yours, but I hope to be able to help you in some way, Max."

He frowned suddenly, a wave of emotion, almost of guilt, washed over him. "There is a lot of work to do, it is true," he admitted ruefully. "And I have neglected the estate for the delights of London for the last few years. But now…" He sat up again, draining the tankard and holding it out to her for more. "Now, my dear – I have – no – we have a lot to do."

Her expression was one of quiet enjoyment. "Will we have to go to London very often, Max?" she asked him.

"Not if you don't want to," he replied. "We will go for a month every Season, just as my parents used to do. I think that will be sufficient, do you? Unless…" A sudden thought struck him. "Unless of course, you would rather go for longer."

She shook her head. "No, Max, not at all. I have had my Season – I have enjoyed this last year with Georgiana and, of course, meeting you, my darling, but it became slightly too hectic occasionally."

He paused before drinking down his second tankard of lemonade. Thoughts came unbidden of his cold-blooded plans, made in the scented boudoir of his mistress, of leaving his bride for several months of the year to return to the hedonistic delights of the city.

He was going to marry a milksop, he recalled, get her pregnant and leave her to bring up his heir. He would join her occasionally to rusticate, to hunt and shoot and fish and generally carry on behaving as he always had done, leaving others to run his estate, letting it get more and more run down with an absent landlord taking no care or interest in his lands or the welfare of his tenants.

His father had known what he was about when he had put that clause in his will, Max realised with a jolt. His father knew him better than he had known himself and he thanked God that he had had the good sense to reject every milksop London and Davina had thrown in his path over the course of the last six months.

His bride of six days watched the different play of emotions crossing his expressive face. He was lost in thought, staring out to sea, his eyes dark and brooding, his brow furrowed, his expression sombre.

"What is it, Max?" she asked gently.

He forced his thoughts back to the present. His expression lifted and he managed a somewhat rueful smile at her.

"I was thinking of my birthday, Callie," he explained. "I might be thirty years old next month, but I think I finally grew up the day I met you."

He reached across and took her hand and in a gesture that

touched her more than anything else he had ever done before, he pressed it against his cheek.

For a moment neither spoke, but the sound of footsteps behind them caused them to look around to see two of the Trevellyan staff, come, as promised, at 4 o'clock to take them back to the house.

She stood up as they approached, carefully brushing the sand from her damp and creased clothes, and turned laughing eyes to Max. "This afternoon has ended all too soon," she said. "May we come again?"

He passed his tankard over to her to pack in the picnic basket and, like her, picked up his discarded shirt and jacket, trying to make himself look faintly presentable before returning to the house.

"We will spend many days here, Callie," he promised. "And perhaps even take an occasional moonlight stroll."

"Oh Sir Maxim, how romantic," she responded and together, looking far more disreputable than when they arrived some hours earlier, sun kissed, damp and happy, they made their way slowly back up the steep steps to the house.

Their month in Cornwall passed far more quickly than either of them had anticipated.

Within a few days of their arrival, Callista had met the rest of Max's cousins and their families, when they were entertained to a lavish family dinner at Lady Sarah Tremaine's home, where she met Sir Henry and their two sons, Sir James Trevellyan, the patriarch of the family, together with his vivacious wife and their four children. The evening was informal, the meal was delicious and, once the children were taken away to bed, Callista was able to sit and talk comfortably with the two women, listening to their tales of marriage and motherhood that made her laugh and brought a blush to her cheeks on more than one occasion.

Having never known her mother and with her Aunt being far

too cold and distant to ever indulge in such frivolous conversation, Callista was delighted with their unconventional manner and their comfortable easy-going attitude.

She could hear roars of laughter coming from the men they had left behind in the dining room and she had no doubt that Max was getting a roasting from his older cousins. She smiled at Sarah as they heard the men but Sarah merely sipped her coffee and remarked coolly that Max should be thankful that Hugo was not here to make sport of him.

The evening was a success and was followed a few nights later by another, more formal affair up at Trevellyan Manor where Sir James and his wife introduced the newlyweds to their friends and neighbours. Callista suddenly found herself amongst several families who were home from London for the winter season, meeting once more and renewing acquaintances with some familiar faces from the world she had so recently left behind.

Max was an attentive escort, never abandoning her to strangers whilst he went off to seek amusement elsewhere. He danced occasionally with his cousins and once with the Mayoress of Truro, much to that lady's delight, but the majority of the evening was spent firmly by his bride's side and they made an attractive couple as they danced and laughed and joined in with the spirit of the evening together. On one occasion, as a spectacularly attractive blonde haired woman waltzed past them, dressed in a vivid blue gown, Max took in a sharp breath as the thought of Davina flashed through his mind. Instinctively he found himself clutching Callista closer to him, a strange feeling of panic almost overwhelming him. He pulled himself together at once and shook off the feeling, apologising to his wife for startling her. She, however, had followed his eyes and where Max had felt nothing but alarm, she felt a quiet despondency creep up on her. Her eyes glittered strangely for a moment but taking her cue from Max, she said nothing and instead smiled brightly up at him and continued their dance uninterrupted.

They returned to Penhallow when the evening drew to a close, promising to see their cousins again the following weekend at the Truro Assemblies, a monthly highlight in the Cornish social calendar.

If Max thought Callista was unusually quiet on the journey home, he said nothing, accepting her explanation of feeling tired. It had indeed been a hectic day, starting early that morning with their journey to Trevellyan Manor, a tour of the estate, followed by the Ball. They should have accepted their host's invitation to stay, but seduced by the magic of Penhallow, they had refused, preferring to return to their honeymoon home.

They sat together in companionable silence, Callista staring out of the carriage window, looking up at the dark August skies, staring up at the millions of bright stars. It was almost midnight by the time they reached Penhallow and she had to shake Max's shoulder to awaken him. He yawned and laughed as he realised he had fallen asleep.

"My dear, what a laggard you must think me," he apologised.

"No, merely that you have had a good dinner followed by far too many wines," she replied. "We have certainly had our share of entertainment these last few weeks."

They left the carriage and walked up to the front door of the Hall. Lanterns were arranged along the long driveway and flanked the entrance door of the house. The Butler was still up, awaiting their return and as they entered, he paused to lock the front door behind them.

"Did you have an enjoyable day, Sir Maxim?" he enquired.

"It was very agreeable, thank you Peters," Max replied.

"Cook has left a cold collation in the small Salon, Madam, should you require anything to eat before you retire."

"Thank you, Peters," she replied, "but I think I will go straight to my room. Is Alice still up?"

Peters acknowledged her with a slight bow of the head. "Yes Madam, I believe so."

Max turned to her. "I will be with you in a moment," he told her and as she smiled and left him, she saw him accompany the Butler into the small Salon.

Alice was awaiting her mistress, half asleep in the armchair in the bedroom, lit by a single candle and the light of the full moon streaming in through the window.

Tired but strangely restless, Callista undressed and slipped on her fine lawn nightgown, pausing to remove the pins from her hair, sitting down at her dressing table whilst Alice hung up the beautiful rose coloured evening gown, brushing it down and arranging it so the creases would fall out.

"Did you have a good time, my lady?" she enquired.

"I did, Alice, but I must admit I am relieved to be back."

Alice came over to the dressing table and picked up the heavy silver hairbrush. Quietly she started to brush out the tumble of auburn curls, smoothing the hair, effectively soothing Callista as she closed her eyes and felt the smooth rhythm of the brushes through her hair.

"Thank you, Alice," she sighed. "Go to bed now and I'll see you in the morning."

"Yes madam." Alice replaced the hairbrush and curtseying, she left the silent room.

Callista moved over to the window and stood for a moment staring out at the moon. It was a clear, still moonlight night; she gazed out at the reflection of the moon sparkling on the iridescent blackness of the sea, shimmering and glittering in the distance.

She still felt strangely restless; she was tired but she could not think about sleeping. Something was troubling her and she knew this feeling had started the moment at the Ball when Max had been startled by the entrance of a beautiful blonde woman. For a moment they had both thought it was Davina and Callista admitted to herself the unease she experienced every time she thought of Max's childhood sweetheart.

As she slipped between the cool sheets of the bed, the door opened and Max entered. She lay back on the pillows as he undressed and joined her in the bed. She turned to him and smiled. His face was slightly flushed, his hair was ruffled and he yawned as he leaned over to kiss her.

"What a day!" he exclaimed. "I do not believe we stopped once

– I think our honeymoon has turned out to be more hectic than I was expecting."

He pulled her into his arms and together they lay in close silence, his arms around her protectively and she laying safe next to him, her head resting on his chest. He kissed her softly and she snuggled into him, holding him close, revelling in the feel of his taut body next to hers.

A few moments later, the sound of his steady breathing told its own story.

She could not sleep. She could not get the image out of her mind of the first time she had seen Lady Davina Fitzpatrick, at Georgiana's coming out Ball. She remembered the way she had clung to Max as they waltzed around the Wetherbys' Ballroom, the predatory, hungry expression on her face as she had gazed up at him. She remembered also the way in which Max had held Lady Davina; he had danced with her as if he could not bear to let her go.

She sighed in the darkness of the bedroom. Her heart felt heavy as she slipped out of the bed and pulled a heavy shawl around her shoulders. She stood beside the bed and gazed down for a moment at her sleeping husband. She was suddenly overwhelmed by the feelings suffusing her, love, longing, and a deep despondency at the thought of losing him to another woman.

Something drew her to the window again and she looked out at the scene below her.

She pulled on her thin slippers and quietly, not disturbing him, she opened the bedroom door.

It was after midnight as she slipped down the stairs and made her way through the sleeping house to the Ballroom. She walked across the wide dance floor and opened one of the French windows that led out onto the terrace. Soon she was running across the grass towards the door in the garden wall. The bolt slipped back soundlessly and the door opened. She stepped out onto the cliff top path and stopped for a moment to gaze around her at the spectacular night-time view of the cove below her.

Guided by the light of the moon, she made her way down the

steep path to the beach below. She walked quickly, breathing in the cool night air, walking to clear her head, walking to dispel the image of her husband with another woman, walking to calm the anger that had arisen in her as she thought of Davina Fitzpatrick. She did not know why the sea called to her that night. The freshening wind was stirring the waves, and she could see the white-topped surf crashing against the beach by the light of the full moon. All she knew was a primitive, instinctive urge to be out of the house, to be by the sea, to breathe in its cold salt spray, to cool down the rage gripping her so fiercely that if Davina had appeared in front of her, she would have attacked the woman with the ferocity of a she-wolf.

She reached the sand and ran down towards the sea. She did not feel the tears running down her cheeks; she only felt the burning anger of jealousy, the hopeless rage of unrequited love, the longing for the love of a man who had given his heart to another woman.

She ran along the edge of the water until finally she stopped and looked up at the moon. A feeling so overpowering filled her body, an urge, a compulsion that stopped her. She dropped her shawl onto the sand and she turned her face up to the moon, a huge silver disk in the inky sky.

She raised her arms, reaching out for the moon, her lips moving in a wordless prayer, but whether it was to the God of her father or to an older, more pagan deity she could not have said.

Max could see her on the beach as he ran out of the garden, wearing only hastily pulled on breeches. He had awoken to find her gone and the bedroom door open.

He had no control over the panic seizing him. He was shaking with fear at the thought of losing her and as he ran soundlessly through the garden, he could only pray that she was unharmed, unable to sleep and had gone for a walk in the moonlight.

The sight he beheld caused him to stop in his tracks.

She was alone on the darkened, moonlight beach. It seemed to him that he could hear voices, a lovely, melodious sound just on the edge of his hearing. He watched her, the white of her nightgown appearing silver in the moonlight. There, facing the pounding surf, she lifted her arms to the stars and moon. Dazzled with wonder, the music in his ears seemed filled with joy and he watched as light, shimmering moonbeams slid down from the sky to brush the tips of Callista's fingers, the ends of her flying hair. For a moment it seemed she was like a candle, straight, slim, incandescent, lighting the edge of the world.

He felt dizzy then, a sudden flash of some half-remembered dream overcoming him. Callista, kneeling with her arms held up to the sky, her head thrown back in supplication to the gods of the moon and sky. She was in a strange, alien landscape surrounded by flowers and dressed in rough woollen robes.

Then there was only the sound of the surf, the pearl-white light of the moon and a woman standing alone on a beach.

A woman who lowered her hands to cover her face and sink to her knees in the damp sand, weeping.

He moved then, the spell was broken; the music was just the pounding of the surf and he ran down the steep path, a man possessed with anger and apprehension.

She heard him and stood up, turning to face him. She stepped back, alarmed at his speed and the expression she could see on his face. In the bright moonlight, it appeared contorted in anger.

She stumbled as a wave crashed behind her and she fell backwards, into the water, down a deeply shelving ridge of sand. She gasped with the cold and struggled to stand up, suddenly frightened by the depth of the water and the speed of the incoming waves. She could not find the bottom and she went down under the water once again as another huge wave smothered her.

She could feel the pull of the undercurrent and as she struggled to the surface again, the thought crossed her mind, albeit briefly, how easy it would be to give up, to give in to the sea and let it claim her in its icy embrace.

Then she heard his voice, screaming her name and she surfaced, floundering in the deep water, crying out to him.

It was over in moments. He ran into the water, dived through the waves to swim out to her, where the undercurrent was dragging her away. She felt his hand in her hair, she felt herself pulled to the surface and then the strength of his arm as he put it around her neck to tow her back to the safety of the beach.

He stumbled to his feet and lifted her into his arms, carrying her out of the water and onto the sand, finding her discarded shawl and wrapping it around her as she shivered in his arms.

He pushed wet hair out of his face and gripped her shoulders. His eyes were an angry arctic blue. "What the hell do you think you were doing?" His voice shook with emotion. "I thought I'd lost you – I thought you were going to drown."

She raised her wet face up to his and he could see tears shimmering in the deep green emerald of her eyes. "I – I'm sorry," she whispered but could say no more as she found herself crushed against his chest as his arms went around her, bands of steel, holding her tightly.

He was whispering her name, over and over again, into her hair. He was trembling almost as much as she was, but it was with a fear, an anguish he could not yet put a name to, of losing her to the ocean.

Despite the cold, despite the icy chill of the night, despite the salt-tanged sea spray drenching them both, despite everything, she raised her head to his and saw his eyes. Then she found herself being kissed with such tenderness, such warmth that she felt the weight in her heart lift, soaring away on wings of happiness.

Exhausted, mentally and physically, on shaking legs, they made their way off the beach and up the steep path back to the cliff top. It was a tortuously long journey that night but Callista felt only the strength of his arms, holding her, sometimes carrying her, but constantly supporting her every inch of the way.

Lihanna 9

The days passed peacefully enough for Lihanna and her General, days when he allowed her to accompany him as he went on his patrols, evenings when together they would return to the compound, eat a meal together, and talk until the sun set over the horizon and the fires burned low. Nights when it became more and more difficult to bid him goodnight and leave him for the warmth of her fur-lined narrow cot. He kept his promise though. He did not touch her, nor embrace her again even though her body ached to feel the strength of his arms around her, the feel of his lips crushing hers, the restrained gentleness of his hands upon her. He would ask permission from his superiors and her brother, the King, for her to become his wife and not until then would he claim her for his own. She would remain pure, inviolate until they were joined together in the hand fasting ceremonies of her people.

Two months into her captivity, Julius returned to his quarters, his face serious, his demeanour once more that of the resolute Roman General, ready to crush any rebellion against him and his masters. He came to her, as she stood at his entrance, surprised at his early return.

"General, what is it? What is wrong?" She was suddenly anxious, for her family, her mother and for him.

His eyes sought hers and his hands reached out to take her own small white ones in his.

"I have to take a battalion of my men and march West, Lihanna." He paused, his eyes boring into hers, brooding, dark, intense. "We have been informed of an uprising of Celts, led by an army of your Druid priests. I have been charged with subduing this rebellion and I must leave at once."

She looked down at his hands, holding hers so securely. She swallowed a suspiciously large lump in her throat. "Will you take me with you?" she whispered.

His hands gripped hers. "I cannot. It is too dangerous and you are too valuable to…. to Rome." He paused as she looked up into his eyes. "And to me," he finished. He took a deep breath. "You will be safe here. My guards will protect you and ensure no harm comes to you. "

"And you? Who will protect you?" she demanded.

He smiled, a curiously warm and amused smile, touched by her concern, nevertheless his tone hardened. "I have no need for bodyguards, Lihanna. I will survive this skirmish and will return."

For a long, wordless moment they stared at each other. She could not tear her eyes from his. She found herself unable to look away and he, too, seemed incapable of movement. She did not know who moved first, but suddenly his arms were around her, pulling her close, holding her against the lean hardness of his body. His mouth came down on hers and his kiss sought and found a response which surprised and frightened her in equal measure. Her lips moved against his and her arms went up around his neck so she could press herself closer to him.

Lihanna could not tear herself away from him. She responded and returned his kiss with equal passion and when he eventually lifted his lips from hers, her eyes were glazed with the feelings he had aroused in her.

He withdrew his arms from around her and put his hands on her shoulders, pushing himself away from the soft curves of her pliant body.

She was shaking slightly and reached out her hand to touch his mouth. He caught it and pressed a kiss against it. "Come back to me, Julius Maximus," she whispered.

A smile light up the darkness of his eyes. "Your heart and mine are as one, Lihanna," he replied. "I will return and we will be together. You will be my wife before winter comes."

He kissed her once more and reluctantly left her to gather up his armour and his weapons.

She watched him as he left the camp, riding his horse at the head of a column of his Centurions, the bright red plume on his helmet *a beacon in the light of that dark afternoon, the dull light shining on his armour and short broadsword at his waist. He rode a great black stallion and it reared suddenly as he passed his quarters. He controlled the horse in one fluid, easy movement and his head turned once to see her standing in the entrance of the tent, standing between two of his best men, posted to guard her, to protect her until his return. He saluted her and for a moment their eyes locked before the column moved off and he led the marching Centurions out of the village, heading West to where the reported uprising was taking place.*

She waved once to his disappearing back and took time to look around the village, now almost unrecognisable as the home she had grown up in, quickly changing into a new encampment, a new Roman fortress.

She found herself the subject of scrutiny and she saw the familiar figure of Daveth, labouring with some of the other men, carrying rocks and stones to build and secure the fortress.

He was watching her with that intense expression on his face she remembered from their childhood. He had been determined to become one of the Druid priests even then and had been proud and pleased when he had been chosen to become an apprentice. Eager to join and determined to succeed, he had been the most zealous, the most passionate of all the apprentices and had surpassed all the other young men in every test of their faith and courage.

She smiled at him but the smile froze on her face as he frowned and looked away, carrying on with his labours and turning his back on her.

She returned to the luxurious confines of her prison. Disturbed by Daveth's attitude and concerned about Julius, she went into her small curtained bed chamber, where she had slept – ten feet away from her Roman jailer – a slight smile lifted the corners of her mouth – she wished he was with her now and wondered how much longer that arrangement would have lasted. Tradition and customs of her tribe would not allow her to willingly give herself to any man without the permission of her parents and the ceremonial joining of hands – the rites of marriage performed by the Druids in the site of the sacred stones. She remembered the feelings which had flooded her body each time he had kissed her – no man had ever dared to treat her so – her father would have had them flogged for daring to touch her. Yet her father was no longer with her and the whereabouts of the rest of her family remained a mystery. This Roman, this Julius Maximus Aurelius wanted her – he wanted her for his wife and her heart soared with this knowledge. She knew he loved her, that her feelings towards him were reciprocated and she longed for his safe return.

The memory of his kiss flooded her mind, made her smile but she could not suppress a strange shiver of foreboding as another memory, that of the cold unfriendly glare from her old friend Daveth, came back to her as the sun set once more behind the great forest.

Chapter Seventeen

Lady Joanna Langley watched with some amusement as her guest jumped up and ran to the window for perhaps the fiftieth time in the last hour.

"Georgiana, my dear," she remonstrated. "They will be here soon. Max's letter said the 1st of September and he would have informed us had their plans changed."

Georgiana sighed and re-seated herself beside her hostess once more. "I am sorry, Lady Joanna, but I was sure I heard their carriage."

Lady Joanna smiled indulgently at her young guest. Persuaded by the young woman to intercede on her behalf, she had requested the pleasure of Georgiana's company for the month of the newlywed's honeymoon. Georgiana therefore was able to enjoy a month with her newly betrothed husband to be, with Lady Joanna attending as a chaperone. Leaving her parents to return to Yorkshire to attend to the matter of arranging her forthcoming nuptials, Georgiana spent the month in a whirl of social engagements with Damon at the Assemblies in Bath, Balls with their neighbours, meeting Damon's tenants and friends and generally basking in her newly found happiness.

Georgiana picked up the letter from her mother she had been reading. Full of information and details about wedding arrangements, she smiled and raised laughing eyes to Lady Joanna.

"Oh dear, I think I had better intervene before Mama bankrupts the estate. She is talking about inviting Royalty to the wedding and getting Papa to hire Westminster Abbey."

Lady Joanna chuckled as she listened to Georgiana reading

the letter from her mother. Lady Amelia did seem to be taking the wedding of her only daughter to the extreme. Where once Georgiana would have concurred with her Mama's plans and ambitions, now she would have been happy with the type of quiet country wedding her cousin had enjoyed, surrounded by family and friends and forsaking the Society wedding her Mama was determined to provide.

Georgiana stood up and moved gracefully over to the writing desk placed conveniently beside the window. She seated herself in a rustle of silk, golden autumn sunshine highlighting her primrose coloured gown as it settled around her. She opened the desk and picked up a piece of embellished writing paper and a pen, searching through the drawer for ink.

"I must write to my parents and tell them to stop all this nonsense. It is my wedding and I want it kept simple and elegant – I will not have Mama turning my day into a circus. I have only agreed to London as it is too far for our respective families to travel to either Yorkshire or Wiltshire."

Her eyes were sparkling with good humour but she had a determined set to her chin as she started to scratch out her letter. Lady Joanna watched her approvingly. She was becoming as fond of Georgiana as she was of Callista and had enjoyed this past month in her role of unofficial chaperone.

She had seen much of Damon and was pleased to see he had shaken off the shadows of his past. There was nothing about him that reminded Joanna of his dissolute father, and she was heartily glad of it. Joanna had felt nothing but pity for Damon's mother, saddled with a wastrel of a husband and a hoyden of a daughter. She had watched their father ignore Damon and indulge Davina's every whim, the wilder the better, until she had become so out of control that their poor mother had finally just given up. She had watched Davina growing up to be totally spoilt, thoughtless and self-centred and when the family had finally married the child off to a rich Irish peer, Lady Fortescue had died not long afterwards. Fortunately for Damon, a year later and a hunting accident had seen the widower follow his wife, leaving

Damon to start his attempt to rescue the estate and the family fortunes.

Now, with his fortunes restored through his hard work and careful management, Damon was engaged to Georgiana, and Lady Joanna had never seen him so happy. They were expecting him over that evening to join them in welcoming back Max and Callista, and as Lady Joanna picked up her embroidery and Georgiana wrote her letter, neither were aware of the maelstrom that was about to shatter their peaceful existence.

The carriage clattered into the driveway of Moreland Hall and Max observed with a wry smile the way in which Callista leaned forward to gaze out of the window at the approaching house. It was far older than Penhallow, a substantial, solid, mellow building with red ivy covering part of the walls. In the dying rays of that sun-filled afternoon, it glowed with a beauty Max had never noticed before, but he saw it through his wife's eyes as if for the first time and he was struck suddenly with the knowledge of how much he loved his home. Guilt weighed heavily on his shoulders as he recalled how sadly he had neglected his estates for so long, and he realised with a newly developed maturity how hard Damon must have worked to restore his own home over the last few years. Luckily his finances and his means were never as straitened as Damon's and now he determined to improve his estates as never before. He found himself quite looking forward to immersing himself in the management of his properties and resolved to send for his estate manager first thing in the morning to arrange what he knew would be a lengthy and difficult meeting.

"Max, it looks so beautiful, does it not?" Callista squeezed his hand and he turned to her, a smile lighting his face as he looked anew at his wife.

He had always thought her attractive. After four weeks of marriage in which he had experienced happiness he had never expected to find with another woman, he thought her beautiful.

Her sparkling eyes, her mobile laughing mouth, her creamy skin and those tumbling curls framing her face – how could he ever have considered her anything less than stunning? Dressed in her travelling clothes of dark green velvet jacket and matching bonnet over a travelling dress of green muslin, the colour enhanced the green in her eyes and as she held his hand, he returned the pressure with a caress.

"Do you like your new home, Callie?" he quizzed her.

"It is indeed a very fine property, Sir Maxim," she replied, smiling at him. "I am very proud to be married to its owner."

The sound of the carriage on the drive had alerted the occupants of the house to its arrival and the door opened to reveal three people coming out to greet them.

The carriage came to a stop and Damon Fortescue strode forward to open the door. Max kicked out the step and he jumped down to shake hands with his old friend before turning to assist Callista out of the carriage.

Lady Joanna and Georgiana came forward and after Damon had bowed over Callista's hand, she turned to them to find herself greeted with a kiss from her fond mother in law and a hug from her cousin.

"Welcome home, Callie," Georgiana exclaimed. "Welcome back – we have so much to tell you and I want to hear all about your honeymoon."

Georgiana turned to Max and curtsied politely to her new cousin in law and he laughed and kissed her fondly on the cheek.

"It is good to see you, Georgie. We believe congratulations are in order."

Blushing rosily, Georgiana stepped beside Damon who drew her hand into the crook of his arm. He gazed down at her and smiled, the happiness exuding from them both almost eclipsing that of the newly married couple.

Lady Joanna ushered them into the house and amid much greetings and laughter, Callista spotted a small head appearing around the banister in the hallway.

Callista turned away from them and approached the tousled haired child.

"Joe? Is that you?" she enquired.

An extremely clean and smart young man stepped out from behind the newel posts.

"Cook said I wasn't to bother yer, Miss, I mean Yer Ladyship. But I just wanted to see you'd come back orright."

Joe had grown since his first appearance on their doorstep only three months earlier. A combination of good food and the attention of a Cook who had taken to the young motherless boy had improved his looks considerably. Gone were the hollow eyes, hollow cheeks and lank hair of the guttersnipe and instead a handsome child with thick blonde hair and striking amber coloured eyes gazed happily up at the woman his mother had described as an angel.

"As you can see, I am very well, Joe," Callista replied, taking his hand. "And you – are you being well looked after?"

"Yes, Yer Ladyship. I like it 'ere."

She laughed softly and touched his head gently. "We will have time tomorrow to catch up Joe," she promised. "You can be my official guide around the grounds and you can show me where you work and introduce me to the people you work with. Are you happy here, Joe?"

He smiled up at her and the happiness his face told its own story. "Yes I am. I'll see yer tomoror then?"

"See you tomorrow, Joe," she promised, and gave his hand another squeeze.

Grinning from ear to ear, he turned and returned the way he had come, going back to the kitchens, happy to have seen her and delighted with her promise to seek him out and for them to continue their daily meetings.

The hall suddenly became very busy with the bustle of unloading the carriages and trunks and luggage being carried up to the master bedroom. It was a hive of activity and Callista, tired after long days of travelling was relieved to be home at last. She removed her bonnet and handed it to her maid to take to her room, before following the rest of the family into the Drawing Room.

Callista went immediately to Max's side as he rose from his seat and held his hand out to her, surprising a pleased smile from Lady Joanna as she watched the interaction between her son and his wife.

She sighed, one of contentment. "It is so good to be home."

Lady Joanna smiled across to her daughter in law. "It is good to hear you say so, my dear. I have always loved Moreland and I will be sorry to leave it, however, Mrs Spencer will be joining me soon and I will move across to the Dower House in the next few days to ensure it is ready for our joint occupation." She looked across to where Georgiana sat next to Damon.

"I understand Georgie has written to apprise you of the situation here?"

"Yes, Mama," Max replied. "Georgiana is to remain with us until her engagement party in October after which she is to return with her parents to Yorkshire and then come back for Christmas."

Georgiana turned her huge cornflower blue eyes to Max and dimpled prettily at him. "I hope you do not mind," she said, slight anxiety in her voice, as if his refusal to allow her to remain at Moreland would completely ruin her happiness. "Damon's arrangements are well under way and the party is only a few weeks away."

"Fear not, sweet cousin," Max replied drily, "I am happy to accommodate you for the foreseeable future. Callie has been looking forward to seeing you and I am also looking forward to catching up on all of Damon's news."

With some relief, Georgiana turned to her cousin. "Thank you both, you so understand. Mama is most anxious that I return with her to Yorkshire but I cannot bear to leave just yet." She sighed. "I cannot believe we are to be neighbours, dearest Callie. Is that not just wonderful?"

Joy shone from her eyes as she surveyed the company. Lady Joanna watched the amused glance exchanged by Max and Callie and the look of utter devotion on Damon's face. She felt very content suddenly. She also felt quite old.

The servants returned with tea and, as they talked, Callista told Georgie all about Penhallow and how Max had been teaching her to swim. Max joined his mother, asking her if she had arranged the meeting he had requested for his Solicitor and Estate Manager to attend him the following morning.

Lady Joanna raised an eyebrow at him.

"I have indeed, Max. They will be here at 9am prompt. They are both exceedingly eager to wait upon you. In fact Hedges has been requesting this interview for some time – I am pleased to see you finally taking heed of your responsibilities, my son."

Max had the grace to appear slightly discomfited by his mother's direct unerring gaze.

"I realise I have a lot of ground to cover, Mother," he replied, "but rest assured I am not looking to leave the estate for several more months and I intend to spend some time with both Hedges and Mr Tremaine to ensure I know exactly what needs attending to."

He spoke with a quiet determination in his voice and Lady Joanna observed his newly acquired maturity with some approval.

"Marriage seems to have agreed with you, Maxim," she remarked.

"If you mean it has made me take stock of my life, then I must agree with you, Mama," he replied thoughtfully. "Callista and I have decided we will remain for most of the year here at Moreland and spend only part of the Season in London." He looked across at his wife and friends with a rueful grimace. "I would not deprive her of some amusements with her family in London but we are both agreed our lives will centre around our home here."

He spoke with simple sincerity and such honesty that Lady Joanna felt almost moved by his words.

It was exactly what she and his father had hoped for. They had worried about his fondness for Society that had so consumed him for the past few years and had been alarmed by the rakish lifestyle he had enjoyed. Troubled by his restless inability to settle down to any of the responsibilities towards his heritage, they had despaired of him. Joanna could only wish her beloved husband could see their only son now.

Her eyes shone with pride as she reached out and gently touched his cheek.

"I am happy and somewhat relieved to hear it, Max," she said quietly. "And we have had correspondence from Italy – we have received a very generous offer for the Sorrento estate."

Max glanced up at the portrait of his father above the nearby fireplace. The Italian estates had been bequeathed to his father from a distant relative. Max had been once, years ago and had fallen in love with the rambling Italian villa, the golden Tuscan countryside, and the acres of ripe grapes providing a wonderful tasty wine. Max had spent six months there, his sojourn spoilt on his return to find Davina married – he frowned at the memory of his anger on discovering her gone, an anger he had directed at his father for sending him so far away and powerless to prevent the marriage. He had been young, foolish and impetuous. As his gaze transferred to where Callista sat laughing with her cousin, he sent up a belated, silent prayer of thanks to his deceased parent.

"I want to take Callista there," he said softly. "I thought next year for our anniversary."

Joanna laughed softly. "I sincerely hope she might be in an interesting condition by this time next year." she said drily, succeeding in bringing a slight blush to her son's cheeks.

"Mama," he admonished her.

"Max!" Callista called to him and he turned gratefully to his wife for her interruption.

"Yes, Callie, what is it?"

"Damon and Georgiana are holding their engagement party at the end of October. It is your birthday two weeks later – can we not persuade Georgiana to remain with us until after your birthday?"

"Of course, Georgiana, you are very welcome to remain with us until Christmas if your parents would agree," he replied.

Georgiana's smile was radiant as she turned her head up to look at Damon.

"I would love to accept your invitation, Max," she replied. "When my parents arrive for the party, I will ask them. Papa would probably agree but I fear my mother is finding the strain of arranging my wedding without my assistance proving a little challenging even for her."

"And expensive," Lady Joanna interjected. "Westminster Abbey, my dear?"

Callista and Max were laughing as Georgiana shook her head and rolled her eyes in mock horror at her mother's extravagance.

"Such nonsense," Georgiana exclaimed. "But it is true I need to speak to her and have a say in my own wedding arrangement. Although I will miss you, Damon." She looked up at her fiancé, gazing down at her with undisguised love and happiness. "And you, Callie – why we have so much to catch up on."

Her artless chatter amused the gathered company, the clock struck the hour of 4pm and Max, seated with his back to the Drawing Room door, did not hear it open as he was laughing at something Damon said.

It was a contented, domestic scene and as he faced his wife, Max was alarmed as Callista suddenly stopped talking and stared at the open door, the colour draining from her cheeks, leaving her eyes wide and huge in her small white face. Then Damon became silent and Georgiana followed his gaze to the door. Max spun round in his seat and stood up as his Butler stepped aside.

"My Lord," he announced, "Lady Davina Fitzpatrick."

The stunned silence following the announcement was interrupted only as Damon stepped forward.

"Davina…" he started. "What on earth brings you here?" he demanded.

Davina was clad head to foot in deepest black. She pushed a delicate net veil away from her white face. Her blue eyes were blazing, her rosebud lips scarlet, the only splashes of colour about her.

The black served only to heighten the radiance of her beauty;

no other woman could have worn such an unrelenting blackness with such stunning success.

Her eyes scoured the room and came to rest at last on Max.

"I went to our home, Damon," she began, her voice husky, breaking with emotion.

"The servants told me you were here – I had to come, please forgive me, Lady Joanna for this intrusion but I needed to find Damon."

Lady Joanna's cold glance at Davina could have frozen molten lava.

"And what, pray, was so important you had to find your brother so urgently?" she demanded.

Davina's eyes never left Max. Her lips parted, sudden tears sprang to her eyes and she held a black trimmed kerchief to dab affectedly at her black eyelashes.

"Callum is dead," she announced to the assembled company. "My husband died three weeks ago and I have returned to live in England."

Grief had not marred any of Lady Davina's beauty; instead, she seemed to glow with an inner radiance. Her white blonde hair was tucked neatly underneath a fetching black bonnet, adorned with a simple net veil and two discreet feathers. Her tall slim figure seemed to have been poured into the elegant silk gown, enhancing rather than disguising the curves of her lithe body and although her white bosom was visible, it was through a sheer black chiffon scarf draped casually around her shoulders.

She held out her hand and stepped forward, stumbling a little. Spurred on by nothing more than a natural desire to prevent her from falling, Max stepped towards her and caught her hand. She gripped it and the look she gave him seared into his brain. It was not the look of a grief stricken widow – it was one of triumph, of success, of victory.

He released her hand at once as Damon also came forward and she turned gratefully towards her brother. He put a protective arm about her shoulders and she leaned against him, as if her legs were too weak to be able to stand unaided.

Max turned to look at Callista. She had not spoken but the look on her face spoke volumes. Her eyes were huge, she was staring at Lady Davina with a look of something almost fearful in her expression. Georgiana was simply dismayed at the sight of her future sister in law; she had no love for Lady Davina and only common courtesy towards her future husband's only sister had prevailed upon her to send a wedding invitation.

"What has happened, dearest?" Damon enquired gently, leading her to the sofa where Georgiana sat.

Davina clung to his hand as she settled herself down beside Georgiana.

"It happened two days after you left me to return to England," Davina explained. "We had thought Callum was improving – his health has been so uncertain these past few years." She directed her explanation towards Georgiana as she spoke.

"There was a terrible storm the day you left us, Damon. Callum was most affected by it, he seemed to take a turn for the worse and his influenza turned to pneumonia. The doctors could do nothing more for him – his lungs were weak and he died a week later."

Damon frowned, her words hung in the shocked silence of the room. "But his sister – she was such a devoted nurse – she had assured me Callum was so much better, how could his have happened?"

Davina shrugged gracefully, favouring them with a faint bewildered smile. She sighed heavily. "I do not know. His sister was as distraught as I."

Her eyes swept the room, her demeanour subdued. "I know we had been estranged but I would not have wished him harm." She gazed at Max and Lady Joanna, entreating them to believe her, her manner almost imploring for their understanding.

Max stared almost uncomprehendingly at her. His feelings were those of bemusement by her sudden and unexpected reappearance into his life, he had not thought to see her again so soon. If he was honest, he had hardly thought of her since his marriage and he was confused over the conflicting emotions her appearance stirred in him. His first thought was of his mother – her anger at Lady Davina's arrival was almost palpable. Georgiana was less subtle in hiding her feelings; despite Davina's reason for this intrusion, she looked simply annoyed. Damon of course was as usual the anxious and loving brother.

It was Callista who was causing him the most concern. She had not spoken, she was staring at Davina and the fearful expression had changed to one of apprehension. She looked uneasy and as her glance flickered between Davina and himself, he realised with a raw, shocking comprehension that Callista was as angry as his mother, as dismayed as Georgiana and – something else – Davina's presence had stirred in his wife an almost primitive dislike she was even now attempting to disguise.

"I am sure," Lady Joanna said, her voice still as cold as ice, "no one would wish harm to another human being, much less one's husband, estranged or not."

Callista meanwhile was struggling to control her emotions. At Davina's entrance, she had experienced again that strange dizzy sense of recognition she had come to expect more often as the months sped past. It was one of familiarity, not because Lady Davina was known to her, but an older, more deep seated knowledge that filled her with a foreboding and a dislike she could not rationally explain. She had dismissed it as a new bride's jealousy of her husband's former love – but she knew it was far more profound and mysterious than that. Something in her subconscious mind was screaming at her to remember, remember and beware – Davina was dangerous – she had always somehow known that on a very conscious level. But now as she gazed silently on the black robed woman – who even in her sombre clothing somehow diminished the beauty of every other female in that room, she felt her senses heighten and the knowledge flooding her being warned her that this predatory, ruthless woman was very dangerous indeed.

A vision – a frightening scene flashed into her mind. She closed her eyes momentarily but behind her eyelids for a split second she saw an image frozen in time. She saw a room, lit up by the lightning flash of a vicious storm. She saw a woman slumped by the side of a bed, unconscious – breathing too deeply for it to be a natural sleep. She saw a man on the bed, the covers pulled back so he lay uncovered, naked and unprotected against the freezing rain pouring in through the wide-open windows of the room. A howling wind blew through the room, putting out the candles and causing the fire to splutter and extinguish in the hearth. She saw Davina – opening the balcony doors ever wider. There was no trace of gentleness or beauty on that countenance. It was hard and unsmiling and as she turned back to the helpless figure on the bed, the cruel, vicious expression on her face caused Callista to shudder.

She opened her eyes and stared directly across at Davina. Her gaze seemed to disconcert the widow and she turned her head away to seek out her brother.

"Dearest, could I prevail upon you to escort me home?" she enquired, her voice tremulous and throaty.

Damon exchanged a regretful glance with his fiancé and stood up again immediately.

"Georgiana, pray excuse me. I must take Davina home and make sure she is comfortable."

Georgiana too, stood up and faced him. "Of course. I trust Your Ladyship will feel better once you are rested." Courtesy, good manners and natural concern for the bereaved woman fought with Georgiana's alarm at the thought of her future sister in law taking up permanent residence with Damon. She was a determined young woman but she did not feel herself equal to the task of insisting Davina make her home elsewhere.

Davina placed her hand possessively on Damon's arm and swept a graceful curtsey to the assembled company.

"I am so sorry to have intruded," she said softly. "I will interrupt your afternoon no longer."

"Damon, Davina – please – return to have dinner with us this evening." Max spoke up at last, suddenly aware of his lapse of good manners and feeling obliged to invite them to return.

Damon, however, frowned as his sister smiled at Max.

"Thank you, Max," he replied. "I think it best if we remained at home this evening. Davina has had a long and arduous journey and I would like to discuss what has happened and what her future plans are likely to be."

He was as stern and as unsmiling as Lady Joanna herself, who nodded approvingly at him. She too had felt momentary alarm at the thought of Davina taking up residence with her brother once more – a threatening cuckoo in the nest of two lovebirds. It was obvious looking at the tall young man in front of her now that Damon had no intention of starting his married life with his wife and sister under the same roof.

Damon bowed his farewell to them all and left the Drawing Room. A sudden silence descended on them all.

Georgiana was the first to speak. Her blue eyes suddenly filled with tears. "Why does she have to spoil everything?" she demanded, her voice tremulous.

Callista was roused at last from the disturbing vision that had so alarmed her. She reached across and took Georgiana's hand in her own.

"Damon will not let her keep him from your side," she said gently. "He is too devoted to you, dearest." Her eyes swept the room and came to rest on Max. "We will not let Davina's presence spoil anything, will we, Maxim?"

Max was standing stiffly beside his mother's chair. Her words were soft, but with the hint of something behind them. Something he had never heard in his wife's voice before, a clear, decisive note of steely resolve. He recognised the meaning behind her carefully chosen words – she did not just mean Georgiana's happiness was at stake here. She was talking about them.

He looked directly into her wide green eyes. He relaxed suddenly and walked towards her. He took her hand and lifted it to his lips. "I will not allow anyone or anything to spoil our homecoming," he said, "and I promise to make Georgie's visit here most enjoyable."

Callista felt the tension leave her body. A smile lifted the corners of her mouth and she squeezed the hand holding her own. "Thank you, Max," she said softly.

They heard the front door closing and faintly, as if from afar, the sound of a carriage driving away over the crunching gravel of the wide driveway. Lady Joanna kept her feelings firmly to herself. She said nothing more about Davina's unexpected arrival. She had seen the look exchanged between her son and Callista. Callista recognised the threat Davina posed to her happiness, to her marriage, and she had made it quite clear in her words and attitude that she would fight Davina's influence over Max to the end. She would brook no interference in her life with her husband, with her future. She was satisfied Callista was more than a match for Davina, but the threat hung over them – a silent menace – and Joanna could only pray that Max was strong enough to recognise the danger Davina posed to his future happiness.

Another pair of eyes followed the departure of the Fitzpatrick's travelling coach as it drove away from Moreland. A pair of watchful amber eyes, staring from the side garden where he had been happily picking herbs with a chattering kitchen maid. Joe watched the coach leave and he was frowning, a crease forming between his eyes. His promise to Sir Augustus came back to him once more, and the hairs on the back of his neck seemed to prickle with alarm. Her Ladyship was in trouble, he realised. He did not know exactly how, but he knew trouble was brewing and as he watched the large coach lumbering away, he knew exactly who was going to cause it.

Chapter Eighteen

They made their way up to their rooms that night after a quiet family evening spent together, telling their honeymoon tales of Cornwall and parties and picnics.

Joanna listened with a quiet contentment, Georgie with undisguised envy. She gasped in horror as Callista told her cousin how she had nearly drowned and how Max had saved her life, and Max replied with a laughing rejoinder of how if his wife had not been so foolish as to be wandering the beach in nothing but her night clothes she would never have placed herself in such a predicament.

As the evening drew to a close, the September sun setting earlier as the year drew on to autumn, Callista found herself yawning, weary after days of travelling and glad to place her hand on Max's arm as he escorted her to their rooms.

They had the suite that had once belonged to his parents. His mother had vacated them, retiring to the best guest room in preparation for her move to the Dower House.

It consisted of two fine bedrooms, connected by the most modern and up to date addition to any gentleman's country house – a bathroom. Callista raised her eyebrows at the room that had been prepared for her. Redecorated for her homecoming, it was a beautiful room of gold and soft creams, with fine hangings on the walls, elegant candle sconces and heavy golden damask curtains. A pale green and cream carpet covered the floor and it was a welcoming room fit for the new mistress of Moreland. She looked at Max with a quizzical expression on her face and promptly accompanied him through to his own chamber, a more masculine room decorated in dark maroon reds.

He watched her with an amused glint in his eyes as she examined his room and as she walked about the room, she finally returned to him. He caught her around her waist and pulled her to him.

"Well, Madam?" His voice was low, husky with the desire she invoked in him more and more.

"Very well, sir," she whispered back to him. "I love my room but I am afraid I have no intention of ever sleeping alone in there."

He kissed her upturned mouth and felt the instant spark of mutual passion ignite.

Her arms went around his neck and she pressed herself against him, abandoning herself in his arms.

"I have no intention of ever letting you sleep alone, Witch," he murmured against the creamy softness of her neck as he pressed urgent kisses against her skin.

"Sir, I fear we will shock our servants," she replied, shuddering as his mouth sent shivers of delight down her spine.

She was melting and exploding all over again. His touch had the power to leave her senses reeling and she revelled in the feeling of helpless desire that coursed through her body.

"I sent them to bed earlier," he replied. "You will have to endure my clumsy ministrations tonight." As good as his word, as he continued to caress her, his hands unbuttoned her dress and pushed it gently from her shoulders.

She stepped away from him only far enough to let the dress fall to the floor, followed by her petticoat and silken shift. With eager, shaking hands she pushed the jacket from his shoulders and pulled his cravat loose, throwing it to the floor to join the growing pile of clothes, unbuttoning his shirt and running her cool hands across the taut muscles of his chest. He groaned at her touch and with almost indecent haste, he scooped her up into his arms and carried her to the bed. She lay silently watching him as he stripped off the last of his constricting clothes, her eyes dark with desire, her cheeks flushed, her hair in wild disarray, her mouth suddenly dry as his nakedness was revealed.

She lay naked against the cool linen pillows and he joined her, his lips and tongue taking her to the heights of ecstasy before entering her, moving as one together until she cried out with the intensity of the pleasure he drove her to.

The crackle of the dying embers of the fire was the only sound that disturbed him as he lay with his sleeping wife safely curled against him.

He stared up at the canopy of the bed, turning his head slightly to look at the glow of the fire in the hearth. He found himself once again wondering at the deep intensity of his feelings as he held Callista. He had never expected to feel this way about any woman other than Davina. Davina's arrival today had stirred in him unexpected feelings. Memories of their love affair returned to haunt him; shame engulfed him as he recalled the cold way in which they had discussed his inheritance, planning his marriage of convenience to a hapless girl. He rested his cheek against Callista's hair, smiling as she made a small, almost mewing sound and snuggled further into his arms. She was definitely no hapless girl. She was a fiery, beautiful, wanton creature who had burst into his life and wrapped her arms firmly around his heart.

Davina had stared at him today with the light of invitation in her eyes. She expected him to visit her, to take up their former relationship and the thought of carrying on their liaison filled him with nothing but disgust. He sighed. He knew he had to see her. He had to tell her that whatever it was they had once shared, it was now over.

She was widowed at last, free of the man she had despised for so long. She had returned convinced he would race to her side at the first opportunity; her confidence had been palpable, so sure, so certain of her power over him that it had felt almost physical.

He, however, had experienced a profound change of heart.

He could never imagine being unfaithful to Callista. She was his wife, she deserved his total and utter devotion and as she stirred sleepily in his arms he realised with a jolt that this girl, this unexpectedly delightful creature he had married for convenience had very inconveniently made him fall in love with her. A sense of awe, of wonder, filled him. He loved her. He loved her with a deep intensity he had never before thought possible and she made him profoundly happy. He desired her with a passion that shocked and surprised him. He had thought the passion would fade after their first few weeks together but quite the reverse had happened. The passion had grown, his feelings had deepened and he had, quite frankly, fallen head over heels in love with his wife.

With a sigh, he curved himself protectively around his sleeping wife and fell into a deep, dreamless sleep beside her.

The morning dawned crisp and clear and following a brief breakfast, Max left his wife and mother to join his Estate Steward and Solicitor in his study.

The study was exactly how his father had left it. He had barely used it since his father's death and only in the few weeks leading up to his wedding when he had been forced to return home with his injured mother had he actually entered the room, to start to unravel years of neglect.

He walked over to the desk, groaning with unread letters and untouched documents and raised his eyes to the portrait of his father, sternly looking down at his only son. Max shook his head and turned away, to face the men who awaited him. His eyes briefly took in the bright flare of red on the burnished gold of the Roman helmet and a smile touched the corners of his mouth as he recalled Callista's wish to see him in fancy dress. The smile disappeared however as another memory came unbidden, a memory of blood and horror and he forced his mind away from the dreams which had haunted him.

"Gentlemen." He acknowledged his waiting staff. "I have

ignored you and my estate for far too long. Please be seated and we will start work – I need to know the worst and how I can repair the neglect of the last few years."

Smiling, relieved at last at the new maturity which had finally reached their young master, Mr Hedges, the family Solicitor, and Mr Bailey, the Estate Manager, seated themselves opposite Max's large oak desk.

He paused momentarily to stop and raise his eyes to his father once again before seating himself in his father's large worn old seat. He smiled at them. "I think I must order my own chair, gentlemen," he began. "My father's seat is a little worn and creaky for me. I fear I will be sitting here for many a long hour from now on and a new chair is the first thing on my somewhat overcrowded agenda."

He laughed softly, no longer finding the look in his father's painted eyes as stern as he had done formerly. He saw instead the kindness and pride his father had taken in him and his responsibilities, from the lowliest servant to the largest of farm houses on his estate, his father had cared for them all and he was finally about to step into his father's footsteps.

"I hope I live up to my father's legacy," he said, more to himself than the bemused estate manager.

"I am sure your father would be extremely proud of you, My Lord," he said quietly.

"Very well, gentlemen," he said, "shall we begin?"

While Max began the arduous work of sorting out years of neglect his cavalier attitude had caused to his estate, Callista toured Moreland Hall with her mother in law. She met her Housekeeper and Steward and Cook, all the servants lined up in the large open hall to welcome their new mistress. It was a large and prosperous establishment and Callista was soon dizzy with trying to remember the names of all her staff. She endeared herself to them all, however, remembering quite a few from her previous introduction on the day before her wedding and apologising quite sincerely to those she had forgotten.

Lady Joanna and the Housekeeper and Cook instructed the new Marchioness on what her daily duties would be, from ordering the daily meals to scrutinising the household accounts. She would meet with her Housekeeper every morning before breakfast and together they would decide on which rooms would be cleaned that day, what social events would need to be prepared for, the Cook would be consulted over what meals would take place, how many guests to cater for. The running of such an establishment as Moreland was a complex and demanding role and Callista felt quite overwhelmed by all her duties by the time she managed to rejoin Georgiana in the Drawing Room. With a sigh, she seated herself beside her cousin and looked enviously at the framed piece of embroidery Georgie was engaged in.

Georgie raised laughing eyes to her cousin. "You have been gone quite an age, Callie," she teased her. "Have you learned all the secrets of your establishment yet, my dear?"

"I have not," Callista replied. "I am quite amazed at the amount of work it takes to run such a house. I fear I will never become as adept as Lady Joanna – she makes it all seem so effortless."

Georgiana thoughtfully sat back in her seat to observe the frown forming between Callista's eyes.

"Callie – you ran your father's house, you organised all the events expected of the Vicar and when you came to us, you were more of a help than Mama ever gave you credit for – my Ball would have been a disaster without you to keep us all on track."

She laughed softly and took Callista's hand in hers. "Come along, Callie, it is time for a little relaxation. I have taken the liberty of ordering a pony and trap and a certain young groom to accompany us. We are going out for some fresh air."

Callista smiled, relaxing at the thought of both fresh air and the invigorating company of young Joe.

"Let us get ready at once," she exclaimed and with renewed energy the two young ladies retired to their bedrooms, coming out moments later wearing short Spencer jackets over their muslin dresses, matching bonnets and carrying warm shawls against the cooler September air.

Joe and another groom were both awaiting them as they left the house. The older groom had insisted on accompanying them. Joe was still a little inexperienced to be allowed to escort the new Marchioness around the Moreland estate alone and unprotected.

The ladies were helped into the little trap and with Joe seated beside her, Callista was treated to a running commentary from him on what he had seen and what he had found out since his arrival on the estate. The older groom, William, frowned at the lad's unbecoming forwardness but Her Ladyship laughed with delight at Joe's description of the stables and the kitchens and he was forced to admit that the lad hit the nail on the head with his account of day-to-day life at Moreland.

Joe was happy, Callista found out. He had made friends, the Cook had taken to him, one of the older stable lads had taken him under his wing and Joe was fast becoming both an accomplished horseman and quite a favourite with the other servants. His relationship with Her Ladyship might have caused jealousy in some quarters but his feisty nature and his refusal to submit to bullying or intimidation from anyone had earned him respect from the other staff.

They trotted through the grounds of the Hall, leaving from the front gates, and Callista told William to take her on a tour of the estate nearest the Hall, not wanting to go too far on her first trip.

"I think this is something I should do regularly," she said to Georgiana. "I need to be able to find my way around eventually."

Joe pointed out a fine house just outside the gates of the Hall. "That's the Dower 'ouse," he explained. "Lady Joanna's movin' over there soon."

It was a large, square and respectable building. Solid and reassuring and Callista gazed at it, pleased that Max's mother would not be too far away from them. Far enough for privacy but close enough to be available for advice when called for.

The little pony trotted past and soon they were approaching the dark shadows of a wood that bordered the property.

"Have you been here before, Georgie?" Callista asked, staring doubtfully at the large trees framing either side of the narrow path they were driving down.

"No." Georgie too seemed a little nervous as they trotted through the wood, sunshine dappling them as the sun tried to break through the heavy boughs of the trees, the green of the leaves turning gold in the autumn sunshine. "Damon's estate is the other way so I have not yet explored this area."

"Begging Your Ladyship's pardon but I thought you might like to see our local historical landmarks," William interjected. "It draws visitors from all over the country – it's a very popular site."

Callista and Georgiana smiled at each other.

"How wonderful!" Georgie exclaimed. "I had no idea there was anything so exciting around here."

"What exactly is it, William?" Callista enquired.

"It's just here, Your Ladyship," William replied and pointed with his whip to a clearing ahead where sunshine lit up a broad flat plain.

"Whatever is it, Callie?" Georgiana was alarmed suddenly as all colour fled from Callista's face.

Callista was clinging on to her cousin's arm with fingers which suddenly dug into her flesh like talons.

The little pony and trap emerged into the sunshine of that September afternoon on to the broad plain which held twenty tall, awesome, standing stones. Grey and majestic, they soared heavenwards, standing alone and straight; twenty granite sentinels standing guard around the broad flat stone which lay in the centre of their stone circle, raised on a platform, supported by four squat granite legs.

Sightseers were walking around the circle, exclaiming at their majesty – at their antiquity and ancient power.

Georgiana was staring at them with undisguised admiration. Callista and Joe however, felt nothing but alarm although neither of them could explain why.

William drew the pony to a stop and he helped Georgiana to alight. He held out his hand to Callista and she found herself stepping out of the little trap with something like trepidation. Driving through the woods had been difficult enough – the sense of recognition and fear had been almost overpowering – standing now amongst the towering standing stones, she felt cold and clutched her shawl around her shoulder in an attempt to stop herself shivering.

She experienced again that feeling which had been growing stronger over the past few months. She closed her eyes and behind her lids she saw a battle; men dressed in fur and leather, long haired and bearded in direct contrast to the clean shaven Romans and the white robed men they all battled. There was a storm, thunder and lightning and rain pounded the battle below – there was noise and screaming and blood – so much blood. She opened her eyes quickly before the dizzying disorientating sensation threatened to overcome her. Her face was white, her eyes a vivid green and she swayed with the intensity of the emotions surging through her.

A small, cold hand suddenly slipped into hers and she dragged her eyes away from the stone circle to look down into the pale face of young Joe. He was looking as distressed as she was feeling and with a deep shuddering breath she managed to pull herself together.

"I don't like this place, Miss," he said. "It feels – bad." He could not put into words his own feelings. Bad was as close as he could come to describing the fear, the sense of hopelessness and evil that he felt emanating from the stone circle before him.

Georgiana was holding Callista's arm, alarmed at the pale cheeks of her cousin.

"Callie," she exclaimed. "Are you unwell?"

Callista shook her head. "I'm sorry, Georgie, I feel a little faint that is all. I will be better presently."

She took a deep steadying breath but her head swam and the vision of a tall blond-haired Druid brandishing a wickedly sharp knife coming closer to her was suddenly as real as the concerned face of her cousin in front of her. With a small cry, she crumpled to the floor as Georgiana screamed out her name.

The scream and Joe's shout of alarm attracted the attention of the sightseers within the stone circle. However, before anyone could come to their assistance, the sound of horses coming closer alerted Georgiana to the sight and sound of two riders heading speedily towards her.

As she and Joe knelt on the ground beside Callista, attempting to revive her, the relief she felt at the sight of her betrothed galloping towards her was tempered slightly by the knowledge that his companion was his sister, Davina. They stopped beside the small group and Damon dismounted immediately running the last few yards to her side.

Davina dismounted elegantly and walked over to where Damon was attempting to revive Callista. Between them, he and Georgiana removed Callie's bonnet and loosened the top buttons of her gown to assist her breathing.

"What happened?" Damon was quizzing them.

"I don't know." Georgiana was distraught. "One minute we were about to visit the Stone Circle when Callista became anxious and stopped, she went very pale and then she fainted."

"It was the Stones," Joe said, his voice low but clear. "She was frightened of them." He looked up into the concerned face of Sir Damon and glared at Davina who was looking down at the small group with undisguised boredom.

A spark of interest suddenly appeared in her eyes. "Lady Langley was frightened, what on earth by?"

Georgiana was flustered and upset. "Callie was terrified of them," she blurted out. "I don't know why but she would not go near them and she just suddenly fainted."

A movement and a moan from her cousin diverted her attention. Callista's eyelids fluttered and Damon stood up, pulling Callista up with him. He lifted her into his arms and carried her over to the small pony and trap as William brought it round for them.

Georgiana and Joe followed and Georgiana climbed into the trap as Damon gently placed Callista next to her cousin.

Georgiana put her arms around Callista's shoulders and smiled gratefully at her fiancé.

"Thank you, Damon. I don't know what I would have done without you."

"We were just on our way over to visit you. Davina had a fancy to ride this way luckily."

Georgiana turned her smile to her future sister in law. "I am grateful you did, thank you, Davina."

Davina inclined her head. "I wonder why Lady Langley felt so distraught at visiting this place," she smiled, her eyes alight.

Georgiana sighed, shaking her head. "I have no idea, she was just so – so frightened."

Callista made another small moaning sound.

"Callie, my dear, did you hurt yourself when you fainted?"

Callista opened her eyes, shuddering slightly as she came back to her senses. "What happened?" she whispered.

"You fainted, dearest," Georgiana replied.

Callista's eyes focused and with a deep breath, she straightened and looked about her, realising for the first time that Damon and Davina were both with them.

"Are you all right now, Callie?" Damon asked, anxiety still in his voice.

She nodded. "I am so sorry to have worried you all," she apologised. Her voice faint but clear.

"I think we had better get you home," Damon interjected.

"Were you coming over to see us for any reason, dearest?" Georgiana asked him.

"We cannot entertain too much due to Davina being in mourning but we were hoping you would all be able to come to dinner with us tonight."

Georgiana's face light up with pleasure but as Callista slumped against her once more, she turned her attention back to her cousin. "I think we had better wait and see how Callie recovers," she said softly. "I will send word."

Davina had been watching the proceedings with a slight air of boredom. "Please pass on our invitation to Max," she said and holding out the reins of his horse to Damon, she returned to her own highly spirited animal and pulled herself easily up into the saddle. She arranged her leg over the pommel and settled the horse as she smoothed her skirts and straightened up, waiting for Damon to rejoin her.

"Will you be all right getting home?" Damon asked, not willing to leave his betrothed.

"Yes, of course," Georgiana replied.

Callista rallied and he could see some colour coming back to her cheeks.

"Thank you, Damon," Callista said. "We will go straight home now – I feel perfectly well now, I assure you."

"If you are sure?"

"We are." Georgiana nodded and holding out her hand squeezed his own hand, smiling into his face.

"Drive on William," he ordered, stepping away from the small pony and trap.

Returning to Davina, he too mounted his horse and together they waited until the pony trotted away from the site of the Standing Stones.

Davina was smiling and Damon looked thoughtfully at his sister. "What is it, Davina?" he asked.

She nodded towards the circle of the tall granite stones. "I was just wondering what it was about a few old stones could possibly frighten anyone," she sneered.

"The area is very atmospheric," Damon countered.

"Atmospheric?" Davina laughed softly. "What rubbish."

Damon pointed to the large, flat altar stone. "Look there," he said. "History tells that human sacrifice was carried out at that spot."

Davina stared over to where Damon pointed. "I suppose if one were weak enough to be susceptible to such stories then presumably the area could be considered atmospheric."

She pulled on her horse's reins and wheeled it around to face away from the Stones. "Lady Langford must be extremely sensitive to be so frightened by a few old relics like this."

Damon shook his head at his sister's cynicism. "For whatever reason, Callista was genuinely terrified. I don't think she will be returning here anytime soon."

Davina paused and a strange, half smile lifted her lips. "She would go half mad with fear, would she not?" she murmured.

Damon frowned at his sister. He knew there was no love lost between Davina and Callista but he did not like the expression on her face, the sudden glint of malice in her eyes and the suggestion behind her words that there would be nothing she would like more than to further distress Callista by any means possible.

He kicked his horse. "Home, I think, my dear," he said firmly and started to ride away from the Stones.

Davina waited, her smile becoming wider as she considered the Stones for another moment before flicking her riding crop against the flanks of her horse and riding quickly after her brother.

Max and his steward rode together through the gates of Moreland and saw the small pony and trap stop in front of the entrance door.

"Thank you for accompanying me today, my lord," Mr Bailey said, his tone sincere and heartfelt.

"Not at all, Bailey," Max replied. "I am just sorry it has taken me so long to realise the amount of work needing doing on my lands."

His face was stern, his feelings in turmoil. Relief that he was at last taking responsibility for his home was matched in equal parts by the dismay on finding out how neglected he had allowed his estate to become.

His Steward and his mother had done their best but the lack of a master's hand was obvious. Run down farms, overgrown fields and woodland, the list of work to do seemed never ending. Many of his tenants were living in homes that were little more than hovels. His feelings of shame and guilt were overwhelming – it was going to take months of dedicated hard work, and a lot of money to bring his estate back up to the standard he desired. His father would have been appalled at the state of disrepair he had allowed his lands to fall into and, not for the first time, Max felt utter relief that the trustees would soon release the money left to him by his father. It was going to be expensive to repair the damage but with good husbandry and careful planning, Max knew it was not an impossible task.

He saw Callie and Georgiana get out of the small vehicle and watched as Callista waved to little Joe as he and William trotted away. He smiled at the sight of them – and at the way Callista's eyes lit up as her husband drew closer.

He dismounted and handed over the reins to his steward. Bailey touched his riding whip to his hat and bowed in the direction of Her Ladyship.

"I will see you again tomorrow, Bailey," Max promised and slapped his horse's rump as Bailey walked the horses around to the rear of the house in the direction of the stables.

Callista was waiting for him by the front door. Her face was pale but she smiled as he joined her.

"Callie, are you unwell?" He was suddenly anxious at her unaccustomed pallor.

She shook her head. "I felt a little faint, that is all," she replied.

Taking her hand, he led her inside where Georgiana was removing her bonnet.

"We went to view the Standing Stones," Georgie explained. "Callie fainted when she saw them."

"Callie!" Immediately concerned, Max stopped and took in his wife's slightly dishevelled appearance. "Are you all right now? Do we need to send for a doctor?"

Callista shook her head firmly refuting the need for medical attention. "Indeed not at all, Max. I am perfectly well. I was just dizzy and disorientated for a few minutes that was all."

The memory came to Max of that night at his mansion in London, when the young musician had played and Callista had been in tears – explaining that she had seen a vision of tall, standing stones.

"I was going to take you myself," he said softly. "You might not have felt so emotional had I been there."

"I'm not surprised Callista felt overcome." Lady Joanna's voice rang out as she joined them in the wide hall. "The place is positively haunted, you know."

"Mother!" Max admonished her. "Please do not alarm Callista in such a manner."

Lady Joanna came closer and examined Callista's pale face with a concerned eye. Colour was returning to Callie's cheeks.

"Callista is obviously sensitive to atmosphere," she said. "And there have been stories of strange sightings and activity at that place for hundreds of years."

Georgiana was agog with curiosity at Lady Joanna's words. "Really? It certainly was very atmospheric."

Lady Joanna took Callista's arm and started leading her into the Drawing Room. "Apparently it was the scene of a major battle hundreds of years ago – there was a lot of death and destruction. I'm not surprised it has an atmosphere." She paused and looked back at her son. "That was where your Roman helmet came from, my dear. Did your father not tell you the story?"

They followed Lady Joanna into the Drawing Room and seated themselves as the Butler brought in the tea tray. Pausing to pour the tea, Lady Joanna handed out the teacups and Max took a sip before he answered his mother.

"Father told me he had allowed some archaeologists to carry out a dig and they unearthed the helmet then. I was away at school at the time and missed the event."

"Yes, but they also unearthed a grave of some sort," Lady Joanna replied. "They were very careful not to disturb the remains, of course, it was all very respectful – but they removed the helmet and some other artefacts. They found the grave near to the Standing Stones and it contained the remains of two people, a man and woman. However, from the description given by the experts they deduced that the woman's remains were much older than that of the man – she had jewellery which proclaimed her to be from a wealthy family – probably a Celtic princess from what they said – the man was a Roman however."

Georgiana and Callista were listening wide eyed to Lady Joanna's tale. "How strange," Callista murmured. "I wonder how they came to be buried together?"

Lady Joanna sipped her tea and smiled graciously at her daughter in law. "The Celts and the Romans fought many battles around here, perhaps marriage between two opposing sides garnered some peace to the people."

Callista smiled, feeling a little uneasy. "They must have loved each other though, to be buried together."

Max bit into a sandwich, realising how hungry he was after the full day out with his Steward.

"She must have died first though, if her remains were older than his."

Georgiana smiled, her eyes suddenly dreamy. "How romantic," she sighed. "He must have loved his princess to want to be buried with her."

Max finished his sandwich and reached for another. "All this talk of death is making me hungry," he exclaimed, causing his wife to laugh and his mother to cast a disapproving glance his way.

"What happened to her jewellery, Lady Joanna?" Georgiana asked.

"The archaeologists handed some over to my husband – there was a lovely golden bracelet which he gave to me but the rest was placed with the family jewellery. I will show you tomorrow, Callie, it will all come to you now anyway. The Roman helmet held a fascination for your father, Max. He had it cleaned and polished and it remains in your study still."

Max paused, considering for a moment his father and the study and the burnished metal of the helmet, its red plume as vivid and bright as it must have been a thousand years ago.

He turned to Callista, noting how thoughtful she was, remembering how pale she had been as she returned to the house.

"Damon and his sister helped us at the Stones," Georgiana

said. "They were on their way to invite us to dinner but as Callista was indisposed I said we would have to let them know later."

Max was frowning slightly. "Georgie, might I ask you to write a note to Damon thanking him but refusing his kind invitation. I have a lot to do tonight and I really don't think Callie should exert herself again today."

Lady Joanna cast a shrewd eye over her son and his wife and noted with some approval Max's concern over her indisposition.

Georgiana drank her tea and looking up at the clock, stood up. "I will write to him now. Please excuse me." Curtseying prettily to Lady Joanna and Max, she took her leave.

Lady Joanna smiled after her young charge.

"I will miss having her with us," she sighed. "However, I know you will be glad to have the house to yourselves soon enough." She refilled her cup and sipped at her tea. "Mrs Spencer has written – she informs me she will be here by the end of the week so tomorrow I really must make sure the Dower House is prepared."

"What will you be doing tomorrow, Max?" Callista asked, realising that she had hardly seen him all day and was missing his company.

He grimaced, shaking his head at the thought of the work ahead of him. "More inspection of the estate, I'm afraid," he replied. "I've only just scratched the surface of what needs to be done."

She reached forward and squeezed his hands. "I will help as much as I can," she said softly.

For a moment their eyes locked and had his mother not been present, he would have kissed his wife there and then. He squeezed her hand in response. "I know you will," he replied.

Lady Joanna's cup rattled softly against the saucer, jolting their attention back into the room.

"Mr Hedges informs me that you will have to go to London soon, Max," she said.

At the mention of his Solicitor's name, Max frowned and

turned back to his mother. "He did not say so this morning, Mama."

"Mr Hedges is the family Solicitor; he does not manage your father's will. You have to go to London to meet with your Trustees."

By the tightening of her husband's lips, Callista surmised that he was not happy with this information.

"I've only just returned from honeymoon," he said, his voice cool. "I did not envisage a further journey to London. I have too much to do here to leave so soon."

Lady Joanna sighed. "I know, my dear, but the sooner you go and get everything settled, the sooner you can return and put the Estate in order."

Max suspected that his mother was determined he should be sent out of the way of Davina rather than any other reason but unwilling to upset Callista, he did not pursue a discussion with his mother.

He merely stood up and bowed stiffly to his mother. "I will make arrangements to leave in a day or two. Bailey is expecting me to accompany him tomorrow so I cannot disappoint him. Excuse me please, Callie, I have some work to do."

Callista watched him walk out of the Drawing Room, realising that his sudden frown and change of mood was down to more than his mother's insistence on him leaving them to go to London.

She looked over to her mother in law, whose calm demeanour and smiling face hid her true feelings.

"Why do you wish him to go to London so soon?" she asked her directly.

Lady Joanna did not look in the least discomfited. "Family business only, my dear. Nothing for you to be concerned about."

Callista opened her mouth to protest but Lady Joanna stood up and held her hands out to her daughter in law.

"Come, my dear, let us go and join Georgiana. Then we must put our heads together and decide what to do about her engagement party. It is only a few weeks away, and in all likelihood

Max will be away for most of that time – it will be up to you to organise the event."

Callista stopped in her tracks. "Will Max not wish me to accompany him to London?" she enquired, not pleased to be parted from her husband so soon after their return.

"Very probably," Lady Joanna replied drily, "but I fear your presence will be a distraction to him and cause him to spend more time in London than we would like."

Lady Joanna swept out of the Drawing Room and led her towards the stairs. Callista paused outside Max's study, wanting to go in and talk to him about his impending departure but Joanna would not let her stop and together they ascended the curving staircase.

Callista stopped once and looked down at the hallway but Max's door remained firmly closed and, with a sigh, she followed her mother in law to find Georgiana, happily writing a letter to Damon and who, upon their entrance asked their opinion over what to wear when Damon visited the following morning. Callista, determined to put behind her the events of that afternoon, firmly turned her mind away from her fainting spell and joined in with her cousin's discussion with Lady Joanna on what sort of gown would be most suitable for a young lady's hotly anticipated engagement party.

Lihanna 10

It was a different servant who brought her food and drink that night. It was one of her own people and although he smiled at her, guarded as he was by a Centurion, he did not speak, but set her supper down in front of her with a bow and left immediately.

The drink was mead. She drank it down thirstily, but grimaced as she realised it had a strange, bitter taste to it. She put down the goblet with a frown and wiped her mouth. She found she could not eat the food placed on the table and pushed it away.

Lihanna stood up and stared down at the discarded goblet with a growing suspicion and dismay. She felt suddenly dizzy and it was with a moan of horror that she stumbled over to Julius' bed and collapsed in a heap onto the thick fur rugs.

She heard the fighting as though through a fog. She could hardly open her eyes and her limbs felt so heavy she could not move them. She heard the clashing of swords and the cries of battle but nothing could make her reluctant body work.

The shadowy figures who entered the dark interior of the tent met with no resistance as they wrapped her in a thick woollen cloak and lifted her from the bed. Her head lolled back and her arm trailed as she was carried from the tent. Only vaguely aware of the fighting, she was carried through the village and she was able to force her eyes open only long enough to see the soldiers Julius had left guarding his quarters were lying either dead or unconscious outside the tent.

She gave up the unequal struggle at last and lapsed once more into unconsciousness.

Chapter Nineteen

Max was unusually silent that night, appearing deep in thought throughout dinner and later, he excused himself and left the ladies to return to his study. Georgiana entertained them however, making them laugh, albeit unintentionally with her description of Davina's waspish conversation the last time they had spoken, regarding the forthcoming nuptials of her brother and Georgiana.

"She seemed quite put out, Callie, when Damon informed her that we would not be expecting her to live with us. Why, I think she fully intended to move permanently into Damon's London house."

As Callista had wondered how Damon was going to juggle his brotherly responsibilities with his marital arrangements, she was quite pleased to hear that he intended to make Georgiana his priority.

A view Lady Joanna concurred with whole-heartedly. "I think the sooner Lady Fitzpatrick sets up her own establishment, whether it is in London or back in Ireland, the sooner I for one would like it."

Callista paused in sipping her coffee and looked over the rim of the fine porcelain cup at her mother in law. Lady Joanna had never been Davina's ally, in fact she had made it plain on many occasions how she disliked the woman, but she wondered just how deeply ingrained the older woman's dislike of Davina could be. Uneasily, she realised it was to do with Max and she found herself silently agreeing with both Lady Joanna and Georgiana in the hope that the beautiful and dangerous Lady Davina Fitzpatrick would soon grow tired of country life and leave them in peace.

The evening drew to a close and the ladies prepared to ascend the stairs to bed. Callista stopped outside Max's study and saw the light still shining beneath the door.

Cautiously, she opened the door to see Max at his desk, pen in hand, reading through some papers.

She went inside quietly and waited silently until he realised he was no longer alone. He was frowning but his brow cleared as he saw his wife standing by the door.

"Callie, I'm sorry, have I kept you up?" he asked, putting his pen down.

"No, Max, I was just on my way to bed. I wondered how long you would be."

He grimaced, indicating the paperwork before him. "I need to clear a few things before I leave for London," he sighed. "Go up, my dear, I'll join you presently."

She moved towards him and stood beside his chair. Bending down, she kissed him gently.

"Don't be long, Max," she said softly.

He caught her hand in his and pressed it against his lips. His eyes sought hers and for a moment she saw something there, some deep trouble, an anguish she had never seen before.

"We will only be apart a few days, Max, surely," she smiled at him.

He nodded, forcing a tight smile onto his lips. "Yes, of course," he replied. He kissed her fingers once more and released her.

Smiling, she walked back towards the door. "I'll send some coffee through for you," she promised and leaving the room, rang the bell for the Butler to organise a tray to be taken in to her husband.

She went upstairs with Georgie and into her bedroom where her maid awaited her. In a few minutes she was ready for bed, sitting beside the fireside waiting for Max. Dismissing her maid, she waited until the fire burned low and the candles spluttered.

It was after midnight when Max came upstairs and found her, asleep on the rug in front of the fire.

With a smile, he bent over her and lifted her gently into his arms. He carried her over to their wide, comfortable bed and carefully lowered her onto the crisp linen sheets. He pulled the covers over her and stood for a moment, watching her as she slept, as innocently as a babe. He bent and pressed another kiss onto her forehead before leaving her to undress. He slipped in beside her and for a few moments listened to her breathing, until, with a heavy heart, he too fell asleep.

Lethargic, sleepily stretching in her bed the following morning, Callista awoke to the sound of her maid moving around the bedroom, drawing back the heavy curtains to let the late summer sun flood the room.

She felt so tired. Her eyes felt heavy and her head was aching.

"What time is it?" she asked as Alice came over carrying a silver tray.

She placed the tray on the bedside table and as Callista struggled to sit up, Alice reached behind her and plumped up the pillows.

"It's after 9, Your Ladyship," Alice replied. "The Master has already left and Lady Joanna asked for a tray be brought to your room. Are you feeling well, My Lady? You seem a little flushed."

In truth, Callista did not feel well but she managed a wan smile at her maid. "I fear I might have slept a little too heavily," she sighed. "I am sure a reviving cup of your splendid tea will put me back to rights."

She leaned back against her pillows, wondering why the room seemed to swim around her.

Alice seemed unperturbed, pouring her mistress a cup of tea and handing the cup and saucer to Callista.

"Lady Joanna is so excited, My Lady," she said brightly. "A letter has arrived this morning by courier, her friend is on her way and will be here some time later today. The servants at the Dower House are busy already making it ready for her arrival. "

Callista took a sip of her tea, the welcoming liquid seeming to revive her a little.

"And my husband, did the Steward say where they were going today?"

"No, My Lady." Alice stopped in her movements, returning

to the bed carrying a dark red gown for Callista to wear that day. "But, begging your pardon, there is such a lot of work to do to the estate – he is likely to be gone all day again just touring around and seeing for himself what needs to be done."

Callista frowned. "I had no idea there was so much need," she said softly. "I had hoped he would take me to meet his tenants this week but it seems I will have to wait a little longer."

Alice smiled at her mistress. "There's plenty of time, My Lady," she exclaimed. "And I understand Miss Georgiana is wishful of a trip to Bath to buy a new gown for her engagement party – she was talking to Lady Joanna this morning about you both going for a few days."

Callista laughed at the thought of her exuberant cousin. As though Georgiana did not already own enough dresses but she thought back to her own engagement and smiled again. There was something to be said for wanting to look one's best for the man in your life.

She put her cup down and pushed the covers away. "Well, if I may not accompany my husband to Town then he can have no objection to me joining Georgie on a trip to Bath," she said as she pulled on her dressing gown. "And in the meantime, unless anyone has any other plan for me, I think a further tour of the estate today is called for."

Revived and refreshed, Callista attended to her toilette and dressed in the dark red dress laid out for her by her maid. The colour normally enhanced her colouring but today her cheeks were pale and it was only with the best efforts of Alice that she managed to make herself presentable, with her hair neatly styled and a white scarf tucked around her neck and into her bodice. Nevertheless, she did not feel quite as bright as normal that morning and it was a subdued Callista who went to find her cousin and mother in law an hour later.

As predicted, Lady Joanna was about to repair to the Dower House to ensure all was in readiness for the arrival of her new companion. Georgiana was eager to engage Callista in a trip to Bath and discussions were in full flow as to the suitability of the two young ladies going alone to that city. Lady Joanna was firmly of the opinion that married lady or not, the new Lady Langley was a little too inexperienced to act as chaperone to the exuberant Miss Wetherby, in a strange city, new to both of them.

"May I suggest then Lady Joanna that Georgiana and I delay our trip until Mrs Spencer has settled in for a few days and then the four of us go together?"

Callista's suggestion met with approval from her mother in law and a slight pout from her cousin but her sunny disposition was soon lifted by the announcement of the arrival of her fiancé a few minutes later.

Damon had come to escort the two young ladies on a further tour of the area. Since Callista's unfortunate episode yesterday at the Standing Stones, he had offered to stand in for Max and show Callista and his bride to be a little more of their future homes.

As Lady Joanna could find nothing to object to with this arrangement, she departed in good spirits for the Dower House whilst the young ladies donned jackets and bonnets and accompanied Damon to his open carriage to take advantage of the warmth of that late summer's day.

Georgiana fairly glowed with happiness as she seated herself beside her betrothed and Callista sat opposite them, with her back to the driver and accompanying groom, young Joe, who, it appeared had managed to convince Damon's driver that he was more or less Lady Langley's personal servant and went everywhere with her. As Damon had raised no demur, choosing to be amused by Joe's demands, he had allowed the young man to come along.

At Callista's request, they stopped at the nearby village of Moreland as she had been quite entranced by the bustling little community on her brief visit weeks earlier before her wedding to Max.

There were houses, a small coaching inn, a Church and quite a variety of shops for them to look around but Callista, taking Joe firmly by the hand, marched the whole party, somewhat bemusedly, towards the small school nestling within the boundaries of the Church and vicarage.

"Miss, 'ere – where we goin'?" the young man demanded, although he made no move to remove his hand from her own dainty white gloved one.

Lady Langley exchanged a glance with Damon and Georgiana and determined not to be put off by the glint of merriment in Damon's eyes, she stopped outside the schoolroom door.

"Joseph – my dear young man, it has come to me lately that I have sadly neglected your education. Why, I do not know if you can read and write and I feel it remiss of me to have overlooked this small detail."

Joe was frowning, mutiny written all over his countenance. "I don't need to go to school," he objected.

Callista crouched down to look her young protector in the eye. "My dear, you will oblige me by going to school – I do not want to think I have failed in my duty to your mother by not looking after you to the best of my ability."

She spoke to him gently but he could see by the light in her eye that she was serious. At the mention of his mother, Joe hesitated. He could argue all day but he recognised in his gentle mistress the same steely resolve his mother had exhibited when she had wanted him to obey her.

He was not going to give up without a fight however.

"But Sir Max needs me in the stables," he protested further. "How am I gonna learn to be a good groom if I'm stuck in 'ere all day?"

Unperturbed by his argument, Callista merely smiled and brushed a stray lock of thick blond hair from his forehead.

"I am sure we can come to some agreement with the stables," she reassured him.

"But the other lads'll think I'm too good for the job," he wailed.

Her Ladyship was not for moving. "You are the youngest lad in those stables, Joe. The other lads are local boys who all, I am certain, came to this very school to learn their letters." She paused and straightened. "All the other boys can read and write, Joe," she continued gently. "I do not want them thinking you ignorant."

With this final statement, she rapped smartly on the schoolhouse door and had it opened a moment later by a plainly dressed young woman, rosy cheeked and merry eyed who was at once taken aback by her unexpected visitors.

"Your – Your Ladyship… Sir Damon…" she stammered and dropped a hasty curtsey as the small party entered the schoolroom.

It contained rows of benches upon which were seated twenty or so children who all looked up at their entrance.

Callista held out her hand and shook hands with the woman. "Good morning – you obviously know who I am but may I enquire as to whom I am speaking?"

Regaining her composure, the woman returned her greeting. "Good Morning, Your Ladyship. I am Mrs Bradshaw, the Vicar's wife and schoolmistress. I saw you at your wedding to the Marquis last month." She stepped back and indicated the children with a small gesture of her hand.

"Children, this is Lady Langley. Please say hello to Her Ladyship."

At once the children executed various bows and curtseys and, as one voice piped up, "How do you do, Your ladyship?"

Callista heard Georgiana stifle a small giggle behind her but she turned to the children and bowed her head in their direction.

"How do you do? I am very pleased to meet you all," Callista replied politely.

A small disturbance at the door announced the arrival of the Vicar himself. Alerted by one of his parishioners as to the visitors to his wife's schoolroom, he had immediately left the vicarage to come over and greet them in person.

"Sir Damon, Lady Langley, what an unexpected pleasure," he exclaimed bowing in their direction. "May I invite you to join me in the vicarage for some light refreshment?"

Damon, on recognising the intent in Callista's eyes moved to speak to the Vicar.

"Why thank you, Mr Bradshaw, but this is just an informal

visit. Lady Callista has only recently returned from honeymoon and she was wishful of meeting the villagers herself."

Callista shook hands with the Vicar.

"Thank you, Mr Bradshaw, I would be delighted to come to tea another day but today I have brought this young man to meet your wife and enquire as to whether there is room in your school for him?"

Whilst the adults had been making their polite conversation, Joe had, meantime, been looking around the room, at the rows of children – some his own age and others both older and younger. The older boys were obviously weighing him up and he bristled, pulling himself up to his tallest height and glaring back at them. Girls were hiding their faces behind the small slate blackboards they held and a few giggles could be heard throughout the room.

Mrs Bradshaw looked down at Joe and held out her hand to shake his.

With a glance up at Callista, who nodded and pushed his shoulder slightly, he took her hand and bowed over it politely.

"Pleased to meet you," he muttered.

Callista smiled down at her young charge, fully aware of his dismay but determined to do the best by him. She knew that she was doing the right thing.

Mrs Bradshaw smiled kindly down at him. "Welcome to our school, Joe," she said. "Would you like to start now?"

Joe looked up in alarm at these words. He was not wearing his best dress uniform it was true but he was clad in the livery of the Langley household and he was aware that he was considerably better dressed than the rest of the boys in that room.

Lady Langley seemed impervious to his dismay and smiled gently at her young charge.

"I think the sooner the better," she replied on his behalf.

Mrs Bradshaw led the reluctant boy over to the front row of the schoolroom and placed him directly in front of her.

She provided him with a slate and a stick of chalk and turned to bid farewell to her unexpected visitors.

With a sigh of satisfaction and deliberately ignoring the suppressed merriment of her companions, Callista waved farewell to the crestfallen young man and allowed the Vicar to escort them outside.

Pausing to thank Mr Bradshaw and discuss with him the times of the services that following Sunday, Callista was suddenly aware of a disturbance on the small village street behind her.

The whole party turned in time to see a large, florid man, red-cheeked and angry, berating in a loud voice an unfortunate creature in the shape of an overburdened and decidedly ancient-looking donkey.

He was providing amusement to the various village folk standing around as he pulled on the donkey's bridle, cursing and shouting at the animal and was not in the least disconcerted when the laughter turned to shouts of dismay when his bad temper led to him producing a large stick and commencing to beat the struggling animal.

Georgiana and Damon stood frozen in shock as Callista, with the light of an avenging angel in her eyes, picked up her skirts and ran down the path leading from the schoolroom.

The villagers, the Vicar and her companions had no chance to react as Callista, filled with fury at the cruelty of the man ran over and wrested the stick from his hand. She then turned it on the man and brought it down on his shoulders in a sold, satisfying thwack.

"How dare you, sir," she exclaimed, her eyes blazing with temper. "How dare you mistreat this animal – he is vastly overburdened and now you expect him to work faster by beating him to death."

The florid man, astonished into silence by the sight of this Lady of Quality berating him so soundly began to make his excuses but Callista was having none of it. Throwing the offending stick to the far side of the road, she turned to the donkey and started removing the load from its back.

Sir Damon and Georgiana had by this time joined her. "Callie, what are you doing?" exclaimed the mortified Georgie.

"I am taking this creature home, Georgie," she replied. "Help me to unburden it."

"That's my donkey!" the angry man started to protest, to be silenced by a single, withering glance from Her Ladyship.

"And this is my husband's land and village," she retorted. "He will not tolerate such disgusting behaviour and neither will I."

By this time, quite a crowd had gathered and all were watching in awe as the new Lady Langley finished throwing the man's belongings into the dusty road.

"Damon," she turned to her future cousin. "Do you have the wherewithal about you to buy this creature?"

Sir Damon would have willingly run the villain through but he recognised the impropriety of so doing and reached into his waistcoat pocket from where he produced a golden sovereign.

He tossed it to the astonished man. "Here – take it – it's far more than this creature is worth but if Lady Langley desires it – so be it."

Murmurs of approval were emanating from the gathered crowd and various school children from Mrs Bradshaw's class were observing the scene from the doorway and window.

The donkey, free from its restrictions, lifted its head and nuzzled the lady removing the heavy weights from its back.

Callista took the bridle and led it into the garden of the schoolroom, leaving behind untidy bundles all over the dusty road.

"Mrs Bradshaw," she called and immediately that good lady appeared.

"Yes, Your Ladyship?"

Callista handed over the reins of the liberated donkey to the Vicar's wife. "Kindly instruct Joe to bring this donkey home with him this evening and tell him I will be looking out for him. In the meantime, would you be so good as to provide it with water and allow it to graze in your garden?"

Mrs Bradshaw curtsied and watched as Lady Langley returned to the road and gave the former owner of the donkey a dressing down the like of which she had never before heard.

The disgruntled gentleman picked up his discarded bundles and to the amused jeering of the assembled crowd he started off down the road leading out of the village.

Damon, deciding that they had provided diversion enough for one day, took Lady Langley firmly by the arm and led her away towards the waiting carriage.

"I think it is time to continue with our tour, Callista," he murmured to her, receiving a grateful smile from his betrothed.

Callista sighed and acquiesced gracefully, content that the wicked animal-beating rogue had been summarily dismissed. She allowed herself to be handed into the carriage and to the delight of the gathered villagers, she waved to them as the carriage drove briskly away.

"Have I totally embarrassed you, Georgie?" she asked her cousin.

Georgiana shook her head, her eyes dancing with laughter. "I had forgotten your fearsome temper, my dearest Callie," she exclaimed. "Woe betide the villains who cross your path."

With that, she gave way to her suppressed hilarity and burst into a peal of laughter. Callista, her temper cooling and the spark of indignation she had felt on beholding the outrage of the beaten animal fading away, smiled in response to her cousin's laughter and cast a slightly worried glance at Damon.

"Do you think Max will forgive me for making such a spectacle of myself?" she asked.

Damon, joining in the laughter with his betrothed, shook his head. "He will only be sorry he missed it," he replied.

Indeed, as Max returned home that evening he was startled to be met by the sight of his wife's protégé, his second best livery stained with the mud and blood of schoolyard fisticuffs, a suspicious looking bruise marring the smoothness of his cherubic countenance, walking down the drive of Moreland Court's immaculate driveway, leading an equally disreputable-looking donkey and cheerfully greeting his master with the news that his first day at school had been a complete success. The donkey belonged to 'Er Ladyship and she had given the donkey's former owner a taste of his own medicine and a right earful.

Max shook his head slightly in disbelief as Joe led his new charge around to the stables, wondering what kind of reception the other lads there were going to give their new acquisition.

He entered the front door to be welcomed by his ever-efficient Butler and the sound of voices and laughter coming from the Drawing Room. Handing his hat, gloves and whip to the Butler, he opened the door and was greeted by more merriment and the sight of his wife, mother, Georgiana, Damon and a lady of indeterminate age, well dressed and elegant who he recognised at once as his mother's new companion, Mrs Spencer.

Callista's smile broadened as she saw her husband and her eyes lit up as he entered. He approached her and bending, kissed her cheek. She held his hand a moment longer than necessary and as he straightened, he raised an eyebrow at her.

"I understand you have made an addition to my stables, Callista?" he enquired.

She felt a surge of colour to her cheeks at his words and was grateful for Damon's intervention once again.

"Indeed, Max, I wish you had been there to witness your wife's fearless defence of that poor defenceless creature."

"Attack, surely Damon?" Max commented drily. "I understand the donkey's owner was no match for my wife. A gross mismatch, in fact?"

Realising she was being teased, Callista joined in with the general laughter and stood up to move closer to her husband and take his arm in the most natural of movements.

"Max. You do not mind our new donkey surely?" she demanded.

"Not at all, in fact young Joe is busy leading him to a suitable new home now as we speak."

"Oh, is Joe back?" She glanced at the door. "I must see how his first day at school went."

Max restrained her with a gentle squeeze of her hand. "Permit Cook to clean him up first, my dear," he continued. "He claims that his first day was a complete success but a ripped shirt and bloody knees beg to differ."

Dismay crossed her features but he patted her hand further. "No, no, Callie. Leave him be – he appears to have thoroughly enjoyed himself."

She nodded. "I only hope he has forgiven me for insisting he attends school," she replied.

Max smiled and leaving her for a moment approached Mrs Spencer.

"Forgive my shocking manners, Mrs Spencer," he apologised. "Welcome to Moreland. I trust you had a pleasant journey?"

Mrs Spencer, seated next to his mother, shook hands with him and bowed her head politely.

"Thank you, Sir Maxim, it was tolerable enough. I was glad to reach Moreland though, I must admit." She smiled around at the assembled company. "I have been highly diverted since my arrival. I am so pleased to meet your new wife and family – you are a lucky young man, Max."

Max and Callista found themselves suddenly looking into each other's eyes for a long, silent moment.

"Yes," he replied quietly. "I am a very lucky man, Mrs Spencer, thank you."

Damon broke the suddenly serious mood.

"When are you planning on leaving for London, Max?" he enquired.

Max seemed to rouse himself from a reverie. "The sooner I go, the faster I will return," he replied. "I want to be back for your engagement party, my friend." He seemed to force a smile onto his face as he looked down into his wife's face. "I will leave tomorrow," he added.

Callista's eyes clouded slightly at his words. "The party is in less than four weeks," she reminded him gently.

He squeezed her hands, longing to kiss her but held back by so many pairs of watching eyes.

"I will be back, I promise."

Silence followed his words, the merriment of earlier dampened by Callista's obvious unhappiness at the thought of her husband leaving her so soon.

Lady Joanna, however, lightened the mood once more. "In the meantime, Max, the ladies of this particular party will be going to Bath for a short holiday."

"Bath?" Damon raised his eyebrow at his betrothed.

"Yes, my dear," she replied. "I have only visited it briefly with you and I did not get chance to visit any of the prodigious amount of shops a lady may amuse herself in."

Damon uttered a theatrical groan. "Perhaps I should accompany you and attempt to curb your spending on your poor dear Papa's behalf?"

Georgiana's eyes were sparkling and her dimples were evident as she retorted to his words. "Indeed no, my lord. You may await my return and be suitably dazzled by the new gown I shall wear to our party."

As Damon had already seen the outrageously expensive ensemble his sister was planning on wearing, he had a sinking feeling Lady Davina was going to attempt to outshine the bride to be at her own engagement party, but ever loyal to Georgiana he raised her small white hand to his lips.

"You will outshine everyone there already," he murmured. "You need no further embellishment, my love."

Lady Joanna and Mrs Spencer exchanged glances as they observed the two young couples before them. A smile passed between them as they, too, remembered their younger days and the devotion of their own dearly departed husbands.

Lady Joanna rose to her feet and held her hand out to her new companion.

"Come, Lydia, let me escort you to your room for tonight. We will be moving to the Dower House tomorrow and we shall take up our residence there forthwith. My son and his lovely wife will soon have the house to themselves."

The two ladies left the young couples alone and their conversation and laughter could be heard as they ascended the staircase to the guest bedrooms.

Max found he was still holding on to his wife's hand and genuine amusement lifted the darkening of his brow. "And you, Callie? Do you intend to find something in Bath to dazzle me also?"

Grateful for the lightening of mood, Callista returned his smile. "I am going to order costumes for your birthday party, Max," she replied mischievously.

Diverted at once, Georgiana was intrigued. "Costumes, Callie? Pray what do you mean?"

Callista turned laughing eyes to Georgiana and squeezed Max's hand. "I have a fancy to see my husband as a Roman Centurion, and to see him modelling that fine helmet he has on display in his study."

Immediately that sense of unease gripped Max. "Callie, no, I don't think so…"

But Damon joined in the general atmosphere of amusement. "Excellent idea, Callie," he agreed. "Perhaps you would like me to join you in wearing a toga, Max?"

Georgiana clapped her hands, entranced at the thought of dressing up in fancy dress.

"Oh Callie, what shall we wear? We must find something unusual, do you not think?"

Callista nodded, her auburn curls bouncing on her shoulders. "Oh, I have some ideas, Georgie, never fear."

Finding himself overruled by his wife and friends, Max gave a slightly shaky laugh. "So be it, I can see I am outnumbered. Now, Damon, are you joining us for dinner? I need to bathe and change. I have been out in the saddle all day; I have ridden miles and am dirty and hungry."

Damon shook his head and reluctantly kissed his fiancée's hand. "Alas, not tonight. I have promised Davina I will look over the legal documents she has brought with her and as she has to meet with our Solicitor tomorrow, we need to settle matters this evening."

"Ah, I fear this evening will be extremely one sided. Just myself and four ladies. However shall I cope?"

Callista laughed. "You poor dear. Still at least you will be entertained. Make the most of it, my husband – soon there will be only the two of us once everyone leaves us. I only hope you will not be too bored."

The expression in his eyes flared briefly for only her to see. It was one of passion and longing and laughter. "Never, my Witch," he murmured.

Damon took his reluctant leave. An evening spent in the pleasant and amusing company of his friends and fiancée was in every way preferable to the task which lay ahead of him. Davina was in a strange mood. In no way did she convince her brother that she was a grieving widow. On the contrary, she gave every indication of relief at the death of her once estranged husband. She made no secret to Damon of her disappointment that Max had married another woman but she seemed accepting of the fact, announcing to her brother that whilst she could never be the new Lady Langley's dearest friend neither did she wish her any ill. She seemed extremely calm and composed and Damon, wrapped up in his forthcoming engagement to Georgiana, was reassured by Davina's prosaic acceptance of the marriage of the man she had once declared to be the love of her life.

Damon circumspectly bade his farewell to Georgiana, promising to return the following day to say goodbye to Max and spend some time with his fiancée before her own departure for Bath.

Gazing after him from the threshold of Moreland, Georgiana waved to him before sighing, stated her intention to change for dinner and leaving her cousins alone.

"I need a bath." Max grimaced. "Would my lady care to accompany me and keep me entertained with tales of your schoolroom adventure?"

Re-taking Max's arm, Callista mounted the stairs with him. "Your lady realised young Joe was quite illiterate and decided it was time to do something about it."

Max shook his head. "And you will never know how sorry I am to have missed the sight of your berating of that unlucky former donkey owner."

His voice was almost mournful and Callista, realising she was being teased all over again, started to laugh.

She was still laughing as he led her into their bedroom. Her smile was radiant as he paused to lock the door behind them but her laughter died completely when he stopped her mouth with his own, pulling her into his arms and devouring her lips with the urgency of a drowning man seeking air. She found herself held against the door, his full length pressed hard against her – his hands caressing her, his mouth demanding and receiving the response he sought. He groaned as he shakily pushed himself away from her.

"I have been longing to do that all day," he whispered hoarsely against her throat.

"Then don't stop," she demanded.

"I need a bath first…" he began but her hands were suddenly at his clothes, pushing his jacket from his shoulders, pulling the cravat from around his neck, her arms snaking up around him again, pulling his head down to hers to kiss him with the same burning desire he had shown her.

His shirt followed his cravat and jacket and he paused only long enough to divest himself of his riding boots before propelling her across the room to fall in a frenzied heap on the smooth covers of their bed. Her clothes joined his on the floor and all gentleness was forgotten, all foreplay dispensed with as they were overwhelmed with the mutual passion which engulfed them.

Moving together as one, driven to the edge of reason, no restraint, nothing holding them back, their coupling was almost primitive in its raw power and when he could wait no longer he drove his seed into her with a cry of ecstasy which was echoed by her own.

Sated, spent, they collapsed together, panting for breath, shuddering, sweating, holding on to one another, loath to let go.

His hands wound into her hair, her lips against his throat, her arms around his lean hard body, pressing her naked body up against his, one of his legs still thrown possessively across hers.

"How am I going to live without you for a month?" she whispered against his skin. "Please let me come with you, Max."

He groaned. Lifting his head, he bent to seek out and kiss her lips with renewed tenderness now that the rawness of their passion had been sated.

"You will be too much of a distraction, Callie," he replied. "I will be busy with lawyers and my Trustees and I want to get it over with as soon as possible so I can get back here to be with you."

To her dismay, Callista felt tears spring to her eyes. Max took her face in his hands and wiped the tears from her cheeks with a tender motion with his thumbs.

"Don't cry," he begged, his voice a hoarse whisper. "I will be back with you as soon as I can and we can start to live our lives here properly. Together, forever." He kissed her forehead, her eyes, her cheeks and finally her mouth.

"I know," she murmured. "But I will miss you."

He smiled then. "What, even in Bath?" he teased her gently.

"Even there," she agreed. "Although Georgie is right – there are a lot of distractions in that city."

"Never mind Georgie's Papa – I shall have to make sure you do not bankrupt me."

Soft, gentle laughter rocked them and they lay together, contented and sleepy, holding each other, warm and tranquil in the cosy confines of his room. There they would have stayed if not for the passing of time and the gentle knock on the door alerting them to the arrival of servants with hot water for a bath. That, together with the knowledge that good manners demanded their presence in the dining room to entertain their guests and hope the evening would speed past as quickly as the past hour had done.

Chapter Twenty

Their parting the following morning was restrained and formal. Standing with her mother in law and cousin, Callista watched with heavy heart as Max supervised the loading of his trunk onto the Langley travelling coach. His personal papers were all packed carefully, carried by a soberly dressed Benson, already seated in the carriage awaiting his master's presence.

He was leaving last minute instructions to his Steward and he was frowning. Annoyed at having to leave so soon after taking up the reins of his inheritance, frustrated at having to leave his bride without expressing his deepest feelings and anxious to return to carry on with all the plans he had been formulating over the past few days, Max was not in the best of moods.

He had been up and dressed early, having breakfasted and spent time with his Steward in the study, going over the work he had ordered be carried out in his absence.

Georgiana had joined Callista in the dining room and, seemingly unaware of Callista's pale faced silence, had chattered inconsequentially about their forthcoming visit to Bath and the imminent arrival of her parents.

Mrs Spencer and Lady Joanna were there to bid farewell to Max and the newly married couple found themselves unable to say their goodbyes in private. That strange dark anguish was obvious in the sapphire blue of his eyes as they sought hers. They were outside the Hall, he was dressed for travelling, the horses were restless and he was unable to do any more than take her hands, facing her, looking down into the shadowed green eyes, noting the pallor of her cheeks.

"I promise I will return soon, Callie," he said softly.

"What have I told you about making promises you might not be able to keep?" she reminded him. Her voice was low, the melancholy evident in every fibre of her being.

He raised her hands to his lips, feeling their coldness and he was frowning as he looked once more into her eyes.

"Callie, are you unwell?" he asked.

She shook her head, forcing a smile to her lips. "Indeed no, Max. Just sad that you are leaving me."

Ignoring the watching eyes, Max bent his head and pressed a kiss gently onto her lips.

"I will be back within the month," he said. "Then we can make plans to celebrate this engagement and my birthday properly."

He seemed to be forced from her side, so reluctantly did he loosen his grip on her hands and walk away to the waiting coach.

He bowed his farewells to his mother and Georgiana and with a nod to his Coachman, he jumped up inside, slamming the door closed behind him.

Callie felt a comforting arm go across her shoulders as her cousin drew closer to her.

They watched as the Coachman wielded his whip and the four horses pulled away from the house, trotting slowly down the wide expanse of the drive.

A horse and rider appeared at the gates and the coach paused briefly as Max exchanged a few words with his friend before starting off again on his journey to London.

Damon carried on down the driveway and dismounted, bowing to the older ladies and greeting his betrothed with a kiss on her hand.

"Do not fret, Callista, " he urged her. "Time will pass quickly and pleasantly enough – and Max will write often, I am sure."

As Max had only managed one letter in the six weeks prior to their wedding, Callista held no great faith in his ability to send frequent letters home but she managed a faint, wan smile.

"I will miss him," she said simply and leaving them, returned to the house to seek out her Housekeeper and Steward and continue with her new duties as mistress of Moreland Hall.

Lady Joanna and Mrs Spencer exchanged glances and wisely left Callista alone, escorting and chaperoning the engaged couple, discussing the visit to Bath and making arrangements as to when they would be leaving and where they would be putting up for their short holiday.

The Langley's had no Bath residence and various options of accommodation were discussed. The merits of two of Bath's finest hostelries were considered and Lady Joanna settled the matter by declaring she had always stayed at The Royal Crescent Hotel and that was her preferred establishment for their sojourn.

As Damon could raise no objection to this, and as Mrs Spencer echoed her friend's sentiments, agreeing that it was superior in every way to other, less fashionable hotels, the matter was settled. The date was set for seven days hence to give time to make arrangements and Damon agreed to write to the hotel to reserve rooms. He regretted his inability to escort the ladies, his sister requiring his services for the next few days to help settle her affairs.

"Indeed," he added, frowning slightly, "we have to return to London. It appears the Fitzpatrick family have raised some objection to Davina's claim on her husband's estate and whilst the bulk of his fortune will be hers, his sisters are demanding they retain the family home and houses in Dublin and London."

"Surely Davina will have no opposition to his sisters remaining in their ancestral home," Lady Joanna remarked.

Damon was frowning, remembering the angry scene he had witnessed when Davina had received the letter from her Solicitor in London.

"No," he replied thoughtfully. "I did not think so either, but the estate is unentailed, Callum's will has not yet been found and, as his widow, Davina is determined to sell the property as soon as she can find a buyer."

"And what of Sir Callum's sisters and the rest of his family, what will become of them?" Georgiana's concern was evident, shocked at the idea that Davina could make her sisters in law homeless.

Damon sighed. He had felt the same pity for Callum's family as Georgiana was feeling now but his sister had been adamant. They had hated her, they had made her life a misery and she was not about to let them live in any comfort or luxury if she could help it.

"It is going to take all my best diplomatic efforts to convince Davina to forgive the Fitzpatricks for their treatment of her," he admitted ruefully. "I think I can win her round, but it may take a while and unfortunately in the meantime it also entails us returning to London."

Mrs Spencer, recognising the look of disgust on her friend's face, hastily interjected.

"Will you be long in the capital?" she enquired.

"No, a few days only. We will not go until you leave for Bath and I may return with Max."

"With Davina also?" Georgiana asked.

Damon smiled at his fiancée and, reaching across, squeezed her hand gently.

"I cannot get engaged without my sister there to witness my happiness," he replied.

Georgiana forced a faint smile to her face, one echoed on the frozen visage of Lady Joanna. "Of course not," Georgie replied. "I would not expect you to."

Her displeasure, however, was made quite clear to Callista later that day as the two young ladies were in Callista's bedroom sorting through the gowns which she was to take to Bath.

"I'm sorry, Callie," she said. "I cannot help myself. I am sure Damon's affection for his sister is truly honourable, but her actions are nothing short of despicable. Turning the Fitzpatricks out of their home indeed."

As Callista had not heard the full story, Georgiana enlightened her.

"And now Damon has told me that she is to go to London to fight the Fitzpatricks' claim to their estate."

Callista paused in her perusal of the contents of her wardrobe to turn to give Georgiana her full attention.

"When, pray is she to go to London? After your engagement party, I trust?"

Georgiana sat down on Callista's bed with a decided jump. "Indeed, no, she is not," she declared. "She is preparing to leave for London within the week and Damon is to escort her whilst we are in Bath."

A cold hand crept into Callista's chest and wrapped icy fingers around her heart.

She stopped her task and sat down on the window seat, facing Georgie. Her mind was racing, her thoughts were in turmoil.

Max could not have known, she tried to assure herself. There was no way on earth he could have known her plans.

"Callista, are you all right, my dear?" Georgie was concerned as the paleness of Callista's face and her sudden silence.

Forcing herself to concentrate on Georgiana once more, Callista smiled at her cousin.

"I am quite well, thank you. I was just thinking what a shame it is we are both separated from our men so soon."

Georgiana climbed off the bed and came over to the window where she joined Callista on the padded upholstered seat.

"Oh Callie, I'm sorry. Do you miss Max already?"

Callista nodded, feeling unexpected tears spring to her eyes. She looked away from her cousin and stared out at the rapidly falling twilight. The nights were starting to darken earlier, summer was over and the chill autumnal evenings were on them.

"Yes, he has not been gone a day yet and I miss him." She sighed and dashing away the sparkling tears, she gave a shaky laugh. "He will be back soon enough and I am just being missish. Pray tell me more of what has been decided for our visit to Bath."

Relieved that she had not upset Callista, Georgiana brightened up as she repeated Lady Joanna's itinerary for their visit and debated the rival merits of the Bath Pump Rooms to the pleasures of London's Almacks.

As Callista slipped between the sheets of her bed that night, she lay awake for what seemed hours, wondering about what was going to happen in London between her husband and the woman who had been determined to have him. Was Max going to be strong enough to resist Davina if she were to try and seduce him?

Callista shuddered at the thought and burrowed herself deeper into the heavy covers of her bed. She slept uneasily that night, her dreams full of unseen dangers and dark frightening shadows. She awoke unrefreshed and lay awake, waiting for the dawn to break, to alleviate the cold darkness of that long cold night.

The days passed quickly enough, although the nights dragged and Callista spent many sleepless nights pining for Max, missing him more than she could ever have imagined.

She filled her days with learning more about the management of the house and its servants, familiarising herself with her staff and getting to know better both her Housekeeper and Cook. She visited Joe often and listened to him as he practised his letters and helped him as he struggled to read and write but she was truly pleased with his progress in such a short time. He was extremely bright and intelligent and she knew she had done the right thing in sending him to school. He still lived with the other stable lads and got up early enough to complete his chores before school, returning after lunch to carry out the rest of his duties with a diligence and commitment which touched her and made her proud of his dedication.

She would join him in the afternoon to visit their donkey, which he had named "Jade" after a particularly bad tempered episode when the donkey had kicked him. He kept Callista amused and entertained and helped fill the gap left in her life with Max's departure.

Arrangements for Georgiana and Damon's engagement party were well underway. Everything was organised and would take place a week after their return from Bath. Invitations had all gone out and acceptances were flooding in, friends and family from

London and the North were due to arrive the day before the party and accommodation in Moreland Hall and the Fortescue home was being prepared ready for the arrival of their guests. Local gentry from all around the two estates were invited and it looked as though the engagement party was set to rival Max and Callista's wedding in its splendour.

One letter arrived from London, to let Callista know he had arrived safely and the first meeting was due to take place with his Trustees imminently. Max was missing her, he wrote, and he could not wait until he was back again in the country with his wife and dearest friends. No further emotion was displayed in his letter and Lady Joanna, on learning of its contents, commented drily that at least Callista had succeeded where she had failed over many years, in receiving any form of correspondence from her son.

Although she did not see Davina again that week, Callista understood that Lady Fitzpatrick had not yet left for London. She was planning on going the same day as Georgiana and her companions left for Bath, due, it would seem, to Damon's refusal to be parted from his betrothed any longer than absolutely necessary, much to Callista's silent relief.

Only one other thing disturbed the smooth running of Callista's life in that first week following Max's departure.

She had decided to try and learn to ride, to surprise Max on his return and had persuaded Georgiana and Damon to assist her.

They seated her on a very placid pony and, with Joe as her groom on his return from school, the four of them would take sedate walks through the pleasant countryside surrounding the adjoining estates. She was a nervous but not an anxious rider. She was as calm as she could be riding such a sedate and good-natured horse and eventually became brave enough to allow them to teach her how to trot comfortably. She was not a natural horsewoman, but determined to become at least proficient, she persevered.

It was whilst out on one of these gentle walking tours that she and Joe fell behind their two companions walked sedately through a part of the woods separating the two estates. Georgiana and Damon were deep in conversation and did not notice Joe and Callista's slower progress. It was Joe who suddenly became alarmed.

"Lady Callie," he hissed, and reaching over, took the mare's bridle in his hands, urging her into a faster walk. "Hold on, someone's watching us from behind them trees." He nodded in the direction of a densely overgrown grove of trees and she raised her eyes from the back of the horse's head, concentrating hard, trying not to fall off.

Callista risked a quick glance over her shoulder in the direction Joe was indicating and she did, indeed, see the shadows of two horses, standing close together, their riders silent, not moving.

Joe's alarm was enough to instil in her a frisson of apprehension. He did not scare easily, she knew that, but for him to become so agitated, she knew his sixth sense was telling him to be wary.

The little mare responded to Joe's urgings and risking a slight kick, Callista compelled the horse into a slightly faster trot than she had been used to.

"Sir Damon, Georgiana!" she called out. "Wait for us!"

Damon reined in immediately and turned to face them, registering the alarm in her voice.

Joe turned his head once more and watched as the silent riders disappeared further into the undergrowth. His uneasiness did not abate until they had reached Damon's side.

"Is there something wrong, Callie?" he asked, his face serious, his voice low with concern.

"I think we were being watched, followed – I'm not sure but whoever it was did not wish to be seen."

Damon was immediately alert, realising with an impotent fury that he was unarmed and he and Joe could offer little in the way of protection for the ladies.

"Joe, lead the way and let's get back to Moreland quickly," he ordered, his voice and manner abrupt with the anxiety he felt. Taking up the rear, he remained still as Georgiana and Joe flanked Callista on either side and hurried the little mare into a fast trot back towards the Hall. Damon followed slowly, his whole body and mind alert and watchful, his eyes raking the undergrowth, searching and failing to see anyone still lurking. He did not for a moment dispute Callista's fears, he could not see anyone but he felt the air crackle with anticipation, realising that Joe's senses had alerted them in time to what could have been a dangerous situation.

They returned, rather faster than expected, to Moreland Hall and as Joe assisted his mistress to dismount, she gave him a quick, hard hug.

"Thank you, Joe," she whispered. "I do not know who or what those people were, but I think they meant us harm. "

He blushed, delighted at her show of affection and pleased that he had been alert enough to recognise danger when it had appeared.

Damon, however, was angry. Whoever it had been, they had remained hidden. They had not wanted to be seen or recognised and whilst he was prepared to dismiss the incident as a lucky escape from a couple of wary highwaymen, he determined that he would not allow the ladies to be placed in such a situation ever again. Their riding lessons would be conducted within the grounds of Moreland Hall and visits further afield would be taken accompanied by a fully armed rider and one of the more stalwart footmen in attendance.

He had already ensured the ladies' visit to Bath would be completed in safety. For his own peace of mind, he had personally picked out the most reliable of the men from both Moreland and his own estates to act as outriders for their journey. He would ensure, however, that they were fully armed and prepared to protect the ladies from any possible harm on their two day journey.

On the day before their proposed visit, Callista, on sending for the Cook and Housekeeper for their normal morning meeting, was perturbed to find Cook was flustered and quite out of sorts.

"Why, Mrs Smith," Callista stood up to greet her staff, "what on earth is the matter?"

Mrs Smith was quite red-faced and although the Housekeeper

had obviously tried to calm her down, she was obviously not her usual composed self.

The Housekeeper attempted to explain.

"We had a couple of unsavoury characters come to the kitchen door earlier, Madam."

Instantly Callista felt her skin start to prickle with that same uncertainty she had felt earlier in the week in the woods.

"What did they do to upset Mrs Smith in this manner?" she enquired, as calmly as she could.

Mrs Smith found her voice at last, raised in indignantly at the effrontery she had endured earlier.

"They were former coachmen employed by Lady Fitzpatrick," she exclaimed. "They have been turned off as they were only hired to escort her from Dublin and they want to stay in the area."

Callista seated the Cook and sat next to her, placing a comforting hand over Mrs Smiths own.

"And what did they want with us, pray?" she asked, her voice composed but inwardly she could feel herself becoming as unsettled as her Cook.

"Jobs, Madam," the Housekeeper added. "They wanted to speak to my husband to see if there were any positions with your household as grooms or footmen."

"Did you call your husband to deal with these men?"

"I did, Madam," the Housekeeper replied.

"But they wouldn't go away, they tried to come into my kitchen and they were quite intimidating, Your Ladyship." Mrs Smith was still unhappy. "I tried to tell them there was nothing for them here but they tried to push me out of the way and force their way into the house," she continued.

Callista felt the same indignation rising in her that her Hook had obviously felt.

"How impertinent," she exclaimed. "I trust they were evicted from our grounds?"

The Housekeeper's expression was that of grim satisfaction.

"Indeed they were, Madam," she answered. "My husband and a couple of his footmen saw them off the premises and out of the grounds. Nasty, rough men they were too. It's not my place to criticise, but why Lady Fitzpatrick would employ such ruffians I can't imagine."

Callista shook her head. "No, neither can I," she agreed. "I trust they will have moved on by now. We cannot have anyone else upset by their presence. I will speak to your husband directly, Mrs Bailey."

Slightly mollified by Her Ladyship's reassurances, the two ladies reverted to their normal discussions and left Callista's morning room later completely satisfied that they had done the right thing in turning away the two ex-employees of Lady Fitzpatrick.

Callista sent for the Steward immediately and it was only when he assured her that the two unsavoury characters had indeed been turned away completely did she feel at ease. She wished, not for the first time, that Max was with her. She felt suddenly unprepared for the responsibility of running the Moreland home and estate without him. Even though she was surrounded with loyal servants and a loving family, she felt unaccountably alone and vulnerable.

Georgiana, as usual, cheered her up and she found herself looking forward to their trip with uplifted spirits as the four ladies dined together that evening. She kept the story of the strangers to herself, not wishing to alarm or upset the others and the evening was spent in a convivial and pleasant manner, with all four ladies agreeing that they would meet early the following morning, ready to depart at 8 o'clock for their journey. Thanks to Damon's ministrations on their behalf, they were to spend only one night in a coaching inn on their way to their destination and, safely guarded by his outriders, they would complete their journey the following day.

Lady Joanna had invitations already to several engagements which, she assured her daughter in law, would be extremely diverting and she would introduce Callista to as much of Bath's society as she could possibly stand.

Callista found her mother in law's acerbic comments and wit highly amusing and with complete accord, the ladies parted company to go to bed early in preparation for their forthcoming visit.

Callista slept uneasily again that night, her dreams disturbing her and she realised as she opened her eyes to the morning light shining through the windows, that she had revisited some of her dark dreams of old, the fear and anguish of those nightmares coming back to haunt her even as she gazed around at the luxurious room in which she awoke.

Her thoughts, as usual, flew to her husband and, with a sigh, wondered if he was missing her as much as she missed him. She rolled over and hugged his pillow, burying her face into the clean linen, a faint aroma of sandalwood filling her nostrils as she breathed in deeply before pushing herself upright, ready to dress and prepare for the journey ahead. She pushed the covers off herself and swung her legs over the side of the bed. She stood up and paused, the room swayed around her and she held on to the upright of the four poster bed for a moment. Taking a deep breath, she smiled softly. It was rather sooner in her marriage than she would have wished but if her suspicions were correct, she might have more news to impart to her husband than he was anticipating.

Lihanna 11

General Aurelius and his Centurions returned to a scene of destruction and came at last face to face with Queen Eithann and her son, the new King, Carmag.

They were as appalled at the scene as he was. They faced each other, their armies at their back, warily taking stock of the other.

"I am here to discuss a peaceful resolution to this conflict, General," Queen Eithann spoke, "but first I demand to see my daughter and ensure she is unharmed."

The General dismounted and almost ran into the deserted tent, stepping over broken furniture and the bodies of his personal bodyguards.

He returned and stared up into the proud, strong face of the Queen, looking down at him from her royal war chariot.

"She is gone. Whoever has done this has taken her." His voice was harsh, abrupt.

Carmag laid a restraining hand on his mother's arm as she would have raised a whip to the Roman.

"Your envoys promised me she would be safe," he replied, as alarmed as his mother.

"She was safe yesterday when I left her," Julius replied, his hand curled around the hilt of his sword. "We were called away by the false tale of an uprising to the West. There was no such rebellion – merely a rumour started to lure me away."

His attention turned to his second in command, left in charge in his absence. They spoke in their own language briefly before he turned back to the Queen.

"Your daughter has been taken by your priests," he told her, "a party of Druids came and attacked the camp late last night – Lihanna was seen being carried out by one of the captured Druids, a man named Daveth."

Eithann and her son exchanged looks of pure horror.

"No!" Eithann almost screamed aloud and half collapsed out of the chariot. Carmag helped her to get down and together they faced the General.

Carmag was almost as tall as Julius, broad shouldered, with fair curling hair and eyes the colour of amber.

"We must get to the Sacred Stones at once," he told Julius. "My sister is in grave danger."

"Why? What is she to the Druids?" he demanded.

Eithann moaned again, the proud Celtic queen almost collapsing against her son.

"They came to my parents when you Romans were slaughtering your way across our country," he snarled at the General, oblivious to the darkening of Julius' brow at the insult. "They tried to persuade them that they could prevent the invasion, call on the gods and by their rites and ceremonies turn you back and drive you from our shores." He looked around briefly at the carnage around them, the partially demolished tents, the bodies, the fires which had destroyed most of the Roman quarters. "They wanted my parents to give up Lihanna to them. A maiden of pure bred royal blood – the perfect sacrifice."

Julius felt his world spin around him and he had to bite hard down on his lower lip to prevent himself from crying out as Queen Eithann had done.

"Sacrifice?" he managed to whisper.

Carmag had already turned away from him and pulling his distraught mother with him, they climbed into their war chariot.

"Come, Roman. If you wish to save her life, we have to hurry – if it is not already too late."

Barking out orders to his men, Julius remounted his stallion and followed the Celts as they thundered out of the encampment, following the rough cart track of a road to the North West. Julius had explored these very roads several times over the previous weeks in the company of Lihanna; he knew where this route led and it was with growing foreboding that he galloped beside the war chariot of his former enemies.

Chapter Twenty One

The autumnal sun was setting as the travel-stained coach turned into the drive of Moreland.

Max leaned forward, the weariness on his face lifting as he drank in the view before him, breathing in the crisp sharp air as his eyes greedily absorbed the sight of his home, welcoming him back after the long weeks of his absence.

The mullioned windows were already alight even though it was barely dusk, but the short autumn day was ending and the stars were already sparkling in the velvet blackness of the sky. The frost was starting to settle on the shrubs and the manicured perfection of the lawns in front of the house had acquired an icy sparkle which added to the beauty of the scene before him.

His eyes scanned the front of the house, searching for that beloved face he had missed so much these last few weeks. His business had finally been completed, spending hour after hour with his Trustees, going over the intricate details of his father's legacies, days spent in meetings with his lawyers, dealing with the minutiae of his father's businesses, his investments, property and estates. Weeks had passed whilst engaging in discussions with bankers and the men who had been appointed as trustees of his father's will. He had no idea of the intricacies and complications which management of his vast wealth entailed but over the last few weeks he had learned quickly.

Max was weary with it all. He longed to be home, to get back to Callista and his country estate, to continue with his work putting right the neglect of years spent pursuing the pleasures of life rather than the more serious affairs of his heritage.

He had no time for entertainments whilst in London. Apart from dinner at his club in the company of old friends, he had eschewed the pleasures London afforded. He grimaced and wiped his hand tiredly across his eyes. A year ago he would have plunged into the social life of London without a care; in the last few weeks he had declined every invitation which had been offered to him. He had dined quietly with his Trustees and old friends of his father, enjoying their reminisces and wishing with all his heart he had spent more time with his father during the final few years of his life.

He had met with Damon on his arrival in the capital, but despite his vow to seek out Davina and speak to her, he had not seen her. She, too, had been embroiled in an exhausting round of meetings with her former husband's lawyers and when he had called at the Fortescue home, he had been disappointed to find her away from home. He had no wish to seek her out to continue their former relationship. He merely wanted to speak to her in private and explain that since his marriage, their connection could not endure. He was committed to his wife and there was no room in his life for his former lover. He owed it to Davina to speak to her in private and tell her, as gently as possible, that he could ask no more from her than her friendship.

Frustrated at not being able to speak to her, he had met with Damon at their club and listened to his old friend's explanation of the problems his sister was having with the Fitzpatrick family. Damon was returning to Wiltshire to rejoin Georgiana as their engagement party was due to take place at the end of October and he was anxious to see his fiancée once more. He was torn between supporting his sister and missing his fiancée and reluctant though he was to abandon Davina in London, his commitments at home forced him to take his leave of her. Davina was more than capable of dealing with the Fitzpatrick family lawyers and, together with her own men of business, she had decided to remain in London until the business was concluded. It was not all going her way, unfortunately, but she was not giving up what she considered to be her rights without a fight.

Max and Damon returned to Wiltshire, travelling together, both anxious to get home. Damon had gone straight to his estates, sending a message with Max that he would call on Georgiana first thing in the morning. Tired and travel-stained, he had not wanted to present a weary face to his fiancée.

Max, meanwhile had urged his drivers to cover the final few miles at a sparkling pace. He longed to see his wife and he felt that connection between them growing stronger the closer he got to Moreland.

The lanterns were alight in the driveway to the house, the glow in the windows was warm and welcoming and as the carriage came to a halt outside the front doors, they opened as the footmen came out to meet their master, the golden ambience from the hall highlighting the entrance to his home.

Max leapt from his carriage as the groom opened the door for him and he bounded up the steps into the hall, all weariness forgotten as Callista appeared, her face suffused with joy at the sight of her husband.

She flew into his arms without a word, he held her tightly and picked her up, swinging her around with delight before placing her feet back on the floor and for a moment their eyes met before he lowered his lips to kiss her soundly. Her response was immediate, her arms tight around his neck.

A sound disturbed them as they stood locked together in the hallway. A sigh escaped her as she reluctantly drew away, discretion finally overcoming the happiness she felt at his appearance.

Max lifted his head and turned to the cause of the disturbance and he saw the Drawing Room door open to reveal his wife's cousin and her parents coming out to greet him.

No flicker of annoyance was allowed to cross his features as his natural good manners reasserted themselves.

"Sir Augustus," he exclaimed, striding forward and shaking the outstretched hand of Callista's Uncle.

"Max," Augustus replied, a broad smile lifting his heavy features, "it is a pleasure to see you again."

Georgiana and her mother curtsied to him in response to his

greeting, Georgie's eyes sparkling with mischief as she saw how discomfited Callista was looking.

Max bowed to Amelia. "Lady Wetherby, forgive my disreputable appearance," he apologised. "The journey has been a long and arduous one from London."

Amelia nodded her head. "Indeed it is, Sir Maxim," she agreed. "We were almost a week travelling here."

"Then forgive me anew, Your Ladyship," Max apologised again, "that I was not here to meet you upon your arrival. When did you get here?"

The hall was suddenly filled with footmen and luggage and at a sign from Callista, Max and their guests returned to the abandoned Drawing Room.

Augustus returned to his seat on the gilded sofa beside his wife.

"We arrived yesterday," he replied affably. "Callie and your mother have made us very welcome. "

Max looked around the room as if expecting his mother to reappear.

"Does my mother not join us this evening?" he enquired.

"Lady Joanna and Mrs Spencer will be joining us for dinner shortly," Callista answered.

"And Damon?" Georgiana could refrain no longer. "Did he return with you?" she asked, her eyes and face animated with the thought of seeing her fiancé again.

Max smiled at her, the weariness evident on his face relaxing as he surveyed the contented domestic scene around him. "He did indeed. We travelled together and I left him at home – he wishes to present a less disreputable figure than myself when he sees you again."

Georgiana sighed. "He cuts it very fine, my lord," she exclaimed. "Our party is only two days hence and the arrangements are very far advanced. I was truly beginning to be concerned."

"He would not have let you down, Georgie," Callista replied gently.

Max grimaced suddenly. "My dear," he turned to Callie, "I

must go and change for dinner. Could you ask that it be delayed for a few minutes?"

"Of course," she replied. "I will speak to Cook directly. Go up and I will attend to it."

She excused herself and accompanied her husband out of the Drawing Room. The door closed behind them and at once she was caught up in a brief, passionate embrace, a hard kiss pressed upon her lips.

"I have missed you." He groaned, sending her heart soaring at his words.

"And I you," she replied. "I thought you were never coming home."

"I could hardly wait to return," he whispered.

With another groan, he pulled out of her arms and with shaking hands, raked his fingers through his long, unkempt hair. "I will be back shortly. I must clean myself up and change."

He moved away from her towards the stairs. Pausing briefly, he gazed at her, drinking in the radiance of her expression.

"You look beautiful," he murmured. "I could not forget how lovely you are."

Her cheeks were pink with the compliment and she reluctantly tore her gaze away from his. In four weeks he seemed to have grown taller and broader than she remembered. He was just as handsome, his eyes boring into hers a darker azure blue and her breath caught in her throat as she realised just how much their mutual desire was burning in both of them.

He turned away and carried on up to his room to find his Valet awaiting him, laying out fresh clothes, supervising the servants filling the bath for his master. Max paused for a moment as he pulled his jacket off – he suddenly felt absurdly happy. He could not remember ever feeling this content and he was smiling as he handed his jacket to Benson. He missed the twinkle of amusement that suffused his old Valet's countenance as he assisted his master to undress. Max sat down to pull off his boots and within minutes he was immersing himself in the bath of hot water, sighing with sheer contentment to be home, with his wife and family, surrounded by the people he loved and realising he was finally in the place he had been longing for these last weeks.

His business was concluded, the inheritance was safely his; he was free at last to undertake all the work needed to his estates and, most importantly, he and Callista could finally start their lives together properly.

Suddenly eager to return to his wife, Max hurried to dry himself and dress in the evening clothes his Valet had laid out for him.

His hair was still damp, brushed carelessly back from his eyes as he left his room and returned to the Drawing Room where he was greeted joyfully by his mother and the rest of his guests but his eyes were for his wife alone, whilst Callista, overcome with happiness at his return, was able to disguise her interesting condition for another evening. No one would guess that the becoming glow to her cheeks and the sparkle in her eyes could be due to any other reason than pleasure at the return of her husband and the marked attention he was paying her.

She had been tormented with doubts for weeks, just knowing Max and Davina were in the same city. She had no way of knowing if her husband and his first love had resumed their close friendship. She sincerely hoped not and had tried not to allow the agonies of jealousy to eat away at her soul these last few weeks. His homecoming this evening had been everything she had been longing for; his delight in greeting her had been as joyous as her own. Every time she looked up from her meal that evening, she found his eyes on her, he was relaxed and smiling and his happiness in being home was obvious for all to see.

Good manners dictated Max entertain his guests, and his wife's family were duly impressed by the attention he paid them, Amelia preening herself in the company of Lady Joanna and Mrs Spencer and taking all the credit for her niece's marriage to Sir Maxim, allowing herself the luxury of gently boasting about her daughter's forthcoming nuptials, smiling with undisguised maternal pride at Georgiana. Georgiana in the meantime was quizzing Max about Damon, how was he, when would he be paying them a visit, was his sister with him?

This last question brought Callista's head around from Augustus, with whom she had been discussing the delights of Cornwall; a county that the esteemed gentleman had never hitherto visited.

Max, however, was laughing at Georgiana's inquisition. His eyes were crinkling with amusement as he answered her barrage of questions.

"Your betrothed is very well, Georgie. He is as anxious to see you as you are yourself, however, the journey from London was a long and arduous one. He will no doubt be calling over first thing in the morning once he has rested and slept – and no, Lady Fitzpatrick did not accompany us from London. I understand she was planning on attending your engagement party but matters to do with her inheritance keep her in London for a few days longer."

Lady Joanna was watching Callista, and saw the pain which crossed her face as Davina's name was mentioned. "Did you see much of Lady Fitzpatrick in London, my dear?" she asked smoothly, aware that Callista would never enquire.

Max sipped with satisfaction the fine wine his Butler had poured for him and the glance he afforded his mother was wryly amused. "No Mama, I did not. I was engaged with bankers and Solicitors and my father's acquaintances for the entire time and only managed a few meetings with Damon. I did not attend any function where Lady Fitzpatrick might have attended."

"Surely she would not have gone out anyway," Lady Amelia joined in the conversation. "She has only recently been widowed, I understand."

Lady Joanna's lip curled at Amelia's words. "If Davina Fitzpatrick wished to attend Almacks – bereavement would not be sufficient reason to stop her."

"Mama." Max frowned at his mother but Georgiana found her words amusing and laughed, breaking any tension before it had chance to take hold of the party.

Mrs Spencer interjected smoothly enough. "I wonder if you have managed to see much of the local area yet, Sir Augustus? Perhaps we could entertain you tomorrow with a tour of the estate?"

Sir Augustus joined Max in drinking the wine before replying. "I believe we are expecting my future son in law in the morning," he replied. "I think it would be appropriate for Georgiana's mother and myself to meet him and discuss the forthcoming party and wedding."

"In that case, if you will excuse us," Max said, "perhaps Callista and I could take a drive out together in the morning. "

Callista looked up, a slight quizzical frown between her eyes. "Of course, Max," she replied. "But where are we going?"

Max leaned towards her and taking her hand, squeezed it gently. "The Stones," he replied softly. "I wanted to be the one who showed you them. To let you see for yourself there is nothing to be afraid of."

Her smile was a little tremulous. She had no wish to return to the Stones but his hand was reassuring, his face earnest, and his smile sincere. "Of course, Max. If that is what you wish."

"It is. Now, tell me, Mama, has my wife totally taken over the running of my estate in my absence?"

Lady Joanna joined in the soft laughter. "Indeed, Max, one more week away and your staff would have forgotten your existence. Callista is extremely popular and very much admired."

Callista could feel her cheeks growing pinker with the compliments but Max looked delighted and he raised his glass to her. "To my wife," he announced, "Lady Callista Langley, the Lady of the Manor."

Amid general amusement, the rest of the party raised their glasses to their hosts.

"Now, tell me the truth, Callie," Max went on ruefully. "What might I find when we go on our tour? More irate donkey owners, an orphanage full of the chimney sweeps of London or a Home for Fallen Women?"

The evening passed quickly, the atmosphere suffused with

happiness, Max and Callista at the centre of a pleasant family party. Callista, on saying farewell to her mother in law and Mrs Spencer, and goodnight to her Aunt and Uncle could never have guessed a year ago how much her life would have changed, how affectionate they both were towards her, how much she loved her cousin and how happy she was that they were to be neighbours.

She accompanied her husband upstairs, her hand on his arm as they strolled up with the rest of the party, no unseemly haste allowed to spoil the ambience of the evening. She curtsied politely to her Uncle and kissed both Georgiana and Amelia, much to that stern lady's surprise.

Turning back to Max, she replaced her hand on his arm and together, unhurriedly, they walked along the landing to their own rooms.

The door was opened for them by Benson and, in the room beyond, Callista's maid awaited her.

Smiling, they entered. "Benson, Alice – you are both dismissed. Lady Langley and I will fend for ourselves this evening," Max ordered, and he held the door open for the servants to leave.

A warm fire was alight and Callista walked in to seat herself at the small sofa in front of the blaze. She turned to face Max as he closed the door behind the servants and he paused for a moment to gaze upon her, her hair shining a rich dark chestnut in the light of the fire, her face glowing with some new tenderness, her eyes dark with desire for him, her lips curved into a welcome smile. She raised her hands to him and in an instant he was beside her, his hands trembling with emotion as he raised them to frame her face. For a long, long, moment they gazed into each other's eyes.

"I have missed you so much," she whispered.

"I feel I am finally home at last," he replied softly.

"You are. You will always be home when you are by my side."

A slight smile touched his lips. "Then I will never leave your side again," he whispered and he lowered his face to kiss her trembling lips.

Time melted away, all the long weeks of separation were forgotten, all the anxious days and long tortuous nights faded into obscurity as their lips met and their mutual passion was finally allowed to blaze as brightly as the leaping flames before them.

The smart curricle pulled by Max's matching bay horses trotted along through the woodland paths at a lively pace the following morning. After a leisurely breakfast, Max and Callista had left their guests to be entertained by Lady Joanna, and awaiting the arrival of Damon Fortescue. Georgiana had been in an agony of impatience and only the sobering presence of her mother had calmed her nerves sufficiently to allow her to regain her composure as she said farewell to the Langleys.

Callista had dressed warmly in a dark blue velvet coat over her walking dress of stiff blue brocade. A bonnet trimmed with matching blue velvet ribbons and kid gloves completed her outfit. They were greeted by a woodland thick with early winter frost as they journeyed to their destination, Max quizzing her about her visit to Bath, laughing at her descriptions of the Balls they attended, how Lady Joanna had been courted most respectfully by an elderly admirer, much to the amusement of the two younger ladies of the party. He kept her mind off their destination and it was only as they emerged from the thickly wooded forest onto the huge flat plain did she falter in her conversation and grow silent as the majestic stone structures loomed large above her.

She found she was gripping Max's arm and he felt the frisson of alarm go through him as she shivered.

He drew the curricle to a halt and gently removing her hand from his arm, he leapt to the ground to tie the reins to a nearby tree. He turned to hold his hand out to his wife and helped her to climb down from the tall step. Her face was unusually pale as he drew her hand through the crook of his arm and together they turned to face the silent circle of ancient power.

They were alone, the cold weather preventing casual sightseers from visiting the site and as Max started forward, he had to hold tightly onto Callista as she found herself trembling the closer they got to the Stones.

"What is it you feel, Callie?" he asked gently, pausing beside the huge grey slab of rock lying on the ground.

She turned wide, tortured eyes up to his. "Fear," she whispered. "I cannot explain it, Max. I just feel overwhelming horror and fear as I stand within this circle and the closer we get to that – altar – the more apprehensive and anxious I feel."

Max was frowning, his eyes scanning the circle around them. "I have never liked this place," he admitted slowly. "I always felt it held an atmosphere of great suffering and unhappiness. When I was a child, one of my earliest memories was waking up in the middle of this site, I was crying and had no idea how I got here. My parents thought I had sleepwalked here – I was only a small child and three miles was a great distance – my feet were cut and bleeding and my nightclothes were covered in mud where I must have fallen. My father told me later that I had told him I had been searching for someone – I had to save them but I was too late, always too late…" His voice tailed off, as if the memory of his father and those far off days of childhood had distressed him.

"How old were you?" Callista asked, transfixed by his revelation.

"I was only about five years old." He grimaced, forcing a smile. "Apparently I had a fascination for the place and was always coming here even though it made me weep every time. That night was the first time I had come alone and my parents had the whole estate out searching for me."

He laughed suddenly, a harsh sound which echoed around the silent plain.

"My father used to ask me who I was searching for but I could never tell him. I just know I was drawn here time after time until eventually it stopped holding such dread and I came to see it as just the ancient archaeological site it has become now."

Callista found herself still holding tightly to Max's arm. She tried to relax but even as she forced herself to look around the Stones, the words of the old gypsy woman came back to haunt her.

345

"I am the High Priestess," she had said. "I tried to save you but it was too late – one betrayed you, and one who loved you lost you."

Callista frowned again, recalling the vision of the white robed Druids who had surrounded her, the priests and priestesses coming closer – some of them wanted to help her but many of them, most of them, had meant her harm.

"Callie?" Max's voice came to her as if through a mist, far away. "Callie, are you unwell?"

She raised stricken eyes to his and it was not her Max she saw, but another man – someone with his eyes, with his features, his face tanned brown by the sun of a foreign clime. "Maximus…" she whispered before the world spun dizzyingly around her and once more she collapsed in a dead faint.

She came back to her senses as he was carrying her back to the curricle. She groaned as she regained consciousness and Max stopped, lowering her gently to her feet where she swayed in his arms and clung to him.

His face was as white as hers. "Callie, are you all right?" he asked, his voice strained with anxiety.

She nodded, holding him as the dizziness passed and the world finally came to rest.

"I'm sorry, Max," she replied. "I don't know what came over me."

Max held her close and turned his head towards the silent, omniscient obelisks. He was frowning. "I don't know why this place has this effect on you, Callie. I don't know what draws me here or why I keep coming back – but I think for both our sakes, it is a place best avoided from now on."

She rested her head on his shoulder as together they gazed at the Stones. She shuddered once more and he hugged her close to him.

"Come," he said. "Let us go home and think of more pleasant subjects." He helped her as she unsteadily climbed into her seat.

"Let us discuss tomorrow night's party with our friends and talk about nothing more serious than what frippery we shall be wearing and how many guests Damon will be entertaining."

She laughed shakily as he leapt up into the seat beside her, taking her hand once more as he expertly turned the carriage homeward. He raised her kid gloved hand to his lips, kissing it gently before turning his attention back to the pair of perfectly matched bay horses.

They drove away from that place of ancient memories and long forgotten tragedies but the gypsy woman's warning stayed in Callista's mind far longer than the standing stones remained in her sight.

Chapter Twenty Two

All Hallows' Eve, 31st October finally arrived and with it Georgiana and Damon's longed for engagement party.

Georgiana, reunited with her beloved Damon, had been giddy with happiness all day and it was with some difficulty that her Mama and Callista managed to get her down to earth long enough to help her change and dress for this, the formal acknowledgement that she would soon marry the love of her life, the equally besotted Damon Fortescue.

Her gown was as stunning and as perfect as she could have wished. A deep cream silk, embellished with the finest Brussels lace, trimmed with tiny roses of the palest pink satin. Pale pink feathers were pinned to her hair by sparkling diamond combs, an engagement gift from her husband to be, and a simple diamond pendant glittered at her throat, matching the single band of diamonds around her wrist, covering long creamy pink satin gloves. She was pale with excitement, but her huge blue eyes glowed with happiness and both her fond Papa and Max caught their breaths as she descended from her bedroom, a vision of loveliness.

Callista could feel no jealousy of her cousin and recognised Max's admiration for what it was – happiness that his oldest friend was going to marry his own wife's beloved cousin. Callista and the other female members of the house party faded into insignificance beside the radiant Georgiana but Max caught her hand and kissed it. "You look lovely, Callie," he whispered, making her blush at the compliment but pleased nonetheless.

She had chosen a new gown for the Ball, one purchased

from the same fashionable modiste in Bath who had provided Georgiana's own creation. Far simpler than Georgiana's gown, the dress was a soft off white silk, silver ribbons underneath the breasts and trimming the edge of the low cut square bodice giving the dress an almost Grecian appearance. Callista wore a silver organza scarf draped across her arms and a circle of iridescent moonstones adorned the plainness of her bare throat. She was no rival to Georgiana but in her own unassuming way she looked every bit as attractive and delightful as Max could have wished.

Georgiana and her parents went ahead of the Langley party. She was to greet their guests with Damon and her parents at her side and they left earlier to take up their positions in the Fortescue Manor house ready to meet and greet their guests, made up of all their friends and local gentry, most of whom had been looking forward to the Ball almost as much as Georgiana. Events of this type were few and far between in their quiet backwater, far from London and Bath and even the local larger county towns could not boast such a prestigious event. The occasional country dance and Assembly were all that the local young people could look forward to and the advent of such a glittering occasion as an engagement Ball was much anticipated.

The Manor was the matter of only a few miles away from Moreland, a smaller estate which bordered Max's lands near the great flat plain upon which stood the famous standing stones. Their families had never fought over the ownership of that plain, however. It had been claimed long ago by the Langley family and the Fortescues had never disputed the agreement, perhaps glad that they did not have to worry about protecting the site and its upkeep.

In consideration of his wife's deep dislike for the historical site, Max ordered his coach driver to go the long way round to the Fortescue home, to avoid the Stones in order that Callista would not have to see them, lit up by the clear autumn moonlight, standing even more solitary and powerful at night than they had seemed during the daylight hours.

Young Joe was their groom that evening and he sat beside the driver, dressed in his best livery, keeping the driver amused and exasperated in turn with his ceaseless chatter and good humoured comments.

Callista and Max listened with half an ear to Joe's constant battering of the driver's sensibilities and smiled at each other as the driver could not help himself any longer and finally laughed aloud at something the child said. Joe and Sir Augustus had resumed their old friendship and they had ridden out together that morning, delighted to be reunited, much to Lady Wetherby's undisguised horror.

Lady Joanna smiled indulgently as she heard the laughter. "That child," she murmured.

"He is indeed quite a character," agreed Mrs Spencer. "How on earth did you come by him, Callista? He is totally devoted to you, I understand."

Callista found Max's hand had closed over hers in the darkness of the carriage but she smiled at the two older ladies. "I met his mother under somewhat straitened circumstances," she explained. "I promised to help her child if anything should happen to her. As, unfortunately, it did. She passed away a few weeks later."

"Oh I am so sorry." Mrs Spencer was genuinely distressed. "I did not mean to pry, I am just glad the child had you to turn to."

"Yes indeed, Joe came as quite a surprise,," Max interjected, somewhat drily. "An old head on young shoulders, I think, is the best way of describing him."

Soft laughter from the ladies, then the conversation turned to the forthcoming Ball.

"I understand there will be almost a hundred people in attendance," Lady Joanna commented.

"I did not think Damon knew a hundred people," Max added. "Still Lady Amelia will be gratified at the crush."

"Max." Lady Joanna admonished him. "Do not be so disparaging about your wife's Aunt."

Callista, however, merely smiled at her husband. "My Aunt will indeed be gratified – as will we all. I am sure Damon has no idea of how popular he really is – I hope tonight will show him."

"Hmm, yes." Lady Joanna was suddenly thoughtful. "He has always been overshadowed, first by that disgraceful father of his and then by that… by his sister. It is time Damon was allowed to shine in his own right. Your delightful cousin has been the making of him, Callista." Joanna bent forward and patted Callista's hand.

The journey was almost over. The carriage turned into the Fortescue gates and started down the drive to the Manor house. They could hear the sound of music before they reached the house, their progress slow, held up by the half dozen or so vehicles and horses in front of them.

The Manor was smaller than Moreland, but it was a square solid building, a respectable size and large enough to allay any fears Lady Wetherby may have had that her daughter was marrying into a disreputable family. Talk of Damon's father and sister had long ago been dismissed and anyone daring to mention their names in her presence had earned the offender one of Lady Amelia's famous cold, piercing stares.

Finally arriving at the front door, their erstwhile young groom leapt down to open the door for them and let down the steps. He bowed smartly as Max descended and waited, as instructed, holding the door as Max assisted the ladies from the carriage.

The party made their way up the shallow flight of steps to the wide front door of the Manor and as they entered, servants took their cloaks and the Butler escorted them to the door leading into the Ballroom.

Callista could see Damon and Georgiana greeting the guests ahead of them. She smiled to herself as she saw Damon laughing at something said to him. Georgiana looked radiant with happiness but Lady Amelia, although smiling as she was introduced to the local gentry, seemed uneasy. It was not long until Callista discovered the cause of her Aunt's uneasiness.

They moved forward, Max offering his arm to his wife as they followed his mother and Mrs Spencer towards the brightly lit and full to overflowing Ballroom. Max leant his head towards her and she had to strain to hear his softly spoken words. "I doubt there have been so many people inside this house in many years."

She fanned herself with her small feathered fan, her cheeks already warm with the heat of the house after the biting cold of the October night.

They walked forward, hesitating slightly as Lady Joanna and Mrs Spencer were announced and went ahead, shaking hands with their hosts. Callista was aware of a slight stiffening of Lady Joanna's demeanour and as they entered the Ballroom, she saw the reason for her Aunt's unease and Lady Joanna's displeasure.

Davina Fitzpatrick stood a little way inside the Ballroom, in the centre of an admiring group of the local young men. She was laughing, her head thrown back to reveal a jet black choker of sparkling stones, stark against the pure white column of her neck. Her dress was of dark grey silk. Trimmed with black ribbons and the tightest of black lace skimming across her bosom, this was no dress of a mourning widow; rather of a woman who wore colours which suited her in a style which was as daring as it was attractive.

She felt Max stiffen beside her, momentarily pausing in the doorway. His eyes were drawn to Davina's and Callista watched in horror as Davina held Max's gaze for far longer than was acceptable, before turning away, back to her admiring audience, a light of triumph unmistakeable in her eyes.

Jostled by guests arriving behind them, Callista walked forward to be greeted by her cousin, who kissed her and squeezed her hands. "I am so glad to see you, Callie," Georgiana whispered. "I must speak to you as soon as everyone has arrived."

Callista nodded, too stunned by Davina's unexpected appearance to be able to speak. Max, his attention drawn back to Damon, shook his hand and offered his congratulations before moving into the throng.

The music started up again and after escorting the ladies to seats, Max acquired glasses of champagne from the attentive footmen, circulating the crowded Ballroom.

The dancing began again and Callista watched as Lady Davina was led out onto the dance floor by one of the eager young men she had been flirting with earlier. She inclined her head in their direction as she passed them, smiling enticingly at Max as he coldly returned her stare.

The noise of the music and the crowd was not conducive to conversation and Callista had to content herself with sipping the glass of wine and watching the dance.

She saw Damon and Georgiana finally able to move away from the entrance to the Ballroom, they made their way to the centre of the room and joined the rest of the dancers circling the dance floor to the music of the waltz.

Graceful, radiant and beautiful, Georgiana moved effortlessly to the rhythm, held confidently and expertly by her fiancé. Callista, remembering her own betrothal, squeezed Max's hand. He looked down at her and smiled but she could see he had been frowning. He seemed distracted, and as she followed his gaze, she felt again that cold hand of apprehension gripping her heart. Lady Joanna and Mrs Spencer were attempting to speak to one another but the noise prevented any easy discourse and they too remained silent until the music stopped and a general buzz of conversation filled the room.

Damon and Georgiana joined them and unable to speak to her cousin, Callista accepted Damon's invitation to dance. Max, as Marquis of Moreland was the most important person there that evening and, as such was the tradition, he offered his arm to Georgiana, leading her out to take part in a lively country dance, the figures of which went on for the next twenty minutes.

The crowd filling Fortescue Manor that evening was made up with members of the local gentry Callista had been getting to know during the weeks of Max's absence. Morning visits with her mother in law to introduce the new Lady Langley to the neighbourhood had greatly increased Callista's circle of acquaintances, several of whom paused to speak to her and exchange pleasantries with the Langley party.

The evening was proceeding in a lively, sociable manner. Callista was claimed for dance after dance but her head was whirling, she felt hot and uncomfortable in the heat of the crush of people.

Returning to her seat following a dance with the son of one of the local squires, she realised she could not see Max. Searching round for him, she could not see any of the other members of her party either.

Standing up, she felt the room swim around her. She felt dizzy and disorientated and found herself longing for a long cold glass of water. She could see Lady Joanna deep in conversation with one of her cronies. Mrs Spencer was being led out onto the Ballroom floor by one of Damon's relatives Callista had been introduced to earlier – she could not recall his name but from the roguish glint in his eyes his admiration for the widow was considerable. Smiling to herself, Callista gathered up the silken wrap on her arm and made her way over to the doorway, to seek out one of the servants and request a long cool drink. As she sipped the cold glass of water, a strange fluttering feeling made her pause and press a hand to her stomach. She had told no one yet of the impending child, but the child within her was reminding her of its presence. Her eyes searched the throng of people, she could not see Max and a sudden cold realisation assailed her as she realised she could not see Davina either.

The music swelled and she started towards her cousin and Aunt when a Footman appeared at her side.

"Your Ladyship," he said quietly. "Your husband has requested that you join him in the Drawing Room."

Alarmed, Callista put down her drink. "Thank you, I will join him immediately."

Wondering what had happened, she followed the Footman out of the Ballroom and across the wide hallway to the door leading into the Fortescue Drawing Room. He would have opened the door for her but something made her hold her hand up and shake her head at him. She had heard voices coming from inside. Voices she recognised and with a sense of dismay, she recoiled from being announced.

"Please leave me," she said softly. "I will go in shortly."

Puzzled, the Footman nevertheless concurred and bowed his head as he left her alone.

Pausing, she turned back to the Drawing Room door and

quietly turned the door handle. Silently the door opened and she slipped through, unnoticed by the two people in the room.

Davina was pressing herself against Max. Her hands were against his chest and Max was holding them. He was holding himself stiffly, his face cold and stern and he was doing his best to remove her hands but she was immovable. Although she was speaking quietly, Callista could hear her words, each one a cold steel dagger through her heart.

"Max – at last we can be together. It's been so long, my darling, but at last my husband is gone, I am free and we can return to London and carry on exactly as before."

Callista could hear the seductive tones of Davina's voice, velvet soft and persuasive. "We have waited so long, Max – I have missed you so much. I cannot believe it has been so many months since we could be alone together – I have missed your kiss, your touch – I have missed feeling your body next to mine…." She threw her head back and Callista could see the slim white column of her neck as she arched her back. "I have had to watch you suffer the humiliation of marrying that – that parson's daughter…"

Trembling with a mixture of horror and rage, the parson's daughter stepped forward into the light of that shadowy room.

Davina saw her first and a strange, half smile played on her lips as Callista moved towards them.

"Why were you humiliated, Max?" she asked, the words almost choking her.

Max jumped as if he had been stung. With a muttered oath, he pushed Davina away from him, anger replacing the sternness of his features. Callista, however was too distraught to notice.

"Callie," he started towards her but she held him at bay with a raised, shaking hand.

"Please tell me what she meant, Max," Callista demanded, her voice shaking as much as her hands.

The expression on his face as he glanced at Davina was filled with loathing. "Lady Fitzpatrick is deluded," he replied. "I was not in any way humiliated. I was honoured to marry you."

Davina moved then, coming to stand between Max and Callie, preventing him from reaching his wife. Her face was twisted with triumphant glee.

"Max was forced to marry you, Callista," she announced. "He had to marry before his thirtieth birthday in order to inherit his father's wealth." She paused, watching the effect her announcement was having on the devastated Callista. "He was forced to choose between you and any one of a dozen other respectable debutantes, otherwise his inheritance would have gone to a distant cousin."

Callista felt the blood drain from her already pale face. She thought she was going to faint, she could feel the beads of perspiration on her forehead and the room was starting to spin. Calling on all her strength, she forced herself to speak.

"Is this true?" she whispered.

Max opened his mouth to speak but he realised that Davina had outmanoeuvred him.

"Callie…" he began.

"Is it true?" she repeated, her voice stronger this time, anger fuelling her, forcing back the faintness, banishing the giddiness by sheer force of will. This was no time to give in to the shaky weakness of her body.

"Did you marry me for money, Max?" she demanded.

"It was not like that, Callista," Max replied, his own voice hardening. "It is true I had to marry to inherit my father's money but I wanted to marry you…"

Davina's harsh, strident laugh cut across any attempt Max had of explaining himself.

She whirled around to face Callista, tall and imposing and her expression one of triumph and evil. "He married you for the money, Callista – he did not love you, he loves me. He always has loved me – he always will."

She laughed again, the sound echoing around the silence of the room.

"He was going to find a nice, respectable, compliant girl, marry her and get her pregnant and leave her on the estate whilst we carried on our affair exactly as before – enjoying everything London has to offer a rich man and his mistress."

Callista's face whitened further. "No…" she whimpered. She shook her head and instinctively her hand went back to her stomach, as if compelled to protect the stirrings of life growing inside her.

Davina stepped forward, a grey spectre, glittering with malice.

"Yes – we had it planned every step of the way. If only we had waited though – who would have thought my husband would have been so considerate as to die so soon? Max and I could have married if he had not already been shackled to a Nobody like you."

Callista stumbled back, away from the tall virago of evil.

"Enough!" Max roared, finally finding his voice as he listened in growing horror and astonishment to Davina's tirade against his wife. "Davina, that is enough. Callista, do not listen to another word. We will talk about this…"

"No." Callista's eyes were huge in her white, stricken face. "No – there is nothing to talk about. You have never loved me – ours was a marriage of convenience – I realise that now…" She backed away from them both. She felt as though she was going to be violently sick and she looked over longingly at the tall closed French doors on the other side of the room.

Avoiding Max's outstretched hands, she pushed past them and ran over to the doors. She paused for the briefest of moments to open the double doors and glanced back. What she saw broke her heart. Davina had stepped forward and was holding Max's arm and she could not tell whether it was a gesture of comfort or one of restraint.

She did not wait to discover which. She pushed open the doors and clutching the thin wrap around her shoulders, she stepped out into the icy cold night air. The cold took her breath away but she paused only to take a deep breath, to fight off the rising nausea and hold back the tears which had sprung to her eyes, blinding her briefly.

With an impatient gesture, she dashed the tears away and

stepped out onto the gravel path at the side of Fortescue Manor. She needed to get away as quickly as possible and without glancing behind her again, she started to run. She ran towards the front of the house and was unaware of the surprise she engendered in the eyes of the various grooms and liveried men waiting with their horses, standing about in groups, stamping their feet and drinking hot toddies to fight off the biting cold of that October night.

"Callie…"

She heard her name called and realised Max was coming after her.

She increased her speed, running as fast as her legs could carry her, down the long drive towards the gates between the high walls surrounding the property.

"Miss." She heard Joe's voice as well in the darkness but she did not stop, she needed to get away, flee, run faster and further than she had ever done in her life before, she needed to get far away from her husband and his mistress and the house and everything in it.

Everything had suddenly tumbled around her ears, her whole marriage was a sham, her life was meaningless, she was exactly as Davina had described, a Nobody, a convenient poor relation who had happened into Max's life at exactly the right time.

She ran towards the open gates and the blackness beyond. She had no idea where she was going, where she would go – she only knew she could not bear to see any of her family just then, witness the pity which they must feel for her.

The horsemen appeared from nowhere. One minute she was running, the next a large black animal was in her path, causing her to stumble and fall, and look up in alarm at the masked man. She was out of breath but she screamed once as he dismounted and seized her roughly, picking her up and throwing her face down across the horse. He mounted behind her and would have ridden away had not a small tornado suddenly thrown itself at him.

Joe shouted and tried to stop the horseman from riding away carrying Lady Callista but even as he jumped for the reins, shouting and swearing using words long since banished from his vocabulary, a second horseman came up behind him and slashed at him with a riding whip.

Joe yelped with pain as the whip found his shoulders but like a gnat maddened at being swatted, he scrambled up again to reach for the reins trying to stop the horsemen riding away with Callista.

Again and again the whip slashed him and a large boot kicked him to the ground making him finally let go of the leather reins. He lay stunned for several moments as the horsemen, their prize lying prone across the saddle, galloped off into the night, Callista's screams cut short as a large rough hand was suddenly clamped across her mouth.

Joe dizzily tried to sit up but he could not move until an arm appeared and gently went under his shoulders, lifting him from the ground. Strong arms cradled the injured child and when he finally managed to open his eyes, Joe found himself being carried by Max.

"'Er Ladyship," he whispered. "The men got 'er – they've ridden off, sir…" He could not speak further.

"Hush, Joe." Max's voice was grim, with a note in it Joe had never heard before, suppressed fury emanating from every fibre of his being. "You were very brave trying to stop them but rest now – let's get you attended to."

"Lady Callie…" Joe whimpered. "The men took her…"

Max's face was stern, Joe had never seen him so angry and he could almost feel sorry for the men who had taken Her Ladyship. They would get what they deserved when his master caught up with them.

"I'm going to leave you with Sir Augustus, Joe, "Max explained gently as he carried the child into the house. "Then I'm going to follow the men who took Lady Callista."

Joe struggled suddenly in his arms. "I want to come too…" he protested.

Max hugged the child briefly, moved by his bravery in trying to save Callie. "No Joe, they have hurt you and you must rest. Don't worry – I'll bring her back."

Joe looked up at him, serious dark amber eyes meeting glittering blue eyes suddenly turned as icy as the cold frosty stars in the heavens. "Do you promise?"

"I promise," Max said, his voice as icy cold as his eyes.

The hand covering her mouth almost suffocating her, Callista struggled against her abductor. The horse was a powerful animal and the extra weight of the woman lying prone across its back did not give it pause as they galloped through the darkness at a breakneck speed, skidding occasionally on rock hard ground made slippery with the icy covering of frost.

She clung desperately to the horse's side, terrified of falling, her stomach churning at the see-saw motion, but her rage and indignation at being treated in this cavalier fashion was causing her to struggle, beating at the man's legs and body with small clenched fists.

His orders were simple, they had instructions on how they were to despatch the woman, and their employer did not care what they did to her in the meantime. He had no scruples about being violent towards a woman and as Callista twisted and turned, landing blows where she could reach, he simply removed his hand from her mouth and dealt her a stinging blow to the side of her head.

She recoiled immediately, her head snapping back, before dropping down against the animal's rough hide. She was stunned but still conscious and lay still for a few moments to recover from the blow, feeling a trickle of blood in the corner of her mouth where his fist had connected.

She had no idea where she was or what was happening but from the glance she had of the man and his companion, she realised they were the two men who had been lurking around the grounds and the village for the last few weeks. She groaned as the discomfort of her position began to hurt but her abductor ignored her distress and simply whipped his horse to gallop ever faster over the frozen ground.

He could not believe his luck. Their quarry had literally run out into their arms. For weeks they had watched and waited and laid their plans. To no avail it had seemed. She had been too well guarded, too well protected by her family and by the staff of Moreland. She had engendered in them all a great feeling of love and loyalty and despite attempts to bribe various members of the staff, no one had accepted a penny to betray their mistress. Threats of violence had prevented any word of the betrayal ever reaching the ears of their masters, but the two men had been vigilant and when no constables or militia had been despatched to arrest them, they realised their dire warnings had worked and the staff of Moreland had said nothing. Their vigilance, however, finally paid off. Watchful and alert for any change in Lady Langley's movements, they had followed the carriage to Fortescue Manor and had decided that they would wait until the Ball was over and attack the carriage as it left for the return journey to Moreland. They reasoned that an evening spent in convivial company, with hot toddies being drunk by the driver and footmen, would lull all concerned into a warm alcoholic daze,. The tired occupants of the coach would probably be asleep on the journey home and a surprise attack in the early hours of the morning would finally bring them their prize.

Then she had confounded them all by running out of the house and straight into their arms.

Their employer had been very explicit in the way they were to despatch Lady Langley and as they made their way through the dark woods, they were conscious that they had to keep the lady alive for a few hours yet – they had found a deserted forester's cottage hidden well behind overgrown trees and it was to this destination they carried their prize. The bright light of the moon obscured by the thick undergrowth, the forest was wrapped in darkness that varied from pitch black to blue, to purple to charcoal grey.

The rider of the horse pulled her roughly from its back and pushed her unceremoniously towards the cottage. Unaccustomed to the darkness, dizzy and confused, she stumbled over the roots of overgrown trees, trying to stay upright and make her way to the ruined building. The men were silent, ominously so – their hats were pulled low ever their eyes and they had made some attempt to partially cover their faces. With an upsurge of hope, Callista wondered if their efforts to keep themselves disguised was due to their wish not to be identified – perhaps they wanted to ransom her and did not want her to be able to recognise them again in future.

Her hopes were dashed as she was pushed into the cottage and her abductors followed her inside, shutting and barring the door as they did so. A meagre fire glowed in the corner of the room, obviously having been left to go out when they had departed earlier, and one of them moved over to it to add a log to the fireplace to revive the flame and bring it sparking back to spluttering life. The sudden glow illuminated the mean interior of the cottage and Callista looked about her with a calmness she was far from feeling. She hugged the thin silk of her wrap closely around her shoulders, shivering with cold and the onset of shock over what had happened.

She faced her abductors squarely. Unwilling to let them see her fear, forcing herself to remain calm, she glared at them with undisguised contempt.

"Why have you kidnapped me?" she demanded, her voice unnaturally loud in the silence of that room.

The two men glanced at each other before one replied. "Because we were paid to," he said, his voice low and guttural, but with an accent she could not quite place.

Taken aback by their response, she rounded on them once more, speaking with a confidence she was far from feeling. "Whoever it was, my husband will pay you more to release me."

The two men were smiling, a sly expression she found disturbing. One removed his hat and the scarf wrapped around his face.

"What makes you think it wasn't your husband who ordered your abduction?" he said, his face splitting into a grin.

The room swam around Callista. Once more she felt the

blackness threaten to overwhelm her. Her stomach churned and she felt the fluttering of her baby stirring once more. Gripping the back of a rickety chair, she clung to it, determined not to show weakness in front of these villains.

Bravely she glared at her tormentor. "Then I will not waste your time bargaining with you," she declared. "What is it you want from me?"

She felt the second man's bold gaze wandering over her shivering body and she drew the filmy wrap more tightly around her shoulders.

She looked around the room at the sparse furniture and locked door. Deciding she had no chance to run away, she sat down on the chair, partly to disguise the shakiness of her legs, partly to avoid the gaze of the men.

"I am thirsty," she announced. "If not for my sake, then for the sake of my baby, may I please have something to drink?"

The two men exchanged a frowning glance. Realising she had an unexpected advantage, she carried on. "Even if my husband were to wish me harm," she continued, "he does not know of the child I carry – he would not wish his heir to be injured in any way."

The first man nodded curtly to his companion and within a few moments Callista was presented with a dirty goblet containing brackish water. Disguising her distaste, she sipped at it. The water was stale but drinkable and she swallowed half the amount to ease the dryness of her parched throat.

Despite the growing warmth of the fire, the room was still freezing cold and she shivered involuntarily.

One of the men noticed her discomfort and almost despite himself he pulled a rough blanket from the narrow bed in the corner of the room. He gave it to her and she wrapped it around her cold shoulders.

He pulled her to her feet and pushed her towards the bed. She was suddenly terrified of his intentions but he merely pushed her onto the coarse, uneven mattress and left her. He pulled his companion to the far corner of the room and she heard a muttered discussion taking place. The second, shorter man was vehemently shaking his head and the occasional glance in her direction made her realise she was obviously the topic of their muted argument.

She pressed herself back against the uneven wall of the cottage, the blanket wrapped tightly around her, the warmth of the fire gradually bringing some colour back to her cheeks. Her head was still spinning. She felt slightly better after the drink of water but the nausea and faintness threatened to overcome her.

Desperately her eyes scoured the room, searching for a way out, a chink of light, an escape. The only window was high above her head, the cottage was made of one square room and the only door out was heavily barred. She felt limp with despair but she refused to let them see it.

The argument appeared to be over. The second man was scowling as he pulled the chair over to sit beside the fire. He produced a pipe and within a few minutes, the air was filled with noxious fumes which made her feel even more nauseous.

The first one, the leader of the two came back to stand over her. Without a word, he bent down and pulled her hands towards him. Stiff with shock, she watched as he produced a length of rope and bound her hands together. He roughly manhandled her until she lay prone on the hard uncomfortable bed and he bound her ankles together.

Almost as an afterthought, he put the blanket back over her.

"There is no escape for you, lady," he said in his strangely accented voice. "But we do not ravish pregnant women… You are safe for tonight."

Realising the argument had not been about releasing or ransoming her, Callista felt the bile rise up in her throat. Forcing it down, she shuddered and held the blanket as if it could provide a shield between her and the two men.

She nodded weakly. "I thank you, sir," she whispered.

He turned abruptly away from her and went back to join his companion next to the fire. Callista stared after them, terrified that their one noble action would be reconsidered in the hours to follow. They did not, however, disturb her. Within a few minutes, the smaller one extinguished his pipe and settled himself on the floor next to the fire. He was soon asleep and snoring loudly until a well-aimed kick from his partner made him turn over and the noise reduced to a low rattling sound.

The other man stared thoughtfully at Callista and, glancing slyly at his sleeping companion he stood up and took a step towards her. Her eyes widened in quickly disguised fear, shrinking further back against the rough wall of the cottage. She could see the lust in his eyes and she knew he had reconsidered his former honourable decision.

Then the light in the cottage seemed to shimmer and she saw even in the dull glow from the embers of the fire the expression on his face change from one of desire to one of horror. He stumbled back and almost tripped over his sleeping companion. Callista glanced around wondering what he had seen and out of the corner of her eye, a shadow moved and she thought she saw the shape of a man holding a short broadsword. Shaking her head in disbelief, she returned her gaze to her kidnapper, but he did not make any further move to molest her, he merely made himself a bed on the floor and sitting with his back to the wall, watched her through the long cold hours of that winter night as she lay silently staring at the ceiling, her lips moving in prayer until exhaustion finally overcame her and she slept fitfully as the first fingers of dawn crept over the horizon.

Chapter Twenty Three

The morning sun struggled weakly to shine on the crowd of men as they slowly walked together in a line across the fields, searching together for a clue to the whereabouts of the missing Lady Langley.

Men from the local Militia had been summoned and, together with every farmer, tenant and villager from the Moreland estate they scoured the countryside seeking the abducted woman.

Max and Damon had been out all night, trying to follow the direction in which the men had ridden away with Callista, until the tangled undergrowth of the forest and losing their way in the darkness had prevented them from going any further. They had returned home to change, rest briefly and change horses to carry on with their search.

An exhausted Georgiana, her eyes red from weeping, had tried to go out with them, but had been prevented by her weary mother from joining the men. They had remained at the Fortescue home, up all night awaiting news of the abducted Callista, wondering and worrying and endlessly discussing why the unknown assailants had snatched her in that manner.

Lady Joanna had quizzed her son quite vociferously on exactly why his wife had been seen running away from him down the driveway. His reply had been short and ill mannered and he did not deign to explain himself further. He did, however, beg Georgiana's pardon for ruining her engagement party and taking away with him every able bodied man sober enough to ride a horse and join in the search for his missing wife.

Augustus had made sure young Joe was being attended to,

harrying the Fortescue servants to make sure the boy received the best of care. Mrs Sinclair helped Lady Amelia to look after the distraught Georgiana and acquitted herself well in ensuring the guests and searchers were kept well provided with hot drinks and refreshments as the former lady of the house, Lady Davina, was conspicuous by her absence.

Remaining in the Drawing Room after the party came to an abrupt end, those guests still remaining dozed fitfully on the furniture, none of them wanting to leave until they received news of the missing Lady Langley.

A slight disturbance just before dawn awoke the sleeping child as he lay in an improvised bed in the servant's quarters. Getting out of bed, Joe opened the door slightly as he recognised Lady Davina's voice demanding her groom ready her horse immediately.

On enquiring whether Her Ladyship was going out to join the search parties looking for the kidnapped Lady Callista, Joe was alarmed to hear Davina actually laugh. It was an unpleasant sound and he recoiled behind the door as the harsh laughter filled the small room.

"No, indeed I am not," Joe heard. "I have other matters to attend to this morning. Now, where is my groom?"

"He is not here, Your Ladyship." The girl's voice was suddenly tremulous. "The master ordered all the menservants to join in the search."

Joe pulled open his bedroom door and stepped out. He looked up at the tall lady and saw the darkening storm of displeasure cross her attractive face.

"I can get your horse ready, Madam," he said quietly.

She looked down her nose at the child, recognising the guttersnipe Callista had rescued from the slums of London. A sneering response was ready on her lips but she paused, smiling to herself.

"Then hurry and do so, boy. I will join you directly."

She whirled away, leaving Joe to hurriedly get dressed. His best livery had been soiled with blood and dirt the night before but one of Damon's staff had kindly provided the boy with some old clothes and it was these rough but clean garments which Joe pulled on, ignoring the soreness of his limbs and shoulders where the kidnapper's horse whip had come down with such vicious force.

Instinct had taken over his senses. He did not like or trust Lady Davina, he knew she meant his mistress harm and her declaration that she was not joining in the search had raised all his hackles.

He ran out to the deserted stable block and with his brow furrowed with concentration, he deftly saddled up one of the few horses left behind, tying it up still in its stable before turning his attention to the glossy, highly strung stallion so beloved of Lady Davina. It was a bad tempered brute but with his natural ability and determination, the boy readied it in time for Her Ladyship as she swept into the stables a few minutes later.

It was just after dawn and the poor light came to Joe's aid as Lady Davina mounted her troublesome horse and pulled away from his steadying hands. She looked as if she could have struck the child herself as she stared down at the silent boy, but there was something about his steadfast, unswerving gaze which stopped her. She set the horse off at a fast trot as she left the stable yards and so intent was she on her mission that she did not notice the small grey horse leaving shortly after her, following her with steady, silent intent.

Max was frantic. They had searched all night and they had found no trace of Callista or her abductors. Wracked with guilt, he could not stop going over in his mind that last, dramatic scene with Davina which Callista had witnessed with such devastating results.

He had not sought a meeting with Davina. The time had long passed when he should have told her the truth. She had been flirting outrageously with him all evening and he had found himself forced to ask her to dance; she had manoeuvred the situation until it would have looked churlish to refuse to dance with her. Their dance had ended and she had taken his arm, leading him away from the Ballroom, claiming to need to speak to him urgently.

The urgent matter had been the good news that she had been waiting for. Her sisters in law had no claim to their late brother's estate, they were forced to give up the fight for a share of his property and everything had been passed over to his widow. There had been no will found to change the decision and Davina had suddenly found herself to be an extremely rich and free woman.

He had had no chance to repudiate her, he had not been able to express his regrets at his change of feelings towards her, barely had he started speaking when she had interrupted him pressing herself against him. He realised now her actions had coincided with the exact moment Callista had opened the door in a scene deliberately aimed to cause his wife the maximum distress possible.

His mother had often called Davina wicked. He could now see why and another epithet crossed his mind now. Evil. She had deliberately goaded Callista – she had purposely measured her words, every one chosen with care and spoken in such a manner to distort the truth to her own sickening twisted version – designed to hurt Callie and wound her so deeply that even if their marriage survived, how would he ever regain her trust?

As he and Damon moved slowly and carefully through the overgrown, long forgotten paths of the forest, they looked for recently disturbed ground and any signs that two horses had pushed their way through the thickly wooded area they now searched.

The weak November sun was barely over the horizon when Max spotted an old path, where the overgrown bushes sported broken twigs and faint hoof marks were evident on the flattened grass. His furrowed brow cleared momentarily and he wheeled his horse around to investigate further. Damon followed him, slowly picking their way through the densely wooded area, finding an old path covered now in moss and weeds.

It led, eventually, to a dilapidated cottage, half its roof gone and a half ruined chimney stack perched precariously at an angle on the remaining shell of the roof. The shutters were closed and the front door was barred, giving the cottage a guarded, secretive atmosphere. Max immediately wondered why such a ruin was so well hidden and why the door had been so carefully locked. He spurred his horse on and jumped off quickly as he reached the old building and without waiting for Damon, he lifted the bar and shouldered open the door.

The cottage was deserted. It showed evidence of having had some recent occupation however as a still warm fire smouldered in the chimney and foodstuffs lay scattered about the floor, as well as a rumpled, stained blanket next to the chimney breast. His eyes raked the room and came at last on the narrow single cot pushed against the wall.

It was empty but a flash of silver caught his attention and striding over to it, he dragged the covers off it to find a thin silver wrap pushed down between the bed and the wall.

Callista had left him a sign. She had been here and this narrow shawl had adorned her shoulders last night when they had left home so full of happiness, looking forward to their eagerly awaited evening of celebration with friends and family.

He stood silently looking down at the gauzy transparent material and said nothing when Damon joined him and took the insubstantial cloth from his hands.

"She was here, Max," Damon exclaimed, excited that this was a step closer to finding her. "The fire has only just gone out; they can't be too far away."

Max lifted his face to his friend, his face pale, his eyes tortured. "She had no cloak, Damon – this was all she had on her... she will be so cold..."

He could not bear it. He covered his eyes with shaking fingers, images of his Callie being cold and frightened and in mortal danger was more than he could stand.

Damon twisted the cloth between his clenched fingers and stared at his friend in dismay. His own resolved hardened. "Max – there is no body, there is no blood. Callie is alive. Otherwise they would have left her here – look around you – there is nothing. They have moved her and are probably even now delivering a ransom note to your home."

Max looked up, his despair freezing into cold, hard anger. He wore the same expression on his face that Joe had glimpsed the night before. It was a look of pure fury and his eyes were an icy arctic blue.

"If they have hurt her, Damon…" he started, his voice almost failing him but he swallowed hard. "I will kill them. I will find them and I will kill them."

Damon gripped his friend's shoulder.

"They will want money, Max," he said, his voice low, urgent. "They are a couple of highwaymen who saw an opportunity and took it – she will be unharmed, my friend – they will not want her murder on their hands. Come, let us leave this place – we will carry on looking and send one of the men back to the house to see if a ransom demand has arrived."

He slapped his friend on the shoulder, breaking him out of his dark reverie.

Max took a deep breath, seeing the sense in his friend's words. He nodded bleakly, unable to speak, swallowing again the lump which had arisen in his throat. He felt nothing but hatred for Davina, fury at the men who had taken his wife and utter helpless rage at the thought of what could be happening to her.

He straightened and with new resolve, he strode over to the open door and marched through, his eyes on the ground, searching for the trail left by the kidnappers.

"There." He pointed to the ground. "Two sets of horse's hooves – one deeper than the other – Callie must be on one of them."

He caught up the reins of his horse and slowly began making his way through the undergrowth, following the trail with determined concentration.

Damon followed, also on foot and only when the hidden path opened up to join the wider one did they remount and follow the trail, realising as they did so that they were on their way towards

Moreland – via the route which led directly to the site of the standing stones.

Max and Damon exchanged a glance and Max kicked his horse to a gallop. They were not too far behind the kidnappers and Max's sense of urgency seemed to grow – common sense told him the kidnappers wanted nothing more than gold to release his wife; instinct told him otherwise and with every step they took, his fears grew.

Lihanna 12

They kept to the edge of the great forest, skirting it but travelling onward, mile after mile until they came at last to the great flat plain. The sun was almost setting as they reached the site of the great Sacred Stones and as they approached, Julius was dismayed to see a large gathering of hundreds of white robed druids, men and women. They were in groups within the Stones, carrying torches, the Stones themselves decorated with huge bunches of mistletoe, and there was the sound of singing, which faded to silence as the combined might of the Roman legion and Carmag's army came into sight.

He could see the great slab of stone and on it, lying flat, with her arms and legs tied to the four corners, was Lihanna. He urged his horse forward, hearing raised voices as the priest standing beside the stone slab was arguing with a Priestess. Queen Eithann was screaming her orders to the Druids, demanding the release of her daughter at once.

Lihanna turned her head as she heard her mother's voice.

She had been dreaming; she had remembered the last time she had visited the Sacred Stones – she had been with Julius and she had made an offering of flowers to the gods, she had whispered prayers and incantations, asking the gods to spare the lives of her family and to grant protection for the man she had grown to love, the Roman, the man who despite the gulf between them loved her as much as she loved him. Thoughts of Julius faded as other memories crowded into her mind. She remembered the great winter celebrations of Yule when the Stones themselves had been garlanded with branches of holly. She remembered Beltane when she and twelve other virgins from her people had taken part in the ceremonies to welcome the arrival of *summer. It had been a joyous, happy occasion, she had been honoured with the task of leading the girls within the circle of stones and lighting the beacons so that the circle had blazed with light as their ceremonies and celebrations had gone on long into the May night.*

She had been closing out the horror of what was happening to her now – shutting down her mind so she could try and ignore the pain in her limbs as they were stretched and tightly tied, her body pressed down onto the freezing cold stone beneath her back.

She saw Julius dismounting from his great black stallion and drawing his broadsword from his waist, running towards her, his eyes blazing with anger and fear and despair.

Daveth's voice was droning on – she could not shut out the sound as he relentlessly carried on with the rites he had started. The Priestess was objecting, trying to reason with him and the other priests who surrounded the slab. They had been summoned here to take part in this ritual – one of massive power and significance and some of them, the High Priestess amongst them, had objected, insisting this was wrong – that nothing could justify the sacrificial slaughter of the dead King's child.

They had been overruled and they protested in vain. Physically prevented from getting close to Lihanna, they were kept back by the young priests, those who flaunted the more normal gentle rites of the Pagans and who believed with a fervour bordering fanaticism, in the old ways, the old, forgotten forbidden ways.

Eithann screamed as she saw the wicked curved knife being held above the prone body of her daughter, her fury and rage rebounding around the ring of stones.

Julius and his men were fighting their way through the priests, desperate to reach the sacrificial altar.

Lihanna's eyes locked onto his. He remembered his last words to her – he remembered his promises to always protect her, that he would let no harm befall her.

The crowd of Druids caught his arms, trying to hold him back and falling back as his broadsword hacked at them, cutting a swathe through the mass of bodies preventing him from reaching her. There was a spurt of blood as one of the Druid's blades found its mark on

Julius' arm. He snarled at the man and his broadsword despatched him to his gods with swift efficiency.

Daveth's voice was reaching a pitch, he was almost shouting out the words of the final rites of sacrifice as Julius threw himself forward.

The knife flashed once in the gathering dusk and plunged downwards.

Julius' howl of rage and anger screamed around the arena of Sacred Stones and one slash of his sword cut Daveth's throat from side to side, almost severing his head from his shoulders. Blood spurted out from his neck over the prone body of the girl lying motionless on the slab.

Julius hacked at the ropes which bound her and pulled the curved knife from her breast.

She opened her eyes, the clear emerald green starting to cloud over as Julius pulled her into his arms, using his cloak to staunch the blood flowing from her wound.

"You promised..." she began.

"I promised to protect you and I failed – I am so sorry, my love." He was distraught, the pain in his heart wrenching him in two, his voice hoarse with grief.

A slight tremulous smile lifted her lips, the rosiness gone. She was white faced. "No, you promised you would come back... and you did..." She paused, her voice hoarse, gasping for breath. "Your heart and mine, Julius," she whispered.

"In this life and forever," he whispered back, holding her close pressing a shaky kiss onto her forehead.

All around them, battle raged, his soldiers and Carmag's army fighting against the warriors of the Druid priests.

She looked up at him, hearing nothing, seeing through fading sight only his tear-filled deep blue eyes.

"In this life and the next..." she murmured.

He pressed a kiss onto her lips and looked up to see Queen Eithann and Carmag standing before them.

He held her in his arms as the tears coursed down his face, crushing her against him, murmuring her name over and over again into the thick auburn tumble of hair.

Eithann was weeping silently. Reaching out, she took her daughter's hand and pressed it to her lips.

"Farewell, my child," she said softly.

His head bowed, Carmag stepped forward and put his arm around his mother's shoulders. The battleground had fallen silent, the warrior priests had been overcome and the victors had turned in dismay to the sight of their proud, noble General kneeling on the ground, holding the lifeless body of his princess in his arms, weeping silently and pressing kisses against the marble cold beauty of her face.

"Farewell, my love," he whispered. "I swear we will be together again one day..."

As if to seal his promise, a flash of lightning lit up the darkening afternoon sky, followed by a clap of thunder and the threatened rain poured down onto the silent armies of Rome and Celt, united in grief as, one by one, they fell to their knees in silent homage to a lost love, a betrayed daughter and the Druid's innocent victim.

Chapter Twenty Four

She was cold, so cold.

The morning frost lay thick on the ground as she was taken from the cottage and made to walk to the waiting horses. The horses were huge, bad tempered animals, ill-looked after and neglected by their riders. She was spared the indignity of being thrown face down across the back of the larger animal as the leader of the two men seated her upright in front of him, holding her tightly so that she was imprisoned against him. The smell of his unwashed body was overpowering, the stench of his breath against her face enough to make her nauseous again, and the movement of the horse made her want to retch. She forced it down, not permitting herself to think about her own discomfort – all she could think about were the kidnapper's words – had Max really arranged all this? Did he hate her so much he would want her to suffer in this manner? Despite everything that had happened in the last few hours, she could not bring herself to believe he was capable of such behaviour.

Yet Davina had told her Max did not love her – Max had not been able to marry Davina and so a suitable alternative had to be found.

The scene she had witnessed, the words she had heard were forever etched into her brain – she could not stop going over and over the events that had led to the situation she now found herself in.

She wanted to cry – she wanted to give in to despair and fear and weep for her unborn child and herself. Married to a man who did not love her, the father of a child he knew nothing about.

She hung her head, turning her face as far away from the rider as she possibly could, clutching the thin blanket around her shoulders, shivering in the cold November air.

She knew now why these men had not moved on, why they had tried to gain employment at Moreland, why they had been watching her whilst she rode around with her companions.

They had been paid to kidnap her – and do what with her? She could not imagine and for once in her life, despair almost threatened to overwhelm her natural courage.

Her thin silk evening dress and slippers were no protection against the cold and despite the rough blanket covering her shoulders, she could not stop shivering. She could see her breath as they picked their way through the eerily silent forest. Dawn was just slipping over the horizon and no wildlife or birds were yet stirring.

It seemed to Callista that they were the only three people left on the planet.

She raised her head to see where she was being taken and her skin started to crawl with apprehension as she recognised the route they were taking.

Silently they went towards the open plain at the edge of the forest, gathering speed as the rough undergrowth gave way to broader paths. The sun brought a pale, watery light to the day and Callista felt her head spinning as she saw their destination, the stark majestic stones – waiting to claim her as she always knew they would.

Feeling ill, sick with apprehension and exhausted, Callista nevertheless started to struggle with her captor. She had been so still in his grasp, he had relaxed his hold on her and he was unprepared as she twisted around and pushed him away from her, throwing herself off the horse as she did so. She fell heavily, the ground was hard and she lay winded for a moment before she pulled herself upright and began to run away from them back towards the cover of the forest.

She gathered up her skirts and ran, losing one of her silken slippers as she did so, feeling the rough ground rip her stockings to shreds. She stumbled but did not fall again, running on just as the riders gathered their senses and came after her.

Branches caught at her clothing, scratching her face, her bare arms and legs but she ran on, oblivious to the pain, intent only on escaping her pursuers, intent on getting away to the safety of the dense heart of the forest.

Blood ran down her face, blurring her vision as it ran into her eyes, but she wiped it away with a hasty, impatient gesture. Her feet were now bare, and she gathered the thin material of her gown up into her arms to enable her to run all the faster, unhindered.

A dizzying feeling of déjà vu almost overwhelmed her as she realised she had done this before, long ago in another time, another life – running through the trees to evade capture, trying to save her life.

The outcome was inevitably the same. She could not outrun the horses and within minutes, the two riders had caught up with her and the smaller of the two, the one called Patrick, leapt from his horse to capture her and bring her to a standstill by the means of a blow to her head. She stopped struggling against him as the blow sent her reeling and she fell once more, her face as white as her gown, streaked now with red as blood from the scratches ran down her face and arms and she lapsed into a semi-conscious state.

She could struggle no more, and overcome by the superior strength of the men, she felt herself being lifted once more onto the horse's back and this time the strong arms which held her in place were uncompromisingly rough – there would be no repeat of her escape attempt.

They rode towards the standing stones and with every step, Callista felt she was growing closer to her inevitable, final destination.

Chapter Twenty Five

Joe kept a careful distance between himself and Lady Davina, following her at a distance, but always keeping her in his sight. He watched as she avoided the groups of searchers still intently looking for Lady Callista and his suspicions grew as she galloped onwards towards Moreland.

The pale November sun was casting a strange yellow glow over the land, struggling weakly to light the world and dispel the early morning frosts which clung to the fields and trees around them. She skirted the great forest and rode past the village, circumspectly keeping out of the way and sight of the villagers. Her behaviour did not seem odd to those local people who did catch a glimpse of her. Well used to her autocratic ways, they were happy to keep out of her way as she rode past them and gave her as wide a berth as she was giving them.

Joe was alarmed to see the direction she was heading. He had the same dread of the area of the standing stones as Lady Callista but he doggedly kept on and followed her as she rode over the great plain onwards towards the ancient circle. Keeping his distance, he made sure she could not see him following her as she rode between the Stones and dismounted.

Joe urged his horse into a faster trot, riding as quickly as he could towards the site, hating the place and feeling nauseous as he drew closer but his curiosity and suspicions were too aroused to draw back now.

He dismounted and tied his horse to a bush at the edge of the Stones, creeping forward slowly, remaining hidden behind the tall granite slabs, just his small head peeping carefully around the edge of the stone to see what was happening.

Lady Davina was pacing up and down, slapping her riding whip against her leg as she walked, and prowling around the central slab as predatory as a tiger, trembling with barely suppressed excitement.

Joe bit his lip to prevent himself from crying out loud as two horsemen appeared and there, with a rough, ragged blanket around her shoulders, was Callista. Even from this distance, Joe could see the blood on Callista's face. She was struggling with her captor, wriggling and kicking and doing her best to free herself from his vice-like grip.

Frantically, Joe searched around his hiding place, looking for something, anything he could use as a weapon against the men holding Callista. He could see only rocks and branches and he picked up some hand-sized rocks, ready to launch them at the kidnappers as soon as he could get close enough.

He started creeping around the edge of the circle, dodging from one stone to the next, careful not to reveal himself to the people within the circle.

They had dragged Callista off the horse and were holding her between them, with some difficulty as she was doing her best to free herself from their grasp. She had little strength left to fight them, but fight them she did.

An ice cold wind blew through the upright stones – a high pitched wailing, keening sound which froze the hearts of the men hearing it. Hardened criminals though they were, this place made them uneasy. For all their bravado, they could not wait to get the deed done and get away from this nightmarish place.

They knew search parties would be out looking for them; every moment they delayed was dangerous. But they had their orders and to receive the rest of their money, they had to follow their instructions to the letter.

They dragged Callista towards the woman in black who awaited them beside the large flat altar stone and as she turned to face them, Callista felt the blood drain from her already pale face.

Then Joe heard the noise. He could see the men looking around nervously, turning their heads and searching the area with their eyes. They were uneasy, they could not work out what the noise was or where it was coming from and Joe too looked around to see if he could solve the mystery.

It was the sound of the wind, a low noise growing slowly louder. Joe was puzzled as he looked behind him as no wind stirred the long grasses or leaves of the trees and branches of the forest at his back. They were still covered in the thick white morning frost, and the forest was eerily, unnaturally silent.

The sound was within the stone circle. The wind caught at the black skirts of Lady Davina's riding habit and blew the blanket away from Callista's struggling form, leaving her dressed only in her white evening gown, soiled with mud and blood, creased and torn at the hem. She was barefoot but she was still trying to kick her way to freedom.

Carefully, slowly, Joe continued to get closer to the group. He could hear them talking now and he became even more alarmed as he caught the words carried to him on the strange wind which howled around inside the stone circle.

Callista and Davina stared at each other. Davina was looking down her nose at the captive – a slow, triumphant smile touching her lips. Her blue eyes were sparkling with glee at the sight of her rival, her enemy, finally brought so low.

Callista glared at her. She stopped struggling as she faced the woman who had engineered this whole kidnapping. The pieces fell into place. She drew herself up to her full height, still several inches shorter than Davina but her head was back and her eyes did not waver as she held Davina's gaze.

Davina seemed to sneer then.

"Afraid, little Nobody?" she asked, her voice carrying on the wind so Joe could hear every word.

"Of you, Davina?" Callista's voice held no tremor as she faced her Nemesis. "Never."

Davina's smile did not waver, her eyes alight with her victory.

Callista looked away from the eyes boring into hers and looked around the space within the stone circle. She had felt terror as her abductors had dragged her closer, but now, standing inside at last she felt her fear draining away. A calmness which had eluded her on her previous visits to this place seemed to wash over her now.

"Why here, Davina? Why did you not let your men kill me last night?"

"Because I knew how much you feared this place. I wanted to witness your death. I wanted to be sure you were really dead."

"Is that why you brought me here, Davina?" she asked quietly. "To terrify me, to make me even more afraid so I would beg you to save me, beg you for mercy?"

A shadow of doubt crossed Davina's face. It was exactly why she had brought Callista here, knowing the effect the Stones had upon her.

"Would it have done any good for me to beg?" Callista went on.

Davina was not smiling now. Instead the look on her face had contorted to one of pure malice.

"No," she replied. "I don't think it would," she conceded at last. "I hated you from the moment we met." Her voice seemed to hiss with the loathing she felt. "There was something about you, Callista, something I could not bear. Something I could not understand, except that I detested you from the start."

Callista shrank back slightly as Davina leaned forward, her face inches from hers.

"Why Max had to choose you, I don't know." The whisper was fierce, the voice as icy as the eyes which were glaring now. "Of all the simpering little girls in London to choose from, he had to pick you."

Callista stared back into those glaring eyes, refusing to let Davina see a flicker of the fear which was coursing through her body.

"But he did pick me, Davina, didn't he?"

Davina's eyes snapped with fury. "For money, you little Nobody," she sneered. "For his father's inheritance. If he had only waited a few more weeks, we would have been together.

There would have been no need for him to sacrifice himself and marry you."

Callista's eyes did not waver as she stared calmly at Davina.

"Just tell me one thing, Davina," she demanded, her voice as steady as her gaze. "Did Max have anything to do with this?"

For a moment Davina was tempted to lie, to tell her that yes, Max had deceived her, that he had participated fully in the abduction of his wife.

A genuine smile lifted her lips and lit her eyes. "No – he knew nothing about this. He did not need to know."

For a moment, Callista sagged against her captors, relief flooding her tired body.

"In fact," Davina continued, suppressed laughter making her voice shake slightly. "He is even now out searching for his missing bride – he has been out all night searching." Davina's voice changed, almost spitting out the last few words. "He dared to reject me – he had the effrontery to rebuff me after all we have meant to one another – for what? You are nothing but a poor relation, a common parson's daughter, little more than a peasant."

Her mood was mercurial, her amusement disappeared at the memory of Max's rejection.

Her eyes narrowed and for a moment Callista saw the glint of evil flash across Davina's face.

"Bind her," Davina snarled at the two men still holding her. "Tie her to this rock."

The wind howled around the Stones. The two men holding Callista's arms could hear something else. The noise was growing, changing – it was becoming more high pitched but the keening sound became clearer, it was the sound of fighting, of a battle, the noise resembled the sound of swords clashing against each other.

Callista stood straight and slim between them as the men looked around them, straining their eyes and ears trying to work out the source of the noise. With shaking hands, they moved to do their mistress' bidding and dragged Callista over to the flat altar stone.

They forced her down onto the icy cold slab and tied her hands above her head to the corners of the hard granite surface.

Callista stopped struggling. That same icy calm engulfed her again as she stared at Davina.

"You are going to kill me," she said quietly, a statement not a question. "Do you think Max will turn to you if I am dead? He will work out for himself your involvement, Davina – you will never have him."

Davina pulled a long, sharp blade from the scabbard she had worn hidden beneath her short jacket, and handed it over to the leader of the two men.

Davina leaned down so that her face was almost touching Callista's. "He will find me here," she whispered. "Bravely injured whilst trying to save you from these two villains – he will adore me all the more for my courage."

She stood up and took a step back from the stone. "Now finish her," she snarled.

Several things seemed to happen at once. Firstly, a flurry of stones was rained upon the two men, hitting them with deadly accuracy, then as they shouted and turned to deal with the onslaught, the noise of the ghostly battle became overwhelming. Pressing their hands over their ears, the terrified men backed away. The curved knife was thrown to the ground in front of the stone altar.

"Can you see them?" Patrick exclaimed. His eyes were wide with shock. He was shaking and terrified and his face had whitened.

Davina whirled around, anger distorting her features. "What are you talking about, you cretin?" she demanded. "There is nothing there."

"Soldiers," the man said. "They're coming for us." He backed away, straight into another volley of stones.

The leader of the two men was made of sterner stuff. He held out his shaking hand to his employer. "Give me my money," he demanded. "So I can get away from this accursed place."

Davina stepped away from the stone slab, towards her horse where a fat purse of gold coins lay in her small saddlebag. She held it out towards him. "Finish her first!" she screamed at him. "Do it now!"

In the distance, they suddenly heard horses' hoof beats, galloping towards them. Joe, picking up more stones to hurl at the two villains, started to shout as loudly as he could.

"Max! Max! We're here, we're here!" He launched more stones, landing each one with perfect accuracy on the bodies of the two kidnappers.

Patrick ran to Joe and knocked him off his feet with a cry of anger and would have continued to beat the child, had he not suddenly turned pale and backed away. Joe looked around in surprise to see what had frightened the man and he saw, quite clearly, a figure standing behind him. A man dressed in a rough brown woollen smock, but with fine furs covering his shoulders and fur boots covering his feet and legs up to his bare knees. The man had wide amber eyes and long blond curling hair, held in place with a wide copper headband. He was carrying a heavy two handed sword, which was held protectively over Joe's prone body. The highwayman had backed away in terror at the sight of Joe's saviour. The man smiled at Joe, silently guarding him and when Joe went to stand up, he shook his head and gestured him to stay down.

The leader of the two kidnappers tried to grab the bag of money out of Davina's outstretched hands but she evaded him deftly and picking up the curved knife, threw it back to him.

"Now!" she screamed, beside herself with anger.

With an oath, he ran over to the altar and paused for a moment to look at the prone, still body of Callista lying tied to the slab.

He raised the knife but stopped himself from plunging it into Callista's heart as a figure came out of the noise and confusion all around him. It was a girl. A wraith – as insubstantial and as ethereal as the morning mists but she came gliding towards him; her face and figure were the mirror image of the girl on the icy granite slab. Her hands were outstretched, reaching for him, her face contorted with anger and as she walked through the stone, through the shivering body of Callista, she came towards him as he backed away, terrified by the very sight of her.

They ran then, abandoning all thoughts of the gold the Lady had promised them. They ran to their waiting horses and started to gallop away from this place which horrified them both.

They were intercepted before they had gone half way by Max and Damon. Fury beyond belief gripped Max at the sight of his wife lying on the stone altar with Davina beside her. The two highwaymen were prevented from leaving by the two horsemen, riding them down with swords drawn and pistols readied. The four men met in the centre of the stone circle and the fight was over almost before it began.

Driven by a passion and a rage he had never experienced before, Max flung himself at them and cut the first man down, driving his sword into the man almost before the man had chance to draw his weapon.

Patrick had no chance against Damon, disheartened by the defeat of his partner, disorientated by the recent events and the strange visions he was seeing, he had no fight left in him and he threw his sword on the ground, holding his hands up in a gesture of surrender.

Davina glared down at Callista, still tied to the slab. She had seen no wraiths, experienced no ghostly visions and could not understand why the two men she had hired for their well known murderous reputations had let her down so badly. She wanted Callista dead but she had had no intention of it being by her hands.

Callista stared up at her, completely calm now. She had seen the girl, the ghost who had so frightened her would-be assassin and recognised at once the girl from her wedding day who had smiled at her from the stairs in Max's house. She could see the man standing guard over Joe and as she smiled at him, he raised his sword, nodding before vanishing once again into the autumn mists.

"Cut me free, Davina," she said quietly. "Release me and I will help you."

"Help me?" Davina's eyes still held that spark of madness Callista had glimpsed earlier. "I need no help from you." She hissed out the words and with a swift movement, brought the knife up to hold it at Callista's throat.

She pressed the tip against the pulse which beat in Callista's throat. Blood oozed out over the sharp blade. "He cannot see if you are alive or dead," she continued. "I could finish you now and he would never know it was me."

Suddenly, from out of nowhere, a small yet determined force hurtled itself against Davina, knocking the knife from her hand. Snarling with an animal fury, Davina scrambled after the knife and turned to finish the task. She gasped in horror and let out a scream as she saw for the first time the two figures standing between her and her victim. The small, wild child, the guttersnipe, his eyes alight with a ferocious hatred, and beside him a woman, a ghost, a white-faced girl wearing a white robe with long auburn hair streaming down to her waist. They formed a barrier and from the expression on the face of the white-faced wraith, Davina knew she would never get to Callista alive.

She backed away, as her henchmen had done previously, and picking up her skirts, she ran to her waiting horse.

"Davina!" A shout from her enraged brother tried to stop her. She realised with that link between them that her twin brother knew what she had planned, he knew now what she had wanted to do and she could not face him yet; she had to get away, run away from all of them, go away and plan her next move. Even in the throes of panic and fear, she could only think of saving her skin and escaping whatever punishment they could devise for her. Kidnapping and attempted murder were crimes even she would have trouble escaping.

She mounted her horse with little difficulty, pulling herself up into the saddle, although the horse was skittish, alarmed and nervous at the sight and sounds surrounding him. She had not heard the battle sounds and the cries of the long departed, but her horse could see and hear it all. He reared as she seated herself but she brought him under control with a slap of her whip.

Max threw himself off his horse and ran the last few yards to where Callista lay. It was his nightmares come true – his Callie in her white gown, covered in blood. His heart was in his mouth as he finally reached her side. He picked up the discarded knife and used it to cut through the ropes binding her to the slab.

"Callie!" He called her name over and over again as he lowered her arms and unwrapped the ropes from her wrists. Her eyes were closed and for a moment he did not know if she was alive or dead. He was shaking with the emotion of finally finding her, reaching her and terrified of being too late.

"Callie, my darling, my angel – come back to me, please don't leave me, please come back." He lifted her from the altar, carrying her cold, stiff form in his arms. He put her down only long enough to pull the jacket from his back and wrap it around her, trying to warm her, trying to breathe life back into her stilled body, the only colour about her being the blood which covered her dress from the wound in her neck. He pressed his fingers against the knife mark and stopped the blood from flowing. Joe flung himself onto Max and Max raised his head from Callie's long enough to look into the boy's amber eyes and see that, like his, Joe's eyes were filled with tears.

"Joe," Max said urgently, "Joe, I don't want to let her go so you must pull my cravat off and together we must bandage Callie's neck to stop the bleeding. Can you do that, boy?"

Joe nodded and went to work, pulling Max's white linen cravat from around his neck and, folding it as instructed, wound it around Callista's throat. They fastened it securely, and Max went back to holding his wife firmly in his arms, kissing her white face, pushing the loosened hair out of her face and trying to warm her frozen body.

They were startled by a sudden scream from the other side of the stone circle. Damon was coming towards them, having tied up the remaining abductor and having given up trying to stop Davina. He would deal with her later, he had decided grimly.

They all turned in time to see Davina's horse rearing and Davina trying desperately to control the animal. It was rearing away from something, terror in its rolling eyes, pulling its head from side to side in an effort to get away. Davina was a superb rider but even she could not calm and control an animal suddenly driven mad with fear.

With another scream, she was thrown from the horse and they heard from a hundred yards away the sickening crunch as her head hit one of the boulders that littered the ground. She lay silently, her head at an awkward angle to her body and she screamed no more.

The horse ran away and Max stared in wonder at the figure he could clearly see standing between two of the upright monoliths. A Roman soldier, dressed in full uniform, holding a broadsword and with a golden helmet on his head, complete with bright red plumage – it was he who had prevented Davina's escape – holding his sword out to challenge any who tried to pass him. Even from this distance, Max could see the man clearly – he was looking at himself, dressed in the uniform and armour of a man from two thousand years ago.

Max could not tear his gaze away from the soldier – their eyes met and locked and an understanding older than time passed between the two men.

The soldier raised his right arm bearing the sword in a gesture of salute, just as Callista shuddered in Max's arms. Max immediately broke eye contact with the soldier to look down at his wife. When he looked up again, he saw the soldier had gone, disappeared into the mists swirling now around the stone circle.

"Lady Callie…" Joe's voice broke and the tears streamed down his face, tears of joy as Callista's eyes fluttered and she opened them to look up at first Joe, then Max who had her pressed tightly against his heart.

She took another deep, shuddering breath.

"Callie…" Max whispered and pressed another kiss against her cold white forehead. "Callie, my love, you're safe now, I've got you... I'll never let you go again. Oh my darling..."

As if aware he was babbling, Max struggled to contain his emotion and contented himself with holding her against him, his cheek pressed against hers, rocking backwards and forwards, kneeling on the damp ground, holding her, protecting her.

Joe was openly weeping and Max looked up at him and smiled a little shakily.

"Well done, Joe," he said quietly. "We heard you shouting and I saw you bombard those evil men with your stones – you stopped them from hurting Lady Callista any further." He actually smiled grimly as he recalled the scene they had witnessed. The two men, being attacked with a veritable barrage of stones, Joe yelling and the men unable to defend themselves, seemingly dazed somehow.

"There were ghosts here, sir." Joe managed to speak at last. "We could hear what sounded like a battle and I saw a man – he frightened them away, sir. I would have been killed if he hadn't frightened one of the bad men."

"I saw one as well," Max said quietly. "A Roman soldier. He stopped Lady Davina from escaping."

At the mention of Davina's name, Joe scowled, a look of pure hatred marring the cherubic childish face. "She was going to kill Lady Callie," he exclaimed.

At her name, Callista roused herself from the faint she had fallen into. The last thing she could remember was the girl – the girl from her wedding day – protecting her and Joe from Davina's madness. There had been another – a man so familiar it felt as though a member of her family had stepped forward to protect them.

"Max." She breathed his name.

Blue eyes sought hers, darkened with anxiety and fear, his brow furrowed with concern over his wife.

"Are you hurt anywhere else, dearest?" he asked her, gently.

She actually managed a shaky smile. "Everywhere," she admitted. "They were not gentle with me."

Horror and anger chased across his features. He glared over

to where the fallen highwayman lay and wished he had taken his time in killing the scoundrel. His partner was seated next to his fallen companion and Max smiled grimly, he would extract revenge from the second perpetrator of his wife's misery.

Callista shook her head weakly, "No, Max," she whispered, knowing exactly what he was thinking. "No revenge – I am safe now – you have saved me and all I want now is to go home."

She reached up and touched his cheek. He caught her hand and pressed a kiss onto her palm. "She was lying, Callie," he said softly. "I love you. I always have."

He kissed her upturned face once more, gently. "In this life and the last – I have always loved you, my Princess."

Wordlessly they stared at each other, the mists of time clearing briefly as Julius Maximus held his Princess Lihanna once again. She smiled at him. "In this life and forever," she replied.

Carefully, gently, Max stood up and lifted her into his arms. "I think I can walk, Max," she protested, but he shook his head.

"You have no shoes, you are freezing and you have been injured. I will get you home and get you cared for before I come back and help Damon."

They both looked over to where Damon was kneeling beside the still body of his sister. He stood up and, bending down, carefully lifted her into his arms. Grief was etched into his face, grief for his sister, for the child he had once loved and the loss of the woman she had become. He carried her over to the waiting horses and signalling to the defeated highwayman to stand, he laid his sister's body across the saddle of his horse. Patrick held the horse for him as he did so.

As Max, Callista and Joe approached, the captured man turned to them. "We didn't hurt her, sir," he exclaimed. "We just abducted her as the Lady demanded – we didn't hurt her or the child, sir."

Max stood stock still, staring in contempt at the man. "You were going to kill her," he retorted. "If it hadn't been for this child, you would have succeeded."

Patrick shook his head vigorously. "No sir, I meant the baby.

She – " He pointed to Davina. "She said we could do what we liked to your Lady – but we didn't, sir, we didn't touch her."

Max and Damon stared in astonishment at Callista. She raised her head from where it had been resting on Max's shoulder.

"It is quite true, Max," she sighed. "They respected the fact I am with child and did not attempt to ravish me."

Max lifted his wife onto his horse and stepped towards the crestfallen highwayman, his face darkened with fury. "You may not have ravished my wife," he snarled, "but she has obviously been ill treated and if she loses my child thanks to your treatment of her then God help you."

He turned back to Callista and a genuinely happy smile finally lit up his countenance. "A baby, my love?"

She returned his smile, a little colour back in her cheeks at last. She bent forward and touched his face with fingers that shook slightly. "Yes, a baby, conceived in Penhallow, I believe."

Max swung himself up into the saddle behind her and placed his arms protectively around her, the news of a child both stunning and delighting him and making him only too aware of what he had come so close to losing. His hands went to her stomach and held her.

"Elinor always said Penhallow was a magical place," he said softly and kicking the horse gently, started the walk home.

Damon and Joe followed them. They parted at the edge of the forest, Max taking Callista and Joe back to Moreland, and Damon returning his sister to her ancestral home, escorting the captured highwayman as he did so, the man too dispirited and frightened to do anything but obey the instructions given to him.

Max felt the hairs on the back of his neck go up on end before they had ridden a hundred yards.

He stopped the horse and turned. Joe drew his own pony to a halt and together they looked back at the tall, majestic stones. There, standing together were the Roman and his Princess. He had his arm around her and, together, they raised their hands in farewell to Max and Callista and Joe.

"Can you see them, Max?" Callista whispered as she felt the strength of his arms tightening around her.

"Yes," he replied. "I think they saved your life, my love."

"They did," Joe said quietly and squeezed the hand Callista reached out to him.

They watched then as the ghostly lovers, reunited after millennia apart, walked back into the swirling mists of time in the centre of the Stones and, together at last, disappeared forever.